I AM JUDEN

UNDERCOVER IN THE SS

By

Stephen Uzzell

For my mother and father,
who gave me everything
and asked for nothing in return.

CONTENTS

AUTHOR NOTE

In the annals of World War Two heroism, the name Haim Michael Klar deserves to be as widely known as Oskar Schindler. Although Haim may not have saved lives on Schindler's scale (the truth is we cannot know; the facts are few and far between), his individual sacrifice was almost beyond comprehension. During the final years of the war, Haim impersonated an SS officer at Auschwitz and helped ease the suffering of prisoners, who regarded him as their 'Guardian Angel'. When we consider that Haim was also Jewish, his courage in walking that most precarious of tightropes is astonishing.

I first chanced upon fragments of Haim's biography several years ago, in a series of Holocaust testimonials to the Association of Descendants of The Shoah, based in Illinois, USA. To my knowledge, it is the sole record of his endeavours.

Haim's extraordinary double-life was like nothing I had encountered in years of Holocaust research. I had become accustomed to stories such as Oskar Schindler, 'the good German', but stories of Jewish resistance are very few and far between. Nechama Tec has written about the Bielski Partisans in *Defiance*, and Leon Uris documented the Warsaw Ghetto Uprising in *Mila 18*, but there are precious few others.

My original intention was to expand upon the brief details of Haim's life, with a view to writing his biography. Unfortunately, my attempts at contacting the Illinois organisation proved fruitless. Out of respect, I decided not to pursue the matter any further. But the story had its hooks in me, and would not let go.

I felt I had no choice but to write an account, lightly fictionalised in nature since there were so many gaps in his life story. And so the novel *I Am Juden* was born. All I knew was that my protagonist, Jozef Siegler, arrived at Auschwitz late in the war as a Nazi. I started there, at the end, and worked back in time, imagining how a resourceful Jew had ended up in an SS uniform. I don't know for sure if the real Haim ever met Untersturmführer Amon Göth or Gusta Dawidson Draenger, leader of the Krakow Ghetto resistance, but since he was active at the same time and at the same place, it would seem a reasonable assumption.

My only wish was to bring this extraordinary story into the open before it faded away for ever. I hope I have done it justice.

To Haim – to life.

Stephen Uzzell
Brighton, UK, 2019.

PART ONE

1

When our mother Elena was one year old, rioters drove her family out of their home village. The Russian government blamed the Jews themselves for exploiting the masses, who were now - quite justifiably - fighting back. In 1900, Jews were officially forbidden from settling in any rural areas, or from buying property.

When Elena Shapiro was three, thousands of 'illegal' Jews were rounded up by the police and expelled. One morning the six year old Elena found herself excluded first from her own school, and then, after she had calmly marched herself three miles to the next, and seven miles to the next, she found she'd been excluded from all schools in the area. They'd exceeded their Jew quota.

Three years later, Elena's father found himself disqualified from voting in local elections. As an impetuous thirteen year old, his daughter was forbidden by the authorities to change her name to a non-Jewish one, and her pass was stamped indelibly with the three letter word.

In 1899, Elena's nineteen year old former classmate was charged with murdering a Christian lady in order to bake Matsoh bread from her blood.

The first years of the new century saw the worst pogroms yet.

Two thousand Jews were estimated to have been killed between 1903 and 1906, including my grandparents, Elena's mother and father. Countless more were wounded. In Odessa, in Yekaterinoslav, in Kiev...

In Vichob, in the heart of the Pale of Settlement, on Friday September 11th 1903, my father's Heroes of Zion were ready. Radion Siegler had assembled a street of blacksmiths as the first defence against the mob, the other blocks organised into similar occupational lines. But the fight broke out behind them, in the marketplace, between the Jewish peddler of a six-ruble barrel of herring and a watchman willing to pay no more than one ruble fifty copecks. The fight became a brawl; the brawl became a race riot that lasted the weekend and drew in crowds of drunks from nearby villages.

On Monday September 14th, Radion's battered blacksmiths tried to prevent a gathering of a hundred railway employees from plundering the Ghetto while soldiers and police looked on. Eventually the soldiers opened fire, killing forty-two Jews, Radion's mother, father and young brother amongst them. Radion and thirty-five of his League were indicted for bearing arms against Russian citizens.

It was around this time that Elena Shapiro's first boyfriend Jeremiah was called up to fight for Glorious Mother Russia against the Japanese, along with a disproportionately high number of his Jewish peers. As Jeremiah told Elena, with little sense of his own gift for prophecy, it was the only war where you stood as good a chance as being shot by your own troops as you did the enemy. With Jeremiah gone, Elena took to the train tracks to sell whatever she could find along the way, riding from shtetl to shtetl for her daily crust.

Meanwhile, since Radion Siegler was to stand bogus trial for attacking Christians, he felt entirely justified in attacking one more, with an extricated bench slat. He lured the fat guard to his cell, rammed the wooden board into his jowled throat, pulled his tunic to the bars, ripped the keys from his belt and opened the cage. The Heroes scattered in separate directions, to further their chances of escape. With no family or home to return to, Radion took the one course of action he'd spent his life avoiding. He fled.

He would emigrate, to the land that was on everybody's lips: the melting-pot of New York City, where Germans and Frenchmen simmered contentedly side by side, Irishmen and Englishmen, Jews and Russians. All that stood in Radion's way was the matter of five hundred rubles for a third-class ticket across the Atlantic, five hundred more rubles than he'd ever glimpsed. But an enterprising Jew with a box of polish and a brush could earn his fortune on the trains, so he'd heard. So Radion lit out on the Odessa line.

The story of how Elena Shapiro met her stubborn shoe-shiner of a future husband at a quarter-past three on the afternoon of Sunday 8th November 1903 would become the central myth on which the Siegler family was founded. The 2.00PM train arrived over an hour late in Odessa, to the usual fanfare of pandemonium, the pushing and the pulling of suitcases and packages and bundles of bed-clothes.

Elena was in a hurry to board the carriage and set down her basket of braided rolls and eggs; the shoe-shiner would not get off until he was good and ready. And the racket, the yabbering, clacking racket! When it comes to queuing orderly on platforms and allowing existing passengers to disembark, it is well known that Jews consider themselves exempt. But this autumn morning, standing at the edge of the platform in the wind and the rain, Elena decided she was going to hold her ground. She gripped the basket to her chest, for ballast. Inside the train, crouching in fact right beneath the door, the shoe-shiner was finishing his work, not content to leave until he could see the reflection of his own face. Neither was the shinee willing to end the transaction prematurely, to the impetuous anger of the crowds on either side of the door, on the train and on the platform, where Elena Shapiro was doing her best to hold back the tide. If there was one thing Elena hated more than being slowed down, it was being jostled to speed up. But the laws of gravity and physics were as against her as they had been King Canute. There was only one other force of stillness in the whole tapestry: a bearded writer seated behind the shoe-shiner, scribbling in his green book.

Elena could see the disaster unfolding in slow motion. The crush on either side, the shoe-shiner in the middle and Elena and her basket inching ever closer. If he didn't stand up soon, she'd be pushed over the shoe-shiner's skinny rump, and two hundred people would collapse on top of them like mahjong tiles. The authorities would be digging through luggage for a month.

The final cruel shove came right between Elena's shoulder blades, propelling her boots over the threshold of the carriage and her shins into the shiner's buttocks, causing Elena to topple... at which point - goodness me, he moved so quickly -

the shiner deftly pirouetted to his feet and caught Elena in his arms, spilling not even one of her hard-boiled eggs. 'I had you covered all along, Miss,' he said.

'You had me covered?' Elena retorted, thereby commencing the dialectical dynamic of a marriage that would endure two children, one world war and almost provoke a second, according to the complaints of their sleepless, harried neighbours.

∗∗

The boy was born with his boots on, that's what Radion always said about me. Not standing up, Elena would chip in, but mid-stride!

Plop-plop, snip-snip, now you're off, that's it, one foot in front of the other.

I supposed my parents must have carried me for the first few months, but it wasn't long before I was standing on my own. The earliest memory I have is of stumbling onto a train with only a staff in my hand for support, a pint-sized Jacob of the shtetls. In my next memory I am carrying a curious sister-sized bundle called Shoshana.

Mama and papa were always loaded down with baskets of braided rolls, hard-boiled eggs, oranges and bottled seltzer water. As the Siegler clan grew in size and number, so did the baskets. Mouths to feed, mouths to feed. Before long, Elena and Radion were an ambulatory grocers shop, and I was the under-boss.

And then one spring morning in 1910, the walking stopped. We had been migrating south-east through the Ukraine and Moldova, leaving the rails behind to trek over the Carpathian Mountains. When we finally emerged on the Promised Land of the Romanian side, all I could see was wilderness.

'This is it,' mama said, setting down her bags of black cherries and green grapes. 'It's perfect.'

'But it's exactly the same as the last place we saw,' papa began, and then noticed his wife's narrowing eyes. 'Which is to say, Yes, it's perfect.'

He kissed her brow and flung out his arms to the flock: 'Children: this is your new home!'

Which was odd, to say the least. When I had previously pictured a 'home', I'd imagined a house with curtains and a garden path, not this swampy meadow on the edge of a forest. And yet, here we were, stopped and apparently settled, the strange word blowing from Shoshana's lips like a chain of dandelion puffs.

Home-home-home-home-home-home-home!

We sat in a circle and broke bread to consecrate the ground. The only thing standing were the pine trees spearing the sky, but papa soon made short work of them.

By dusk, father and son had cut and dragged enough wood to build not only a home but a shop underneath it. In a matter of weeks we were selling timber to the Jews who started emerging over the mountain in their droves. When the new families had built their own houses along the track that now divided the meadow, papa started cutting the timber into cupboards and shelves and tables. When the houses were furnished, Radion Siegler became the village greengrocer.

In 1914, when I was ten years of age, papa sat us all down before bedtime and explained there were other Jews in Siberia much less fortunate than ourselves. The Siegler family had a strapping son to look after them, while the Siberian Jews had nobody.

When we woke up the next morning, papa was gone.

A dozen Sundays later, mama was sewing in the upstairs bedroom with the older girls. I was meant to be overseeing little Shoshana's homework while failing to complete my own at the shop-counter. Copying by rote was no education, even a ten year old knew that. Mainly I was remembering papa's stories about the long struggle to oppose the Russians in the Pale. No letters had yet arrived from his new adventure in Siberia. But I had memories enough of Radion Siegler's Heroes of Zion for now.

Papa used to get angry that it had taken the so-called intelligentsia of Vichob ten years to take up arms against their oppressors. He'd bang his fist and shout as he recalled how his own Hebrew professor had counselled against self-defence. Papa would mimic the professor's wheezing voice: *The violence perpetrated against our people represents the first stirring of the Russian proletariat. It will do us Jews no good to side with the police against the people.*

That was all very well and good, papa countered, but it was Russian officers supervising the slaughter in the first place.

At first, the professors accused papa of making up wild stories to bolster his view. Gradually news trickled in from across the Settlement that proved Radion had fabricated nothing. State-sponsored pogroms were inconceivable to an older generation raised on notions of tolerance and honour. Yet the violence was becoming a fact of daily life. In Odessa, in Yekaterinoslav, in Kiev...

The stillness of the shop was punctuated that Sunday afternoon by the machine gun rat-a-tat of mama's sewing contraption on the boards above. Even though I knew the noise was coming, I still jerked on my stool, slashing the open page of my exercise book with my pen-nib. Shoshana jumped, too, and then found it all hysterical. The day was almost done and a certain weariness had over-taken my spirits, until the shuddering blast of the Singer revived me.

Shoshana was as bored as I was, slumped at the counter under a tumble of red hair, her page of sums only half complete. It had been hours since the shop-bell had last rung, and yet there remained another thirty-minutes or so until the afternoon's shadows claimed the floor and I could close up and eat supper and help put the girls to bed and finally enjoy a little time to myself, reading something more edifying than the twelve-times table. Tonight I would enjoy a Sherlock Holmes adventure, if I could keep my eyes open for long enough.

'Come on, then,' I said. 'Let's get you ready for bed. We'll do the last sums in the morning.'

'But the magic bell! Somebody might come!'

'Not tonight.' I packed our school-books away in the drawer underneath the till.

'It's still early!'

'Shoshana: it's almost five o'clock.'

I looked out the window to satisfy myself of the lateness of the hour, but there was indeed somebody scurrying along the side of the street towards the shop: Boiberik the bullying butcher, head down, beard tucked into his shirt collar.

I slowly tapped my fingertips along the desk until I felt the end of cotton taped to the brass counter edge. Before he left, my father had rigged up a Radion Siegler Jewish Self-Defence Special, the cotton thread attached to a wooden matchstick and lump of sodium in a petrol can beneath the windowsill. My eyes tried to follow the cotton line across the shop but the grey thread was invisible.

The butcher strode right past the shop door, crossed over and hurried into Mrs. Dvossi's house opposite.

'It's late,' I told Shosana, 'and there's a storm coming. Look.'

I swung the counter open and led my sister onto the shop-floor so she could see through the window for herself. The street was deserted.

'The Mendl's have already got their shutters closed,' I said. 'You want to be tucked up in bed before the thunder

9

comes, don't you?'

'Yes,' Shoshana said, her voice wavering.

'Good.' I stepped over to the door and pulled down the blind. 'Me too.' I turned and smiled, and then jumped when a fist pounded the glass. The fist was attached to the bony wrist of Podhotzur, our drunk policeman.

Shoshana giggled, then said, 'A customer!'

Podhotzur pounded again, the urgency unmistakable.

'Go up to see mama right now,' I said. 'I'll be there in a minute.'

'But the Magic Bell hasn't rung yet!'

'Shoshana!'

I didn't raise my voice often. Once was usually enough.

When Shoshana disappeared back behind the counter, I turned to disable my father's booby trap and unlatch the door. Podhotzur fell in, a skinny youth with tiny round eyes like a bird and very small teeth.

'Mr. Podhotzur, are you alright?'

'Soldiers coming. They were in Bystrica earlier.'

'Germans?'

'Worse.' He coughed. 'Bavarians. The usual trouble. You should get up stairs, turn off the lights.'

'I can't leave the shop while we're still open.'

'So close early,' Podhotzur said. 'If the place looks empty, you might get away with only a looting.'

'If I don't protect the shop, who will?'

Not the policeman, evidently. Podhotzur ducked out the doorway with a shrug and scurried on home. I returned to my position behind the till and practised running my finger along the edge of the counter to the taped threads, flicking back and forth between the two.

I tried to visualise the merry havoc the Bavarians would wreak on our shop displays. The skinned rabbit hanging from the window became a boxing trainer's spring-loaded ball under their fists. That neat pyramid of coffee cans was an invitation to any soldier's boot. The wicker baskets would crumple under a punch and spill potatoes through their splinters. But it was the egg boxes stacked so provocatively next to the front door that I was rueing when a tumble of red curls rose up from behind them as if on the end of fishing line.

'Shoshana!' Sure enough, the rest of the girl followed. 'I told you to get to bed!'

'But the Magic Bell didn't ring. Is it broken?'

'Quick. Come here.'

Somewhere up the street a stone broke through a pane of glass and three soldiers in green tunics lurched into view in front of the shop, two big men grinning through our window and a shorter one gesturing at the door. 'Open up, Little Grocer!'

Shosana darted back behind the stack of eggs and would remain hidden, as long as she didn't give herself away.

'Get down,' I hissed at her through a rictus grin, nodding as I unlatched the door.

Stepping backwards, never once taking my eyes off the soldiers, I retook my position at the counter and tried to stop my hand trembling as my fingers sought the taped cotton thread.

The short soldier pushed the door open, ringing the bell. I glanced at the stacked eggs, but Shoshana stayed hidden. Unlike the other two soldiers who wore spiked helmets, the shorter one wore a black beret. Although the door-frame was no impediment to his height, he removed the beret upon entering and smoothed down his short black hair with vicious slaps, as if attacking his own scalp.

He was ten years older than the others. His pale face was a strange mixture of gauntness at the cheeks and paunch below the chin. The other two were altogether more imposing, ruddy and thick-limbed, but were for now content just to stand there flanking their superior. The bags on their backs looked heavy. I could see no gun barrels protruding and the holsters on their brown belts contained only water flasks.

'Good evening, Little Grocer.' The short man spoke German with a heavy Austrian accent.

'Good evening to you, gentlemen,' I replied.

'My name is Obergefreiter Gruber. I'm very sorry to intrude upon you at this unfeasibly late hour.'

'I was just closing up, Obergefreiter, but it's no inconvenience, truly. Are your men hungry?'

The other two soldiers cheered at this.

'Music to our ears,' Obergefrieter Gruber said. 'How observant you are. We made the right decision in stopping here, I told my men that. I knew it from the sign above the door. What did I say? With a name like Siegler, we can't go wrong.'

The other two grinned.

'May I enquire of your age, Little Grocer, if it's not too impertinent a question considering we've only just met?'

'I am ten years old, sir.'

'Ten years old, Jozef Siegler, ten years old.' I did not interrupt to ask how the Obergefrieter knew my name. 'And it is - please correct me if I'm wrong - but I've always believed it is a fundamental absolute of your people that you eat and drink with a gusto that some may regard – wrongly, of course - as bordering on the obscene? The porcine, if I may be so bold.'

'My people?' I said.

'Pot-bellied greengrocers, of course!' Gruber smiled at his thugs. 'Not that your stomach has yet to develop that particular protuberance. Oh dear, you must forgive me, I've been several days now with only these two intellectual titans for company, and my conversational skills have evidently grown rusty. I'm ashamed to say that was my attempt at small talk. Completely redundant, now that I think about it. You people wouldn't be much good if you didn't know your onions from your elbows, would you? Greengrocers, that is.'

'No, Obergefreiter,' I said. 'I don't suppose we would.'

'Well, then. We are in agreement on that.' He beamed, genuinely pleased and quite, quite mad, I now realised. 'I shall not take up too much more of your time in pleasantries, other than to praise you for the tidiness of your shop. You pass inspection, Little Grocer! What is the expression? You cut the mustard, ja!'

'Thank-you, Obergefreiter.'

'And such refined manners, too. Most encouraging. But to turn to the matter at hand, as I promised. It is neither mustard nor onions nor elbow grease that we require from you tonight, although I see you are well stocked in all three.'

'Tell me what you require and I shall do my very best.'

'What I require is that little black bean which the lowly soldier cannot do without. Unfortunately, we've been lacking its dark, sinewy stimulation for several days now, which is another factor to bear in mind when assessing my conversational perspicacity. I wonder, Little Grocer, if you could hazard a guess?'

'Could it be coffee, Obergefreiter?'

'Why, yes!' He clapped in childish glee. 'Amazing. It's true: you people really do know how to rob a man of his thoughts.'

'How much would you like, sir?'

'Shall we say, three bags full?'

'We only have it in aluminium cans, I'm afraid.'

'Decantable cans, I trust? Aluminium is rather bulky for our pack-packs, you see.'

'Of course.'

For the first time since the soldiers had entered, I lifted my finger away from the taped end of cotton. Maybe coffee was all they wanted after all.

I walked over to the shelf above the eggs, raised a clandestine finger to my lips to keep Shoshana silent, and removed three bags. Crossing back in front of the soldiers, I stopped at the pyramid of coffee cans, unscrewed the lid of the one at the apex and began to pour the black powder into the first bag. To calm my nerves, I whistled as I worked, until the two soldiers inharmoniously joined in. Neither seemed to notice when I stopped.

'Three bags full,' I said when done, presenting the cradled coffee to the Obergefreiter.

'Excellent. And I think some tea, for the sake of variety.'

'Tea,' I repeated. Nobody had yet offered to relieve me of the coffee. 'Of course.'

I set down the coffee on the floorboards, fetched another bag, lifted the pot from the counter and began to pour dried Russian leaves when the Obergefreiter said, 'Indian tea, if you don't mind.'

'Indian.'

'The standard three bags worth, I think.'

'Of course.'

I emptied the bag back into the Russian pot and fetched the Indian tea from behind the counter. Three bags later, six in total heaped in my arms, I returned again to the Obergefreiter. A wisp of Shoshana's curls rose above the boxes but dropped again out of sight.

'Flour, sugar and eggs, I think next. Fresh bread's all very well, but it only stays fresh for a couple of days. Its constituent ingredients, however, may be used for several months. But look at me lecturing the Little Grocer on food economy!'

'Flour, sugar and eggs,' I said.

I deposited the tea next to the coffee on the floorboards, and started collecting the rest of the order. My reappearance at the egg boxes was almost too much for Shoshana to bear and it was only with the severest of facial contortions that I persuaded my sister to remain hidden.

This time, before loading myself up like a cart-horse, I asked the Obergefreiter if there was anything else he required.

'Coffee, tea, flour, sugar and eggs... I do believe that's everything.'

I began stacking bags against my chest using my left arm as a crude shelf when the Obergefreiter said, 'Ah-ah-ah! *Almost* everything!'

I flinched.

'Except of course for your bill, Little Grocer!'

I allowed myself to relax.

'How much do we owe you?'

I finished loading the bags onto my arm, abandoning the calculations that came so easily to my brain. Providing the soldiers left, I'd charge them a nominal amount only.

'Let's call it two rubles,' I said.

'As cheap as that? Good Lord. And here was I thinking you people had acquired a reputation for penny-pinching. Greengrocers, of course.'

I stood laden before him, attempting to smile.

'Well, in that case,' the Obergefreiter continued. 'Seeming as I've got more rubles left than I was expecting, we may as well add a few more items while we're about it.'

A sigh escaped my lips. This was never going to end, none

of it.

'How rude!' the Obergefreiter bristled.

'I'm sorry, sir. I'm a little tired, that's all.'

'No, how rude of us, I meant. What on earth was I thinking? Three able-bodied soldiers standing round gawping while you're working up a sweat with your hands full. Musketier, relieve the Little Grocer of his burden.'

The younger of the two soldiers stepped up and pointed to the heap of goods I was cradling. I shifted the bags in readiness of transferring them. The soldier raised his hand but then promptly slapped it down across my arms in a puff of flour, breaking my hold. Bags and boxes tumbled to the floor, splitting and breaking as they fell. A sticky puddle of egg yolks and coffee powder began to ooze around my shoes.

'Clumsy fucking kike,' the Obergefreiter spat. 'You might wallow in this kind of squalor but we certainly don't.'

I began retreating to the counter.

'I think you'd better go now,' I said.

'Imagine being left to look after a shop like this. So your father could run off and help the Jewish swine in Siberia. If that's your people's idea of family loyalty, I'd hate to see how you treat your friends.'

My finger found the edge of the counter and inched along until it came to the taped thread.

I said, 'My father was more of a man than you could ever hope to be,'

'The Heroes of Zion?' the Obergefreiter said. 'Don't make me laugh. Even the Russians trampled them.'

'True,' I said. 'But there were casualties on both sides. And if you know your history, you'll know how well the Ghetto was defended. Every Jew for miles was on hand with a pick-axe or rifle.'

'And where are they now, Little Grocer?'

I held the cotton and tore the thread away from the tape.

'Do you really think Radion Siegler would leave his ten year old son to fend for himself?' I said. 'My father chased off nakniks like you before breakfast.'

'And who's to do the chasing off now, eh? Not your whore of a mother upstairs, surely?'

I began to wind the thread around my fingertip. 'Tell me, Obergefreiter. Are you familiar with the methodology of Russian duck-hunting?'

'Bavarians hunt kikes, not ducks.'

'I'll take that as a no,' I said. 'Season after season, there's one ruse that the poor old duckies never see coming. Frankly, between me and you, their brains are too small. The hunter lays a long trail of ripe berries across the ground, near a large duck nest. The adult birds are of course unable to resist the temptation. They waddle along, scooping up the fruit in their fat beaks until they're almost drunk on the fermentation, with absolutely no idea that they've been lured right up to very edge of a dark forest – much like the one behind you now.'

'Is this where we're supposed to turn round and gape out the window,' the Obergefreiter said, 'while you pick up that gun under the counter?'

'There is no gun under the counter. But there are twelve men crouching in the forest with rifles raised and three Bavarian soldiers firmly in their sights. That's a ratio of one of you to three of them, in case your maths isn't up to scratch. And one of me. All I have to do...'

I raised a distracting left fist slowly into the air while my right hand prepared to jerk the thread.

'Is give this signal and...'

I yanked the cotton.

The thread cut invisibly through the air, pulling the black match at the window and striking the lump of sodium in the neck of the petrol can. A dragon-bellied roar of combustion blew out the shop's window pane, studding the skinned rabbits with jagged chunks of glass. The soldiers flung themselves to the floor, shrieking.

'Now, Obergefreiter,' I said when the smoke had lifted. 'If you'd like to avoid a similar fate, I suggest you walk out that door with your hands raised high and slither back to whatever Bavarian rock you crawled out from. And know this, please: Radion Siegler's Heroes of Zion are watching you every step of the way.'

***

The scene, unfortunately, has a post-script.

The Obergefreiter turned to his men and pointed to what was left of the window. The soldiers nodded, stepped up to the shop-front, pulled the blinds down over the broken pane and came back to stand either side of their superior.

'Nice trick with the cotton,' the Obergefreiter said, dusting glass from his shoulder as he approached the counter. 'Almost walked into it earlier. Ducked just in time. That was when I saw her.'

The Obergefreiter turned to the stack of egg boxes.

'You can come out now, little Shoshana,' he said. 'The real fireworks are just about to begin.'

PART TWO

1

1938. The year everything changed.

For the past fourteen summers, I had considered myself a good German, employed by the still scandalously liberal University of Kiel in the northern province of Schleswig-Holstein, teaching Humanism and Civil Society in a country hell-bent on draining the tank of both. The campus of Kiel was a rare refuge. We'd absorbed so many displaced Jewish professors from 'superior' Aryan universities since the Nazis came to power that we were regarded as more of a gulag than an academic institution.

History will show the Kristallnacht pogroms of November 1938 as the night when tyranny turned from economic and social legislation to the most concerted military campaign against a civilian population the world has ever seen. But at the time, it was just another riot. My parents Elena and Radion Siegler had survived street thugs in Odessa forty years ago, in Yekaterinoslav, in Kiev, in the Russian Pale.

The final tightening of the Nuremberg Race Laws followed that bleak December: Jews were now prohibited from all German universities, including a flea-pit like Kiel. When my good friend Samuel Ehrlich retired in June, he was presented with a Schatz Grand Sonnerie carriage clock. I was given five minutes to clean out my office before being escorted off the premises by the SS.

With little in the way of savings, I decided to join my mother and Shosana, who had settled in Kazimierz, the old Jewish Quarter of Cracow. Together they ran a large grocery store on Izaaka Street. Our father had never returned from Siberia, where he'd gone to help Stalin's Jews. I reached Poland just in time for a family Hanukkah, 1938. It would be our last.

That new year, I couldn't even find a job teaching kindergarten in Cracow, and had no choice but to help out in the family store, a role I had forsaken as a youth in Romania to devote myself to study. The business had prospered since relocating to Poland – and in my absence - expanding to include a cobbler's workshop next door run by an ailing Polish bachelor called Mordka Zygot, whom Shoshana somewhat spitefully referred to as her 'annex'.

Mr. Zygot had no heir and it was deemed that I would be trained to inherit his customers, until the silly war scare died down and the restrictions on employment of Jews in education was lifted. So, at the ripe old age of thirty-four, I became a cobbler's apprentice. My first job was to remove a pair of DIY heel-lifts a rather vain young man had glued onto his boots and to fit Mr. Zygot's patented orthopedic replacement.

Ever since the army visited my father's store when Shoshana and I were children, my sister had worn a black eye-patch. I survived Obergefrieter Gruber's inspection that Sunday afternoon with only a beating, and my broken leg healed. But Shoshana was part blinded for life because of my stupidity. Not that the young woman of 1939 needed my pity. Shoshana was more than capable of waging her own battles in Cracow, blossoming into a militant Zionist who spent all her evenings at an Akiva youth camp just outside the city, where she was already the only female madritch and trained surly teenage lads in the arts of close-combat fighting. In the evenings after my cobbling, Shoshana would tell me that Akiva desperately needed teachers of Jewish religion and traditions, and though I considered myself an expert in neither, I was keen to lend a hand. There was a growing need for Jewish solidarity in the Polish spring of 1939. Like my father, I heeded the call. In part I missed the collegial fraternity I'd known at Kiel. The Akiva camp where I spent the evenings and weekends was a second family that gradually became as important as my own.

It was during a Sabbath meeting that I first learned of plans for the mass resettlement of European Jewry to Palestine. The Rabi believed it was the only way to survive the coming troubles. Our own mother was weak and discussions began at Izaaka Street on how the three of us might make the move. There was no future for Jewish businesses, not even in Kazimierz.

Over the next few weeks, a plan emerged: Shoshana and I were to lead a mission north to Punsk, to arrange a transfer of Jewish orphans across the border into neutral Lithuania. Onward transit visas would be arranged in the capital of Kaunas, where we had an unlikely advocate in the form of a Dutch diplomat. If Shoshana and I were successful, we would return for the rest of our two families, Siegler and the Akiva camp. We said goodbye to our mother in May of 1939.

Operation Punsk was an initial triumph. With the aid of my language skills and Shoshana's seductive wiles, we managed to negotiate a snowy, moonlit crossing through the mountain border and safely delivered our orphans to Kaunas. But while we recuperated, border-controls began to tighten, mainly due to interference from the Russians. Then, thanks to an inside tip-off at the Dutch consulate, the diplomat's irregular visa-granting came under investigation from the authorities. Fearing exposure, Shoshana and I made the trip east across Lithuania to a sun-dappled Wilno, where we were welcomed by the Hehalutz, the federation of Zionist pioneers.

Along with hundreds more refugees we were taken to Akiva headquarters on Subocz Street in the north-eastern suburbs and welcomed by Akiva secretariat Joziek Rudashevski before being sorted by country of origin, or city in the case of Poles, since there were so many of us. Shoshana and I were introduced to a thick-set man with a wolfish grin called Herman Glik and we three were instructed to select a house of young adults to supervise from a very long list. I chose a large villa adjacent to the Jewish Old Town on Pilies Street, which became our new House of Cracow.

Wilno in the summer of 1939 was a Zionist's dream. The Jewish population of the city already comprised of over 60,000, and while tensions between Poles and Lithuanians were high, dealings between Lithuanians and Jews were relatively peaceful. The hub of Judaic religious culture in Europe since the medieval years, Wilno boasted over 110 synagogues, ten yeshivas and was home to both the Yiddish Institute of Higher Learning and the Strashum Library, which housed the world's largest collection of Yiddish-language books. The archives of Kiel seemed positively bare in comparison. I had not become a religious zealot since leaving the Faculty of Humanism and Civil Society, but I had found a new respect for the traditions and customs of our people. While our house on Pilies Street was considerably less grand and cloistered than my German alma mater, it was a place of purposeful learning as well as living, and I was glad to be once more intellectually engaged. Evenings and weekends, our large central room was a place for discussion, study, and occasionally music, when we had the good fortune of hosting a trio of Romanians who'd brought guitars and violins.

From Monday to Friday, we all worked. The women took care of household chores, which was not satisfactory to Shoshana's way of thinking, and it was often remarked that her girls spent more time learning aikido and boxing than they did sweeping the floors. Herman Glik led Moishe and Baruch and the other young men to work in the forests, chopping trees to be sold as winter fuel. With my large frame and powerful limbs, I was an obvious candidate for the role of wood-cutter, but to Herman's amusement, I found an alternative means of employment.

At the northern end of Pilies Street, near the Cathedral and National Museum, there was a small shoe-repair shop that had a long queue stretching out onto the pavement. When I inquired inside, I quickly saw the reason for this chronic over-subscription: the harried cobbler was balancing his shoe-repairing work while taking care of a backroom full of young children. His wife was bed-bound, Mr. Donelaitis told me glumly, with severe swelling. I explained my limited experience as Mr. Zygoti's apprentice in Cracow, and was given my own green apron before I could say another word.

In part I had missed the fragrance of leather and glue and the supple, satisfying pleasures of the trade, and Mr. Donelaitis was certainly grateful for the help. But there were other reasons for my decision. Every Jewish arrival I knew worked outside the city in large teams and only ever talked to a Lithuanian when one of them arrived on a wagon to collect the logs. I was struck with how insular the life of an immigrant could be. Long after 17th century Venetians compelled us Jews to live in Ghettos, we chose to voluntarily wall off ourselves from a city that had been good enough to take us in. I wanted the best of both worlds. While I was in Wilno, I would work with the local people, and become a part of their quotidian lives in this Baltic paradise, opposite the Catholic Cathedral and the National Museum, yet be able to retreat to communal Jewish living at the end of the day.

For a few months that summer, I achieved something close to happiness. On bicycles, Shoshana and I explored an area of six beautiful green lakes in the north-eastern part of the city, perfect for picnics and swimming. Although we were technically stranded in a foreign city with no plan other than 'wait and hope', I thought we had already reached the promised land. If we could only get our mother to the new House of Cracow, she would be safe. But in that summer, all hopes were short-lived.

On September 1st 1939, the Nazis invaded Poland.

From that point on, Shoshana and I also waged a losing battle with our own guilt. We had abandoned our friends, sister and mother for the good life in Wilno while Kazimierz was under siege. Each day brought worse news. A Nazi lawyer called Hans Frank had been appointed as Chief Jurist of occupied Poland and Frank had imposed a temporary ban on Jewish travel visas while the new administration took charge. Our mother was trapped on Izaaka Street for the time being. We had reason to believe that Cracow was relatively safe, since it was in the middle of the occupied zone now called the Generalgouvernment. Indeed, Jews from the less stable annexes of the Wartheland, from Lodz and Poznan, were already being transferred into the Generalgouvernment, so we were led to believe that citizens of Cracow had found unlikely protectors in the German army.

And then, on September 18th, Lithuania awoke to find not Nazi panzers but Soviet T-34s rolling down the capital's streets. Stalin fought The Battle of Wilno as a counter-blast to Hitler's own invasion. Polish forces in Lithuania were relatively weak and their commanders, unsure whether to actively oppose the Soviets, did not put up much of a fight. By the end of the day the Soviets had secured the airfield and made several thrusts into the city, taking the Rasos Cemetery.

By the morning of September 19th the advanced Soviet armoured units had been reinforced with infantry and cavalry. The people of Wilno were presented with an ultimatum which they could not refuse. In exchange for the return of 1/5th of the Wilno region (including the city), Lithuania would have to accept Soviet military bases in its territory. The alternative was a full-scale Soviet invasion.

The Jewish community initially welcomed both the Soviets and the subsequent Lithuanian administration. Herman Glik argued the lesser of three evils: that we would now not be ruled by the hated Polish Endeks or fall under the occupation of Nazi Germany. Having been well versed by my parents in the history of Russian-orchestrated persecution - in Odessa, in Yekaterinoslav, in Kiev, in Vichob, in the heart of the Pale of Settlement - I was less disposed to see the Soviets as saviours. But I tried to convince myself that Elena and Radion's childhoods belonged to a different century, and those days were gone for good. Many of my fellow Jews had already made that leap of faith. Fourteen thousand refugees from the south made their way to the city, including one remarkable young woman called Vitka Kempner who would become my sister's own madritch.

I returned home from Mr. Donelaitis' shop on the dark afternoon of Sunday October 30th to find a strange young couple seated in a cloud of smoke opposite Herman and Shoshana at our kitchen table, their crossed rifles leaning against the door of my sister's cleaning cupboard. I knew why they had come.

Yesterday was supposed to have been a day of pride for Lithuanians. Six weeks after the Soviets had invaded, their troops withdrew on Saturday 29th and power was once again ceded to the capital. Unfortunately, when the nationalists made their grand reclamation, marching into the centre with the pomp of a full fanfare, they found themselves mere bit-players and their city in tatters. The Soviets had plundered the local infrastructure, taking everything they could carry. They left behind 60,000 Jews, twice as many Poles but only a few thousand Lithuanians. For once, everyone apart from the Jews was miserable. The Lithuanians resented our joy at being liberated from Polish anti-Semitism and the Poles resented our love of the Red Army. Such bitterness coalesced in the streets within minutes of the Lithuanian entrance, and anti-Jewish riots broke out later, under the usual veil of darkness. Several tradesmen were beaten to death defending their properties. The Jews went back to being miserable. In the hospital I volunteered at, I heard rumour that the riots would go for a fortnight at least, up until the anniversary of Kristallnacht, November 9th.

So a visit of the likes we'd received was inevitable. The fight back had begun.

'Our mighty axe-man returns,' the young woman said, rising from the table at my entrance. Vitka Kempner was all cheek-bones and blonde curls, a teenage Marlene Dietrich in military fatigues. 'How was the wood today?'

'Not this one,' Herman said. 'Jozef leaves the heavy lifting for the rest of us. He works all the hours God sends as a fancy shoe-maker up the road, opposite the National Museum. You wouldn't think it, but he's got the hands of a temple dancer.'

'Making shoes on a Sunday,' Vitka said. 'Is business that brisk?'

'It is, but today I've been helping with the children,' I said. 'My employer's wife is ill with elephantiasis and there are five young ones to look after, schoolwork and such like.'

'The day after Lithuanians attack us with crowbars,' Herman said. 'And Jozef's playing au-pair for their kids.'

'That might be the best time of all,' Abba Kovner said, a man of no less distinctive appearance than his young friend. I had seen Abba before at the Strashum Library, poring over an antique Talmud, its yellowed pages a precarious funeral pyre beneath his cigarette. Gaunt and heavy-lidded, Abba was a compelling figure. He wore his hair long and his expression longer. His thick black locks were pushed back today, accentuating the flat wedge of his features, large, hooded eyes, flared nostrils at the precipice of his nose's sheer edge and the tight slit of mouth like a prison hatch. Like Vitka, he wore a military jacket, shirt collar pulled out, and wide trousers over skinny legs, tucked into his boots.

'Jozef's always been a natural with children,' Shoshana said. 'With me as a sister, he didn't have a choice. That's another thing you've got in common, it's crazy. Abba also has a sister, and he was born in Russia.'

'Crimea,' Abba snapped, his customary mode of address. 'Sebastapol, on the Black Sea.'

'Our parents met in Odessa,' I said.

Shoshana adjusted her eye-patch, which had started to ride up and expose the rim of her empty socket. 'Abba's family left when he was young, and he ended up here in Wilno, where he went to art-school. He's a sculptor and a poet.'

'But don't let that put you off,' Abba said.

Vitka said, 'He's actually a pretty decent guy.'

'My brother loves poetry,' Shoshana said. 'He taught Literature and Humanism in Germany.'

'In another life,' I said. 'My mother left Russia and settled in Cracow. I went north, to Kiel. I lost my job last year and headed home, where I trained as a shoe-maker. Then Akiva came calling and Shoshana and I arranged our first transfer of children to Kaunas, and – '. I shrugged as if to say, Here we are now, but Shoshana beat me to it.

'And I've been taking care of him ever since,' she said, smiling with Vitka.

'I was in Akiva when I was a little child,' Vikta said.

'You make it sound like the Girl-Guides.'

I asked who they were with now.

'Hashomer Hatzair,' Abba growled.

Their uniforms made sense now, styled as they were like Bolshevik Revolutionaries. Hashomer Hatzair was a Socialist-Zionist movement formed in Austria-Hungary in 1913, while I was in short-pants, trying to fend off Obergefreiter Gruber and the Bavarian army.

'Vitka's Polish,' Shoshana said. 'Her family are still there, too.'

'In Kalisz,' Vitka said. 'I couldn't bear to stand by and watch the SS abuse any longer. Leaving my parents is the hardest thing I've ever done, but I was sure we could all be safe here.'

'Vitka and Abba just met this morning,' Shoshana said, 'in Subocz Street. Tell them the most amazing thing.'

'We share -' Vitka said.

'The same birthday,' Abba said.

'March 14th,' Vitka said. 'But not -'

'The same year,' Abba said. 'You're 1920, right?'

She nodded. 'And you're 1918.'

I did the maths in my head. Vitka was nineteen, which was slightly older than I'd thought. But Abba... I stared at him, trying not to gape.

'You're only twenty-one years old? I thought you were our age.' I looked at Herman for moral support. 'Early thirties.'

'It has been remarked before,' Abba said. 'I blame my parents for naming me.' In Hebrew, Abba means father. 'If they called me Bubala, I'd still be splashing around the Black Sea, building sand-castles.'

Somehow, I couldn't see Abba Kovner in a baby's swimming costume.

'So many coincidences,' Shoshana said. 'I can't get my head around them.'

'C.G. Jung says there are no such thing as coincidences,' Herman Glik said. 'Or rather, he explains that a synchronicity is a meaningful coincidence. It's about the two halves of the brain talking to each other.' He started to gesticulate now, warming to his theme. 'The left part, the creative part, jumps around time, past, present and future, and notices a time and place when something significant is going to happen. The right part, the logical part, rationalises a reason for us to be in that particular place at that particular time, and – voila! Here we all are.'

It was the most I'd ever heard Herman say, on any subject. The four of us were equally flummoxed by all this left-brain/right-brain philosophizing and I felt duty-bound to navigate a way back.

'Whatever you've come here for,' I said, looking from Vitka to Abba. 'I'm sure it wasn't to discuss Jung's theory of synchronicity.'

'They're organising defence groups to attack the rioters,' Hernan said.

'Which is it?' I said. 'Defend or attack?'

Abba reached into his jacket and pulled out a fistful of flyers, handwritten in exceptional Hebrew cursive script, far more beautiful than my own, and mimeographed. I took a slip and read aloud. 'The Independent Jewish Defence Force in Wilno calls you into the streets to defend the life and honour of Wilno's Jewish population.'

'Join us,' Vitka urged, seizing my wrist in a not altogether friendly fashion. 'Together we can end this pain.'

'You could start by easing your grip,' I said, shaking my hand free. 'My father tried to stop the rioters in Vichob and was arrested for his efforts. It was Russians attacking us then, but I believe my point is still valid.'

'So what are you going to do?' Vitka asked, crossing her arms. 'Make shoes?'

'I'll do everything I can to ensure the safety of the Jewish people, by arranging transfers to Palestine.'

'And after the Kaunas children, how many transfers has that been, exactly?'

I didn't know, but it was very few. With the Dutch consul under investigation, there was precious little opportunity. All other foreign embassies had closed. The special certificates could only be issued by Sochnut, and the Jewish Agency was already overwhelmed. And even Sochnut had stopped facilitating transfers for anybody over the age of eighteen. Meanwhile, hundreds of new refugees flooded into the city every day.

'I'm afraid what I told you has not changed,' Shoshana said to Vitka. 'My brother will not fight.'

'Violence does in truth recoil upon the violent,' I said.

'Sir Arthur Conan Doyle.' Abba had recognized the allusion. '*The Adventures of the Speckled Band.* Do you know how Sherlock Holmes finished that sentence?'

I nodded, for I did.

'And the schemer falls into the pit which he digs for another,' Abba said. 'Make no mistake, the Nazis are hard at work at that task as we speak, Mr. Siegler. The whole of ope shall be our burial pit.'

'They wouldn't get their hands dirty,' Vitka said. 'They'll make us dig our own graves.'

'This is true,' Abba said. 'The days of Sherlock Holmes fighting off a poisonous snake with an iron poker have long since passed.'

'And my sister was right, Mr. Kovner,' I said. 'Principles do not change. At least, mine haven't.'

'Yet,' Abba said.

I felt regret at discomfiting my sister, if that's what I had done, but I was not ready to take up arms against our oppressors. For now, our business was done. I rose to excuse myself, but was stilled by Herman's hand against my forearm.

'Let us at least find the others and say Kaddish to honour those who fell last night.'

Herman knew I didn't like to participate in prayer, although I hadn't disclosed to him that I was an atheist. He also knew he had me in a difficult position, for I wouldn't further embarrass Shoshana in front of her new friends by declining his cleverly-worded invitation.

'Perhaps you'd like to lead the Prayer of the Dead,' he said, 'as you weren't here last night.'

'I could never do it as well as you, Herman.'

'Unfortunately I think you're going to get a lot of practice.' We rose to gather our Akiva house-mates in the living room, but Herman was not done yet. 'I heard some of your Lithuanians toasting their overnight success as I walked past the Tappo D'Oro this morning. One of them said, This'll be a great city when we get rid of the Old Town.'

'I told you,' Abba said. 'Mass burial pits, that's how.'

'It's an old joke,' I said. 'But I don't think it's meant to be anti-Semitic.'

'Oh, Jozef!' Shoshana said. 'Honestly.'

'No, let's hear the Professor out.'

'When I heard the joke it was 'get rid of the whole town', not 'Old Town'. Lithuanians are sick of being pushed about by one nation after another, Austro-Hungarian, Polish, Russian. They want to see the back of all of them, not us.'

Herman said. 'So they beat the Jew to death in the street?

If you'd been with us last night instead of your precious shoe-maker, you'd know what I mean.'

'Herman,' Shoshana cautioned. 'Don't.'

'Look where he works. Even the street he chose for us. Everybody else I know lives cheek-by-jowl in the Ghetto. Your brother picked the only Akiva house outside the Jewish Quarter.'

'Vitka and Abba found us without too much difficulty,' I said. 'We're not exactly in hiding.'

'Come on, boys,' said Shoshana. 'Play nice.'

Once again I felt ashamed for squabbling in front of our guests.

I observed Kaddish with the rest of the House of Cracow, once the quorum of ten males had been achieved. Our committed militants took their rifles and left shortly after prayers, with seven new part-time recruits to their Independent Jewish Defence Force.

From everything I have heard, our youths were a boon to the IJDF, and even helped to reign in some of what I regarded as Hashomer Hatzair's more provocative tendencies. I certainly didn't begrudge their involvement. Moishe and Baruch and the others were young men fully able to decide their own paths of action and did not need my counselling on how to spend their evenings. Even after a day of wood-cutting, they still had energy to burn, and I was pleased to see this put to constructive use. It's true, I felt safer knowing they were on patrol.

My only concern was that, with Vitka and Shoshana taking prominent roles while Abba matriculated from art-school, the IJDF was predominately run by women. This was not a problem to me, knowing full well Shoshana's strength of body and mind, but I wondered how some of our lads would handle the situation, not always holding the most enlightened views on sexual equality. Luckily, Moishe and Baruch seemed used to it, having been schooled how to box by my sister's punishing fists.

***

Like us, Herman Glik had left behind loved ones in Cracow. Although he was a tough, sinewy specimen, the heart that beat inside Herman's chest was as broken as my own. I thought long and hard about his rebuke, but could find no bitterness towards the man. He was one of life's natural protectors - especially of my sister, to whom he'd taken quite a shine, another factor in our tussles - and saw me as a weak link in his new family unit.

Perhaps I was. But it wasn't cowardice that compelled the actions Herman found so disreputable.

When I was first presented with the list of available Akiva houses, I didn't know the geography of the Jewish Quarter. I chose Pilies because I had initially misread it as Polis Street, and my mind then equated it as a place of safety for the youths in our care. This was several months before I realised the truth of security in Wilno, that more often than not policemen would join in the beating of Jewish riot victims rather than trying to make peace.

As for my work and friendship with Mr. Donelaitis, I had nothing to apologise for. He was a kindly man who paid well, far more than the wood-cutters earned, and as my wages went into the same common pot as everybody else's, the whole of the House of Cracow prospered from my employment. As Shoshana said, I did enjoy looking after young children. But our own street-fighting Akiva youths now looked more to my sister and Vitka Kempner than they did to me. Meanwhile, as Mrs. Donelaitis' elephantiasis advanced, her family came to depend increasingly on my support, both in the shop and their apartment outback, and I was glad to help. The poor woman was bed-bound on a permanent basis, the swelling having spread from her legs to her arms, which were as purple as bruises. Dr. Todras visited twice a week to lance the fluid from her limbs, which was the sum total of her treatment.

As a result of Herman's words, I doubled my efforts to stay in contact with mother on Izaaka Street. For a brief spell during Lithuania's independence, we could still send letters to the Generalgouvernement. Mother was able to reply through the Red Cross. The news was not encouraging. Under the German regime, Jews and Poles had been prohibited from keeping foreign currency, and before long jewellery and gold were added to the list of illegal items. I found some solace in Shoshana's phrasing, that it was 'Jews and Poles' who were equally affected. The discrimination was not being pursued along racial lines, as Abba and others were warning.

But then at the end of November, Hans Frank announced that 'all Jews and Jewesses over the age of nine must wear a four-inch armband in white, marked with the star of Zion on the right sleeve of their inner and outer clothing.' Transgressors, Frank warned, 'would be punished with imprisonment'.

On Monday December 4th, five weeks after meeting Vitka Kempner and Abba Kovner, Mrs. Donelaitis died in her bedroom from satellite tumours which had grown beneath her swollen skin. Although the illness had been a protracted one, her death came as an enormous blow and the shop remained closed after the weekend.

I spent the day with the grieving father and children and after they were put to bed, offered to stay to allow Mr. Donelaitis and friends to drown their sorrows in the city. What I did not find out until I got back to the House of Cracow early Tuesday morning, was that Moishe and Baruch had also been drinking in the Tapa D'Orro, letting off steam after an IJDF training session with Vitka.

My two house-mates had been in a typically raucous mood and were out-doing each other with a string of ribald jokes. 'If your wife keeps coming out of the kitchen to nag at you, what have you done wrong?' Moishe asked. 'You made her chain too long.'

After much pounding of the table, Baruch countered. 'How do you turn a fox into an elephant?'

'I give up.'

'Marry it!'

It was as this point that one of Mr. Donelaitis' friends approached the pair, whose noise had already emptied one end of the bar. 'Look, we're just out trying to have a quiet drink tonight,' he explained. 'Would you mind keeping your voices down a little?'

'It's a free country,' Baruch said.

'No thanks to the likes of you,' Mr. Donelaitis' friend said. 'I'll have you thrown out on your ear if that's what you prefer.'

'Why don't you guys leave?' Moishe asked. 'We're not doing anything wrong.'

'Yes,' Baruch said, still engaged in a battle of one-upmanship with his peers. 'Go home, old man, to your elephant wife.'

The friend winced when he saw Mr. Donelaitis face drop, then laced his finger's behind the back of Baruch's head and drove his face into the brass-rimmed edge of the bar, snapping his nose. Before he could repeat the move, Moishe swung his tankard into the side of the man's forehead, and a localised riot erupted.

Mr. Donelaitis said nothing of the encounter when he returned that night, but he was so drunk he could barely speak. He fell across the sofa and I let myself out.

When I got back to Pilies Street after midnight, Herman and Moishe were sipping pear brandy at the kitchen table, Moishe's arm in a sling, one eye squeezed shut under a glistening purple contusion. Shoshana was tending to Baruch upstairs. He had taken a far worse beating.

'Who did this?' I demanded.

'Your precious shoe-maker and friends,' Herman said. 'Where have you been?'

'At the cinema,' I said, too embarrassed to tell the truth.

'Well I hope you enjoyed yourself.'

'Mr. Donelaitis' wife died this morning,' I said. 'His friends were taking him out for a drink....'

'This is exactly what I'd warned you about - ' It wasn't, but before he could continue, the front door resounded with a barrage of knocks. 'God damn it, what now?'

'I'll go.' If there was any chance Mr. Donelaitis' friends had found out where Moishe and Baruch lived, I wanted mine to be the first face they saw.

But it was the imposing figure of our Akiva Secretariat I saw through the peephole. A stern, bespectacled Joziek Rudashevski stared back, a frown of grim determination darkening the brow beneath his fedora. Rudashevski was so overwhelmed with refugees these days, he rarely left Subocz Street. The attack on my young house-mates was appalling, but it was tame in comparison with recent assaults, and hardly warranted a personal house-call from our leader. When I opened the door and saw the little boy standing before him, I realised that Rudashevski hadn't come about Moishe and Baruch at all.

'Mr. Secretariat,' I said. 'Please come - '

That was as far as I got before my sister sprang up at my side, a wooden bat raised over her shoulder. 'If those bastards think they've come to apologise...'

I stopped Shoshana before she could bludgeon our leader unconscious. The little boy just stood there on the doorstep, not even a flinch.

'Two of our lads have run into trouble in town tonight,' I said by way of apology. 'Tempers are running rather high.'

The Secretariat nodded, placing his hat over the still-raised end of Shoshana's bat like a mute over a trumpet. He ushered the boy inside our hallway but when the child moved, it was with a stealth and stillness that seemed designed to render him invisible to adult eyes.

'My young friend Jacob has just arrived from Cracow,' Rudashevski said. 'A glass of hot milk would seem in order.'

'Of course,' I said. 'Please come through.'

Our house was already full, and the wrong age group for little Jacob. All our charges were at least ten years older. Perhaps the other Akiva properties had already taken their quota of new arrivals, and we were next on the list.

Whatever the boy's fortunes, the sight of Moishe's purple swollen face at the kitchen table could not have been the welcome for which Secretariat Rudashevski had been hoping – to say nothing of the rearing cobra of my sister at the front door – but again, the boy's face betrayed no emotion. I wondered what those heavy-lidded eyes had already seen.

Herman helped Moishe to his feet and took him by the arm to bed, while Rudashevski and Jacob sat in their places and Shoshana and I prepared five hot milks. When our guests left thirty minutes later, none of the milk had been touched.

Jacob Schmiel was ten years old, but looked like more like

a grandfather in his black suit and lime green shirt fastened at the collar. He wore a thick mop of brown hair long over ears that stuck out like Peter Pan's and his face was divided by two large brown eyes, darker than the eyebrows barely distinguishable from his skin. A long thin nose opened out like a tea-spoon above a pair of lips that looked sewn together from mismatched mouths, the upper lip thin and resolute as any British soldier, the lower one as fit to burst as a ripe tomato.

The last few days had been cold in Cracow, and on Sunday morning Jacob had been caught in the street by German soldiers and forced with many others to clear snow from the railroad tracks. Their job was to keep the trains running. The Nazis had started using cattle-wagons to round up Jews from the countryside. Yes, cattle-wagons. On any other night, that fact alone would have been the most shocking part of Jacob's story. When he returned to Josefa Street, two blocks away from my family's apartment, he learned that his mother Sara and older sister Leah had been killed.

Three months after Hitler's invasion of Poland, December 3rd was ordained as the first Aktion against the Jews of Kazimierz. It was nothing more than a glorified raiding party. The first anybody knew of it was the declaration of a daytime curfew. Anybody showing themselves in the streets or on balconies would be shot on sight, which seemed an absurd threat, until the residents saw what happened next.

The SS stormed into their buildings, rammed open apartment doors, flung mattresses from beds, slashed cushions and upholstery, hauled out the contents of cupboards, smashed open desk drawers, blew up safes, tore rings from fingers and necklaces from throats. One of Jacob's friends had pleaded to keep his school-satchel. The SS broke his arm. When they asked Sara and Leah for jewellery and furs, Jacob's mother said she had none. They shot her daughter first, forcing Sara to watch. The mother met her death without witness: her ten year old son Jacob was shoveling snow to keep the cattle-wagons running.

When the boy finished talking, we noticed that Herman had returned from Moishe's room and was standing in the

34

doorway, hands clutching his jaw like a vice.

'Izaaka Street?' Shoshana gasped.

'Josefa and Izaaka,' Jacob said. 'Also some of the bigger apartments closest to Kazimierz.'

'We have family there,' I said. 'Elena Siegler, our mother.'

Jacob understood what he was being asked. 'I don't know. I'm sorry.'

'So what are we supposed to do?' Shoshana cried, looking from Rudashevksi to the boy and back again. 'Send a letter to the bloody Red Cross?'

Herman staggered stagily over to the table and crouched down to hold my sister, but Shoshana brushed up and ran from the room. We heard a series of thuds up the staircase and then the slam of her bedroom door.

'Go to her,' Herman told me.

I made my apologies to Secretariat Rudashevski, kissed the top of Jacob's mop and left to comfort my sister.

She lay facing her windowless bedroom wall, sobbing softly. I crossed the carpet to her bed, stooping to pick up the discarded eye-patch. The elastic strap had snapped as she'd ripped it from her face. I folded the black fabric and slipped it into my back pocket to repair in the morning. She wouldn't be needing it tonight.

I sat on the edge of the bed and turned round to face her, pressing a tentative palm against the mattress next to her pillow. When she didn't flinch at my presence, I lifted my hand and held it to her hot forehead. Like a cat, she shrugged her neck, sending my fingers back to brush her hair. Eventually she groped a hand over her shoulder, found mine and tugged it down to her chest. The rest of me slowly followed, lying down against her back. We stayed like two spoons in a drawer until the sobbing stopped and her breath evened out. I heard Herman say goodbye to our two callers. The front door clicked shut. It was one o'clock in the morning.

Shoshana wriggled around from the wall to face me, our noses touching. I waited to hear Herman climb the stairs, but his foot-falls never came.

'Hello, big bird,' she said.

'Hello, little...' I was uncertain how to continue the

metaphor. We hadn't been this intimate since childhood, and even then I didn't recall pet-names. 'Little worm?'

As she snorted, a little green bubble popped at the end of her nose. 'Worm? That's charming!'

'Lovely, warm, wriggly little worm.'

'Oh, that makes me feel so much better.' She pressed her knees against mine to let me know it wasn't true. 'The world's an awful mess, isn't it?'

'If it's not, it'll do until the mess gets here.'

'What are we going to do?'

'The Red Cross will help, you know they well. They got mother's letters here and they'll do it again.'

'Letters? It's a bit late for words.'

'We don't know that.'

'We don't know anything. That's the problem.'

'We know she's already handed over their foreign currency, that's what the SS were looking for. As long as she does what's asked, she'll be alright.'

Shoshana massaged a crick in her neck, shifting away until the back of her head knocked against the wall.

'What happened was sheer madness,' I continued, sensing that more than a stiff muscle had come between us. 'But the SS are just throwing their weight around, showing who's boss. They won't keep that level of violence up for long. They can't. They're fighting the Red Army, not us.'

'I think they're more than capable of doing both.' She rolled round to face the wall.

'Then we'll just have to double our efforts.'

'Even if we had an Akiva for every Aktion, it wouldn't be enough. Vitka was telling me about the Sicarii, in Jerusalem.'

'Palestinians?'

'Jews.' Her voice was muffled against the plaster. 'Fighting the Roman occupation of Judea, seventy years after they killed Jesus. Judas Iscariot was a Sicarius, it's where his name comes from.'

'And the Sicarii?'

'The world's first assassination-squad, and they were Jews. Those guys could show the SS a thing or two about terror.'

'How?'

'Sicarii means 'dagger-men'. They went around with small knives hidden in their robes – they were the original cloak-and-dagger. Women, too. They'd wait for public gatherings, the bigger the better, then pull out their blades, stab as many Romans as they could and disappear into the crowd.'

'You think that's what your Jewish Defence Force should be doing?'

'It's a start.'

'Roman centurions didn't have submachine guns,' I said. 'Can you imagine what the SS would do if the Sicarii tried that in Cracow?'

'So what do you suggest?'

'What we came here to do last year. Get as many of our people to safety as we can. I agree that Palestine is the answer, but the Palestine of today, not fifteen-hundred years ago. There are good people in Kaunas trying to help. We go back there and we try again.'

'Last year the SS weren't breaking down doors on Izaaka Street. How can we stay here while that's happening?'

'Because to help anybody, we need to stay out of prison. Lithuania is safe. We've got thousands of Jews flooding out of Poland every day. You and Vitka Kempner are going to head back in? I know how useless you feel. But you have to listen to me.'

'Useless?'

'I know how useless you feel, because I feel it too. But I got you this far, didn't I?

'I didn't realise I was such a dead weight.'

'That's not what I meant,' I said. 'Right now the only person I can keep safe is you, and that's what I have to do.'

'I'm sorry.'

'You have absolutely nothing to apologise for.'

'Good. You may have realised it's not my strong point.'

'I wouldn't want you any other way.'

'We're stuck with each other then. Look, I need to try and get some sleep. Hopefully things will make more sense tomorrow morning. Night, Big Bird.'

I kissed her neck before rolling off the bed onto my feet.

'Goodnight, lovely Little Worm.'

I found Herman Glik at the kitchen table, slumped behind an almost empty bottle of pear brandy. It turned out that Secretariat Rudashevski had one more piece of intelligence to deliver. After seeing Shoshana's reaction to the first part, he'd decided to spare us and tell Herman in our absence. Tongue loosened by the brandy, Herman now relayed the story to me.

While the regular SS were brutalising the apartments of Kazimierz, a small detachment of elite Einsatzgruppe men, Special Duty Groups, had been dispatched to our local synagogue, the Stara Boznica. The Einsatz rounded up the devout at prayer, and drove in a group of small-time Jewish gangsters who'd been drinking across the road. As if this wasn't sacrilegious enough, the Einsatz broke open the temple's Arc, removed the scroll of Torah and placed it on the floor before ordering the entire congregation at gun-point to file past and spit at the parchment. Everybody complied, apart from a Jewish gangster called Max Redlicht, who refused. The Einsatz shot Max Redlicht for his disobedience, then shot everybody else and left the synagogue in flames.

I didn't sleep much that night.

Knowing Shoshana to be an early-riser, I dressed at dawn and crossed the corridor to her bedroom to tell her that I was wrong. The world made even less sense than it had last night. I was all out of hope. Shoshana and Herman and Vitka and Abba were right all along: if the Nazis got their way, Europe was to be the burial pit for an entire race.

I knocked on Shoshana's door, but there was no answer. When I stepped across the threshold, I saw that I was too late. My sister's wardrobe was open, the rail bare, and her bed made with fresh sheets, ready for the new occupant.

My little Sicarii sister had gone.

2

Every Tuesday after Shoshana disappeared, I trekked across Wilno to the Red Cross office, but no letters arrived. On my first visit, I pulled my identification card from my back pocket and a small black square fell out onto the floorboards. Shoshana's broken eye-patch. She didn't have another. Together with Herman Glik, we mourned my sister's departure, both blaming ourselves, as if a stern word could have stopped her. I had tried that, in my clumsy way.

The new year brought nothing but bad news from Cracow, and none of it from my sister or mother. The Nazi invaders of Poland continued systematically identifying, tagging and trapping the Jewish people with bureaucracy. Between January and March, all Jews were required to register their homes. After the SS raids of December 3rd, I no longer believed German assurances that Jewish property rights would be protected. The lie became apparent two months after the registration deadline closed. In May, Hans Frank announced that Cracow was to be the 'racially cleanest' city in the Generalgouvernment. An enormous deportation programme was scheduled. Of the 68,000 Jews left in their 'protected' property, only 15,000 essential workers were now given leave to stay. Greengrocers were not on the list. While my mother (and hopefully sister) were penned in on Izaaka Street, there remained a slim chance of bringing them to safety. Once they were resettled in the rural areas of the Generalgouvernment, they would be lost for the duration. All I could do was wait and hope and make shoes, although not for Mr. Donelaitis, who had moved away to live with his niece after his wife's death. I opened a small workshop in the Pilies Street basement.

After seven months of Lithuanian independence, the Soviet Union made a proposition to Wilno on midnight of June 15th, 1940, demanding that an unspecified amount of soldiers be allowed to enter our territory, and that a new pro-

Soviet government be formed, to be known as - of course - The People's Government. What else could Lithuania do but agree? The process of dividing Eastern Europe into German and Russian spheres of influence that had begun with the Molotov-Ribbentrop Pact was now complete. Lithuania joined Latvia and Estonia in the Russian sphere.

Almost immediately, the NKVD, the Soviet secret police, scheduled their own enormous deportation programme. 21,000 political and social elites including many Jews, were sent to Siberia, where Radion Siegler had last been destined. Thousands more were shot in NKVD prisons. The Soviet regime outlawed Zionism in all its forms, closing down Jewish organisations and political parties and taking over Jewish schools and cultural institutions, decree by decree. With Akiva now illegal, the House of Cracow on Pilies Street was forced to disband, along with the others. I scooped up a trio of lost souls who'd found themselves homeless and we moved into a one room apartment on a steep hill behind the train station. Herman Glik joined Vitka Kempner and Abba Kovner in what was left of Hashomer Hatzair, now an underground organisation rocked by the Soviet's ultimate betrayal. Anti-Semites to the east, anti-Semites to the west. The so-called saviours of the Jews hated them almost as much as the Nazis.

On the second Tuesday of the Russian invasion, a minor miracle occurred: the Red Cross office received a letter from Shoshana. She had managed to find a friendly farm outside Cracow in Novy Sacz where our mother was safe. She would not divulge details, but was hard at work on a plan to secure our transit north to cross the border into Lithuania, near Punsk, where we had taken the orphans last May, and found our Baltic Jerusalem. They were coming to Wilno soon. All being well, we would once again seek an escape to Palestine. Shoshana didn't expect to get her old bedroom back, but she couldn't wait to see Pilies Street again. The letter was dated June 13th. I wrote back with news of the Soviet deportations.

Six weeks later, I was still awaiting her reply. Towards the end of July, the Soviet authorities ordered all foreign embassies to leave Kaunas. But news started reaching Wilno that two consuls had received twenty-day extensions. Far more wondrously, the Dutch consul had reportedly once again been granting visas. Not to Holland this time, which along with the rest of the free world had barred Jewish immigration, but to two Dutch colonial islands in the Pacific, Curacao and Dutch Guiana, via Japan, assisted by the only other foreign consul left behind, a Samurai diplomat called Sempo Sugihara. The story sounded absurd, but I could not discount it before visiting Kaunas in person. I was not alone.

At Kaunas train station I joined a steady stream of Polish Jewish refugees who were making their way through the cobble-stone alleys of the Old Town to the Japanese consulate. But despite the promise of sanctuary, the mood was fearful. Rumour was rampant of a supposed atrocity that had taken place in Kaunas only last night. A group of Jews had been seized in the street and dragged into a garage, where their mouths were stuffed with high-pressure hoses. When the water was turned on, Jewish stomachs were said to have burst like balloons.

The crowd outside the consulate was already in the thousands when I arrived. A desperate group of youths climbed over the compound walls and were met – not with armed guards – but by Mr. Sugihara's wife bearing platters of sandwiches. Everything I had heard was true. Mr. Sugihara was working night and day to help as many people as he possibly could. I left my place in the queue and ran to the nearest Red Cross office where I mailed instructions to Shoshana to come immediately, although my previous letters had gone unanswered.

For the entire month of August, Sempo and Yukiko Sugihara sat writing visas by hand, hour after hour, day after day. They were issuing over 300 travel permits a day, which was normally one month's work. Every morning I gave up my place in line to check for a reply from Shoshana, and every time I came back empty-handed, with a few more hundred people lined up before me.

The Sugiharas stayed in Kaunas well past their twenty day extension, and when they were eventually escorted out by Russian soldiers on September 1st, they carried on signing visas through their train window until the moment the carriage left the station, but it was still not enough.

There were no more letters from Poland awaiting when I returned to Wilno, and no more to come.

A year passed. One fine summer morning thirteen months after the Soviet army invaded Lithuania, I returned on bicycle to the green lakes of Verkiai. There was no Shoshana by my side anymore– I even found myself missing Herman Glik – but I was pleased to leave the increasingly hostile city behind, if only for a couple of hours.

My solitude was disturbed by a small crowd that gathered around a young couple's portable transistor radio a little further along the lake shore. I joined them to listen to the reports. Earlier that morning, Foreign Minister Molotov had announced to the Russian people that the German army had attacked north-western Lithuania. Within an hour, rockets would be falling on Wilno. It was June 22nd, 1941.

The speed of Hitler's offensive took everybody by surprise. That morning, the city enjoyed a beautiful summer's day. After lunch, we were a city at war. German-Soviet tensions had been escalating all year, but the Lithuanians made few contingencies. When the warning sirens sawed through the blue air that afternoon, I recognized the finality of its announcement: the life we'd known was over. Jerusalem had fallen.

I cycled back from the lakes through empty streets. Our tenement behind the railway station was lucky enough to be equipped with a usable cellar. The cool subterranean atmosphere doubled as an over-flow kitchen ice-box during the summer. Now it would be our air-raid shelter. Our tiny ball of a janitor, Mrs. Ormandyova, ushered me in, gave me a tin-hat and directed me through the maze of chairs, blankets and limbs. Each apartment was assigned a section of wall for food storage, some industrious families having furnished theirs with cupboards and doors. A few even had padlocks.

Except for a bottle of milk and a dish of butter, our shelves had nothing. My house-mates were slumped on the floor against the wall, in various states of withdrawal and, in Benno's case, near-catatonia. I soothed them as much as I was able, until the German planes began to grind overheard, and the heavy bombs started dropping.

Boom, crump, crump, crump.

Boom, crump, crump, crump.

The planes were far enough away to ensure our safety, for the time being. The train station was a likely target, but it was the north of the city sustaining most of the damage, the historical Jewish Quarter that the Soviets had already decimated by decree.

After a couple of hours of relentless bombardment, my house-mates became drowsy with boredom and I was able to pick a path through the huddled masses towards the exit. As I stepped out the front of the building onto Pelesos Street, I was overwhelmed by a sense of excitement that contained neither dread nor panic, but pure awe.

From the top of my hill, the city resembled the ruins of an alien civilisation: Wilno pierced with great flames, rocked by explosions, its dark expanses along the banks of the Neris to the west glittering with a constellation of fires, all of it trapped beneath a pink dome of rocket flare and the fierce pounding of Luftwaffe engines. For all the demented savagery, I am ashamed to admit I had never felt more alive. I drifted down the hill, into the rising smoke.

A new wave of planes flew over when I reached the bottom, and proceeded to repeat the manoeuvre every five minutes, motors clanking furiously like a blacksmith's forge. The first time I saw a batch of incendiary bombs tumble from their Iron Cross bellies, I felt the thrill of witnessing a birth. Thirty shells dropped within seconds. They radiated the streets like forked lightning, and left behind clusters of bright pin-points that spiked into yellow flames. Soon the whole of Old Town would be consumed.

I headed north along Didziogi Street, flanked by Konstantino Park to my right, and crossed onto old Pilies. The greatest of all the fires was directly ahead of me, beyond the University Square. Enormous flames tore into the sky from a balloon of bright smoke and out of this haze there gradually emerged the formidable arch of the Roman Catholic Basilica. The Cathedral stood grand and imperious, its contours slowly growing more defined, the way a skyline solidifies at dawn. At the flames' zenith the sky was molten red, but directly overhead, making a halo in the heavens, was a cloud of smoke all in pink. Through a rip in that delicate veil there shone a bewildered point of light, a lone star of the age-old celestial variety.

As I drew closer to the Old Town, I was joined by other shadows who'd ventured out from their shelters. With neckties wrapped around their mouths, they resembled a troop of sand-blasted cowboys stumbling through the desert. I recognized some faces from Akiva meetings, but all I could see were eyes and noses. Nobody talked. Silently, as if our words would alert the thundering planes, we spread out across the road.

The old house I had shared with Shoshana and Herman and Moishe and Baruch was untouched but at the far end of Pilies Street, bombs had fallen on a number of premises near Mr. Donelaitis's old shop, blowing four of them to pieces. Not a shelf or saleable item remained, only piles of earth, bricks and beams of timber. Rescue workers were sifting through the rubble, clawing into the ruins where people were still buried. Seven dead had already been recovered. Four long bodies and three short ones placed in a row along the curb like alternating piano keys.

When I signalled our readiness to join in the search, the workers waved us on.

We floated clockwise on broad and empty avenues round the flaming ghost-ship of the Cathedral, turning right on tree-lined Gedimino into the devastated heart of the city.

There were so many buildings burning all around that firemen had given up trying to put them out. Instead they nursed the victims, occasionally stopping to extinguish their lamps as another flight of bombers passed overhead. I watched one of them bundle a man to the ground as a screaming rocket tore across the sky, then immediately leave him to smother a woman who was on fire across the street. The fireman rolled her on the ground to put out the flames.

We stopped at the left bank of the Neris, joining another

team of rescuers who were pointing at a land-mine suspended from the Green Bridge like a chandelier, its parachute caught on the railing. While we lifted a wooden bench from the promenade to block the entrance, a woman in white appeared from nowhere on the other side of the bridge. She wore a bridal gown with a red ribbon across her chest that turned out to be a bloody gash. Utterly oblivious to our shouts, she began to totter across the river, hands outstretched as if walking a tightrope.

She made it all the way past the landmine to our side but her mind was already gone. From what we were able to piece together, she'd been riding to church with her father when the first bombs fell. We scanned the right bank of the river, but the twin spires of St Raphael the Archangel could no longer be seen.

On the corner with Gedimino and Orzesko were the remains of a house I'd observed yesterday flying the Lithuanian flag, a banned symbol under the Russians. An aerial torpedo had fallen on a stand of trees between the properties, reducing trunks to splinters and caving in the roof where the flag had fluttered. The rest of the house was collapsed beneath.

I stopped at the shattered trees, stooping to pick up a corner of poster that had been pinned to the bark. Proclamations like these had been appearing across the city all year, produced by the far-right Lithuanian Activist Front, whose leader was the country's Ambassador to Germany, Kazys Skirpa. The nationalists blamed the Bolsheviks for ruining 'the fabric' of their country, for the brutality and the mass deportations. In the crude typography of the poster, 'Bolshevik = Jew'. The LAF advocated German intervention but the fragment I held in my hand went a step further, stating that:

1. The old rights of sanctuary granted to the Jews in Lithuania by Vytautas the Great are abolished forever and without reservation.

2. Hereby all Jews, without any exception, are strictly ordered to immediately leave Lithuania.

3. Should it become known that Jews guilty of grave crimes, manage to escape in secret, the duty of all honest Lithuanians is to take measures on their own initiative to stop such Jews and, if necessary, punish them -

While I was reading, one of the men from my team cried out. A small white hand had managed to push its way up through the rubble of the roof.

I crumpled the paper in my fist, tossed it into the wreckage and carefully clambered up the mountain of brick and timber towards the roof's gable. The weight of the blast had fetched the attic, bedsteads, wardrobes and all, right down from the top of the houses to the ground floor.

We laboured until our hands bled, removing debris piece by piece around the boy's groping fingers. Slowly we discovered the miracle that had saved him from being crushed: the explosion had blown his bedroom door off its hinges across the room, where it had fallen over his bed, resting on the top and bottom frames, creating a protective wedge.

For the moment, he was safe. But the closer we got to him, the more the roof began to crack and groan under our boots. It could fall at any moment. Using lengths of broken floorboards, I fashioned a crude scaffold around the boy's head while the rest of the team cleared the wreckage from below.

Several hours later, we pulled him out, quite naked, as grey with dust as we were and bleeding freely from flying glass and scratches of jagged wood. His collarbone was cracked.

The boy's parents lay beneath the son's room, entombed in their bed, the father's arm shielding his face.

With dawn the bombing grew less regular and then stopped altogether. The emergency services were out in number. As wordlessly as we had come together, our team dispersed towards a dozen different destinations.

When I reached my tenement at the top of Pelesos Street, Mrs. Ormandyova came rolling out of the cleaning cupboard that doubled as her office, buzzing with indignant concern.

'Look at you! Dusted like a bow-tie pastry! Where have

you been all night?'

'No need to worry about me, aunty,' I said, taking her fingers in my ashen palm. 'I was safe the whole time.'

'But what have you been doing?'

'There were lots of us out there and we all looked after each other.' This did not satisfy her; she pulled my hand towards her apron. 'The damage to the Old Town is unbelievable. You've never seen anything like it.'

'And what happens now? Will they be back tonight?'

'I would think so. If not before. But what about you, aunty. Do you have everything you need?'

'Of course I do,' she scoffed, returning my hand with a theatrical pluck. 'What do I need.'

'And everybody else is well?'

Wagging her finger, she said, 'Everybody else stayed put in the cellar.'

'Good,' I said. 'Now, if you'll excuse me, I'd like to take a bath.'

'No hot water. They hit the gas works.'

I found Selig furtively poking around the kitchen, up to his usual tricks while the city burnt. The shelves looked suspiciously full, as if he'd been shopping. He banged the cupboard door shut as soon as I entered. Dimly regarding the layer of ash settled on my shoulders, he said, 'I wish you told me you'd be spending the night out there.'

'No need to fuss about me,' I chuckled at the sink, soothing my fingers under cold water. 'There's lots of people who needed help.'

'Not what I meant. If I'd known you weren't coming back, I'd have got forty winks in your bed.'

'You're welcome to it anytime, you know that.'

As he nodded and walked out, a dried bratwurst fell from his jacket sleeve. 'I was looking for that,' he said and scooped it up.

Inside my bedroom, I closed the door, leaned back against the wood and sighed. Under my sheets, a torso jumped, and a greasy mane of black hair poked out.

'I keep saying my room's too light to sleep in,' Wolf

groaned. 'Are you going to be long?'

'Just picking up some clean clothes.'

'Do I have to leave?'

I thought about throwing Wolf out, but I'd already made my mind up. He would have detested his time in the shelter, and probably spent the night working himself into a silent rage. Besides, there was too much for me to do to sleep.

'You rest up,' I said. 'I have a feeling you're going to need it.'

Wolf groaned again and flattened a pillow over his head.

I scrubbed myself in the bathroom, toweled, dressed, and went back out to the streets.

While teams of Jews were out combing through the wreckage, the Lithuanian Activist Front were going door to door, to buildings that still had doors, hunting for bearded Bolsheviks and executing them in the street, their gun-shots drowned out by German shelling. When the Nazi troops rolled in that afternoon, Lithuanians welcomed them with garlands of wildflowers.

There was an immediate exodus of three thousand able-bodied Jews east into Soviet territories, leaving behind the old, the infirm and in some cases, the very young. When I returned home that evening, Selig, Benno and Wolf had fled, together with half the building. Running never once crossed my mind, which was odd, because despite my size, in all areas of life I had previously considered myself a coward. There just wasn't a choice that I could see. However bad things were for me, there were thousands of people in far worse situations, most of whom had nobody at all to which they could turn.

The Germans didn't form their own civil administration August 5th, but there was no reprieve. The Provisional LAF Government lasted for forty-three days and on every single one of them, a new anti-Jewish directive was published. The public murder, raping, robbing and humiliation of that first night were to be avoided because they distressed Lithuanian women and children. But 100 new orders were issued in the brief life of the interim government, perpetrated by Lithuanians, against their former neighbours and employees.

General policy was of course dictated from Berlin, but it was the relish that the Lithuanians displayed in implementing the strategies that was so distressing.

When the executions ceased, the daylight snatching of Jews for hard labour began. 300 were initially taken, on the understanding that the smallest insubordination would result in more prisoners, brothers and friends of the condemned. The authorities of course needed no such pretext. Men unfit to work were also taken, told to bring along a towel and soap. But they were never seen again. All Jewish establishments were closed down immediately, including prayer houses. Jews were dismissed from gainful employment. Jews were forbidden to use sidewalks, forced into the middle of the road with the horse and carts. On many main and side streets, Jews were prohibited from even walking on the road, and had to make city-wide detours in order to complete the shortest journey. Jews were officially identified as 'Jude', and then a few days later reclassified as 'Jud', as if the 'e' was a waste of a perfectly good Aryan letter. In July, all Jews over ten had to wear the star on their arms. Jews first lost the right to rent property, and then to own. Jews were ordered to move from our apartments into single rooms shared with other families. All property deeds had to be handed over. Bank accounts, radios, jewellery and furs.

Days passed in a fever dream of déjà vu. Every abuse that had been inflicted upon my family in Cracow and the Russian Pale was now being visited upon the Jews of Wilno. So well-oiled was the machinery that it took the Nazis three months from invading Poland to their first raiding party in Kazimierz, while the hired hands of the LAF needed only six weeks to drive us to the same precipice of fear.

If they'd wanted to, they could have massacred us wholesale that first night and the Lithuanian women and children wouldn't have lost too much sleep. But where was the sport in that? The steady, incremental process of the daily orders was designed to inflict maximum psychological torture, for every Jew knew what was coming. Every Jew had family or friends who'd fled Poland with nothing but horror stories, like little Jacob Schmiel. And the LAF and the Nazis knew that we knew, and they revelled in the knowledge.

3

Every evening before curfew that sweltering summer, a long line of Jews formed behind the choking fumes of the bus station newly decked with swastikas. Peasants flocked to the city to trade spoiled produce too wretched for pigs to eat. We queued to hand over the last of our belongings, the watches, clothes, pots and pans that the authorities had not yet seized. Jews were banned from all shops. The food market was open to Aryans from six in the morning, and Jews were still permitted to arrive after eleven, when the stalls were bare. An underground economy had started to flourish, which the Germans were permitting, providing they received their cut.

Two soldiers were sniffing around the peasants' stalls, trying to work out if a box of mouldy cabbages was worth breaking into a sweat. There were a couple of dozen people in front of me, and only three peasants left with anything to trade. I had a bag of Mrs. Ormandyova's aprons and baking trays to barter, and strict instructions not to return home empty-handed. No square meals had been served in our building since the weekend. There were reported sightings of a bunch of rogue carrots on the third floor, but intelligence had so far been unable to confirm their existence.

After we shuffled up a few yards closer to the meagre display, the man in front of me turned to his friend and said, 'Crazy but I remember when we used to come here to catch buses.'

'What I want to know,' his friend said, 'is what they'll take when we run out of pots and pans.'

'Sod the pots and pans,' the other man said. 'What happens when they run out of Jews?'

At the front of the queue, the two soldiers had spotted something of interest in the last transaction. They started following an elderly couple tottering arm in arm away from the buses, allowing them to leave the station-yard before the shorter snub-nosed soldier ordered them to halt in the middle of the road. As I looked on with a blooming sickness, a smartly-dressed lady commuter with a briefcase stopped at my side, raised a hand over her mouth and pretended to fix her hair.

'Watch that one,' she said, with a flick of her chin to the shorter German. 'I saw him near the Green Bridge, up to no good.'

I hadn't seen the soldier before but I did recognize the smartly-dressed woman as a University librarian, from the old days of about ten minutes ago when Jews were allowed to sit in the Rare Book Reading Room. She was a middle-aged matronly type who still wore her hair in the plaits and buns of her youth.

'On Ukmerges Stree, outside the bus repair shop,' she said. 'He must have a thing for buses, this one. Maybe he still plays with his toys at the barracks. A young Jewish girl walked by with a bag in her hand. Inside was a loaf of bread, a radish and some butter and cheese. The German poked around, left the radish and bread but took the butter and cheese for himself. The girl cried that the butter and cheese were for her sick little brother, that she'd worked very hard for the food. Tears rolled down her face, but the soldier took no notice.'

Now he was shouting at the elderly couple, who clearly did not understand German. The old woman was offering her recently-purchased marrow in apology, but the taller of the soldiers knocked it out of her hands with his baton and stepped on it, bursting the green skin under his boot heel. The old man took off his cap and held it between his hands like a boy before the headmaster's desk. He was asking in Yiddish what they had done wrong. In answer, the snub-nosed German brought his baton down on top of the man's bald head. His wife shrieked. When the old man tried to raise a hand in defence, the other soldier grabbed both arms and twisted them behind his back. The German struck him again and again until blood poured from his scalp down over his eyes. I could watch no longer.

I gave Mrs Ormandyova's bag to the two men in front of me and asked them to take any food to our tenement behind the railway station. The librarian bent down and put her briefcase at the men's feet and said, 'I'm coming with you.'

She could not be dissuaded. With our hands above our heads, we stepped out of the line and walked to the head of the queue, past the peasant's stalls and out the bus-yard into the road.

Struggling to keep my voice under control, I called out to the soldiers in German. 'The old fool only speaks Yiddish. Let me translate for you. I'll get whatever it is you're looking for.'

'Single file only, you filthy Jewish swine,' the taller one roared when he let go of the man and span round. 'Don't you know the rules?'

The old man collapsed to his knees, but the blows kept coming.

'It's my fault,' the librarian said. 'I told the Jew to walk with me. My name is Ona Simaite and I work at the University. My identity papers are in my purse.'

'What are you doing with this Jewish pig? Are you both Communist traitors?'

'I don't speak Yiddish,' she said. 'I'm a Lithuanian, I speak German.' She pointed disdainfully at the old man on the ground. 'This sort of thing isn't good for anybody. How about we try to keep it off the streets?'

Amazingly, the short German stopped hitting the man. 'You're right,' he said.

I started reassuring the man in Yiddish that he would be safe when his assailant drew the pistol from his belt and calmly fired into the side of the old man's bald head. He crumpled to the ground and his wife went down of her own volition a second later.

The snub-nosed German turned his gun on us.

'At least one of you is coming with me.' He grinned at Mrs. Simaite. 'Your choice, Mrs. Librarian.'

Before she could answer, I said, 'Go back for our bags.' Adrenaline tasted like a copper penny on my tongue. 'Mrs. Ormandyova, remember, Pelesos Street. Whatever you can take her.'

The soldier let the librarian comfort the sobbing woman and signalled for me to start walking, but my feet didn't get the memorandum. A felled tree, I swayed a little in the breeze.

I stared down at my shoes and willed them to move before the rest of me could come crashing down. The miraculous happened: I twitched my right foot in front of my left like a cured cripple. Shifting my weight from one leg to the other, I jerked forward. Not exactly walking, but it would do.

There'd been rumours of summary executions, but nothing had prepared me for what I'd seen. My mind replayed the scene like a nightmare caught in a loop. The frenzy of that first night of LAF killings was supposed to have stopped. Being executed for not walking in single file? Such punishment belonged to the realm of fantasists like H.G. Wells or Aldous Huxley, not the world I thought I knew. It seemed inconceivable that the German army would allow such behaviour to continue unchecked. The librarian was sure to report the soldier for this, his second abuse of power. Taking a young girl's cheese and butter was one thing, but cold-blooded murder...

And now I was the one being led away. Presumably the snub-nosed soldier wasn't going to kill me, or he'd have done it by now. But the unalterable fact remained that I had been captured by Nazis. One didn't meet many Jews who'd lived to tell that particular tale.

What about the people I was leaving behind, Mrs. Ormandyova and the other old ladies of the block? I trusted the librarian to do what she could today, but who would look after my building tomorrow, and the next day? I managed to persuade myself they'd be better off without me. It wasn't hard to do. My intervention had just got an innocent man shot in the head. In this fashion, I was able to persuade myself to keep moving forward.

The urge to make a break for freedom lessened with every corner we turned, the Germans shouting directions at my back, Turn, turn, turn. I was their obedient little doggie who walked without a leash. I didn't need to feel a weighty chain around my neck to know it was there.

Without an old man to batter, the two soldiers sounded much more like reasonable young adults, their conversation not that different from the likes of Moishe and Baruch. When they weren't barking orders at me, they bickered with each other about football teams and attractive young actresses and generally gave no indication of where we were heading. I tried to read clues in the city's twisting topography. But the further we travelled from the centre, the less familiar the streets became, and the more worried I grew.

From the position of the setting sun, I knew we were going east, in the direction of the great forest of Verkiai. But I was not eager to return to the lake shores with my current companions. And then, without any fanfare, we took a right turn and I recognized my surroundings: I was back where it had all started. Subocz Street, the site of the old Akiva headquarters where Shoshana and I were taken upon arrival. The house had been re-appropriated last year under the Russians, but I wondered if my captors knew of my connection. If they had identified me as a former Zionist activist, my goose was well and truly cooked. But the soldiers made no announcement as we neared the old house, and when I first caught sight of it, I forbid my body from betraying any shimmers of recognition. It was merely a coincidence, not one of Herman Gilk's meaningful synchronicities.

The house was freshly whitewashed and a new fence now enclosed the front garden. Mother and father weeded the flower-bed on their knees while a baby squirmed behind them on a red blanket, surrounded by a cache of soft toy guns. The father stood as we passed and raised his trowel in salute at the soldiers.

Half a mile away, I could see two long, low brick apartment buildings, one in front of the other like draught pieces. These were known as the Cheap Houses, where the more left-wing members of Hashomer Hatzair had lived when they first arrived in the city, the likes of Vita Kempner and Abba Kovner. Unlike the more homely Akiva HQ up the street, the Cheap Houses had limited resale value to a good Aryan, and had not yet been reassigned. Many of the windows were broken or boarded up. These Houses also had a new wooden fence built around the perimeter, but it wasn't to stop a young child toddling out into the road. The fence reached as high as the third floor windows, and was strung with barbed wire.

When we reached the entrance, it was locked but

unguarded. The taller soldier produced a long key from a latch in his tunic, and secured the gate again after we'd entered. I was ordered left and followed the fence along the shadows between the two Cheap Houses to a newly constructed garage workshop. Terror seized me as I recalled the story from Kaunas of Jews being forced to swallow hoses, and their stomachs bursting. But this looked like a place of labour, not death. There was a single olive drab Kubelwagon outside, and a random collection of Lithuanian vehicles lined up outside the garage doors. Coal lorries, furniture vans, tippers, just about every type of transport apart from a funeral hearse.

We walked to the front of the line and into the workshop, a hive of industry at seven on a summer evening. The first thing I noticed was that none of the mechanics wore overalls. Secondly, none of them were mechanics. About a dozen strong Jewish men toiled miserably on a miscellaneous cross-section of trucks and vans. Civilians like myself, snatched from the streets and put to work as slaves.

Guarding the workshop, a portly soldier slumped on a chair against the wall with a rifle across the mound of his lap. Behind him was a large-windowed corner office where my two captors had retreated, joining three more soldiers playing cards at a cluttered table, none of them older than university undergraduates. The prisoners were all ages, from a fair-haired teenager hosing down a milk-float to a tanned and wiry man in his sixties called Dusan who offered me a cigarette. Dusan was a rarity in the garage: an ethnic Lithuanian and a proper mechanic.

The vehicles, he explained through crooked yellow teeth, were like us. Requisitioned. Taken in by the police to be used by the German army while superior machinery was assembled. The territory of the Reich was expanding quicker than its factories. We had been brought here to test the automobiles' road-worthiness, lest their brakes fail and injure good Nazi soldiers, and generally bring the vehicles up to military specification. Anything that wasn't safe got bumped down the line to be repaired. Those that were in good shape had to have a certificate issued before they were resprayed and camouflaged. The current batch had to be in Kaunas by nine o'clock tomorrow morning. That was the extent of my induction.

The work alternated between the toxic and the excruciating. Dusan assigned me to the team converting petrol and diesel oil powered vehicles into natural gas powered ones, Hitler's latest pet-project. I was the new 'Sucker'. Nobody told me what had happened to my predecessor. My job was to siphon out the fuel-tanks into enormous barrels, and then drag them outside while the engines were being replaced. Through a process of trial and error, I worked out how hard I needed to draw on the greasy tubes, but not before it had cost me two separated ribs from coughing up all the petrol I'd swallowed. Pulling the full barrels outside was hard enough, but with one hand keeping my rib-cage together, it became an endurance of Herculean proportions. There were five engines to convert inside the workshop, thirteen more lined up beyond the doors. If the Germans saw that I was incapacitated, I didn't fancy my chances. The job didn't strike me as coming with much of a medical benefits package.

But compared to some, I had it easy. The fair-haired teenager with the hose-pipe was picking up some particularly unsavoury attention from the portly guard. All evening he'd been haranguing the boy for not washing the vehicles with enough 'elbow grease'. This devolved into a slew of increasingly odd questions about the boy's physique. Eventually, unhindered by either the other prisoners or his fellow soldiers inside the gambling den, from where he'd been banished, the guard roused himself, strolled over to the boy and demanded to see his muscles. Before the boy could respond, the soldier's hands were all over his arms, pushing up his t-shirt and fondling his biceps. When the soldier returned smirking and sated to his seat, an erection was proudly tenting his trousers beneath his sagging stomach.

But the most distressed person I saw that evening was not a prisoner. After nightfall, our labour was interrupted by a jaunty horn blast from outside. The soldiers weren't expecting visitors, and came out their card den with guns drawn. Dusan and I were pushed out first, as a human shield. Climbing down from his mud-splattered Horch 108 was a lean and rangy SS officer with slick hair pushed back over his ears and a thin moustache. While his uniform was immaculate, the body inside was in a state of some disrepair: wild-eyed and drunk, he lurched across the courtyard, his athletic body a jangle of leaden limbs. Dusan and I were quickly pushed back inside, but we'd already seen the extent of the man's dissolution. There followed much hearty hailing and war talk before the SS man was brought into the workshop. When he saw the wretched prisoners sweating over the vehicles, his face drained of all colour. He collapsed. The soldiers hefted him to his feet and hustled the man into the office, but we had all seen the impossible: those cold SS eyes brimming with tears.

The office blinds were promptly lowered. For twenty minutes, we prisoners were left completely unguarded. We could have fled, but remained, whispering, hypnotised. Eventually, one of the soldiers came out with the keys to the Horch and ordered Dusan to clean and valet.

From the Belarussian newspaper and food-wrappers we found on the back seat, we deduced the SS officer had come from the Eastern Front. Everybody had heard horror stories about what was happening on the lawless steppes. Although I have no evidence, and don't even know the officer's name, I suspect now that he was one of the 'brave and fearless' leading the Einsatzgruppe units. The man we saw that evening was a human wreck, glued together purely by the power of military discipline.

A little after ten o'clock, an air of what I can only call 'normality' settled on our little band. Banished again from the office, the portly soldier had retaken his chair against the wall. He angled it now so he could see little beyond the fair-haired lad with the hose-pipe. The 'elbow grease' taunts resumed, although the boy scrubbed the yellow van so furiously between blasts that he might have done the paint stripper's job in addition to his own. I could hardly bear to watch, but I would not look away. Like the narrator in a Franz Kafka story, I yearned to find the person in charge of this madness. Look here, I'd explain, there's been a terrible misunderstanding. This boy should be at home, tucked up in his bed. His parents will be frantic with grief. Sort it out, could you, old chap? But the senior officer was a drunken ruin and the only other soldier I knew had earlier blown an old man's brains out for walking arm in arm with his wife.

'Right,' the portly guard grudgingly huffed. 'Looks like I'll have to show you.'

He swung to his feet and lumbered over to the lad with his arm outstretched. 'Don't worry, I'm not going to touch you. Give me the hose.'

The boy turned off the tap and surrendered the pipe.

'Go on,' the guard said, motioning to the tap. 'Full blast, don't hold back'.

The boy twisted the nozzle until the hose thickened like a powerful snake. Whistling while he ran it across the windscreen, the guard beckoned for the boy to step closer and observe his technique. I wondered why he felt the need to instruct the boy now, so late in the day. We had cleared the back-log of vehicles from the courtyard; after the yellow van, there was nothing more to be washed. The boy approached. From a point-blank distance, the guard jerked the hose and fired into the boy's face, then shook it up and down, dousing him from head to foot.

Dropping the hose, the guard folded over with laughter. He managed to wheeze, 'Said I wouldn't touch you.'

The pipe span on the floor, hissing and spitting, until one of the men scrambled to turn it off. Still grinning, the guard walked out the rear door and came back a couple of minutes later with a towel and a pile of clean clothes. The boy looked around for somewhere to change, and his gaze settled on a tall lorry jacked up in the corner that had previously had three cherries painted on its side.

'Uh uh,' the guard nodded with an artfully pained smirk. 'Can't have you dripping all over the workspace, I'm afraid.'

The boy looked from me to Dusan, who could do nothing but shrug.

Clothes slopped to the floor as the youngster unpeeled layers from his white skin. We'd all stopped working now, but none of us knew where to look, except the guard.

'Don't worry about it, we all shrivel up a bit when we get

cold,' I heard him say. 'We'll soon get you warmed up.'

When the boy was finally dressed in a too small t-shirt and trousers, the guard put an arm around his shoulder and led him away. I didn't see either of them again.

We cleaned and mopped the garage to Dusan's satisfaction and were left wondering what would happen next. A ferret-faced soldier I had not seen before emerged from the office, with the resolute expression of a man who had drawn the shortest straw.

'Everybody outside,' he said. 'Let's get you home.'

I'm not sure anybody believed him, but the magic word had been spoken, and it cast a powerful spell.

Home.

We assembled in the courtyard. The only vehicle left was the SS officer's gleaming Horch. The passenger car could have taken six at a squeeze. There were eleven of us, plus the soldier.

'Single file,' he ordered. 'Two metres apart and no talking since we're past curfew. You've worked well tonight, so don't make any trouble now.'

A foolish voice cried, 'We have to walk?'

'He means you needn't escort us,' I said quickly. 'We can find our own homes.'

'Orders are orders. I need to personally see you're taken back where we found you, otherwise we get into trouble. The Red Cross are very hot on missing people. There's a war on, you know.'

'So are we being taken home,' someone asked, 'or back where we were picked up?'

'Where we found you,' the soldier patted the chest pocket of his tunic. 'All details here. And I'll need statements from neighbours to prove you're safe and sound, so we'd better get a move on or we'll be knocking up little old ladies.'

'What about the young lad who got a soaking?'

The soldier removed the details his pocket, unfolded it and traced his finger down the margins of a long list. 'Lives in Paupys, just over the river. He's probably home by now. Come on, the city's not getting any smaller while we stand here.'

I fell into line behind Dusan, with whom I'd struck up a

rapport based more on wry smiles and wrinkles than the twenty-odd words we'd spoken. Since Dusan wasn't Jewish, I was surprised to see him still with us. He must have committed some kind of infringement, or else was just unlucky enough to be the first mechanic the soldiers found.

The line started moving along the barbed wire fence between the shadow of the Cheap Houses to the gate, still open from the arrival of the SS officer.

We left the compound behind and marched back along Subocz Street. The old Akiva house was dark and shuttered for the evening. I wondered if I'd ever see it again.

The soldier stayed behind at the end of the line, shouting directions as my two captors had done from the bus station. This one also gave a stern yell whenever anybody turned round or tried talking. Singing, however, was tolerated, despite the curfew. We went through a prayer book of holy songs before settling on Ani Ma'amin to guide us into the unknown. Between verses, somebody hit upon the idea of chanting the location of their capture (and supposed return), so we knew where we were meant to be heading. Before long, a virtual street map of names was yipping up and down the line, and the soldier was none the wiser. To us, hearing those familiar street names was as reassuring as Ani Ma'amin's' principles of faith.

Returned to the civilian world, under the streetlights' watchful glare, I became hopeful that the soldier was telling the truth. If the Germans wanted to harm us, they'd have done it in the garages, out of sight and sound, not on our own front-door steps.

The suburbs slowly receded. We criss-crossed our way north-west towards the bombed out Old Town, where most of us had been snatched. Above us on Gediminas Hill, the western tower of the castle had scored a direct hit, one side completely shorn away. A platform of scaffolding was raised now around the stump like Bruegel's Tower of Babel, although those mythical turrets were still in the process of being raised, while ours had been razed.

The closer we drew to the city centre, the more halting our progress became, as rocket craters and rubble blocked the narrow streets. The soldier drove us on. Scenting home, or at least release from bondage, we spurred our bodies.

At Gediminas Avenue and Lukiskes Street, we had no choice but to come to a complete stand-still. A procession of dapper, briefcase-carrying gentlemen appeared round the corner, and the line kept coming until a hundred had swallowed up our pavement. From the trimmed beards and beautifully cut overcoats and trousers, I recognized these men as the remnants of the city's Jewish intelligentsia.

Coated in oil and grease, one hand tucked into my shirt to clutch my separated ribs, I wondered what specimen of poverty the professors took me for, and if they'd ever believe that I had once belonged to their tribe, in Germany of all places. Our two groups stared open-mouthed as we passed, each silently berating the other for allowing themselves to get caught up in such foolishness. Three soldiers brought up the rear, and then the troop was gone, disappearing into the night.

The ferret-faced soldier ordered us to make a loop through a narrow vaulted backstreet, and on the other side of the road, the five shining domes of the baroque prison chapel glinted under the moonlight. It was easy to forget that yards away from the national parliament, in the very heart of the city, the gun-towers of Lukiskes prison speared the sky. The complex was originally built by Tsar Nicholas II to detain his enemies. Half a century later, the Russians invaded and their secret police put the building to a similar use. Now the prison was under the control of the Nazis.

We marched past a group of four SS officers smoking at the gates. I could see the refuge of the Savicko Street turning about twenty yards further down the road, but behind me an unfamiliar voice called a halt. I heard our ferret-faced soldier shout, 'I have orders to escort these men home.'

'Curfew papers will need to be checked,' the SS officer replied with a certain exaggerated weariness.

'Come on then, men.' Our soldier cajoled us back. 'This won't take long.'

He stood in the middle of the road like a patient crossing-guard while we reassembled on the other side. After the last of us had lined up before the gate, the soldier started to confer with the SS officers, although at no point did he remove our list of addresses from his tunic pocket. I was watching the two so intently that I did not see the other three SS officers break away and fan out behind us. The first I knew was when they charged with batons raised, shrieking German curses. We panicked like a flock of backyard hens. No hope of flight, we could only burst forward, through the prison gate which had come open. On the pavement outside, the SS fell about laughing at their stunt. My capture, commencing six hours ago outside the bus station, was now complete.

We crashed into a courtyard where several hundred other prisoners waited in rigid formation while their names were called by an officer on a raised platform at the front. Behind the church hulked the fearsome cell-blocs, the profane grafted onto the sacred by Tsar Nicholas' sleight of hand. Together with a flood of new arrivals who poured into the yard from the corners, we were directed to an area of the yard that had been partitioned off. I recognized the red rope and brass stanchions from the days when Jews were allowed to make deposits at the Bank of Lithuania.

I lost sight of Dusan and my fellow mechanics and was now shuffling forward amongst strangers. As I surveyed the ranks, I was encouraged (as much as a feeling of cheer could flourish) by what I saw: the courtyard was stocked exclusively with able-bodied males, from burly teenagers to solid, forty-somethings. Unlike the academics and poets being marched along Gediminas Avenue, we had been brought here for our strength and productivity, handpicked by the SS as a connoisseur inspects horseflesh.

This was confirmed by the officer who now strode up and down the line, demanding only our ages. I don't think a single one told the truth. The last time most of these men had seen fit to lie about their date of birth was when they'd rushed to sign up for Germany in the Great War, twenty five years ago.

There were perhaps fifty of us in the rope lines, and we were quickly processed. Scarcely had I come to terms with my new confinement than we were led away, filing along a yellow, crumbling brick wall covered with graffiti towards the prison interior. We stopped at a little window crossed with bars in a heavy handle-less door. A buzzer went off, and the door clicked open.

Inside we squeaked along a twisting corridor that deposited us inside a large function hall last used as a ballroom. A fug of cigar smoke clung to the walls like mould. On stage, a string quartet's circle of chairs was arranged around a stand of empty brass lecterns. Dining tables were pushed to the sides of the room to clear a space for dancing.

Once we were all inside, SS instructions came thick and fast, the last: Stand-still, Move over there, Don't talk, Answer in German. Each order contradicted the last, a policy seemingly designed to elicit vicious truncheon blows, which were not shy in coming. While our panic was subdued, more officers filed into the room clutching cardboard boxes. They lined up against the far wall and placed the boxes at their feet. The doors were closed and bolted. A loudspeaker was passed from gloved hand to hand, finally coming to rest at an immense, sweating officer who stepped out from the middle of the line, puffing his cheeks like a trumpeter. The loudspeaker crackled to life at his chest with a jolt of static feedback.

'Attention, attention. Thank-you for remaining quiet. In the last few hours, we have received intelligence of a significant threat from Bolshevik terrorists. The city centre has been evacuated. You have been brought here for your own protection. Our troops are working through the night to apprehend the aggressors and return your streets to safety. This is expected to take several hours. You will remain here under our care until the morning. Please assist us by remaining calm. We will shortly be relocating from the front of the building into the more fortified blocks, where you will be protected from any explosions. Due to overcrowding, some of you may be sharing cells with existing inmates. To eliminate the risk of violence, we ask you to deposit all valuables with us for safe-keeping. All jewellery, watches, money and other sundry valuables. Individual bags will be issued, together with name-tags and pencils. Fill and clearly identify your bag and tie it securely with a firm knot. You will receive a numbered ticket upon receipt. Do not lose this ticket. In the eventuality that any mislabeled bags are lost, the German government will honour all valid claims. Belongings will be stored in the armoury vault overnight. You may nominate up to five men to be responsible for transporting the bags and remaining with them until morning. Rest assured, the German army will not sleep until the terrorists have been apprehended. We thank-you for your understanding in these matters. Please continue to act in an orderly fashion while we expedite your security.'

A third of the officers picked up their boxes, removed handfuls of miniature pencils and paper tags and began handing them out. While we started writing our names and addresses, the remaining officers distributed the leather pouches. The pencils were cheap and a few broke as they pressed against our palms, but we were not shouted at or hit for damaging army property. Some of the SS officers even made jokes about inferior Polish workmanship as they tossed replacements. I removed my watch, wallet and the last few Litas from my pocket. To protect the smooth face from being scratched by coins, I wrapped the watch in tissue paper before placing everything in the pouch, using my wallet as an additional buffer between copper and glass. When we were finished, the officers put the filled pouches back in the boxes and tore us numbered red tickets from a thick book, as promised. Two prisoners volunteered to watch over the bags and were directed to the full boxes. I thought about putting myself forward, but decided I'd rather look out for people than property. The whole process took less than five minutes.

A few men asked for permission to kneel down as the boxes were being stacked against the wall. I wondered if they were going to pray but instead they removed their shoes and pressed the tickets into the soles. I placed mine in my shirt pocket.

We were marched out of the ballroom towards the blocks, but separated into groups of five along the way. I wondered if these were to be our cell-mates for the evening, but instead an officer took us to a long corridor of dark green wooden doors. Four of us stood outside while the first in our group was taken in. I was third in line. If what we'd been told about the terror threat was true, I wondered if this entire pantomime was a prelude to a mass interrogation. The Germans didn't need an excuse, of course. But if their assurances had been designed to minimise resistance, the strategy was a great success. Part of me feared I would never see the prisoner again, but he appeared unharmed after a couple of minutes, rejoining us against the wall. We were forbidden to ask him about the interview. Unnecessary conversation, we were told, would add to the atmosphere of confusion and jeopardize our safety.

When it was my turn, I was called into the small room and told to sit opposite two SS officers, one of whom would ask questions, he explained, while his colleague printed my answers on an index card. There were four plastic boxes of cards on the table. The room had no windows and one bare light-bulb on a frayed cable.

The officer in charge had a soft, kindly face but his brow was permanently furrowed and he kept pinching his nose between the bridge of his narrow spectacles as if in some discomfort. He began by asking my name, date and place of birth. I answered truthfully, in impeccable German. The kindly officer stared at me, one eyebrow rising.

'Are you Jewish?' he said.

'I am.'

'You don't look Jewish.'

'I'm afraid I can't help that, sir.'

His questions had departed from the script, and the second man stopped recording my answers.

'Mother and grandmother?'

'We are Jewish through and through.'

'What a shame. How do you speak German so fluently?'

'I worked in Kiel for fourteen years. My friends were German.'

'Worked as what?'

I was about to say I'd been a professor when I recalled the procession of intellectuals being marched away on Gediminas Avenue.

'I was a shoe-maker.'

He inclined his head at this, lowered his spectacles and peered at me above the frame.

'A shoe-maker?' he said. 'A shoe-maker in Kiel?'

'Yes.' An inexperienced liar, I was terrified of giving myself away. I needed to retreat to the more comfortable territory of the truth, or at least the partial truth. 'And here in Wilno for a spell, on Pilies Street.'

'What happened?'

This was more difficult. I could not mention Akiva, or the arguments with Herman Glik, or what had happened with Mr. Donelaitis' friends. So I decided to condense my timeline and bring the truth forward by a year or so.

'Our shop was bombed.'

At this, my interrogator closed his eyes, jutted his chin, took the index card his colleague had started writing, tore it in half and dropped the two halves in the basket by his side.

'Return to Herr Siegler his belongings,' he said, dusting his hands with two short claps.

'Yes, sir.'

I followed the second officer out of the room, past my group of four and back to the ballroom.

'One moment.'

He disappeared inside.

For the first time since being pushed through Lukiskes gate, I was left unguarded.

Several minutes expired.

The officer came back without the leather pouch but cupping my belongings, which he thrust at me. I slid the wallet and coins into my pocket and tried to fasten the watch around my wrist but my fingers would not stop shaking. The ballroom door had failed to shut and between the panel and the frame, I saw a half-empty box of pouches in the middle of the floor. A dozen or so had been ripped open, their contents scattered and raked into piles.

My escort was already leading the way up a flight of stairs and had yet to realise I'd remained behind, or that I'd glimpsed his colleagues' rampant thievery. There was nothing I could do except follow.

We walked up several stairway, leaving the administrative centre of the prison and ascending the main towers. If I craned my neck upward, I saw a web of walkways and landings and through their iron lattice, a hundred locked cells. My escort stopped at what must have been the fourth or fifth landing and led me to an open door.

I stepped into the cell and darkness stole over my head as the door swung to. The room had looked empty, but I didn't risk moving until my eyes accustomed to the gloom. There was only one source of light, a small window near the ceiling of the opposite wall. Its bars dissected a wan moon, casting the brick walls a sickly green. A single open hole in the corner for toilet purposes. One bunk bed, unoccupied.

Now, irrevocably, my capture was complete. Several times tonight I'd reached that same conclusion, each of them prematurely. If only I'd known I was still free, at the garages, in the streets, before the prison gates, five minutes ago, outside the ballroom's secret spoils.

This cell was the end, I knew it in my bones. And most likely the end of liberty for every Jew brought here on this most wretched of evenings. To have escaped the Soviet gulag for the German concentration camp, which is where they were surely heading. Frying pans and fires. Lukiskes prison was in the hands of a rogue flock of SS vultures, picking over the last of our possessions while we shuffled obligingly into penal servitude.

Yet I been singled out from the multitude. I wiled away my hours on the bunk trying to work out why. For telling them I was a shoe-maker? My interrogator had stared at me as if I'd claimed to be the Second Coming. Was it possible that the phrase 'A Kiel shoe-maker' was some kind of double entendre I didn't understand? What exactly had I confessed to? I couldn't see how a man of such humble trade could engender the officer's ire. Perhaps a Jewish doctor could have failed his loved one, as Mr. Donelaitis' friends evidently believed, but it was difficult to conceive the damage a cobbler could inflict. Misplaced one of my interrogator's father's best brogues? Pinched his daughter's toes a little too tightly in the measuring? Was it my reference to the German bombs that had so angered the officer? Perhaps we were all supposed to pretend they'd never fallen.

Whatever my crime, I was certain of my fate. No records of my incarceration now existed. The interrogator had ripped my index card in half and dropped it in the bin. My meagre belongings were to be burnt or buried at my side. No SS officer would be discovered six months from now, when the war was over, wearing the stolen watch he'd forgotten to drop. The Nazis had wiped their hands of me, with that most casual of gestures. Clap, clap.

Next!

The footsteps came before it was light, heavy boots clomping down the corridor. A key scraped the lock. I sat up in bed, knocking my face against the bricks so hard I chipped a tooth.

The brightness from the corridor was dazzling after my entombment, but I had enough sense about me to be sure of what was happening. Instead of ordering me out, the SS officer escorted a new prisoner in.

A bald man about my age glanced around the cell like a travel-correspondent at the city's last remaining hotel room. One hand jiggled coins in his pocket, while the other scratched stubble on his cheek. He cast a furtive glance towards the bunk, and I thought he might wink, but instead his face grew impassive when he saw me and he gave a sombre nod.

I shifted on the bunk and the wood creaked. The next sounds were the man's boots shuffling in a small circle, followed by the swish of fabric against his legs and a deep sigh as he settled his spine against the bare wall. I had to stop breathing to make out a soft scratching and a wrinkling of paper and then a match exploded in a shower of sparks and our eyes briefly met through the glare. The room filled with smoke.

I let him enjoy the cigarette in silence, waiting for the stub to be ground against the floor before I spoke across the room with a boldness that could not be denied.

'My name's Jozef. Jozef Siegler.'

I was beginning to doubt whether I had in fact spoken aloud when he said, 'Ronen.'

'How long have you been here?'

Another long pause. 'A few hours.'

'Snatched?'

'Mm hm.'

'We were put to work in a garage before coming here.'

No answer.

'You?' I said.

'I was coming back from my mother's apartment.'

'You have family in the city?'

'Some.'

'Mine are in Cracow.'

'You're Polish?'

'No. But I lived there for a while. Born in Romania.'

'Jewish?'

'Of course. Yourself?'

'You don't look Jewish.'

'You're the second person to tell me that.'

'Who was the first?'

'The man who put me here,' I said. 'I've been mistaken for a German before.'

'Could be useful, this day and age.'

'I lived there for many years.'

'In Germany?'

'Kiel. Schleswig-Holstein.'

Ronen's meagre font of replies appeared to have dried up with my disclosure. I sensed he'd been testing me, and I'd failed.

'I left because I thought Wilno would be safe,' I said. 'Now look.'

'Safest building in the city, this prison.'

'They told us the same thing,' I said. 'Depends where you are, I suppose. Inside or out.'

He lapsed into silence again.

'What's it like out there?' I asked.

'Dead.'

'Quiet?'

'Evacuated. Three square miles, I should think.'

'Has everyone been brought here?'

'Only the men. Nobody's seen the women.'

'Your mother?' I asked, trying to keep the alarm from my voice.

'She's outside the city. She's safe.'

'Good.'

'Will you pray with me?'

I was taken aback by the man's intimacy.

'If you'd like me to.'

'You'd rather not?'

'I'm not especially religious.'

'It couldn't hurt, at a time like this.'

'No. Not so much.'

'Well then. Eight people lost their lives last night when their bus failed to stop at a German checkpoint. Let's say Kaddish.'

'Without the quorum?'

'Eight of them, plus you and I makes ten.'

'If you're sure.'

'Perhaps you're right. What do you suggest?'

'The Birkhat?'

'OK, yes, better,' he said. 'You'll lead?'

I bowed my head, closed my eyes, then peeked – stupidly - to see if Ronen had followed. Without the light from his cigarette, I could see nothing.

'Barukh ata Adonai Eloheinu,' I began. 'Melekh ha'olam, hagomei lahayavim tovot, sheg'molani kol tov.'

'Amen,' Ronen said. 'Mi sheg'molkha kol tuv, hu yigimolkha kol tov. Selah.'

'Selah,' I said.

The prayer complete, Ronen settled back, making himself as comfortable as a brick wall allows. One shoe was kicked off, then the other. He stretched his legs and sighed, rubbing a muscle. Then came the soft brushings of his tobacco and cigarette paper, the careful rolling and the striking of the match. His face appeared in chiaroscuro and was gone. Behind the glowing red ember, he said, 'Do you want one?'

'I never acquired a taste for tobacco.'

'No cigarettes and no God,' he said. 'You really are alone in the world.'

'I was. Until five minutes ago.'

He spluttered smoke at this, but a good-natured laugh came wheezing through. For his second cigarette, Ronen craved companionship.

'I'm sorry if I was short with you earlier,' he said.

'Don't worry about it.'

'I wasn't sure who you were.'

Ronen had been testing me; I was right. Thrust into a cell with a stranger who looked like a German, of course he was suspicious. That's why he'd asked me to lead the prayer.

'My name is Jozef Siegler,' I intoned grandly. 'And I am a shoe-maker.'

At that, he leant forward and dashed his cigarette against the concrete floor. Plunged into darkness, I could sense my words had the same effect on my cell-mate as they had on our gaoler.

'Say that again,' he said.

'Jozef Siegler,' I ventured. 'Do you know me?'

'You make shoes?'

'I used to.'

'Where?'

'On Pilies Street.'

He said, 'Is that what you told them before you were locked up?'

'Yes. Why?'

He laughed. 'Because I told them the exact same thing.'

'You're a shoe-maker?'

'Thirty years, chap and child.'

'This is... ' Words were failing me. 'Most odd.'

'Yes it bloody well is.'

'The Germans are known for their order and efficiency. Could they be confining prisoners according to their trade now?'

'Where's the sense in that?'

'Where's the sense in any of this?'

'True.' He tapped the ground. 'There a special circle of hell I don't know about?'

'Probably.'

'They entered the boat in pairs, just as God had commanded.'

'Sorry?'

'Two by two. Maybe the Germans are building an ark. If this war goes belly-up, they're going to need an escape plan.'

'You're not serious?'

'The fuck do I know. Maybe they just need more shoes.'

'I'm glad you've got a sense of humour. I think we're going to need it.'

'Hang on, I'm being serious now. Prisoners wear a uniform, right?'

'So I gather.'

'And special shoes?'

'I would imagine.'

'And you'd imagine, as of the last few weeks, there's suddenly a lot more people in jail?'

'Demonstrably true, I'd say.'

'Well, then. I reckon they're going to put us to work.'

'In here?'

'Prisons have all sorts of workshops. Did they give your valuables back?'

'Yes.'

'Same here. See. I tell you, we're getting special treatment.'

'They had me working on car engines earlier,' I said. 'At least making shoes is something I can actually do.'

'Me and you both. I tell you, this is our meal ticket!'

'I wouldn't get too carried away.'

He fell silent for half a minute and then started sniffing, one after the other in rapid succession. It was the sound of laughter, until a couple of halting sobs escaped his lungs and I realised it was the opposite of laughter.

He was sobbing.

To hear a stranger so utterly undone, in such close quarters, was almost too much for me. We were both grateful for the veil of darkness.

Luckily Ronen was soon back in control of his emotions. A harder sniff, crunching and resolute, then: 'I'm sorry.'

'No need, old chap. I'm sure you're right.'

'About what?'

'We're here because the Germans need us. Or else we've made things more complicated than they really are.'

'What do you mean?'

'Maybe the SS were telling the truth about the Bolsheviks.'

'You think? We're here for our own safety?'

'A big Russian attack is coming sooner or later. Maybe tonight was the start. Either way, we could be going home in the morning.'

'Now there's a thought.'

'I'm sure it'll all be over soon.'

Lulled by self-delusions, we grew weary. Conversation flickered out like a candle and after an hour or so of restless turning, I drifted into merciful sleep.

I awoke to grey light seeping through the window above my bunk. It was 7.10am. From all around came the sounds of the prison returning to life. I wondered how I had slept through it until now: the shouting and clanging beyond the cell-door, horses snorting outside the window, the whistles and shouts, the trundling wheels of wagons.

My cell-mate was still on the floor by the door, but he had been joined overnight by a plate of bread and two metal cups. The way Ronen sat cross-legged next to them reminded me of a child playing picnic with their dolls, but the food and drink was no figment of his imagination. I tried to banish the phrase 'ritual last meal' from my mind.

'Breakfast,' Ronen said, grinning at me. 'I waited for you. Half each?'

I crawled off the bunk onto my hands and knees and lumbered over.

There was one brown unbroken roll between us, and a fine dusting of crumbs on the plate. I suspected Ronen had polished off a first roll by himself, but I did not begrudge him. The sustenance had certainly improved his mood since last night. I let him go ahead and tear the second roll in half, and insisted on taking the smaller piece for myself.

The first bite was wasted because my mouth was so dry the bread was almost impossible to swallow, sticking like wallpaper paste to the back of my throat. But after a sip of water the meal became quite enjoyable. At least we were being fed: the Germans wouldn't waste supplies on a pair of walking corpses.

We ate quickly, in case our captors realised their mistake.

I rose to relieve myself in the corner, but found the bucket full.

'Sorry,' Ronen said. 'Weak bladder.'

A minute after I'd drained my cup the door opened. The guard read our names from a clipboard; we identified ourselves.

'Come with me.'

We collected our meagre trinkets and warily stepped into the corridor. No other prisoners were outside their cells at this time of morning. We descended the landings with only guards as our witnesses, and they had no interest in our movements. It was as if we had already ceased to exist.

We followed outside to a stable courtyard where black horses were being groomed and saddled, through an archway into a rectangular park of army vehicles that overlooked Gediminas Avenue. I inhaled my first taste of freedom, so far away, so close. The handsome apartments of the city looked the same as they had last night: no signs of Bolshevik terrorism.

The guard led us to an olive drab truck, unlocked the wooden doors at the rear and indicated with a shove to my back that we were to climb in. Ronen and I sat opposite each other on benches while the guard shut the door. The truck's roof was tarpaulin, six covered windows along the sides. I waited until the guard walked past to take his place behind the wheel before jumping up from my bench to peer through the gap in the fabric.

We rolled out of the prison gates onto the street and slowly ground our way north, crossing the river at the Green Bridge. The last of Wilno fell away behind us, the factories and warehouses on the outskirts where Ronen had been certain we were heading.

But he was wrong.

We would never see the city's ruined spires again.

4

We crossed the Neris River a second time at Lazdynai and turned off the main road to Guoptos onto a dirt track through lush forest. Across from me, Ronen turned white as a china plate and muttered a prayer as we bumped along.

'Come look at all this greenery,' I told him from the window. 'The colour's meant to sooth travel sickness.'

'You fool.'

'Old wives' tale?'

Ronen shook his fists at the tarpaulin roof. 'This is who God sends me.'

'For what?'

'My last day on earth.'

'What are you talking about?'

'Ponary. The forest. You must have heard.'

'No, I haven't. Please stop talking in riddles.'

'It's where they bring people.'

'For what?'

Ronen stared at me a long time before saying, 'Many roads lead to Ponary, my friend. But none go back.'

The deeper we went, the more my thoughts conspired. Bird song conspired with dappled sunlight to strike as much oppression into the human heart as any Lukiskis prison cell. Could it be true? That shoemakers were brought here, away from the city of witnesses, in order to be disappeared? For what, crimes against shoe leather?

We rumbled on, passing a murky brown lake and a crooked little church. At the next turn, an expanse of trees in the distance, sheer as a cliff face. In the middle of the foliage, I spied the red, white and black of a Nazi flag. I followed its pole down until I came to the top of a chimney, and below that a tessellation of roofs. I kept quiet, praying that we would pass on.

We reached the wooden perimeter fence and drove round until coming to a thick-legged watchtower. If there was a guard in there, I couldn't see one. A little further along, the truck slowed to a stop and I heard our driver speaking to men outside. Jumping over to a far window, I prised the fabric apart and squinted through. A dozen Lithuanian soldiers lined along the fence, three SS smoking at a folding table behind them.

'Well?' Ronen couldn't bring himself to look. 'It's bad, isn't it?'

'Hard to say. Barbed wire and soldiers.'

Ronen let out a low moan, which I was unable to console.

The truck was on the move again. We were leaving the garrison behind, entering the compound. The gates were pulled shut behind us; the soldiers on the other side.

We drove half a mile along a smooth tree-lined track, towards the fluttering flag. Emerging into the open, the driver took us forward and looped round a sad grass roundabout in the middle of a concrete lot, stopping under the flagpole. Finally I saw the camp in its utilitarian entirety.

On the left of the cluster was a cubed block that I took to be SS bunks, from the circle of broad-backed officers chatting outside. Next to the accommodation were five individual red-brick units linked by a zigzag of saw-tooth roofs with glass sides. Behind them was the chimney I had spied earlier, dwarfed by the backdrop of towering trees. On the right was the most impressive structure of the lot, low but very long. At three hundred yards, it was twice the length of the other two buildings combined. Unlike the SS bunks, this brick snake comprised of only one floor, deep, spacious and bright thanks to the bank of skylights that ran the entirety of the sloping roof. It looked like it had once been some kind of factory.

The driver opened the wooden doors. Neither of us moved.

'Out!'

I rose from my bench, hand outstretched to Ronen, whose shoulders appeared stuck to the tarpaulin. Eventually he grasped my fingers and I pulled him towards the doors. We stumbled out into harsh sunlight.

Instead of being ordered onto our knees to be killed, we were left to stand blinking while the driver hurried away into the shadows. He paused at the top of five cream coloured steps, framed between two supporting columns under the zigzag roofs in the centre of the complex.

'This way,' he called. 'Quickly.'

Again Ronen refused to move.

'We're safe.' I mustered all my conviction and continued. 'Look where we're going. Nobody gets executed inside a building with Doric columns.'

'So what do they want?'

'I don't know. Information.'

'About what?'

'About anything they choose, as far as I'm concerned.'

'And then what?'

'They'll let us go.'

Surprised as I was by my own facility with fiction, nothing prepared me for what we found at the top of those five cream steps. For a second I was back in my old Faculty at Kiel, ensconced behind stained glass and oak staircases. The marble lobby must have been where the factory owner brought clients when he needed to make the best impression. Now it was a couple of shabby Jewish shoemakers being escorted up the hand-carved bannisters by a Wilno prison guard.

I paused, trying to decide why my feet felt so strange. They no longer ached. I looked down: a thick red carpet was tacked to the steps. I hadn't walked on such luxury for many months.

'Stop dawdling,' the guard shouted. 'I haven't got all day.'

I followed up towards the light from the elegant painted window that crowned a wide double-doorway, paneled with frosted glass. The door was left open for Ronen and I to enter.

The room was wide, tall and turquoise, and had it overlooked the French Riviera, the arched windows could not have transmitted a greater sense of vivacity. Between the curved glass, the walls were wood-paneled, dark brown column-bases rising to vanilla porticos across the ceilings. The fittings resembled the architecture of a sumptuous chocolate cake. Parquet tiles accounted for four-fifths of the floor, upon which three uncluttered desks lay in parallel slants. The fifth strip was given over to a strip of scarlet carpet along the right wall, delivering us to the far corner where a birdlike silver-haired man with a limp bow-tie and a grey cardigan stood at a large desk, right arm raised in salute as our driver approached.

'You're late,' the man said in German, his voice thin and reedy. Behind him was a frosted glass door with a 'Herr Direktor' brass plaque.

'My apologies, Herr Ritter.' Our guard switched to a halting school-boy Deutsche. 'The journey was slower than expected.'

'Did they give you any trouble?' Herr Ritter dabbed his nose with a corner of handkerchief concealed in his fist.

'No, sir.'

Twitching his flat little head to us, Herr Ritter commanded our approach, speaking now in Polish. 'Identify yourselves, who's who?'

'Ronen Kesselman.'

'Jozef Siegler, Herr Ritter.'

He chopped the air, swatting away my civility. 'Let's get down to business. What can you tell me about Eva Braun's trip to Florence last year?'

I wasn't sure I'd heard properly and asked Herr Ritter to repeat the names.

There was nothing wrong with my hearing.

Eva Braun? Florence, Italy? What on earth did I know about Hitler's girlfriend's holiday?

Did Herr Ritter belong to the Gestapo? Was that why we'd been brought here, to be interrogated? Maybe Ronen was right all along.

'Either of you?' he snapped. 'Florence, 1938. I haven't got all day.'

I wondered if I was back in my cell, still dreaming. Morning had not yet broken. There would be no bread and water slipped through the door, no truck drive out to Ponary, no enchanted factory in the middle of the forest.

The clock on the wall behind Herr Ritter ticked remorselessly forward. Dreaming or not, one of us had to attempt an answer.

'I'm afraid there's been some kind of misunderstanding,'

I ventured. 'I've never been to Florence.'

'Who cares where you've been, Jew,' Herr Ritter spat. 'I was asking about the purpose of Eva Braun's visit, not yours.'

Next to me, Ronen woke from his trance. Grinning like a seminar student who couldn't possibly believe he'd stumbled on the correct answer, he said, 'I saw *The Wizard of Oz*. The red shoes.'

The fool. What was he thinking of?

'My friend is confused,' I cut in, eager to spare further humiliation. 'He knocked his head in the cell last night - '

Herr Ritter astounded me by saying, 'Proceed, Kesselman,'

'In 1938, Signore Ferragamo created the platform sandal for Judy Garland, and named it The Rainbow in tribute to her most famous song. Eva Braun went to Ferragamo's Via Mannelli shop in person to purchase a pair.'

I was stunned. It was more than I'd heard Ronen say all night.

'Correct,' Herr Ritter said. 'At least one of you knows what you're talking about. How can any self-respecting shoe-maker not have heard of Salvatore Ferragamo?'

As Herr Ritter stared at my hands, I became so fascinated with a drip of white liquid beading on the tip of his nose that I could not answer.

He asked, 'Where have you worked?'

'In Wilno, on Pilies Street.'

'For whom?'

'Jan Donelaitis.' This provoked a raising of the Ritter eyebrows and a corresponding rolling of his lower lip. 'Before that I was in Kiel.' In full swing now, I switched tongues, reacquainting myself with the harsh Schleswig-Holstein accent. 'I also speak fluent German, Herr Ritter.'

'You'll do, then.' He wiped his nose with his fist and turned to the prison guard. 'I'll take both.'

'Excellent,' the guard said.

'Fifty each, as agreed.' Herr Ritter unlocked a desk drawer and pulled out a metal box, from which he doled out ten notes into the guard's hand.

One hundred Deutschmarks heavier, the guard saluted,

turned with a crisp kick, and walked out.

'As of now,' Herr Ritter said. 'You two belong to the Moda Wehrmacht Uniform sub-camp, Leatherwear and Accessories division. Wait downstairs and you'll be shown to your workstation. Dismissed.'

He sat down at the desk, picked up the telephone, hooked an index finger in the rotary dial and paused, slowly raising a dismayed face at our continuing presence.

We backed away, twisting into opulent sunlight.

The lobby was empty when we floated back down the oak stairs.

Turning to Ronen, all I could think to say was, '*The Wizard of Oz*?'

'It's not bad,' he said. 'For Hollywood.'

'I wouldn't know.'

'Lucky one of us does.'

'Very true. If I was wearing a hat, I'd doff it to you right now. Looks like we'll be working together after all.'

Ronen inhaled lustily. 'Get a load of that country air.'

'I hate to remind you, but we are in an SS camp.'

'Do you see any soldiers?'

'Not right now.'

'In my book, 'not right now' is an improvement. Enjoy the peace and quiet. And if you can't, be a good chap and don't spoil it for those who can.'

He grinned, took out his tobacco pouch, finessed a cigarette and tossed it into his mouth. With rhythmic clicks of his fingers, he stepped across to the entrance and smoked in the doorway while our guard's truck rattled around the grass island.

'Auf Wiedersehen.' Ronen flicked his butt towards the departing wheels. 'You jumped up speck of Lithuanian fly shit.'

A suspiciously cheerful whistling came from the direction of the barracks and a voice called our names. Ronen was out the door before I could stop him.

When I caught up, he was talking to another civilian, a tall man with a head of red curls and conspicuous spray of freckles across his broken nose.

'Oswald Zgismond,' the youth said, extending a hand of elongated fingers before me. 'Head of the Julag Welcoming Committee.'

'The what?' I said.

'We're here to work,' Ronen said. 'That's all we need to know.'

'Alright then,' Oswald Zgismond said. 'The shift's already started and we'll be finishing an hour early tonight, so I won't waste time showing you the bunks.' Pointing over his shoulder to the flat-roofed cube we were leaving behind, he said, 'That's where you sleep.'

This was the most shocking thing I had heard so far, and I tried not to choke. 'You don't expect us to sleep in the soldier's barracks?'

Oswald wrinkled his nose as if I'd blasphemed. 'How much did Ritter tell you?'

'Not much,' I said. 'Herr Ritter seemed somewhat... ' I searched for the apposite word. 'Distracted.'

'Big day, a lot on his mind.'

Oswald reached an iron door at the end of the long brick snake and led us onto a deserted factory floor, topped off by large skylights. We passed a staircase that led up to a huge structure of steel pipes joined together like a tree trunk.

'What did this place used to be?' I said.

'Corrugated cable-works, originally, during the Great War. It's been empty since 1920. The Chaze moved us in a couple of days ago when Gestapo HQ got too cramped.'

I presumed this Chaze he spoke of was the boss, Julius Ritter.

'We started off on Gedimino Avenue, in the basement, making luxury goods for commissioned officers. But no, to put your mind at ease, Comrade Siegler, you won't be bunking down with the SS. Regular soldiers aren't allowed in the camp, on the Chaze's orders. Artisans are very sensitive, they can't be disturbed. If you want quality footwear, that's the cost. Last time they tried coming in without warning, the Chaze wanted to chop their balls off.'

Ronen was rubbing his hands at this news. I wished my mind was as optimistic as his, because to me, something seemed terribly wrong. That the curt and unfriendly Julius Ritter, he of the dripping nose and limp bow-tie, could inspire the Yiddish nickname Chaze, meaning 'Protector' or 'Fatherly Friend', was difficult enough to conceive. That he had either the inclination or authority to threaten the SS with castration was quite impossible.'

Oswald said, 'There are no permanent guards here, no resident Commandant.'

'No beatings or abuse?'

'It's not that kind of camp.'

'You've got a garrison outside your fence.'

'And I told you, that's where they stay. A couple of truckloads rotate in every two days from Wilno, Lithuanians and a few SS. Keeps things fresh. We don't know them, they don't know us. There's no trouble. Everybody gets on.'

We crossed the floor and followed Oswald up a second staircase on the far side. Along a narrow walkway and out onto a balconied area overlooking another floor, this time a very busy one, as many as fifty tailors hard at work in the uniform room, polishing, burnishing, and making final quality checks. Every face was a mask of deliberation, committed but content, and much more well-fed than the ones I'd seen last night in the prison courtyards.

I said, 'So what's the catch?'

Oswald chuckled. 'It's not what, it's who.'

Ronen glanced my way.

'The Chaze?' I said.

'The clients he brings, for sure. Ever wondered what it's like to measure the in-step of the Nazi Party Chancellor, Martin Boorman? Kneeling down with your head six inches away from his foetid, corpulent groin?'

'Not particularly.'

'You want to pray you never find out. We're talking about the most senior SS men who come here for personal fitting. The words 'exacting' and 'meticulous' don't even come close to describing them. But it gives you some idea of the standards we have to keep. Pressure most craftsmen can't imagine.'

I didn't take the opportunity to point out I'd only been making shoes for a year, since Signore Ferragamo had first glimpsed Judy Garland's red slippers, in fact. Meanwhile, our own Oz was at the far end of the balcony, leading us back down to another room behind yet another door. By the time the tour was over, I wouldn't be able to find my way back to Reception, let alone Wilno.

We passed through the unmistakably pungent leather store, roll after roll of raw crust calf hide, suede, and shell cordovan, all wrapped up in the seals of the very finest European tanneries.

The clicking department next, where the leather was cut, Oswald explained. Moda's signature product was a new flying boot for Luftwaffe pilots, designed to enhance comfort, but also to save their lives. In the advent of an unforeseen landing behind enemy lands, a pilot could usually find a disguise of clothing on a washing-line without too much difficulty, but replacement footwear was much harder to come by. The silk-lined Breakout Boot was the German army's response: a cunning, multi-purpose invention that necessitated the most complicated cutting template I had ever seen. In the advent of an emergency bail-out, the pilot could easily detach his boot-legs to leave behind civilian Blucher shoes. As if this wasn't difficult enough, the clicker also had to factor in a concealed pocket in the inside leg of the right boot to sheathe a small penknife. After refashioning his boot leg into a non-military looking Blucher, the pilot could be safely on his way.

Gimping and hole-punching came next, in the closing room. First with trusty awl and hammer, then a variety of ingenious hand-operated machines I had not seen before, and finally the press-knife.

Lasting, perhaps the most critical stage of production, was done in three discrete stages: toe-lasting first, then side-lasting, and finally seat-lasting. The machines, however, ran simultaneously, creating quite the din, although I was not alone in finding the monotony strangely pleasurable. It was here that Ronen and I parted company, to meet again for noonday soup. My erstwhile companion could not wait to get his hands on the very latest in lasting contraptions while I, lacking all knowledge of the mechanized world save for my mother's sewing machine, was escorted back to the clicking department.

Ronen and I had only been cell-mates for a short while but in these strange days, constancy was in short supply. How rare, in the summer of 1941, for one Jew to be able to say to another, 'Let's meet for lunch', with the certitude that both would keep the appointment.

After five minutes of cutting the breakout boot, my hand cramped from gripping the knife so hard.

After ten, my head ached with the intensity of concentration.

The clicking proved as fiendish as it had looked. But the work was rewarding and the atmosphere in the room was never less than congenial. There were twenty of us at the benches and although conversation was sparse, it was neither strained nor curtailed by anything but our own dedication to the job. After a year of sundry and often degrading menial labour, my fellow artisans were grateful to once again be using our fingers to craft an object of ingenious - if cruel - beauty.

At twelve, all work stopped and the entire factory decamped to the canteen for thick tomato soup with a generous chunk of bread and enough tea to drown a wild boar. Schumann's piano concerto played through loudspeakers in the four corners.

I ate at a long table with my fellow clickers, as was the custom. Ronen was on the other side with the lasting department, quite as cheery as when I'd last seen him. Through a series of hand gestures, we arranged to reconvene briefly after lunch to compare first impressions. Freed from the workbench and lubricated by sweet tea, tongues wagged incessantly during the meal. Had mine not been one of them, I would have contended the noise rivalled the din of the lasting machines.

Revelations came fast and frequent around our table. I was astounded to discover that my team of twenty included not just one family unit, but two. A pair of twins worked side by side while husband and wife (perhaps wisely, for marital harmony) kept their distance in the clicking room, but away from the benches talked to nobody else. Keeping families together was one of the Chaze's key policies. A happier worker was a more productive worker, he argued. Lists of parents or siblings and their last known whereabouts were submitted to Oswald Zgismond's little red book every Saturday, like a lottery. But Moda had the best odds in Central Europe: barely a week went by without another mother being reunited with her child, or some other miracle.

The language of wonder was common currency when my team discussed camp life. *The miracle of Moda. An island in a sea of horror. Finally, someone heard my prayers.* If talk turned to the Chaze himself, it was with the hushed reverence normally reserved for a saint. I nodded along, but found my fellow clickers' adulation difficult to reconcile with the ill-tempered little man who'd purchased Ronen and I like cattle and displayed about as much concern for our welfare. But are we not asked to judge a man by his actions, rather than his words. In providing refuge for a hundred Jewish craftsmen (the number rising by the day), Herr Ritter had acquired his own grateful tribe. Or an army of slave labour, making him as rich as Croseus. Ronen and I had simply exchanged one prison wall for a better-appointed one, but I didn't want to appear ungrateful as I sat there dunking bread in the man's tomato soup.

Especially not since today, I discovered, was the Chaze's birthday – the 'big night' to which Oswald had alluded. Festivities were planned for later that evening, when the man himself would be joining us. A family of bakers had been steadily squirrelling rations from the kitchen for a sponge cake and two young violinist sisters had managed to acquire instruments for a celebratory recital. The Chaze would be providing the wine – surely a joke.

Oswald appeared at my shoulder during my third cup of tea and offered to show Ronen and I to our bunks.

We followed through the silent, resting factory, past the foyer's oak staircase and stained windows into the cubed building where I'd seen the SS men loitering, in brazen defiance of the Chaze's edict. Perhaps they wanted a one-way ticket to Russia. Through a ground floor window, I saw now that I'd been mistaken: the four men in the courtyard were nothing more than wooden tailor's mannequins on wheels, draped with partially stitched jackets and trousers.

'Clever, eh?' Oswald said. 'Better than a scarecrow to keep the bastards away.'

Regarding the living quarters, I had been expecting a drawback sooner or later. Moda would provide a basic cell for sleeping, not unlike Lukiskes, but perhaps more crowded. Instead, Oswald threw open the un-bolted door of a freshly-painted bedroom, complete with curtains, a desk, and wooden shelves. True, it had a proper bed instead of bunks, but there was only the one. I could sense Ronen trying to get my attention by coughing into his hand, but I stared straight ahead, nodding politely at the four walls as Oswald concluded his spiel.

'This gets the best of the morning light,' he said. 'But the opposite one overlooks the forest and is a bit quieter.'

I was about to ask, 'The opposite what?' when Oswald said, 'I'll leave you two to sort it out between yourselves. The bell goes in five minutes, then straight back to work.'

Without waiting for an answer, he walked back to the stairway.

Ronen turned, speechless, and for once, I was inclined to agree.

Our own private bedrooms? With better furnishing than the student dormitories in Kiel? I walked in a circle around my new room as if examining a museum exhibit. I tried the bed, gingerly siting on the edge of the mattress. When no concealed snake or steel-trap sprang up behind me, I swiveled my feet round and lay down with my head on the clean cotton pillowcase.

I closed my eyes. Without doubt the last twenty-four hours were the strangest of my life. Last night I'd been working at gun-point in a greasy garage, sucking out engine oil until I vomited. Then I was thrown into prison. Now I was part of a hand-picked band of artisans working in the middle of the forest, well-fed and generously accommodated.

I slipped my fingers into my jacket pocket and removed the three black and white photographs, curled by the warmth of my chest. Shoshana striking a karate pose in our Pilies Street garden. My mother as a beautiful young woman at a crowded harbour on the Black Sea. Both sister and mother in Cracow last year, before the Nazi purification of the city began. The photographs had not left my side since I departed for Kaunas and Yukiko Sugihara in June. I lined them up on the shelf above the desk, spacing them out against the wall.

'Knock knock,' Ronen said, hand raised at my open door.

'Ah, my fellow guest from across the corridor,' I said, attempting some levity. 'Come in, good sir.'

'Did you want to see the other room?'

'Lord, no, I'm fine here,' I said. 'Unless you wanted to swap?'

'No, no, it'll do me. I prefer quiet to sunlight any day of the week.'

'Good. What do you think then?'

'You should see the toilets. Nobody to ask permission, no bucket. A proper lavatory, with a flush.'

'I've never known anything like this.'

'Me neither, my friend.'

'I hate to be the voice of caution, but when things are too good to be true, usually it's because...' I let the silence finish my point.

'We've just seen a hundred happy souls in that factory who disagree. Are they all putting on an act?'

I could not answer.

'Why would they?' he pressed. 'Good work, own clothes, enough food, these rooms. Everybody's due a bit of good luck sooner or later. I wouldn't question it if I were you.'

'I know. You're right.'

Ronen's capacity for self-delusion was almost as impressive as my own. We would enjoy the sunshine while it lasted. He gave my room the customary tour of inspection, stopping at my pictures on the shelf.

'Nice,' he said.

'Sister and mother.'

'Where?'

'Poland. Near Cracow.'

'Not the Ghetto?'

'They managed to get out,' I said. 'To the countryside.'

'Probably safer there.' Ronen reached up to the picture in the middle. 'May I?'

'Sure.'

He turned it over and checked the back where I'd scribbled my name last night in the Lukiskes ballroom.

'You put them in those little leather pouches they handed out?'

I shrugged. 'I had no choice. They were returned as soon as I said the magic words.'

'And your wallet?'

'All of it.'

'Strange,' Ronen said. 'I got my money back, but not the photo of my parents. Why would that happen? They'd give me the money but not the photo. Doesn't make any sense.'

I didn't tell him what I'd seen through the crack in the ballroom door, the mountains of jewellery and purses and photographs that were never going to be returned. The picture of Ronen's parents must have been lost in there. It was only because I'd been one of the first to be processed that I managed to get mine back.

The bell began ringing from the factory floor at that point, and we returned to our respective departments for the afternoon shift.

As Oswald had promised, we finished an hour early, in honour of the Chaze's birthday, which might have explained why Herr Ritter was so grumpy that morning. When you reach a certain age, birthdays stop being a cause for celebration. Either Ritter had left the camp since, or he never came out of his office, for I hadn't seen hide nor hair of him all day. In the Chaze's absence, party preparations had begun well before the end of shift. Scores of women started making their way back to the canteen after three o'clock to deck the walls with ribbons and lay the tables for cake and wine. A little after five, the final bell rang and the various departments hurried to their pre-arranged positions. I followed the clickers outside to the flagpole where the prison guard had deposited us from his truck. The closers were already out there, slouching in the fierce afternoon sun. It was the two smallest departments who had been selected to welcome the Chaze's return, about forty of us in all.

After a few minutes, we began to attract the attention of the SS garrison stationed on the other side of the fence. Soldiers started to crowd around the gates, just as we were doing in front of the factory. Separated by a hundred metres of concrete road, the two groups watched each other in silence, until the soldiers retreated back to the sides and the gates swung open. A gleaming black Daimler nosed through the opening and glided down the hill towards us. My co-workers stood tall and rigid, a pose that to the watching SS must have looked like deference not devotion.

The Daimler circled the grass island and came to a halt under the becalmed flag. Bright sunlight bounced off the car windows, shielding its occupant from our stares. After a minute of uncertain idling, the engine fell silent and the driver's door creaked open. Herr Ritter's grey cardigan emerged from the darkness. I was about to start clapping when my neighbour placed a firm hand on my forearm and said, 'Not here.'

Without acknowledging his audience, Herr Ritter strolled round the rear of the vehicle and opened the far side passenger door. I was expecting him to lift out a crate of wine, but instead he stepped back as an enormous Marschsteifel black boot swung out and planted itself on the gravel like a tree trunk. A grey-green flared hip followed, then the second boot and a tight eight-button woollen tunic with the double lightning bolt studded to the black collar.

I gasped, but those around me broke into smiles at the sight of the uniform.

What was happening? Surely the beloved Chaze wouldn't have been so crass as to invite an SS officer to his birthday party? Unless this was one of the senior Nazi clients that Oswald had warned about, come for a surprise fitting. But there seemed nothing unexpected about his arrival. If anything, it was waves of relief spreading across my co-workers' faces. In contrast, the SS man's jowls trembled against his starched collar and his clenched mouth carved a crevice into each sweating cheek. There was something swinish in the pink stripe of features beneath his field cap, the broad snout and dark narrowed eyes.

Out of the car he towered well over six-feet, with the malicious physique of a rearing bear. His scent too was overpowering, an opulent musk of leather and spice. As the officer turned to face us - a Hauptsturmführer, according to his insignia - the crowd raised their right hands in salute and parted, forming a guard of honour that stretched to the ornate Administration block. With his broad back to the perimeter fence, his stern mask slipped and a transformation stole across his face: eyes crinkled into benevolent chinks and a set of crooked teeth flashed between his lips.

Finally, I understood.

Herr Ritter was his secretary and glorified chauffeur. When we'd met him upstairs, I saw the Herr Direktor sign behind his desk, and assumed he was the man in charge. The true proprietor of the camp, the much-loved Chaze - the Protector, our Fatherly Friend - wasn't a beleaguered businessman with a limp bow-tie but an SS officer, Hauptsturmführer Jansen Gerternberg.

We followed the two men inside. The Chaze swiped the cap off the top of his bald head as soon as he was through the doors and released the strangle-hold of his collar's top button. Cutters and closers swarmed behind him, offering best wishes, clapping his shoulders, seizing his meaty fingers. It was a kind of adulation I had never seen before, more fitting for a Hollywood starlet than a hulking brute of a Nazi warlord.

But unlike the parade I'd just witnessed, the affections were genuine, on both sides. I studied the Chaze's round face for signs of duplicity. There was one slight roll of the eye at a particularly unctuous greeting and a split-second when the muscles of his cheek tired and his grin threatened to collapse, but otherwise the German clearly considered himself amongst friends. Of all the extraordinary sights I had witnessed since the Nazi party came to power in 1933, this reception was by far the most bizarre.

Camp Moda's hundred-strong workforce were waiting in the canteen, and unleashed a mighty cheer when Herr Ritter ushered the big man through the double-doors. Confetti and streamers rained down and the two pretty violinists began to play a waltz on a podium behind the gargantuan iced cake, as big as a buckled hat-box. Chilled bottles of wine from the Chaze's own reserve – Perrier-Juet Brut champagne no less – were dispensed into fluted glasses by a fleet of young artisans in radiant white shirts. Most of my co-workers looked tipsy after a couple of sips. I didn't even need that much. My head couldn't have felt lighter if it was inflated through the ear with a bicycle pump.

I wondered if Herr Ritter or the Chaze might step up to the podium and make a speech after mingling with the well-wishers and cutting the cake, but it became evident it was not that kind of affair. If anything, the Chaze actually became less visible as the night proceeded, disappearing at one point to change out of his uniform, and spending most of the evening in the canteen's far corner behind a protective huddle of Herr Ritter, Oswald Zgismond and an older man on crutches, missing the lower half of his right leg. A bemused onlooker might have concluded this wasn't a party for the Chaze at all, but rather a celebration to mark the beginning of Camp Moda, and our own good fortune at finding refuge.

The thought was a sobering one, even after a glass of champagne, and I retreated into my own circle of solitude. Where was the justice in a world where one man could be plucked to safety while Mrs. Ormandyova and the remaining Jews of Wilno were subject to the terrors of the Snatchers, of forced labour, imprisonment and worse?

Perhaps sensing my disenchantment, Herr Ritter appeared at my side with another bottle of Perrier-Juet.

'Thank-you, no,' I said, blocking with my fingers. 'Not just yet.'

'Don't be silly. You can't talk to him with an empty glass in your hand.'

'Talk to who?'

But my nostrils already knew the answer: the perfume of spiced leather betrayed mein host. As I whirled round, Herr Ritter thrust the bottle at me, splashed the bottom of my glass and said in German, 'Jansen, allow me to introduce our newest recruit, a very useful cutter from Kiel.'

I was face to face with the Hauptsturmführer himself, although from his heavy-lidded, impatient stare, he clearly didn't share my excitement at the encounter.

'Good evening, sir,' I stuttered. 'It is an honour to work for you.'

He nodded, rubbing those jowls that up close bristled with salt-and-pepper stubble. 'You were brought in last night?'

'Transferred this morning, sir,' I said, not wanting to correct the great man.

'From Luskiskis?'

'Yes, sir. But I'm not a convict. I was part of a group - '

'Siegler completed his apprentice with J.P. Donelaitis,' Herr Ritter said, wisely cutting short my blather. 'Formerly of Pilies Street, opposite the Cathedral.'

The Hauptsturmführer clicked his tongue. 'Unless he trained with Signore Ferragamo on the Via Whatever-the-fuck in Florence, you can spare me the details.' He forced his face to relax, flashing those crooked teeth. 'Please, Mr. Siegler, forgive my manners. We had a very rough night, as I'm sure you know. Welcome to Camp Moda. You're part of the expansion of these works now, and you'll be safe here, I give you my word.'

And with a wink, he was gone, lumbering back into the crowd, in as much as a man of his size was able to make himself scarce.

The only other time I heard Gertenberg speak that evening was when he raised his voice at a freckled youth who'd had the temerity to enquire if there was any news about when his mother might be joining the camp. The youth had submitted her name and address six weeks ago, and had heard nothing since. 'Who do you think I am, the Red Cross ?' the Hauptsturmführer snarled, momentarily silencing the violinists. But his annoyance was short-lived and the freckled youth was shepherded away by Oswald Zgismond, who once more added his mother's name to his little red book.

While the Chaze himself was more present as an aura than a man, conversation rarely strayed from the subject of his exploits. Over the course of the evening, I was able to piece together a serviceable biography of the man.

Jansen Gerternberg's humble background bore little resemblance to the rest of the elite SS. He was born in the Francovian town of Herzogenaurach in the first year of the new century, which made him as old as myself, although his bloated size added an extra decade to his appearance. In common with most of Camp Moda, he had trained as a cobbler. His father worked in a shoe factory, and it was always supposed that Jansen would follow in his footsteps. But the son possessed a rogue streak of ingenuity. After serving as an infantryman in the Great War, he returned home and started making sports shoes in his mother's laundry room. Through his father, he became acquainted with the Zehlein brothers, who produced spikes for track shoes in their smithy. Gradually the two businesses merged, until Gertenberg became the dominant partner, and was able to buy the brothers out. By the 1928 Olympics, he was equipping many of Europe's top athletes and come 1936, the company's reputation had spread to America. Jesse Owens won his gold medal in Berlin wearing Gertenberg shoes, although Jansen had sold up by that point, and gambled away a succession of small fortunes in the intervening years.

In 1933, when I was lecturing at Kiel, Gertenberg joined the Nazi Party in Silesia and served in the Wehrmacht. He married in 38, entered the Luftschutzpolizei a year later and served in a police reserve unit in Poland.

When I met him, Gertenberg had only been in Wilno for six weeks, arriving with the Nazi invasion of June 1941. His rise since then had been spectacular. In the basement of Gestapo headquarters in the former courthouse of Tuskulenai Manor, Gertenberg was assigned to an SS Komando workshop using Jewish artisans - one of whom was Julius Ritter – to manufacture leather goods. As Officer of the Watch, Gerternberg's chief duty was to lead a small unit of SS men who steered the Jewish workers to and from the Manor each morning and night, to protect them from roving semi-legitimate Snatchers like the two Lithuanian thugs who'd murdered the old man outside the bus station and marched me to work in the garage.

In a city fuelled by a black market economy for luxury goods, the leather workshop flourished. After only a week, they outgrew the Gestapo basement and needed to be rehoused an old Jewish school nearby. Impressing greatly as Officer of the Watch and flaunting his own credentials as a successful pre-war shoe manufacturer, Gertenberg was promoted from Jew escort and put in charge of the expanded workshop.

Under his control, the Gestapo work detail acquired a lucrative sideline outfitting senior Nazis with hand-crafted clothes and accessories for wives and girlfriends. Money and business were slushing in, justifying the faith his superior's had placed in the industrious officer. With his crooked teeth and bulbous nose, Gertenberg was hardly a poster boy for the genetic purity of the SS. But he was proof that the German army respected the ability to turn a Reichmark as much as the rest of the Weimar.

Of course, Gertenberg never missed an opportunity to profit personally, in backhands and bribes. But he also gained a reputation as a fair and decent employer, and made sure his workers were cosseted from the horrors of the streets. After a month in new premises, the workshop ran out of space again. Gertenberg managed to requisition an old abandoned cable-works factory in the middle of the Ponary forest, installed the whole Kommando only last week and Camp Moda was born. The rank of Hauptsturmführer was added to his accomplishments.

Gertenberg was a chancer with an eye for the comfortable life. But he was a profiteer with a conscience, a rare enough commodity in times of war. The men and women in his employ enjoyed a privileged life of protection compared to the rest of the citizenry. In his private life, he was said to be considerably less disciplined, as if the two spheres could not exist without some give and – mostly, it must be said - take. He was a glutton who added three inches to his waist-size every month, an inveterate gambler, an egotist and a serial womaniser, with a mistress for each mistress. His favourite saying was reputed to be, 'If God didn't want to me to sin every day, why did he make seven of them, and seven days of the week?'

On the last weekend of every month he returned to his family in Silesia and played the doting husband and father to twin boys. But even his own children had no exclusive claims on his affections if there was another underdog to champion. One of the legends I heard most often that night was the time the Chaze turned up late for his son's football match, found them winning comfortably, and switched his support to the other team. Whether true or not, it is the story that best encapsulates the man. In that famous irregular grin I saw the botched dentistry of an irascible charmer who'd been born poor, and pulled himself up by his boot-straps, even if he now wore thigh-length Marschstiefels. Most of that birthday evening, it was the chubby, carefree boy I saw, a mischievous glint in his eye and the last remnants of the snuggle-toothed grin he'd almost outgrown.

And now the Chaze was a man, when the darkness did descend upon his brow, there was a remedy. Well before the end of the evening, I saw him put his arms around the two pretty violinists – seventeen if they were a day - and steer them out of the canteen towards his office.

Turning to the old one-armed man now standing next to me, I said, 'Haven't they done enough tonight in terms of services rendered?'

'Did you see them complaining?'

'No. But what would you think, if you were their father?'

'He's one of us, that's what counts.'

One of us? Blessed was the shoe-maker indeed, to walk away with a couple of beauties like that for the night.

5

After the peculiarities of that first day, life at Camp Moda returned to its prosaic routines. There were no more early finishes, no more nights of champagne and iced cake. The Chaze's appearance in our midst became a rarity, and I wondered if what I'd seen could really be true. Oiling the wheels of business kept him occupied in Wilno, where he maintained a grand apartment on Parliament Square that by all accounts put our Art Deco reception rooms to shame. The day-to-day running of the Camp was left to Herr Ritter (ordering, invoicing and a multitude of such invisible upstairs work) while Oswald Zgismond oversaw the factory floor.

Conditions were never less than reasonable but our shifts were long (twelve hours with a thirty minute lunch) and the exacting nature of the handiwork took its toll on fingers and wrists. Double-shifts at short or indeed no notice were commonplace, and unrecompensed with extra food or sleep. But no matter how great the demands placed upon his workers, the Chaze's stature continued to swell, much like the great man's waistline. A weak boss would have commanded no respect at all. We were here to work. Not only did we accept that, but most were grateful for the opportunity when they remembered what was happening outside. Camp Moda was hard but fair, and the Chaze a decent employer. The more I learned about the man, the more convinced I became that his dealings with us Jews were the only honest transactions in his life.

While Wehrmacht uniforms and the ingenious new flying boot were the Camp's bread and butter, it was the sideline in luxury accessories that provided the cream for the Chaze to skim. For this most closed of workshops, he recruited the highest skilled leather workers, personally travelling the width and breadth of the Baltics to collect his next artisan. It was their fine gloves and belts and handbags and ladies shoes – boxes of tissue-lined delights that blocked corridor after corridor – which were loaded into the Chaze's

Daimler to be gifted upon his superiors at Gestapo headquarters. If there was anything left over at the end of the week, Herr Ritter negotiated an arrangement with the local farmer who supplied our dairy produce. After a delivery to the canteen, his truck would depart with treasures to be sold on the Wilno black market, with a healthy percentage of profit funneling its way back to Herr Ritter's desk drawers.

There were days when I believed I was the only man in Ponary not in on the graft. The Chaze grew ever richer, indulging his appetites for French cuisine and horse-racing. But a generous proportion of his gains went directly into the Camp's coffers. Our nutritious and filling meals, I learned from Herr Ritter, were paid for out the Chaze's own pocket. Had my co-workers known, they would have undoubtedly petitioned to make him a Ger Toshav, the Righteous Amongst Nations, the highest honour for a gentile who had helped Jews.

Days passed and I saw no sign of the Chaze's 'exacting clients' whose fittings we'd been warned about during our initial tour. I was beginning to think it was a scare-story dreamed up by Oswald Zgismond to keep new arrivals on their toes.

I also saw precious little of my former cell-mate. Come evening Ronen was too tired to chat, preferring to doze in his rooms before lights out, while I had taken to strolling around the factory grounds before sleep. What interaction I had with Ronen was confined to the row of bathroom sinks first thing in the morning, where we would take turn with the shaving brush and paste.

We were joined at the mirrors by Ernst Bau, the one-legged man I'd seen huddled with Herr Ritter during the birthday party, and had spoken to briefly at the end. Ronen and he grew quite close, as older members of a workforce will tend to. They were an odd couple to be sure. I took Bau to be a man of some influence and stature, perhaps a rabbi who had survived by shaving his beard. He was certainly no longer able to work leather, if he ever had. He was employed as the barrack cleaner, although as far as I could tell, spent most of the time dozing in his mop cupboard, or reading a newspaper with the assistance of a wooden library-style turning rack.

Although Ronen didn't mention the various money-making schemes I'd already observed, it didn't take him long to uncover the Camp's less guarded secrets. On our third morning, his razor hand positively shook with excitement as he told me that not only did many workers have family at the Camp, but it was possible to request names from Oswald, or Ozzie as he had taken to calling him. I professed astonishment. Ronen might have lost the photograph of his parents, but he was convinced the real thing would be joining him before the summer was out.

I urged a sense of caution, although it was true that in the seventy-two hours since our arrival, another pair of siblings had been reunited and now hefted rolls of raw crust calf hide together in the leather store all day long. But I could not forget the endless columns of old men and women being marched through the city on the night of our arrest, or the piles of stolen loot I'd glimpsed in the Luskikes ballroom.

Camps like Moda where you were allowed to keep your valuables were few and far in between. The gruelling Konzentrationzlangers of neighbouring Stutthof were the rule to our exception. And from all reports, conditions in Wilno were growing more perilous by the hour for those Jews who remained.

Deep down, Ronen knew all this. It was he who'd spooked me with whispers of shootings in the woods as we'd rattled our way here that morning. But three days later, such speculation had been tucked away in a dim corner of his mind. Camp Moda could be dangerous that way.

On the morning of August 16th, we were woken an hour earlier than usual, with no reason given. Breakfast was a bowl of thin, watered-down porridge, no egg or toast in sight. When I left the canteen to start work, I noticed the doors to the accommodation block had been padlocked shut and a red sign proclaimed 'NO ENTRY: CLOSED FOR ESSENTIAL MAINTENANCE'.

'Is everything OK?' I said to Hirschel, the absent-minded clicker with whom I shared a bench.

He gave a mystifying wink. 'Nothing to worry about.'

I tried to heed his advice and concentrate on my work. If the accommodation block was closed, I told myself, bad luck came in threes, and this morning's fill was my lot. It was certainly well overdue. But then, just before lunch, Herr Ritter paid a rare visit to the clicking room and requested my presence outside in the corridor.

Whenever an employer makes an unscheduled appearance in my day, I fear the worst. Perhaps that is the lot of the working man. Even after a lecture at the sedate University of Kiel, I lived in fear that the Head of Philosophy would knock on my door, to upbraid me for a controversial interpretation of Nietzsche or a joke I may have cracked about the city burghers. As a Jew in Nazi-occupied Europe, you might conclude that a smattering of paranoia was well placed.

'Don't fret,' Herr Ritter said. He was the only man in the Camp to speak to me in German, but usually only a curt, Gutten morgen. 'You haven't done anything wrong. Quite the opposite, in fact. You're earning some glowing reviews.'

'I am?'

'A man of your intellect shouldn't look so surprised, Herr Siegler.' He straightened his polkadot bow-tie. 'It's time for you to really start earning your keep.'

'I can work faster. I was unforgivably slow this morning.'

'There's nothing wrong with your work, and everything right with it. On your first day, I believe you enquired of Oswald Zgismond what was the drawback of life in Moda?'

'Yes, but I didn't - '

'Do you know the name Hinrich Lohse?'

'Of course.' I drew back, perplexed by Herr Ritter's change of tact. 'Reich Commissar for the newly designated Ostland region.'

'Very good.'

'He was Oberprasident of the Province of Schleswig-Holstein when I lived in Kiel.'

'Exactly so. Yesterday he was in Kaunas. And at 1.30 this afternoon he will find time in his busy schedule to be our guest. The Reich Commissar has requested a fitting for a pair of Adelaide semi-brogues. We are extremely honoured to receive a man of his stature, naturally.'

Hinrich Lohse's stature was five foot one, in heels. If he looked like a sour, baby-faced accountant, that's precisely what he was. A baby-faced accountant with a toothbrush moustache, and a pair of thick round spectacles behind which his eyes blinked like gormless goldfish. We used to call him FF, the Fat Führer. Tell a newspaper cartoonist to caricature a Nazi, and he'd end up drawing Hinrich Lohse. Tales of the man's temper were legendary in the cafes of Kiel. An avid horticulturalist, he had once been summoned from the garden by his valet to take an urgent telephone call. When the Oberprasident found himself addressing a dead line, he repaid the courtesy by fracturing the valet's cheekbone with the receiver.

'Word of our craftsmanship is spreading far and wide,' Herr Ritter continued. 'Great news for the camp, but it presents challenges, in terms of recruitment. The labour pool, shall we say, is an ever diminishing one. Today, the Reich Commissar's appointment will be conducted by Joziek Seidel, one of our most eminent lasters.'

I was relieved to hear that I would be spared. Joziek was a stoic sort and a gifted craftsmen, whom even Ronen rated highly.

Ritter said, 'You will be his apprentice, his shadow.'

A shadow: I could just about live with that. Our initials were the same, after all. A J.S. for a J.S.

'If you feel I am ready, Herr Ritter.'

'You are there to watch and learn, to listen but on no account to talk. If the Reich Commissar feels so much as the need to comment on your presence in the room, then clearly you were not ready, and your position may need to be reviewed.'

'I understand, sir.'

'Of course you do.' Herr Ritter smiled like a business traveller whose wife had just walked into his new favourite bar. 'Seidel will collect you from the canteen after lunch.'

I returned to the clicking room, but could only hang my

head and count the grooves on the bench.

Hirschel gave my arm a light squeeze. 'You'll be fine. We've all been there.'

'Who did you get?'

'A nobody, compared to the Reich Commissar.'

'How did it go?'

He snorted, the tip of his nose and the right corner of his mouth pulling into a mirthless smirk. 'Why do you think I'm stuck in here?'

The department took lunch together in the canteen as usual, but for once I was in no mood for small talk. My silence was contagious, enveloping the table like a thick mist. Not even the ubiquitous Schumann or Mozart played today. Lost in my thoughts, I picked at the scabs that Herr Ritter had left.

First there was his mild rebuke concealed amongst the compliments: a man of my intellect shouldn't look so surprised. What had he meant by that? Herr Ritter was known to measure his words like pieces of gold: every last one accounted for. A man of my intelligence? I had come close to disclosing my previous life as a professor to Ronen in Luskiskes, but had thought twice. There was nobody else with whom I would have confided. Since the subject of my intelligence (distinctly average, whatever was claimed) had not been raised in even the most innocent context since my arrival, I was forced to conclude that Herr Ritter had somehow found out the truth about my previous occupation from elsewhere. Yes, I had switched careers. One would be hard-pressed to find a European Jew in the 1940s who hadn't. In the three years since leaving Kiel, I'd become a solid shoe-maker, if not an exceptional one. But I'd never claimed to be anything else. Was this a hanging offence? Was my 'fraud' about to be uncovered? With the Reich Commissar drafted in as an unwitting stooge? Highly unlikely.

Perhaps I'd been selected because I'd worked in Kiel. I spoke fluent German and knew the Schleswig-Holstein area well.

If so, it still made no sense. Herr Ritter had expressly forbidden me from talking to the man.

And then there was the matter of the camp's reputation,

'spreading far and wide'. Herr Ritter gave the impression that we were struggling to cope with a flood of VIP fittings. Yet this was the first since my arrival.

I was being manoeuvred by shadowy forces beyond my control. There was nothing to do but submit, and pray that Camp Moda would continue to keep me from harm.

Although I'd been going through the motions of eating at the long table, no discernible tastes had yet troubled my palate. Upon glancing at my dish, I saw why. The usual tomato soup had been replaced by a thin watery stew. None of my fellow clickers had seen fit to comment on the substitution.

In fact, nobody was talking at all, in the entire canteen. The silence reminded me of the artful vigil we'd maintained under the flagpole that first evening, awaiting the Chaze's arrival.

I thought back to this morning's early alarm, the meagre porridge, the closing of bedrooms for so-called essential maintenance... Finally, the day was starting to make a modicum of sense.

From the moment the Camp had woken, it was putting on another display. All sense of contentment and joy had been banished for the day. This time the intended audience wasn't a garrison of faceless soldiers on the other side of a fence, but the most powerful Nazi in the country. It seemed utterly inconceivable that an entire SS work camp would conspire to dupe the visiting Reich Commissar, but that's exactly what was happening. My own tribulations paled into insignificance for a handful of sweet, fleeting seconds, until Joziek Seidel's hand came to rest on my shoulder.

'It's time,' he said, solemn as an executioner.

As I rose to follow, not one of my co-workers raised their heads to watch us go. Ronen sat determinedly swirling his spoon in his stew, as if motion alone could thicken the broth. But today even daydreams were curtailed: the back to work bell rang before the two of us reached the exit. Lunch was a paltry fifteen minutes. Joziek and I were to await the Commissar's arrival while our co-workers returned stony-faced to their labours.

We passed through the cool oak reception lobby out into

a barbarous August sun, from which the solitary flagpole offered scant resistance. It was 1.20pm. With any luck our guest would be punctual and we would only be lightly grilled as opposed to charcoaled. To pass the time, I asked Joziek for a breakdown of the fitting procedure.

The first meeting normally took an hour to measure and assess the feet, and discuss the models, toe shapes, leathers and decoration that the client desired. Since the Commissar already knew what he wanted - a pair of Adelaide brogues - today's appointment might only take thirty minutes. After this, Joziek would begin making the bespoke 'last' that would give Hinrich Lohse's shoes their unique shape and personality. Hand carved from a block of kiln dried Beechwood, the last incorporates every contour and measurement of the foot so as to make it as comfortable a fit as possible. The finished last then shapes the paper patterns from which my team of clickers will cut the various components. The inner sole is soaked in water, attached to the sole of the last, and left to dry for a long period so that it assumes the correct shape to walk upon. This process takes time to perfect. Providing he was happy, the Commissar would be expected to return in a week, for the first of several trial fittings.

As Joziek explained the intricacies, I was alarmed to see my guide's eyes grow watery and his nose require the constant ministrations of the tissue he kept up his sleeve. I hoped it was only the heat that was provoking him. I suggested we step back into the shadows to cool down.

Joziek's lips curled in derision and for the first time I heard a distinctly adenoidal twang as he said, 'Do you suffer from hay fever or something?'

'Not that I know of.'

'Well then,' he said, with an emphatic blow of his nose. 'If I can stick it out, so can you.' Above us, I heard a window frame swing and click shut. 'Besides I don't think we've got long to wait.'

A minute later Herr Ritter appeared on the cream steps behind us and we stood to attention as the perimeter gate opened and the silver shark of a sleek, finned Tatra 87 sped down the slope.

Crunching to a stop under the flagpole, the driver removed a long wooden stick from the trunk at the front – the air-cooled V8 engine was mounted at the rear, beneath its fin – and proceeded to help his passenger out, via the ignominious loaning of his own arm and shoulder together with the stick. Herr Ritter pushed past us cursing to hold open the door.

The Fat Führer had not aged well in the years since I had left Germany. Where many men acquired a dignified gauntness in their late fifties, the Commissar's cheeks had continued to plump. The hair at his temples was razored to the point of invisibility, but piled suspiciously high on his head in a pompadour that reminded me of a baby's frilled bonnet perched upon his brow. The toothbrush moustache had lost a few more bristles, and could now be mistaken as a shadow of his unimpressive nose.

Despite these ravages, the man had never looked happier. In place of his usual doleful pout, his lips were smiling, an unusual arrangement. More alarming than his seeming inability to hobble without a stick, was the fact that the Commissar appeared to have grown two inches in height.

The problem with his foot, I learned from his salutary exchange with Herr Ritter, was only temporary in nature, and paradoxically explained the reason for his good cheer, if not his gain in stature. En route from Kaunas this morning, the Commissar had stopped at a friend's villa to shoot Red Grouse, and bagged a brace for evening supper. While returning from the fields, the party's Lithuanian groundsman had happened to mention a Jewish partisan who was rumoured to be hiding nearby and stealing chicken eggs. Having succeeded with the gamebirds, the Germans considered themselves sharpened for a spot of Jew-hunting, and spent the next hour stalking through the corn. Once more, they bagged their quarry, an adolescent boy in rags who fell out of a tree and broke his neck after being winged by the Commissar's shotgun.

'Sprained my ankle in the heat of the battle,' he told Herr Ritter, shrugging off his driver's yoke and limping towards us.

'Damned nuisance, second time this year I've gone over on it.' He grinned, wheezing through small teeth. 'Worth every minute, though, most fun I've had since Nuremberg.'

'I trust you'll be leaving your Krieghoff in the car this afternoon,' Herr Ritter joked.

'You know damn well I'm no trigger-happy thug. In fact, I've gone on record that the manner of these executions we hear about on the Eastern Front simply cannot be justified.' The Commissar stopped in front of Joziek and I, putting his stick down squarely on my foot, pinning my little toe under its rubber stopper. I resisted the urge to squirm.

He said, 'Where is the sense in the destruction of manpower that could aid the war economy?'

Once an accountant, always an accountant.

'After all,' he said, 'Who'd make our shoes then? Fear not, Ritter, your pampered poodles are safe.'

With that, he released me. Joziek and I followed them in. I tried to get another look at the Commissar's height to disprove the notion he had grown, but he was already limping up the steps, and when we entered the reception lobby, Herr Ritter was leading him into the ground floor fitting room, and once inside, he was seated. The room was bedecked in the time-honoured fashion with previous clients' lasts, in much the same way that an upmarket restaurant displays photographs of esteemed customers upon the walls. Hinrich Lohse's moulds would no doubt be taking pride of place.

There followed a couple more minutes of small talk, during which the Commissar spoke of his children, and bemoaned the fact that his new Ostland responsibilities kept him away from the family home. He was particularly disappointed to be missing this week, when the children were expected to harvest their crop of green peppers. The Commissar had built them a three-foot square garden box, based on exciting new horticultural theories of economy. Three square feet, he crowed, warming to the theme, one of the simplest lessons a father could teach his child, and one that would improve any German's lot in life. Herr Ritter excused himself during a lull in the gardening conversation; I had been advised he would watch through the one-way full-length mirror.

After a meek young girl in plaits had taken the Commissar's drink order (Earl Grey tea, slice of lemon, warmed thimble of milk), Joziek removed a pair of Adelaide brogues for inspection, and proceeded to get down to business, describing the quality of the finish as the German turned the shoes over in his lap, all trace of the nasal congestion gone now we were inside.

'You will see the shoe shape is refined and elegant, with an accentuated waist. The waist shape under the arch is highly pared back; not only elegant but also likely to be highly supportive to the arch of the foot. The welt is nicely bevelled, while within the waist it is pared almost flush with the upper up to the junction of the welt and the heel. The heels are pitched inwards.'

The Commissar nodded along, as impressed with the supple course of Joziek's words as he was with the leatherwork. I could see why Herr Ritter had chosen him as my mentor.

Joziek continued. 'The uppers are very finely sewn, and great care has been taken in the design and finish, such that the lines seem to flow through the shoe harmoniously – the downward curve of the vamp, for instance, coincides exactly with the position of the heel, and so on. Turning the shoe over, you may find – as might be expected – that it has a channelled welt, and there is a prominent fiddleback to the waist.'

'I'll take them,' the Commissar said, struggling to his feet. 'Do you have a size nine?'

Joziek chuckled nervously. 'Very good, sir.'

But Lohse wasn't joking. We'd never thought to ask if he had attended a shoe fitting before. Evidently the old bean-counter had not. He expected to walk away this afternoon with a box under his arms as if he'd bought them over the counter at Batas.

'Herr Ritter has details of my account. Might as well take two pairs while I'm here.' The Commissar thrust the shoes at Joziek, who was too stunned to take them. His considerable gift of the gab had deserted him and he stood there, mouth flapping.

'I see the Commissar's sense of humour is as sharp as ever,' I said, committing all three of Herr Ritter's sins – moving, speaking, and even touching the great man as I relieved him of the inspection shoes. 'If you'd like to make yourself comfortable, my colleague will remove your boots and begin measuring your feet.'

Lohse stared red-faced at my intrusion, nose twitching. I half expected Herr Ritter himself to come crashing through the mirror.

I blundered on. 'We should have you out of here in fifteen to twenty-minutes, sir, no longer.'

Eventually the Commissar grumbled his acquiescence.

'I thought you Jews were meant to have a sense of humour,' he bristled, doing a good job of passing off embarrassment as indignation. 'Let's get this over with.'

I retreated and tried to make myself invisible while Joziek assembled his measuring tools. He knelt at the man's feet and began unbuckling his calf-high jackboots. I thought he was working in a very sensitive manner, but the Commissar grew visibly uncomfortable with his efforts, would not sit still, and twice insisted on removing the boots himself, but Joziek apologised and insisted on trying again. It was during these remonstrations that I heard the adendoidal twang return to Joziek's voice.

I strained to look over my mentor's shoulders. The angle of the ceiling's lampshade was just right to allow me to see what Joziek could not: the right length of Lohse's black trousers was stained with dusty yellow pollen, from his exploits in the corn-fields. Joziek's nose was inches away.

I watched as his poor eyes began to water. He had to stop unbuckling the boots to wipe away the tears, and then he started to sniff, three, four times, each one growing louder.

The last thing I remember seeing was Joziek's face undergo a seismic eruption, seemingly sucking into itself before exploding in a shower of phlegm. His hands jerked up instinctively to catch, but to no avail. A string of mucus shot through his fingers and splatted the centre of the German's left boot.

'Good God, man,' Lohse roared, with no sense yet of the

scale of the insult to his footwear. 'I didn't come here to catch your filthy germs!'

It didn't take him long to realise he'd caught a lot more than that. He endeavoured to lean forward and peer past his stomach to his boots, and I watched the Commissar's face turn purple as the green blob trembled on his shin, and then start to slide.

But my eyes were drawn down the length of the leather, to the bottom of the Commissar's boot, where an odd wedge-shaped obstruction was lodged under his heel. No wonder he had sprained his ankle: the man was walking around with what looked like a child's wooden brick trapped under his foot! When I craned my neck to check the other boot, I saw a second triangular block in exactly the same position, and I realised what I was looking at. I had seen this kind of amateur heel-lift before, on the counter of Mr. Zygot's counter in my mother's shop in Cracow.

Spitting profanities, the Reich Commissar fumbled for the pistol holstered at his waist, but the folds of his stomach were preventing its release and he could not stand up without his walking stick, which had been placed in the umbrella stand. It was this impotent delay that saved Joziek Seidel's life.

'Herr Lohse, sir.' I knelt at his side and raised my hands in supplication. He swiped them away like a bear.

'Never. In. All. My. Life - '

I put my wrists together to block his blows and stood my ground. 'I think I know why you keep spraining your ankle, sir.'

His fingers paused at the holster. 'How could you possibly know?'

'Your boots, sir. I believe they may be dangerous.'

'Dangerous!'

'With your permission, if I may ask my colleague to give us the room, I would wish to speak to you about your heels.'

It was only when I made reference to the heels - his most shameful of secrets - that the Commissar's fight left him like a bull stunned by a cattle-prod.

'In the strictest confidence, of course,' I added.

'He'd better get out before I bash his filthy nose in.'

'Seidel,' I said. 'Outside. Now.'

When I opened to door to eject him, Herr Ritter was seething against the oak panel, miming a string of invective worse than the German's. I re-entered the room, removed the walking stick from the umbrella stand and handed it to the Reich Commissar, in case he felt more comfortable with a weapon in his hand.

'Let me just wipe this clean,' I said, mopping the mucus up in my handkerchief. 'Hayfever, sir, nothing contagious I can assure you. Now, I have a confession to make, Commissar.'

I tossed the handkerchief in the waste-paper basket and began to pace the room.

'I have not always been a shoe-maker. For ten years I worked as a teacher in the fair city of Kiel, in Schleswig-Holstein. I only mention this, because during my time, I became familiar with seeing your good self in the newspapers and news reels. And I was a little taken aback when I saw you again today, and confess I wasn't sure it could be the same person. I am bracing myself for a blow at this point, sir, but would I be correct in suggesting you have gained two or perhaps three inches of height in recent weeks?' Before waiting for an answer, I dropped to my knees in front of him and said, 'Your boot – may I?'

Now he was relaxed, the boot slipped off like Cinderella's slipper.

'Just as I thought,' I said, holding up the offending heel. 'I cannot say who fitted this sir, but I would hazard it was not a professional shoe-maker. Such height-enhancing lifts are a common cause of foot pain and injury. Anything inserted above ½" will mean that the heel is not held firmly in place by the boot, and the wearer will tend to walk 'out of the shoe', if you understand my expression?'

'Out of the shoe, yes. That sounds right. I thought it was just a case of getting used to the extra height.'

'It is common for the wearer of such lifts to be prone to spraining or even breaking an ankle after losing control. The ankle will roll to the side with the foot tucked underneath.'

'That's exactly what happened today, yes. I knew I wasn't

that badly out of shape.'

'Any shoe-maker worth his salt knows that inserts which add more than ½" of apparent height should be avoided, sir, due to this very risk.'

'You can remove them?'

'Of course.' It wasn't difficult: the lift came away in my hand. 'And if the Commissar cared for my colleague to continue his measurements, we could see to it that your new shoes were specifically designed to accommodate such an additional height. The trick is to raise the full foot rather than just the heel, and to use a heel-cup and side support to keep the heel in place while adding height.'

'You can do all this here, on site?'

'Certainly, sir. It may take a week or perhaps longer, but I guarantee you will never walk more proudly, comfortably or indeed more safely.'

'Splendid.' He placed his other leg up on a chair for me to remove the lift. 'I daresay I could have a pair of these things made the same way?'

'Any shoes or boots you desired, sir. I'm afraid you would need to enquire the price from Herr Ritter, for it would be a little higher, given the additional and specialist nature of the work.'

'You will personally oversee it?'

'It would be an honour, sir, to assist the Oberprasident of my former dearly-beloved province.' I paused at the door, inclining my head, weary from obsequiousness.

'Just you, mind,' he said. 'I can't have any Tom, Dick or Harry knowing my particulars.'

I released my grip on the door handle. 'Forgive my confusion, sir. Would you prefer I didn't call my colleague back into the room?'

'To have him sneeze all over me again? What did we just agree, that you would personally oversee the work. Or am I losing my sanity as well as my wallet here?'

'Of course not, sir. As agreed.'

I turned to collect my thoughts along with Seidel's tape measure, shrugging helplessly into the mirror for the benefit of Herr Ritter.

And that was how, on the afternoon of August 16th, 1941, I came to perform my first bespoke shoe fitting, a pair of height-adjusted Adelaide brogues for the Reich Commissar of the newly ordained Ostland region.

Within hours of Lohse's departure, word spread from the Camp's radios of the real reason for his presence in Kaunas the previous day.

On the morning of August 15th, the Reich Commissar announced a raft of new anti-Jewish directives which made the initial purge of the interim LAF government seem restrained in comparison. Effective immediately, all Baltic Jews were required to wear not one star but two, on the chest and now back; not to use any public transport; not to visit parks, playgrounds, theatres, cinemas, libraries or museums; not to own cars or radio sets.

But more than this, it was the first we'd heard of mandatory Ghettos outside of Poland. In the space of one day, twenty-four hours before leaving for his grouse hunt and shoe fitting, the Commissar had personally overseen the removal of the twenty-six thousand surviving Jews of Kaunas from their homes to the small suburb of Vilampole, in which, henceforth, they were to be confined. All Jewish property outside the designated Ghetto area was to be confiscated. The amount of living space that each Jew was to be allowed?

Three square feet, the same as Hinrich Lohse's children's garden box.

6

While my co-workers sought solace in each other's company downstairs that evening, I retreated to my bedroom. The extra supper originally conceived as recompense for the Reich Commissar's visit had turned into a wake for the Baltic brothers and sisters caught up in yesterday's resettlement and I wanted no part of it. The more Herr Ritter attempted to strengthen my position within the Camp, the less I felt I belonged. I had not survived five years of Nazi persecution to become their glorified wardrobe consultant.

Yet in my heart, I knew that was the only role I could play.

Abba Kovner offered me a chance to fight when he showed up at our kitchen table in Pilies Street, and I'd sent him away with grandstanding talk of pacifism. My failure to act had cost me dearly, with the flight of Shoshana. Her photograph on the shelf above my desk was starting to fade. Soon I would be entirely alone in the world, and I deserved every minute of it.

I was rescued from maudlin iterations by a knock at the door. My neighbour Ronen, I supposed, come for the lap-dog's report.

But it was the lofty, tousled head of Oswald Zgismond that poked round the top of the frame.

'The man of the hour,' he said. 'Will you be joining us later?'

'Perhaps,' I lied.

'It'll pass, you know.'

He asked if he was intruding; I shrugged, backed up against the wall on my plump pillow and picked lint from my sheet.

'Talk about being thrown in at the deep-end.' Zgismond turned the chair from my desk and sat at the foot of my bed. 'Julius should never have sent Joziek in his condition. His nose was redder than a baboon's backside.'

It took a few seconds to realise that Julius was Herr Ritter. I'd never heard his first name spoken before.

'He's very proud of you.'

'Pride,' I scoffed, releasing a handful of lint to stream through the dusk.

'It might not feel like it, but you've done a great thing today. When we get out of this mess, you'll never have to buy a meal again, the way those people downstairs feel.'

'To think that they're... celebrating?' I said. 'Makes me feel even sicker to be honest.'

'They're enormously thankful for what they have here, it's not the same thing. Everyone's got loved ones beyond this forest. As of tonight, we're all prisoners.'

'Some have bigger cells than others.'

'Not for too much longer,' he said. 'Moda can take in a lot more, and we will. Measures are already underway. But it comes at a price. As you know.'

'Yes. Yes, I do.'

'I'm sorry I have to ask but we need to know. Did Lohse say anything else?'

'About what?'

'The conditions. Pampered poodles, or the like.'

I tried to wave it off. 'That was a joke with Herr Ritter before he'd even set foot inside the building.'

'Precisely. Lohse's never been here, so that means we've got a reputation beyond the quality of our goods, and that's not good for anybody.'

'He didn't see a soul outside of the fitting room.'

'Old man Bau didn't limp out of his cupboard?'

I smiled, despite myself. 'He did not.'

'No more comments we need to know about, you're sure?'

'On a day like this, you're worried about your reputation? About what kind of show you put on?'

Zgismond's talk horrified me. Labour camps had been operational in Germany since the mid-1930s. The Nazi press liked to gloat how they'd fooled the International Red Cross on inspections of the likes of Esterwegen, Oranienberg and Dachau by painting and renovating, planting trees and flower beds and staging football matches between convicts. Inmates were coached on what to say to IRC delegates, and too terrified to reveal the truth about the hunger and the beatings.

Camp Moda was no Dachau, but our levels of deceit today had been on a par, even if this time it was to trick the Nazis themselves. But we had our own Nazi in charge, the elusive Gertenberg. It made no sense.

I said, 'Where is the Chaze tonight?'

'I'm sorry?'

'Did he even know about Lohse's visit?'

'He arranged it.'

'Yet he was not here in person to receive his superior.'

'What's on your mind, Jozef? Come out and say it.'

'Did he know what you were up to? Closing the bedrooms, the canteen substitutions?'

'You think Ritter could have authorised any of that himself? He's only the foreman.'

'Then I don't understand. Why would the Hauptsturmführer risk everything – his life – for us?'

'Don't flatter yourself, comrade. Gerternberg's only loyalty is to his bank account. He's a businessman first and foremost. When Stalin wins this war, the Chaze'll be churning out fur caps in Vladivostok. Play your cards right and you might be fitting out the Politburo for new boots. Or you can sulk and find yourself out of a job.'

'That almost sounds like a threat.'

Zgismond smiled, rose to his feet and neatly tucked the chair under the desk.

In an attempt to clear my head after Zgismond had left – it was the closest I'd come to an argument at Moda – I left the building for one of my solitary perambulations around the perimeter fence. I confess, had I found a hole in the wire that night, I might have slipped away. But in the end, my fate was sealed by a discovery of a very different nature.

I walked to the western end of the accommodation block, keeping my distance from the soldiers on the other side of the fence. They had no need to stray beyond their garrison huts, and the back of the factory was mine to roam. As long as inmates were in bedrooms by Lights Out, our movement was largely unrestricted – another luxury of the camp I had taken for granted.

It didn't take much pumping of oxygen to the brain to realise how shamefully I'd acted. Oswald Zgismond had come to me in kindness and compassion, but I was too adrift in a fog of self-pity to see, convinced that having spent twenty minutes measuring the hairy toes of a high-ranking Nazi was the utmost sacrifice a man could make. While Zgismond tried to absolve my conscience, I'd moped on my bed, sighing and fluttering my eyelids like an imperious high school princess. Worse still, I had been deliberately obtuse, accusing my co-workers of celebrating in the canteen when I knew the opposite to be true. The fool who goes looking for an argument with a friend is an even bigger putz if he claims victory on finding one. I owed Oswald an apology. He'd been right about the Chaze, too. Everyone knew of his gambling habits and addictions to the high-life: a man of those weaknesses would do anything to cover his tracks. If Gertenberg was prepared to lie to his own wife, the deceit he'd practised upon Hinrish Lohse was small-fry.

The only comment of Zgismond's that still left me uneasy was his parting shot. Was my lack of experience really so obvious that I had been rumbled? However well Messrs' Zygot and Donelaitis had trained me, I couldn't hope to compete with some of the finest artisans in Eastern Europe, men who'd had the craft handed down by fathers and grandfathers. Yet Julius Ritter had chosen me this afternoon. Why? Ungrateful as it seems, I couldn't shake the feeling that Hinrich Lohse wasn't the only one to have had the truth concealed from his eyes. I made up my mind to track down Zgismond before lights out, not to offer my fists but to seek answers.

In the meantime, I was lost. I'd strayed beyond the buildings' glare into untamed wilds of overgrowth, with only moonlight to guide me. Up ahead, about ten metres from the fence was a clearing in the trees and what looked like a free-standing brick wall, covered with leaves and twine. Intrigued, I approached, trampling a path through the spongy floor.

The wall had a thick roof along the top and wasn't a wall at all, but a series of fronts concealing a network of narrow trenches with coffin-shaped portals built into the brick. It was an air-raid shelter from the Great War, when the factory was producing steel cable. As I stood at the opening of the main passageway, wide enough for single file entry, I wondered if I was the first person to explore since the plant had ceased production. I squeezed between the mossy walls, my mind racing with memories of H. Rider Haggard stories, intrepid explorers of lost temples, painted faces hidden between cracks, blowpipes poised.

I struck a match and entered. The shelters themselves were empty except for things that scuttled in the dust. I passed through the cold and clammy chambers, one after another, enough to accommodate the entire cable workforce in its heyday. I was nearing the thin column of light at the far exit when my shin collided with something soft but substantial on the floor, like a padded armchair. Another match flaring in my hand, I stepped back and peered down at an upright battered suitcase. There were two others behind it, standing the same way, as if patiently awaiting their owner in Lost Property.

I tried lifting the handle of the one I'd walked into but it was far heavier than a box of clothes had any right to be. I could feel the contents sifting back into place as I let the case sag to the floor. It sounded like a hoard of hardware, screws and nails. There was a chalk inscription on the side of the case, a name I had not heard before:

HAHN Irene, DOB 1929

The other two cases were marked the same way, hand-printed in chalk, presumably by the owners :

EMIL HUBSCHEIN 4/6/32

WAISENKIND HANA FUCHS 13. JULY 1941

This last case dated from only a month ago.

None of the names were familiar as Moda prisoners, although of course I did not know everybody. I couldn't understand for a moment why Irene or Emil would have left full cases out here with the beetles and rats, even if they'd arrived at the camp fully laden, which almost nobody did. Like me, most inmates had been brought in from other work-details, or snatched off the streets with no more belongings than the contents of their pockets.

On my knees, I lowered Hana Waisenkind's case to its side and tried the brass buckle.

It wasn't locked.

I lifted the lid, revealing a jumble of discarded wealth, more than one person could possibly have owned, unless Hana was a princess. More money than I had seen in my lifetime: gold and silver coins, bank notes, stocks, certificates, foreign currency, real estate assets, ear and finger rings, necklaces, spectacles, bracelets, watch-cases, lockets. I estimated I was gazing at the combined loot of a hundred different Jews.

The other suitcases were filled the same way.

Supper was over when I returned, the barrack landings busy as a tenement fire escape in July, neighbours exchanging gripes for gossip before bed. I made straight for my room, unable to look a fellow prisoner in the eye.

My mind was a jangling bag of billiard balls that night, one thought constantly knocking into the other. Who did all that jewellery and paperwork belong to? Why was it hidden? Who were Irene and Emil and Hana? After hours of twisting my sheets into damp knots, I resolved to take the only course of action available: to check the air-raid shelter again at first light, when I could see clearly. There had to be something I'd missed, a sign or notice that would explain. No point jumping to wild conclusions based on one moment of moonlit madness. Partly mollified, or at least soothed by the semblance of consolation, my mind was able to settle and still. Cooling sleep anaesthetised me a little after three o'clock.

I snored straight through the siren, and awoke to the sounds of the barracks performing its morning ablutions, rushing water and hissing steam from the bathrooms. I had missed my chance to slip out to the shelter before breakfast. Providing I could stop myself from blabbing about what I'd seen, the earliest I'd be able to return was dusk, in the lull between supper and lights out. It was going to be a long day.

I stepped out of my room and almost walked into a neat pile of striped clothing that had been left outside. Glancing down the corridor, I noticed Ronen's door also had a pile outside, as yet untouched. While I stood there scratching my head, Elise Trachten came out of the women's bathroom at the far end, dressed in a brand new black and white striped smock.

I grabbed my pile of clothes and jumped back inside. Vest, trousers, hat and coat: I laid them out on my bed in disbelief. From my window I saw a stream of Jews walking to breakfast, all dressed in the same stripes. I donned my new uniform and followed them out.

More changes were afoot in the canteen. Only porridge and water were served. Not one of my table of clickers commented or looked remotely disappointed; it was as if everybody but me knew what was going on. Perhaps they did. After my grilling last night about Hinrich Lohse's 'pampered poodles', Oswald Zgismond had returned to supper, where the workers were still coming to terms with the news of the Kaunas Ghetto. I later learned that a collective decision had been made, and I was now witnessing the consequences. In the interests of collective self-protection, Ernst Bau had led a successful petition for a harsher regime, surely an unprecedented move in the history of penal servitude.

From now on, every day would be inspection day.

I was careful not to point out that the fortune stashed in our air-raid shelter could have bought us all breakfast at the Narutis Hotel, for the rest of our lives.

At twelve o'clock I learned from my supervisor that Herr Ritter wanted a word with me before lunch, as he had the previous day, when he gave news of Hinrich Lohse's arrival. This time, I was to report directly to his office on the first floor of the Admin Block. Wondering if there had been an overnight adjustment to Lohse's order, I made my way through the insistent rhythms of the factory's machines to climb the oak staircase, pass under the painted window and into the grand turquoise room I'd first glimpsed with Ronen Kesselman.

The typewriters were idle; the secretaries took their lunch earlier than the rest of us.

Herr Ritter was not at his desk either either, but the frosted glass 'Herr Direktor' door in the corner was open. I could hear voices from the inner sanctum. As I approached along the strip of scarlet carpet along the wall, a voice bid me to enter.

Compared with the bright, lavishly appointed room where Ritter and the secretaries worked, the Chaze's office was little more than a closet. Ritter was scrawling notes on a piece of typed paper at a small table in front of the window while Oswald Zgismond stood clutching a black file at his side, next to a bust of Adolf Hitler. Behind him on the wall were two maps of Europe. The only other décor of note in the drab office was a black SS jacket discarded on the back of a leather armchair in the corner. Zgismond remained standing, but gestured for me to take a seat opposite Herr Ritter.

'So,' the old man said, finally laying his pen down. He raised a bunched handkerchief to his nose and wiped the tip. 'What is it you'd like to ask first?'

I stammered, all bluster.

'Don't be afraid,' Herr Ritter coaxed. 'You're amongst friends.'

'Now I really am worried.' I grinned, looking from one to the other for signs of a well-wrought joke. 'I don't have the faintest idea what you're talking about. Sir.'

'Look,' Ritter said. 'You've been here long enough, I don't doubt for a second that you've preserved your integrity with the rest of the workers. But this is an opportunity for you to discover the truth.

'About the new uniform?'

'About the suitcases,' Zgismond said. 'We know where you went last night, Jozef. And we'd like to set the record straight.'

Blood pulsed against my ear-drums and the room flashed black on white, like a reverse negative. I nodded and pushed back against my chair, appraising the two again in the light of Zgismond's transparency. The time for duplicity was over, on all sides.

'Alright,' I said. 'I realise I'm in no position to make demands, but I'd certainly like to know what's going on.'

Herr Ritter went first. 'The contents of those suitcases were legally obtained, every last ear-ring and necklace. You must understand that.'

'I saw 'legal obtaining' in Lukiskis,' I said. 'And it wasn't pretty.'

'This is different,' Zgismond said. I couldn't stop myself from scoffing at the distinction. 'Everything you saw in the shelter was the result of police raids after deadlines to hand over property had expired. Due process was followed every step of the way. Nobody's allowed to keep this stuff anymore, you know that. Lithuanians, Poles, Jews...'

'So where did you get it?'

Behind me, a closet door opened and I heard the soft click of a light switch cord.

'From me,' the Chaze said, walking out, drying his hands on a small towel. I tried rising to me feet, but he stopped me. 'Sit, sit. You're our special guest.'

The three of them smiled at that. I suspected I was about to have my throat cut.

The Chaze had put on weight since his birthday, and it wasn't sitting well on him. Already a big man, there was a weariness in his limbs this afternoon, as if they were finding the strain all too much.

'Believe me, there's more diamonds sloshing around in Tuskulenai Manor than anyone knows what to do with,' the Chaze said, slowly circling the table. 'So I helped myself to a couple of cases, big deal. You think running an operation like this comes cheap?'

He paused behind my chair, hands on my shoulders. The perfume of leather and spice was more pungent than ever, but it was mixed now with the rank odour of his sweat, and something deeper, riper.

'Any idea how much vodka alone it takes to keep those soldiers on the other side of that fence? How much I have to spend on birthday presents to keep the Armoury Inspectors from making a day-trip out the city?'

Releasing my shoulders, he began to circle again. 'You think you've paid a price to keep this going, well guess what, we all have. This is a good thing, for everybody. If you don't want a place here anymore, all you've got to do is say the word. Fine, no problem, I can pick up ten more like you before supper. But if you're here, and you're working for me, you cannot have any second misgivings. Are we clear?'

'Clear,' I said.

Herr Ritter looked up at the big man, stopped behind the armchair in the corner. They really were a strange pair: the Bird and the Bear.

'There are over a hundred lives at stake in this camp,' Ritter said, dabbing the white drip on his nose. 'And we're expanding all the time, bringing in whole families where we can. After yesterday, quicker than ever, I'd imagine. Let us help you, Jozef.'

'Yes,' the Chaze said, 'Help. That's what I'm talking about.' He removed his Hauptsturmführer's jacket from the chair and began buttoning up in front of the mirror on the back of the door.

'My family are in Poland,' I said. 'There's nothing to be done.'

'Let us help *you*,' Ritter said, correcting his emphasis. 'Help you to help us. And I mean more than carrying out bespoke shoe fittings, although you certainly earned your keep in that regard.'

'Lohse's very impressed,' the Chaze said, squaring his chin while buttoning his collar. 'Called me personally. The sneezer not so much. He's on the fast train to base-camp.'

Base-camp meant Stuthof, the nearest concentration camp in northern Poland. I hoped he was joking.

'With your looks, and your fluency of the language,' Herr Ritter said. 'You could pass for anybody.'

'I'd say he's already proved that.' The Chaze poked a pick between his crooked incisors in the mirror. 'Ten years at the University of Kiel. Not bad for a humble cobbler.'

The office was filled with the sound of the wooded point squeaking against his teeth.

'How did you find out?'

'It wasn't difficult,' Ritter said. 'When you told me you'd lived there, we searched your employment records. You're an extremely valuable commodity.'

I didn't know what he meant, and I managed to say as much.

'Let us get you papers.'

'What sort of papers?'

'This sort.' Ritter removed his wallet from his trousers,

unfolded his identity card and pushed it across the desk. I leaned forward. The scrappy yellow card told me nothing I didn't already know, that he was Julius Ritter of Aryan descent, German, born in 1893.

'What am I looking for?'

'The one thing you won't find,' Ritter crowed. 'The letter J'.

In Nazi-occupied Europe in 1941, the letter J didn't only stand for Julius, but Juden.

'You?' I said. 'You can't be...'

'It's alright.' The Chaze twirled past me with a surprising grace for a man of his proportions and placed his hands over the Führer's bronze ears. 'Hear no evil, see no evil.'

'He's...' I studied Ritter's face like a mystic reads a palm. 'You're Jewish?'

'Julius Ritterstein, from Gdansk. Yasher koach, my friend.'

'Best bookkeepers in the western world,' the Chaze said, producing a thick cigar, biting the end off and spitting to the floor. 'If Hitler had a Julius Ritterstein to dot every 't' and cross every 'i', we might actually win this thing. I knew he was too good to wear the tin star the first time I saw him at Gestapo. So I told him to throw it away.'

He sucked on the cigar, the flame flaring, until it was lit and smoke leaked out his mouth like steam vent.

'Simpler times,' Ritter said. 'Much has changed. Even out here, we have to be careful.' Turning his attention back to me, he folded his card back into his wallet. 'The work was completed before we left the city. But don't worry, we can get more. We use a very good man, total discretion. He gave a discount for taking the 'stein' off at the same time as the 'J' – six letters for the price of five.'

'Now you believe he's Jewish?' the Chaze said, cigar wagging in his mouth like a baby's arm. 'Or we need to drop trousers? No? Good.' He took a pound of my cheek in his hand and pinched it very lightly. 'So what do you say, Professor? You going to help us out?'

Before I could answer, a flushed secretary burst through the door.

'Please, sir. You'd better come and see.'

'What is it?' the Chaze said.

The secretary pointed out to the turquoise room's front window, where her colleague stood, clutching a glove to her mouth. As our Council of Four approached, I saw a large garrison of SS troops assembled at the gates, and a column marching up the driveway towards us.

Unbeknownst to the Chaze, who had received a complimentary call from Hinrich Lohse the previous evening, the Reich Commissar had been appalled to see drunken soldiers dozing in the huts outside the fence and outraged to discover they had not set foot in the camp since arriving forty-eight hours previously. The men were all dismissed from their positions overnight.

A new permanent detachment had been deployed, the secretary said. SS Einsatzkommando 3, under the command of Unterscharführer Rausch, fresh the success of the Kaunas Ghetto, with strict instructions to be based inside the compound at all times.

I had heard the term Einsatzkommndo once before, in a report from Cracow. They were the Special Duty Group who moved in after the first Kazimierz Aktion, rounding up Jews in the Stara Boznica synagogue, before shooting them all and setting it on fire.

There was no time to lose. Fraternizing with the camp leaders was a punishable offence, so Oswald Zgismond and I lurched downstairs before the soldiers entered the buildings.

Even Herr Ritter collected his belongings from that beautiful room for the last time and followed us down, installing himself in a hot and airless office behind the leather store. Not that Commander Rausch would be availing himself of the spare desk; the Unterscharführer believed very much in 'hands on' management. I wondered if Ritter would continue the pretence of his Aryan nationality from his new position on the factory floor, and what any of this meant in terms of the work we had pledged. No doubt the four of us would re-group and take stock, but for the foreseeable future, everything was changed.

Apart from the secretaries banished to their turquoise tower, nobody else in the camp knew of the soldier's arrival or the change in regime it signified. It was down to the three of us to communicate with maximum haste and minimum alarm what was happening.

I thank God for the foresight the Chaze and Ritter had already shown, the changes to food rations, and the uniforms. Imagine the contemptuous report if we'd had a full-scale examination yesterday, instead of a bespoke shoe fitting for one very large and exhausted man with a bad limp. Well-fed, content, jovial Jews strolling around in their own clothes like they owned the place!

Moda had to look every inch the furious hive of disciplined, high-quality artisanship that the Chaze had built his reputation on, or we were doomed. What the three of us agreed not to disclose as we raced down the oak staircase was that Commander Rausch's men were here to stay. The knowledge was dangerous, and could have unleashed a general panic. For safety, we judged, our comrades should slowly work out the truth for themselves.

We divided the factory into thirds to cover, each of us managing to get word out that a snap inspection had been called. The prisoners took the news in their stride. Most of them had been resigned to as much, after the 'pampered poodles' comment of the previous day. As one of them shrugged, 'We knew this day was coming. By a miracle of Moda, we're actually prepared.'

And so we were. When Unterscharführer Rausch entered the clicking room after twenty of the most anxious minutes of my life, flanked by his deputy and finally the Chaze, nobody at the benches batted an eyelid.

And, more importantly, nobody called him the Chaze.

Lunch was our next test. The bell rang shortly after the inspection party had moved on, and there was an awkward pause where nobody was quite sure what to do. Knowing that I had recently been admitted into Herr Ritter's inner-circle, the supervisor looked to me for direction.

'Business as usual,' I told him. 'We go, we eat, we come back.'

For the second lunch running, there was no piped-in music. We queued for the same thin watery stew as yesterday, seemingly from the same batch. Scraps of rotting cabbage disintegrated under my quizzical spoon. Tomato soup was now as rare as liquid mercury.

The main change in the canteen was the seating arrangements. Instead of sitting with our work teams, we had to squeeze in at a reduced amount of tables in order to accommodate the new garrison. Forty soldiers occupied the two tables nearest the entrance, where they could best keep an eye out. Back in school in the shtetl, you would have to sit with the teachers if you couldn't drink your milk without slurping. Today our master's had steel helmets with death-head insignia. I was heartened to see the soldiers were at least fed the same stale soup as the rest of us. Their predecessors used to have three-course meals delivered to their huts, courtesy of the Chaze.

Ritter was eating with us now, I noted, although he had not yet exchanged his bow-tie and cardigan for a uniform. Another change, when our bowls were dry: before returning to our labour, there would be a roll call, to ensure all prisoners were accounted for.

Roll call involved standing completely still in front of the Admin Block, underneath the flagpole – henceforth to be called the Appelplatz – while the Kapo, a prisoner functionary, counted the number of prisoners before reporting to the SS officer on duty. Since we had no Kapo, one first had to be chosen, which took a little time. The Chaze was invited to make a selection. I was relieved when he walked up and down our lines and stopped in front of Oswald Zgismond.

The eventual tally was a hundred and fourteen, but it took poor Zgismond two re-counts to arrive at.

Wasted minutes, Unterscharführer Rausch announced, would be doubled and added on to the end of the day. With that, we were sent back to start work.

The afternoon shift wore on much like any other, except

that every twenty minutes we were interrupted by a chubby, pink Lagerführer called Nickel who insisted on making each man and woman stand ten inches away from their workbench while he patrolled between us, scouring the floor. Every scrap of leather had to be accounted for, he shouted, as if we were deaf. Jews stole like rats. It was our nature.

In between Nickel's patrols, news spread from the rest of the factory floor: Rausch was leading a delegation on a tour of the perimeter fence, to check for weaknesses. While my comrades groaned, my thoughts turned instantly to the air-raid shelter on the southern side of the compound.

Three bags full.

The Chaze wouldn't have had time to move them.

It was no good, I couldn't concentrate on my work. Laying my work down on the bench, I told the supervisor that I had to speak to Herr Ritter on an urgent matter concerning the work I was doing for Hinrich Lohse.

'Five minutes,' he said.

I didn't need even that much. The large pink guard had taken up permanent residence on a chair in the corridor. As I emerged through the doorway, Nickel raised his legs as if to trip me.

'I thought you lot had been scurrying around. Where do you think you're going now?'

'Toilet, please, sir.'

'Get back inside. All temporary sanitation release permits must be applied for in advance.'

Temporary sanitation release permits was not a word string I had ever heard before.

'Yes, sir. Can I ask how much advance is needed?'

'Twenty-four hours,' he snapped, as if was the only logical answer.

'I'll be sure to do that in future. However, on this occasion, I also need to speak to my boss, Herr Ritter. As I'm sure you know, we are currently outfitting the Reich Commissar himself, Hinrich Lohse. He will be returning in a couple of days for the first fitting.'

'Bullshit.'

'I assure you it's true. I myself took his foot measurements only yesterday.'

'Where's your proof?'

'I could show you the Adelaide brogue I'm making, if that would satisfy you?'

'Work order?'

'None was given to me. At least, not in writing.'

'Nice try. Without proof, you're not going anywhere.'

'But the Chaze is my proof, you must ask him!'

It was obvious that a pig like Nickel would not speak Yiddish, and I believe I might have got away with my indiscretion, had I not compounded my foolishness by gasping as soon as I realised what I'd said.

'What's the Chaze?'

I made a split-second decision that, for the future of the hundred-plus prisoners in the camp, if I had to incriminate anybody, it couldn't be Jensen Gertenberg.

'Herr Ritter,' I said. 'It's a nickname we have for him.'

'What does it mean?'

I gulped and said, 'Boss.'

I'll need to get permission before I let you out of my sights.' He shooed me away. 'Go on, shut the door.'

Back inside, I passed on the news about the temporary sanitation release permits, to stop anybody else wasting their time.

'Twenty-four hours?' Hirschel groaned. 'So they're staying another day.'

'If he's being serious,' I said. 'I suggest we do what we can to satisfy them for now.'

And so we began the process of inventorying the capacity of our bowels, in order to submit requests for the next day. The supervisor drew up a list of names, and next to them wrote our preferred 'release' times, one per shift so as not to appear overly demanding. When the schedule was complete, the supervisor suggested it might be better if I was the one to submit the application.

I knocked to leave the room. Nickel shouted, 'What now?'

'We have our sanitation release paperwork.'

'Come.'

I approached Nickel's chair, and placed the application at

his boots as requested.

He bent down to pick it up, nodding judiciously as he studied the columns. As his finger traced down the list, he stopped halfway and brought the sheet closer to his eyes.

Behind the paper, he started growling, then cleared his throat, hacking volubly.

Finally, with a wet whistling hiss, he hocked out a spit-ball with such velocity that it tore a hole right through the middle of the sheet, which he then proceeded to crumple and hand back to me.

'Application denied,' he said.

That night after roll call, most of the soldiers retreated to the huts at the entrance gate, leaving the estimable Lagerführer Nickel outside the barracks door and six on guard in the courtyard beyond the windows. On my first day in Moda, I had gleefully spied a cluster of wooden mannequins in SS uniforms out there. Now we had the real thing.

In the brief period of relaxation before lights out, conversation turned to how long Rausch's inspection would last. No other work teams had been told the same twenty-four hours nonsense but most men agreed with Hirschel, that the soldiers wouldn't be leaving in a hurry. Some were more concerned than others. Almost half the men were convinced that the SS reinforcement was a good thing, despite their petty vindictiveness. For weeks now, in the face of German setbacks on the Eastern Front, rumour had suggested that that the Chaze and his garrison could be redeployed at any point, leaving the future of Moda as a specialist labour camp in doubt. A strengthened military presence could only bode well for our long-term survival, or so it was argued. I feared the worst of both possible worlds.

Oswald Zgismond was nowhere to be found amongst our number that night. I hazarded that he had been kept out of the barracks in case of reprisals for his beating of old man Blau, until I was put straight by a diligent Czechoslovakian hole-puncher called Libor, sent to Moda from camp Stuthof. Once selected, Libor explained, Kapos never slept with the rest of the men. The duties of Polish Kapos went far beyond keeping count at the Appleplatz. Over time they became more like prison wardens, accountable for the performance of the men's work, for their cleanliness, for even the solid workmanship of new bunk-beds. The Kapo soon learns how hard he must drive his men. The moment the SS become dissatisfied with him – and they always found a reason - he is no longer Kapo, and must return to sleeping with his men. Libor recalled one such Kapo who fell out of favour: on his first night back with his former friends, they beat him to death.

Shivering beneath my blanket, I turned over and find the shadow of Ronen Kesselman kneeling at my pillow, softly sobbing.

'Hey,' I said, putting my hand on his shoulder. 'What's wrong? We've got through worse.'

'At least I could pee in prison. The guard threated to have me sent to Stuthof if I didn't stop pestering him.'

'We can get the doctor to certify you,' I said. 'Something in writing. They'll have to respect that.'

'Like they respected Ernst?'

There was no answer for that.

'You may need to wear something,' I said.

'I'm wearing this uniform, aren't I?'

'Something like...' Bereft of a tactful phrasing, I didn't pursue the idea of some kind of sanitary pad.

'I usually need to go twice a night, even on a good day. Do you think the guard will let me out?'

I thought back to Nickel's reign outside the clicking room. 'Probably best not to push your luck tonight.'

He groaned. 'I don't know how my parents will cope in here. My dad's even worse than I am, up and down every five minutes.'

I pushed myself up. 'Everything's changed now, Ronen. The old ways aren't the same anymore. There won't be any special favours from now on.'

'No, no, Oswald promised me he'd find them.'

'Shh!' someone piped from a nearby bunk. 'The fool's going to get us shot.'

Ignoring him, I tried to talk to my friend. 'You have to accept... It might be a while before you see your parents again.'

'You're right,' he said. 'Do you think if we wrote to the prison, their photographs might have turned up?'

'Definitely not,' I said. 'They're gone, and they're not coming back.'

Again, the coward called, 'If you don't shut him up, I will.'

'Try to get some sleep,' I offered weakly, and followed up with a lie. 'Things will seem better in the morning.'

I could see Ronen wrinkle his lips and brow, giving this last remark much more thought than my weasel words deserved. Apparently consoled, he said, 'You always know best, Jozef. Good bye, old friend.'

If I'd listened more carefully that night instead of worrying about my own welfare, I might have been able to stop what happened next. Ronen hadn't wished me 'good night' but 'goodbye'.

***

The next morning, the usual ritual: canteen, Appelplatz, another fumbled count. Ernst Blau was still with us – I could see his bandaged head in front of me – yet somehow Oswald Zgismond contrived to arrive back at his original tally.

A hundred and fourteen faces sunk into a hundred and fourteen palms.

Of all the Jews in Europe, the Chaze had picked the one who couldn't add up.

Zgismond was about to learn the consequences of falling out of favour with the SS, when from the side of the factory came the harsh piping of a patroller's pea-whistle, followed by a soldier's shout for help.

Rausch calmly raised a hand as he considered his actions. With the same hand bunched into a fist, he extended the long barrel of his index finger and pointed out six of the meanest looking soldiers. The men immediately unholstered their pistols, sprinted past us, through the courtyard and disappeared behind the barracks.

While we stood waiting, I managed to catch the eye of Herr Ritter, two rows ahead of me, at the far end. I mouthed the only word that I could think of.

Suitcases?

Ritter frowned, unable to read my lips.

I tried again, contorting my face to exaggerate each syllable, then stepped a foot out of line so he could see my body. Stooping, I dropped my arms and picked up two imaginary heavy handles.

At last, Ritter understood. *Suitcases?*

I nodded tiny, furious increments.

He winked back: they're safe.

I tipped my head back and blessed the cloudless sky.

The riddle of what exactly the patrol had found was answered when the seven soldiers marched back past the barracks, the last two dragging the limp body of a male prisoner by his wrists. The man had been caught trying to cut the wire fence with a knife he'd taken from the tool box. The soldiers dumped him in a heap at the front of our formation, under the flagpole.

While the lead soldier conferred with Rausch, the name of today's elusive hundred and fifteenth comrade passed up and down the ranks like a contagion of sneezes, until it reached me, where it stopped.

Ronen Kesselman!

At the front, a decision had been reached. The count was now complete. The Kapo had been saved, but the escaping Jew must pay the penalty for being caught.

Two soldiers pulled Ronen moaning to his feet – he was alive - pushed him back against the flagpole and tied his wrists above his head so he could not slide down.

The rest of us marched past in single file, to start our working day.

Ronen was scared he couldn't cope with the new regime, and tried telling me last night. Instead of reassuring him, I told him he'd never see his parents again, that he was on his own, and had to toughen up. He must have decided there and then to escape.

Later that morning, we received a valuable lesson in the Nazi doctrine of Collective Responsibility. The camp was to be punished for Ronen's transgression in three distinct stages:

Firstly, it was announced over the loud-speakers that prisoners were to have their heads shaved. Each department was given a specific time to report to the bathrooms. Any attempt to delay the process would result in the wasted minutes being added on to the end of the morning shift.

All pampered poodles were shorn. The two genders were treated differently in one respect: the women had all their hair cut off, while us men had one thick, white stripe shaved down the middle, leaving two sides of hair intact, to ridicule us even further.

The second punishment followed the theme of eviction: prisoners would no longer sleep in barracks. The huts outside the camp's entrance were deemed unfit for military purposes, and soldiers would be moving into our former quarters, after due fumigation. Since Jews could not very well be housed on the open side of the fence, alternative accommodation would be provided. From now on, we were to sleep in the stables, unused since the cable factory had closed. Prisoners with experience of carpentry were selected to cut wood from the forest and begin work immediately on the construction of three-tiered bunk-beds. For mattresses, there was straw.

To the din of the factory's machines was added the incessant hammering of posts and nails.

The carpenters worked hard. At the end of the shift, twelve bunk-beds had been made. We would be relocating en masse to the stables later in the evening and could draw straws for the available bunks. But not before the introduction of the third stage of punishment: from now on, soup would only be dispensed after roll call.

As we returned to the Appelplatz, I realised that the carpenters had been busy with more than just bunk-beds.

In the middle of the car-park stood a black gallows.

Ronen already dangled limply from the flagpost; he had been out in the August sun all day.

Was that not punishment enough?

A group of SS with bayoneted rifles formed a semi-circle before the gibbets. The rest of the soldiers stood at the side of our rows, machine guns aimed at us. One of them made a phantom lunge, and laughed when we flinched.

Orders were barked more harshly than before, the air thrummed with menace.

'Caps off!' Zgismond suddenly shouted.

We knew not why, but one hundred and fourteen caps came off at once.

'Cover your heads!'

Just as quickly, the caps were back.

Two SS headed towards the flagpole, released Ronen from his chains and carried the condemned man on his final journey to the scaffold and up onto the chair.

With his back was to the gallows, his face turned towards his judge, the Chaze, our Protector who was about to sentence one of his own Jews to death.

Burnt by the sun, Ronen's cheeks now turned pale, but his hands were still.

He shook his head as if emerging from a doze, eyes clearing to take in the hundred prisoners, the dozens of SS guards surrounding him.

Three SS assumed the role of executioner as Zgismond looked on.

The Chaze stepped forward to read the verdict, halting after every word.

'In the name of Reichsführer Himmler...Ronen Kesselman...attempted to escape the camp...'

All eyes turned to Ronen.

He appeared composed as he stood in the shadow of the gallows, apart from a steady gnawing of the lower lip.

'According to the law...Ronen Kesselman...is condemned to death. Let this be a warning and an example to all prisoners.'

Nobody moved.

I closed my eyes and considered what my friend's last thoughts might be.

I heard the pounding of my heart.

The dozens of dispossessed souls I'd seen marched through the city on the night of our arrest no longer troubled me. But this man, my old cell-mate, leaning against his gallows, upset me more than I could ever say.

'Where is merciful God?' somebody whispered behind me. 'Where is he?'

At a sign from the Chaze, the executioner stepped up to the condemned man.

The SS wanted to blindfold Ronen, but he refused, shaking his head with that bullish belligerence I knew well.

After the longest of moments, the hangman put the rope around his neck.

The SS kicked his chair away.

The trapdoors were sprung, the body fell, and the rope went taut.

My own body jerked to attention, but I kept my eyes open. I whispered, 'Good night, cell-mate.'

'Caps off!' Zgismond screamed, his voice quivering. As for the rest of the prisoners, they were weeping.

'Cover your heads!'

A hundred and fourteen prisoners paid their respects.

Ronen swung in a slow circle, his bound hands twisting open and shut as his head jolted and his legs frantically pedalled the air, loosening his trousers. His pale, hairless legs and buttocks glistened in the dusk.

An awful silence descended on the camp as the sun dropped amongst the trees.

When the only thing moving were the ropes, the executioner yanked on Ronen's legs, and we heard the last cracking of his neck.

After that, we were ordered to file past and look deeply into his extinguished eyes, the tongue lolling from his open mouth. The soldiers made sure everyone stared him squarely in the face.

Finally, we were given permission to go back to the canteen for supper.

We forced ourselves to eat, for fear of what tomorrow would bring.

7

The death marked me greatly. It is no exaggeration to say I was not the same man afterwards as I had been before. None of us were.

I had only known Ronen for six weeks, we were by no means close. It was the manner of his murder as well as the act for which I grieved. The hanging was no unruly street killing, but official government policy. And the charade with our caps that Oswald Zgismond had been forced to lead us through, to show our respect. It was almost too much.

But to the SS, due process had been followed, or what passed for it in a work camp. 'According to the law,' as the Chaze himself had intoned. I could not believe what Germany had allowed itself to become. The country that had employed me for ten years to instruct its young generation in the doctrines of Humanism and Civil Society. Evidently, I had not done a very good job.

The Chaze could not be blamed for Ronen's death, nor his edict seen as an act of betrayal. If anything, he deserved my pity. He must have been suffering as much as I was, but could not show it. Camp Moda was investigated because of rumours of leniency, Rausch now watching every day for proof. His initial onslaught of rules and regulations was specifically designed to prompt a situation to test the Chaze's will, and Ronen was the first casualty. Anything less than total ruthlessness would have called his entire camp to account.

After Ronen's death, days passed without incident. The disagreeable Nickel was rotated away from the clicking room, as if his superiors understood perfectly that his personality was best enjoyed in short doses.

After the implementation of twice daily roll calls, the shaving of heads and being moved to the stables, we were largely left in peace at our work. On occasion, even the rigours of roll call were dispensed with, leaving Zgismond to take a more civilised head-count while we were seated in the canteen. On these days, we were not allowed outside at all. We attributed this to a lack of manpower. The garrison's number had already shrunk by a third. A common assumption was that Rausch's original heavy-handed blitz was only ever intended to be short-lived. However vital the camp's contribution to the war effort, there weren't enough prisoners to warrant so large a detachment. But I heard other rumours as to what the soldiers had been deployed for, rumours I chose – like others before me – to ignore. Out of the SS who remained, we even succeeded in making a few – I hesitate to call them 'friends' – acquaintances amongst our new captors, as soldiers started approaching on the sly with shoe requests for their wives or families, in exchange for an extra bread roll or blanket.

In this way, Camp Moda slowly resumed its old ways of graft and craft. I was sure the Chaze had found a way to take a tasty slice of the action for himself. But of course I was no longer privy to what went on at the top. For all the harmony of the new normal, there was no way for the Council of Four to meet.

Only once was I dispatched again to the turquoise tower in daylight hours, on the afternoon of August 16th. A week had passed since the initial visit of Hinrich Lohse – the true architect of the camp's misfortune and the one man I could and did hold responsible for Ronen's death - and we were ready to receive him once more. A pair of Adelaide brogues awaited his fitting, and much of the secretive repair-work had been completed to his collection of heels. After making a nuisance of myself by repeatedly asking for news of the Reich Commissar's return, I was ordered up to Hauptsturmführer Gertenberg's office to find out in person, like a naughty school-boy sent to the headmaster.

When I got there, the Chaze was almost horizontal on his chair, telephone propped on his enormous belly, hairy ankles crossed on the desk. He motioned for me to step inside, and offered a scoop of Linde ice cream he was eating. I declined. He twirled his finger in the air to suggest the telephone call would be over soon. As I sat opposite and waited, I assumed it was the Chaze's long-suffering wife on the other end of the line.

'Absolutely, yes, no question about it.' He feigned conviction in his tone but mugged otherwise to me, fingers and thumb snapping together like a bird's insistent beak.

'The last lot were drunk and lazy, typical Lithuanians. One of them even had the... ... what do you call it - the *tempurity* - to tell me he'd rather be in Russia than out here guarding my shoemakers – I told him it could be arranged... Ha! You did? Excellent, sir, excellent.'

He raised his spoon in a silent toast, and winked before taking a sip.

'Now, I'm not going to pretend Rausch hasn't put the wind up them, and that's probably a good thing. But, all due respect, there's a fine line between guarding and terrorizing, am I right? We've already had to put down one escape attempt... And bear in mind, the first four weeks, we didn't have one... '

The Chaze sat up a little in his chair for the reply; I sensed a mild rebuke.

'That's... er... a little harsh, if I may say so, Commissar, but, yeah, you might have a point. Anyway, you'll see the changes for yourself, very soon now. Thank-you for taking my call, Sir... Heil Hitler.'

When he put the receiver down, he saw a drop of ice cream had landed on his dress shirt. Grabbing a handful of fabric, he pulled it up to his face and licked.

'Jozef Siegler, man of the moment, just talking about you.'

What on earth did Hinrch Lohse think of this uneducated slob, his mangled vocabulary and Silesian street slang, his causal assumptions of intimacy?

The Chaze said, 'How you holding up?'

'Me personally?'

'You, the camp... I've been remiss, not done my rounds, I know.'

'We're... Morale is... improving, I'd say.'

'That's good. You know, I'm sorry about your friend, Roni. You two came here together, I remember that. What happened was unavoidable. Sure you don't want some ice? Vodka, hint of vanilla.'

'They might smell it on my breath.'

'I'm working on a couple of things, I want you to know that.'

'Things, sir?'

Glancing at the walls, as if fearful of being monitored, 'I can't go into any details right now. But I haven't forgotten.' He tapped the side of his swollen red nose.

'That's good. Do we have a date for the Commissar's next appointment?'

'August 20th.'

I counted on my fingers. 'That's a week today.'

'It's not a good time, right now. Lot of people looking to be resettled. Organisational nightmare.'

'Will we be taking in more prisoners now, or has that...?'

'Has it what?'

'Have plans changed?'

'I'd say that's a little above your position, wouldn't you, inmate?'

'Very good, sir.' I got up to leave. 'Thank-you for your time.'

'Relax, I'm joking with you.'

'Yes, sir.' Again, I tried to smile, but my jaw refused.

The Chaze swung his feet off the desk and leaned forward, using his elbow as a prop. 'Can you keep a secret?'

'I believe you know I can, sir.'

'Rausch has never met Lohse. I've been building it up, little by little. How Lohse isn't ready to come back out here yet, how he's worried about his hay fever, blablabla. Eyes running, red nose. Very, what's the word, self-*conscience* about his appearance, a man in his position, always in the papers.'

I ignored the mangled vocabulary. What was he talking about? Lohse didn't have hayfever, Joziek Seidel did. I was worried that the Chaze had drunk himself into a stupor and was confusing reality.

'Rausch is such a little brown-noser, he won't be able to resist.'

'Resist what?'

'He'll be out there under the flagpole when the old guy's Tatra pulls up, and the first thing our friend's going to say is,

I see your hay fever has cleared up, sir. Imagine the look on the old guy's face, first time back here since you know what...'

'Very good,' I said. 'Yes, good plan.'

The Chaze shrugged, stuck out his bottom lip. 'He screws with me, I screw with him.'

'Of course. Everybody's screwed.'

'Amen.' He winked again and raised his spoon. 'I'll drink to that.'

In the end, we were spared at least one embarrassment: Hinrich Lohse's second visit on the 23rd was first postponed and later cancelled altogether, without reason. In a rare moment of privacy in the canteen, Julius Ritter pulled me aside and whispered that 'it wasn't politic' for the Commissar to be seen in the area.

I didn't understand what he meant until the evening of August 25th.

Earlier that day, we learned that Rausch had taken the Chaze out into the forest, along with a handpicked unit of soldiers. The prevailing rumour had it that they were going to hunt Jewish partisans. Alone at my workbench, I started to believe that the real quarry was the Chaze himself. The man's time had finally come.

Could it really be so? A high-ranking member of the SS had to at least be subject to the same 'law' that had a claimed a lowly Jew like Ronen Kesselman. Professional soldiers didn't take men out to the woods and shoot them. But as afternoon turned to dusk, I began to wonder if the darkness was coming for us all.

While the others were playing cards in the stables, I heard vehicles approach on the long drive, and jumped up to take a look. There was the Chaze, being helped out of a Kubelwagon, a little stiff but otherwise intact. I was so relieved that when the lights out order was barked shortly after, I fell asleep as soon as my head hit the rolled up sweater I used as a pillow.

The soft chanting of my name awoke me. Straining through the darkness, I made out the untameable curls of Oswald Zgismond kneeling at my side. The Kapo had not slept with us since his selection, and only ventured into the stables these days to inspect our bedding for lice.

'Come with me,' he whispered.

'Where to?'

Zgismond passed me my shoes and said, 'Come.'

The moon was low, illuminating the Appelplatz like a Kreiglight. From the direction of the canteen, I could hear soldiers laughing and drinking, music playing. Checking my pocket watch, I was amazed to see I'd only slept for twenty minutes. It wasn't yet midnight.

I followed Zgismond through the shadows, around the back of the factory and behind the Admin Block to a Fire door. He pushed it open. We slipped inside, passed through an empty storeroom and emerged into the famous oak-paneled lobby. The stained glass glowed a spectral moonlit blue.

Zgismond led me up the staircase, into the grand open-plan office, garish green now, and along the silver strip of carpet to the Herr Direktor's door in the far corner. He paused, knocked, and we heard a grunt from inside bid us enter.

A candlestick flared on the desk, and behind it I made out the broad bulk of the Chaze's torso, glistening in a white vest, a medallion round his neck, the pendant hidden under the cotton. He pushed forward a sealed bottle of vodka and three glasses.

We took a seat around the desk. As Zgismond poured, the Chaze reached a powerfully simian arm down to the floor. I noticed then that he was wearing only boxer shorts, no uniform trousers. At his feet was a bulging manila folder. His fingers tapped around on the wooden boards and came up clutching a second bottle of Smirnoff tucked under the chair, which he swigged from the neck. Two-thirds of the vodka was already gone.

'I tell you,' he said, smearing his lips. 'Nobody will believe what they're doing - '

The door creaked again and Julius Ritter entered the room. He nodded at us, smiling.

'Gentlemen. I was beginning to think my invite was lost in the post.'

The Chaze said, 'It's an abomination against God, that's

what it is.'

'I wouldn't go that far,' Ritter said. 'Just don't think of doing it again.'

'Julius, sit.' Zgismond rose and pulled out a third chair.

Eyes adjusting to the gloom, Ritter took in the scene before him, the bottles, the Chaze stripped to his underwear, the Manilla folder.

'Where's your uniform?'

'Burn it,' he said. 'After today, I'm done.'

Ritter paused next to me before sitting down. 'What's he talking about?'

A third glass thumped to the table. 'Here.'

Zgismond poured. Without knocking glasses, we drank.

At the Chaze's behest, Zigmond refilled our glasses. We tossed premium Smirnoff back like it was moonshine.

The Chaze bent over his considerable gut, scooped up the pile of folders and handed them to Ritter.

'See for yourself,' he said. 'It's all here.'

'See what? You're not making any sense.'

But the Chaze could not bring himself to say more. The evidence he had taken from Gestapo HQ would do the talking for him, as it will now for me.

The first document chronicles the early days of the German invasion.

Operational Situation Report USSR No. 17

The Chief of the Security Police and the SD
Berlin,
July 7, 1941
38 copies

21st copy

Operational Situation Report USSR No. 17
....
Einsatzgruppe C
Location: Minsk
First summary report of the activity of Einsatzgruppe C

in the Polish and Russian sections of Byelorussia.

1) Organisation and March Route

One June 23, Einsatzgruppe B met in Poznan in order to continue the march towards Warsaw the following morning. According to the order of RSHA, contact was established with Army Group Centre and the commander of the Rear Army Group Area 102 in Warsaw. As was agreed, Sonderkommando 7a started the march on June 26 attached to 9th Army HQ and Sonderkommando 7b on June 27 to 4th Army HQ. Sonderkommando 7a marched via East Prussia in order to enter Wilno with the troops. After being relieved by the Einsatzkommando 9, it proceeded on road 4, and turned south towards Minsk, the capital, and arrived on July 4.

Sonderkommando 7b marched via Brest, Kobrin, Pruzhany, Rushana, Slonim, Baranovichi, Stolpce, via Route 2 towards Minsk and arrived there with the Vorkommando on July 4.

Einsatzkommando 9: Proceeded towards Wilno on June 29 according to instructions issued by the commander of the Rear Army Group Area.

Einsatzkommando 8 proceeded, according to orders of the commander of the Rear Army Group Area, to Bialystok on July 1, and marched on with the two commands towards Slonim, Novogrudok and Baranovichi. The staff continued towards Bialystok on July 3 with the advancing units of the Rear Army Group Area.

In conjunction with the commander of the Security Police for the General Gouvernement, six supporting units were set up for Byelorussia, who relieved the Sonderkommandos and Einsatzkommandos on July 3 and advanced from Warsaw to the assigned areas.

Based on these tactics, all towns in the Polish and Russian sections of Byelorussia are occupied as far as the fighting zone. A supporting unit is posted in Brest, one supporting unit in Pinsk and another in Slutsk with the aim of marching into Gomel after occupying the area. One supporting unit is posted in Bialystok with the task of also taking care of Bielsk. One supporting unit is in Wilno, with the task of also taking care of Grodno and Lida. One supporting unit will be moved forward to Minsk in order to assume the work in Minsk after Einsatzgruppe C will march on Moscow.

Einsatzkommando 8 is stationed, until further notice, in Bialystok. Einsatzkommando 9 is stationed in Wilno so that it can be moved via Minsk towards Moscow at a later time. The staff of Einsatzgruppe C [1] *has been posted in Minsk since July 6 with its headquarters in the Soviet building of the USSR.* [2]

Because of the encirclement and due to the highway system, a rear and a front line cannot be delineated. Thus the Sonderkommandos 4a and 7b, as well as their staff, are constantly in the fighting zone and have been exposed on the highways to Russian sniping. At this time, Minsk is still in the fighting zone. Army Group B HQ is located 150 km in the rear in Baranovichi. After consultations in Minsk, Sonderkommando 7a was transferred from the 9th Army HQ, which is to march to the north of Moscow, to the newly formed 4th Armoured Army HQ. Sonderkommando 7a is joined by a Vorauskommando with translators and persons familiar with Moscow, under the direction of SS-Standartenführer Dr. Six. The former Army HQ four is now Army HQ 2, and Sonderkommando seven has been put at its disposal.

In the course of further advances, the towns of Gomel, Mogilev, Vitebsk, Orsha, and Smolensk are to be bypassed.

2) Police Work

According to the instructions by RSHA, liquidations of government and party officials, in all named cities of Byelorussia, were carried out. Concerning the Jews, according to orders, the same policy was adopted. The exact number of the liquidated has not as yet been established. On June 22, almost all the officials of the Communist party has fled, probably following higher instructions, and had taken with them all well-prepared documents. It is likely that some of the officials will try to return. Some will be identified with the help of the network of informants. The city of Minsk was an exception, although the officials had fled from there; surprisingly, the documentation remained intact in the sole government building - the house of the BSSR Soviet that had not been destroyed. On the other side, in destroyed Minsk, the NKVD and the internal party materials were destroyed by fire caused by the bombardment. Evaluating reports on Minsk follows.

....

Special report on the political situation and activity in the area of Wilno

Police Matters The Lithuanian police branches in Wilno, subordinated to the Einsatzkommando, were given the task of drawing up current lists of names of Jews in Wilno; first intelligentsia, political activists, and wealthy Jews. Subsequently, searches and arrests were made and 54 Jews were liquidated on July 4, and 93 were liquidated on July 5. Sizeable property belonging to Jews were secured. With the help of Lithuanian police officials, a search was started for Communists and NKVD agents, most of whom, however, are said to have fled.

A search was also started for hidden weapons of the Polish secret military organisations, of which the Lithuanian police has yet not made an accurate estimate. The establishment of a Jewish Quarter is being prepared. Upon suggestion of the EK, the Jewish Quarter will be declared to be out of bounds to military personnel by order of the Field Command HQ.

Tucked away at the end after that numbing litany of military advances, buried under the bland miscellany of Police Work and Police Matters – indeed, you may have stopped reading by that point - was a cursory mention of the beginning of a process that would slaughter up to one hundred thousand Lithuanian Jews.

In Wilno, it began on July 4th, less than a fortnight after the first Nazi bombs fell, and the night of my arrest. As we were being marched from the garage workshop, we came upon another procession of press-ganged Jews at the corner of Gediminas Avenue and Lukiskes Street. Unlike us manual labourers, covered in grease, engine oil and sweat, these were a dapper, briefcase-carrying crowd, smart beards and overcoats, professors and academics, as I had once been.

I'd been spared thanks to my new career as a shoe-maker, but the killings followed me to Ponary.

The first executions took place in the forest on the July 8th. One hundred Jews at a time were brought from the city, to what they believed was a 'waiting zone'. Here, in what had been a popular Jewish holiday resort, they were ordered to undress and to hand over whatever money or valuables they had with them. They were then marched naked, in single file, in groups of ten or twenty at a time, holding hands to the edge of the pits dug by the Soviet army to store fuel. They were then shot down by rifle fire. After they had fallen into the pit, no attempt was made to see if they were all dead. If anyone moved another shot was simply fired. The bodies were then covered from above, with a thin layer of sand and the next group of naked prisoners led from the waiting area to the edge of the pit.

I remembered Abba Kovner's warning, delivered before I sent him packing from Pilies Street for fear-mongering:

The whole of Europe shall be our burial pit.

The Aktions continued without respite. In addition to the SS's own methodical tallies, the Chaze had been given the following diary entries – 'flesh upon the bones' - by a Polish journalist called Kazimierz Sakwowicz he knew, who lived at Ponary.

27 July 1941 Sunday

Shooting is carried on nearly everyday. Will it go on for ever? The executioners began selling the clothes of the killed. Other garments are crammed into sacks in a barn at the highway and taken to town.

People say that about five thousand persons have been killed in the course of this month. It is quite possible, for about two hundred to three hundred people are being driven up here nearly every day. And nobody ever returns.

30 July 1941 Friday

About one hundred and fifty persons shot. Most of them were elderly people. The executioners complained of being very tired of their 'work', of having aching shoulders from shooting. That is the reason for not finishing the wounded off, so that they are buried half alive.

2 August 1941 Monday

Shooting of big batches has started once again. Today about four thousand people were driven up, shot by eighty executioners, all drunk. The fence was guarded by a hundred soldiers and policemen.

This time terrible tortures before shooting. Nobody buried the murdered. The people were driven straight into the pit, the corpses were trampled upon. Many a wounded writhed with pain. Nobody finished them off.

The three of us passed the papers back and forth for an hour, sound-tracked only by the occasional clink of glass or the splash of more vodka.

I have never drunk more in my life, nor been more sober.

It was impossible to process in the space of one night what the Chaze had taken six weeks to absorb. He assured us he'd read every word, over and over until he could recite whole sections verbatim, but he'd still struggled to believe it was true.

Until today, when the authorities at Moda had received an 'invitation' to attend the Ponary liquidations. The Chaze had even been given the opportunity to fire a few shots himself.

'How could we not know about this?' I asked, numbed. 'It's only a couple of miles from here.'

'The Aktions aren't every day. When Rausch is told of one, he seals the buildings. Nobody in or out. Plus, factor in those damned lasting machines, it's a miracle we haven't all gone deaf.'

'But...'

'There is no but,' the Chaze said. 'Feels like the end of the world, doesn't it. Book of Revelations. I hate to tell you, but the bastards are only just getting started.'

'How?'

'Something big's planned for August 31st. I'm not hearing any details at the moment, but I'll find out. Something ugly.'

Julius Ritter's voice broke and he tried to pass it off as the remains of an undigested supper. He repeated his question. 'Are we safe here?'

'For now.'

I said, 'And in the meantime?'

'First thing tomorrow,' the Chaze said. 'I'm sending all this to Canaris.'

'What's Canaris?' I hadn't heard the name before, but it sounded like the bird - canaries in the cold mine, warning of danger. Perhaps there was some kind of clandestine support group.

'Not what, but who,' the Chaze said. 'Admiral Wilhelm Canaris, chief of the Abwehr.'

'A Nazi?' I hissed, momentarily forgetting that I was talking to one. 'What's he going to do?'

'You'd be surprised. He's been sending the Vatican reports of atrocities in Poland since 1940.'

'The Pope knows about this?'

'Not Ponary, not yet. But Canaris is getting ready to send his Pastor to Sweden, where he's meeting a British Bishop. I'm going to make sure a copy gets back to ten Downing Street. And there's the resistance movement in the Kaunas Ghetto, the partisans of the People's Army. We get stuff in to them through the couriers.'

'We need to get this information out,' I said. 'Not into a closed Ghetto.'

'It goes in, it comes out. The leader of Akiva Halutz – you heard of them?'

I nodded.

'Guy called Rado Lieber, he gets to travel to all the other Ghettos, working for the Jewish Communal Self-Help.'

'And the Nazis allow this?'

'At the moment. While they still care. It looks good to the

Red Cross.'

On top of what I'd read about the Ponary massacres, I was now being asked to accept on faith the existence of a network of a secret agents extending from the Vatican to the fields of Great Britain that might have been ripped from the pages of *The 39 Steps*, with Hauptsturmführer Gertenberg standing in for the dashing Richard Hannay.

'Why?' I said.

'Why what?'

'Why... Why you?'

'Why?' the Chaze said.

Putting down his glass, his fingers rose to the silver chain around his neck. As he tugged it free, the pendant caught against his vest and a tiny silver point poked through the fabric. Leaning forward, I could see the outline of five more under the cotton, arranged in the shape of a hexagramatic star.

Julius Ritter seized my hand and placed his other index finger over his lips. He jerked his head over to the doorway: around the gaps in the frame, light was seeping in from the turquoise room we'd previously left in darkness.

We held our breath as footsteps padded along the scarlet carpet and stopped outside the door.

Two quick knocks in succession, the confident rap of one who expects an immediate answer.

'Jensen?'

Rausch, the Chaze mouthed, tucking the star under his vest.

'That you in there burning the midnight oil?'

The handle turned.

Oswald Zgismond darted forward and blew out the flame.

'Hold on!' the Chaze shouted, lumbering up and lunging past. 'I'm not decent.'

He cracked the door, positioning himself in the opening. 'Sorry, I've got company.'

Rausch sniffed. 'Anyone I know?'

He gripped the top of the door and scratched his armpit. 'Clara and Zara.'

'You old dog! Two for the price of one, eh.' And then, in an excessively gay voice that suggested Rausch too had been seeking liquid solace, he called, 'Good evening, ladies,'

When we didn't answer, the Chaze said, 'Aw, look. They've gone all shy.'

'I don't know why. Nothing I haven't seen before, right, girls. Anyway, I won't keep you. Just wanted to make sure you were alright. I thought you looked a bit green in the gills out there this afternoon.'

'Not me,' the Chaze said. I saw him flash his trademark crooked grin. 'Must have been all those leaves, making you colour-blind.'

'Maybe so. It's good to hear, anyway.'

The Chaze lowered his hand and scratched his cheek. 'You sure you're feeling alright, Irm?'

'Me?' Rausch said. 'Never better.'

'Cos if you're looking for, I don't know, some distraction tonight, my girls are always happy to share. You know that, right?'

Zgismond found the neck of the vodka bottle in the darkness. His fingers gripped the neck and lifted it from the table. Silently pushing back his chair, he tiptoed over to the side of the door and raised the bottle over his head.

Rausch leant closer to the Chaze until he was less than a foot away from his Kapo's face. He whispered, 'I believe they gave me crabs last time, so with the best will in the world, I'll pass.'

The Chaze and Zgismond stood either side of the door while Rausch walked back along the scarlet carpet.

'On or off?' he said, pausing at the light switch by the exit.

'Off,' the Chaze said, and we exhaled as one into the darkness.

8

After that evening, nothing happened for a week, and then on August 31st, as predicted, something ugly broke loose from its subterranean moorings and surfaced in our back yard. In a strange way, those last seven days of drudgery were the hardest of all to endure. My soul, pierced by the death of Ronen Kessselman, had now been flayed alive. It was the little things around camp that hurt the most. When we were prohibited from going outside the next day, I forced a smile as the others celebrated another reprieve from the dreaded Appelplatz, whose gallows still cast a shadow, even over the most beatific August day. I ghosted across the factory floor that week, flinching at phantom gun-shots from the trees. The knowledge of the liquidations gnawed away like a cancer, but our Council of Four had sworn an oath of secrecy in that candle-lit office. Inside the camp, there was nothing to be gained from revealing the truth, not yet, not unless we wished to precipitate a doomed uprising. In the world outside, the Chaze lived up to his promise and by the end of August 26th, the dossier was on its way to Sweden. I never doubted the man again, and burnt with shame when I remembered how I'd condemned him as a drunken wastrel. To have lived and breathed twelve months within the SS, as a Jew, with the express intention of protecting as many of his people as he could, was the most extraordinary sacrifice I could conceive.

From the afternoon of Sunday 31st, events tumbled after one another in dizzying succession. Any account will inevitably feel like a race, but I shall endeavour to record each development with the clarity it demands. The process started exactly as the Chaze had forecast, but with one minor surprise.

I did not sleep all weekend. According to the Chaze's intelligence, the Gestapo in Wilno were about to stage an attack - on Germans, no less - in collaboration with Lithuanian nationalists. By an audacious use of propaganda, the attack would be blamed on Jews and used as pretence for the biggest purge yet. The operation even had a codename: The Great Provocation. The Chaze was certain it would happen by the 31st; the ensuring 'reprisals' were essential preparation for creating the Wilno Ghetto, which had already been scheduled for the first half of September.

Sunday was a day off in the camp, although there always plenty of work to be done, washing our bedding and uniforms. A little before 4.30, I requested a short break from Lagerführer Nickel and was escorted by Oswald Zgismond to Herr Ritter's office behind the leather store, to inquire about the Reich Commissar's rescheduled appointment, my usual pretext. Despite not being able to freely converse – a soldier was on patrol outside Ritter's open door at all times – it was a comfort to merely be in his presence.

While the three of us spoke intently about a visit that none expected to take place, Ritter's telephone rang.

'Unterscharführer,' he said. '... I see... Yes, that can be done without too much difficulty... We are under no obligation to help, though, surely... Very good. I will have the list sent up as soon as I am able.'

'List?' Zgismond said, checking that the patrolling soldier was not within ear-shot. 'List of who?'

'The Jewish Council have been in contact. They've got a persistent young chap just walked in trying to track people down. Friends and relatives taken away for labour who never came back.'

'Ponary.'

'Probably. Rausch has agreed to check our records to see if any of them ended up here.'

'Why?' I said. 'Why help the Jewish Council?'

'Think about it.' Ritter dabbed a handkerchief to his nose. 'Why wouldn't he. Today more than ever, no? So thanks to Abba Kovner, that's another job I've got to do. Some day off this turned out to be.'

My face must have betrayed me, because Ritter said, 'Abba Kovner, you know him.'

'We met last year,' I said. 'Shortly after I arrived from Cracow. He was organising an Independent Jewish Defence Force.'

'Did you join?'

'No. I took the coward's way out.'

'Don't blame yourself. It wouldn't have helped.'

'Maybe not. But he's still free, and I'm trapped in here.'

While Abba Kovner was searching for the missing, the process was already underway that would see many more Jews murdered, the condemned marched to Ponary, and when the fuel pits were full, forced to dig up corpses and burn them to make more room. Three thousand would be killed in just four days.

News of The Great Provocation was being broadcast on the evening news when I returned to the stables.

'At 2 o'clock, shots were fired from a house on the corner of Szklanna and Wieka streets, into a group of German sentries standing around in the square outside the Pan Cinema. Passers-by, together with German soldiers, broke into the house and identified the cowardly bandits as Jews. Their rifles were still slung over their shoulders. The attackers paid with their lives for their act – they were shot on the spot. To avoid such hostile acts in the future, new and severe deterrent measures are being taken. The responsibility lies with the entire Jewish community.'

Immediately after, the mass expulsion of Jews from Glezer, Gaon, Szawelska, Strashun and Niemiecka Streets – the same area that would soon become part of the Ghetto – began, 'in retaliation'. Germans stormed into each house, into each attics and cellar, and dragged out every person they found: women, men, and children. The streets were coated with blood, and corpses lay everywhere. Herded together into an endless column, the survivors were marched through the nocturnal streets. Nobody knew what would happen to them. The wailing reached the sky.

In order to facilitate the next round of clearances, Hans Hingst, Regional Commissar of Wilno published the following notice on the morning of September 1st:

'All Jews, men and women, are forbidden to leave their homes from today from 3 o'clock in the afternoon until 10 o'clock in the morning. Exceptions will be made only for those Jews and Jewesses who have valid work-passes. This order is for the security of the population and to protect the lives of the inhabitants. It is the duty of every honest citizen to cooperate in preserving quiet and order.'

The Aktions continued until September 3rd, when the area the Jews had been expelled from was fenced in and two Ghettos were set up, a larger and smaller. On the 6th of September, approximately 30,000 Jews were forced into the larger Ghetto, known as 'Ghetto I' and 11,000 of the oldest or most infirm into the smaller Ghetto, known as 'Ghetto II'. Both sections were crowded to the point that they resembled ant colonies. A surplus of 6,000, for whom there was no room or were too frail to survive the relocation, were deported to Lukiszki prison and from there to Ponary.

Judenrat councils were set up in Rudnick Street, in line with Nazi policy of putting the Jews in charge of their own punishment. Various bureaucratic departments were created, providing the illusion of permanence, offices for everything from Food to Health to Lodging to Education to Employment. But the Director of Employment could do nothing for those prisoners unfortunate enough to lack work-passes; they were given jobs as sport for young German soldiers. Men were strapped down with timber then forced to run to the top of Tymin Hill, the soles of their feet beaten for every stumble. Women were yoked to wagons and ordered to pick up horse dung with their fingers.

The able-bodied were marched out of the Ghetto every morning at first light, to labour in factories, construction sites and army units. Workers carried prized white passes, detailing their names, profession and employer addresses. But even these certificates couldn't stop a one-way trip to Lukiszki if the Lithuanian police decided they didn't like the cut of a man's gib. The lucky worker who endured twelve hours of laying train tracks under a guard more brutal than the noonday sun would upon his return to the Ghetto be subject to searches at the main gate, where the Jewish Police checked for prohibited items such as food and milk. If a worker was stopped by Lithuanian police outside the Ghetto, even the shoes on his feet could be considered contraband. Even worse when the Gestapo decided to monitor the gate, prying mouths open with crowbars and confiscating the smallest morsel of bread trapped between molars, sometimes the molar itself, if it was filled with silver. For 'importing' food in this manner, a man could be beaten bloody before being sent to his death. By this way, the smuggling of contraband into the Ghetto was controlled.

But still, goods managed to find a way in, and a way out.

Before three weeks had passed, the Chaze had a conduit of his own, a kashariyot, literally, a connector, one of a handful of brave young Jewish women – usually pretty, it must be said - who traversed the Ghettos, smuggling secret documents and underground newspapers, medical supplies and forged identity cards, and whatever else they could conceal about their person. The woman, known only to the Council of Four as X, was a svelte, green-eyed beauty from Warsaw whom the Chaze had used to smuggle his Ponary dossier into Sweden. X was now back in Wilno, and had infiltrated Ghetto I.

A tentative message-delivery system was set up with the help of the baker who delivered our bread, an impassive Lithuanian not immune to the lure of cold, hard Reichmarks. Our first communique was a cautious exercise in information-gathering and read:

'Please tell us what is happening. Ha'aretz yearns to know'.

Haaretz was short for *Hadashot Ha'aretz, News of the Land of Israel*, our oldest daily newspaper.

After leaving the back of our canteen, the baker returned to his shop in the city, where he was later visited by X, who took the message home with her to the Akiva leaders within the Ghetto. Their reply was couriered back to the shop two days later by the same woman. For the baker's next delivery to Camp Moda, he prepared a special batch of loaves along with the usual pastry delicacies for the SS, with the Ghetto's response concealed within.

By this time, Ritter had succeeded in having me assigned to the food-squad, in addition to my usual leather-clicking duties, and I was able to intercept the fragments of paper, and pass them on to Zgismond or Ritter and eventually back to the Chaze. To everybody's surprise, it worked. The Ghetto's reply read:

'Situation very dire, but thrilled to hear of your existence?? Much to discuss.'

And so the dialogue began. It was through these messages that we first contacted family members on the Ghetto prisoners' behalf and then began building up a picture of the conditions they were living under. The decrepit water and sewage systems were straining under the demands of a population a hundred and fifty times bigger than ever intended. Regular blockages led to outbreaks of dysentery, while precious clean water leaked out through burst pipes. Overcrowding and the correspondent worsening of sanitary conditions led to a sharp increase in mortality rates, not to mention swarms of fleas and lice that wouldn't have been out of place in Ancient Egypt. The German authorities displayed a sign at the main gate: 'Warning – Danger of Epidemics. Entry to Non-Jews is Strictly Forbidden!'

Very quickly it became apparent that as well as sending messages in, we needed to put our efforts into bringing people out. We could not free anybody, but we could ease their suffering. Camp Moda was no longer the paradise I had first encountered, but it was still about the best we could hope for. And we had Zgismond as Kapo, another useful buffer.

There was no official word from Gestapo HQ, but the Ghetto was never conceived with longevity in mind; it was a holding bay on the road to Lukiszki and Ponary. Rescue became our overriding preoccupation, and the sole subject of discussion at the next Council of Four meeting, five snatched minutes behind the din of the lasting machines on a wet Wednesday morning, September 24th.

'I'm a glorified leather goods salesman,' the Chaze said. 'They only put me in charge of this place because they appreciate fine shoes, and we make a lot of money. A guy like me doesn't get to start sniffing around a sealed Ghetto, not unless he's found the next Bruno Magli.'

Silence, or what passes for it behind a row of 1,500 kg lasting machines.

'So you find him,' Zgismond said.

'Do you even know who Bruno Magli is?'

'Even better,' Ritter said, 'you find ten of him.'

'Oh, just like that?'

'Just like that.' Ritter threw his fist open like a triumphant magician.

'And why do I need ten more shoemakers?'

'Because our production lines are already going flat out. Because we've got orders flying in left, right and centre.'

'Have we? Why haven't I seen them?'

The corner of Ritter's moth twitched into a sly smile. 'Because I haven't concocted them yet.'

It was ingenious, but there was a problem: work-passes. If Edith Liebgold had a white card in her pocket saying she was a cook, how was the Chaze going to convince her jailer's otherwise? But, of course, every problem was an opportunity in disguise. We might not have figured out how to help Edith Liebgold yet, but she already had a job, and a degree of security. There were hundreds, perhaps thousands of poor souls trapped inside without work-passes, forced to endure the most obscene daily degradations. These were the very people who needed our help the most.

We put in a request via our baker, and names of the jobless started flooding in, hidden in the usual way. So great was the uptake from the Ghetto that we had to increase our order from three deliveries a week to five, citing spoilage of loaves caused by the prolonged heat-wave.

This increased traffic did not go unnoticed by my bête-noir, Lagerführer Nickel, who was already suspicious of my continued requests of meetings with Herr Ritter to discuss yet another meeting that never seemed to take place. When I was transferred to the food-unit, Nickel had started showing up to check on me, convinced that I was stealing rations. Of course I wasn't, and he soon lost interest, or so I thought. But Nickel was a more sophisticated creature than he let on, and had been monitoring deliveries from a discrete distance.

Early one morning, as I was fetching a tray of loaves from the back of the baker's van, I heard the spring-loaded click of a metal tab dropping into position against a firing pin, and squirmed as the cold steel of a gun barrel pressed into the back of my neck.

'Turn around very slowly and put the tray on the floor,' Nickel breathed into my ear.

The pressure eased from my skin and I complied, setting the tray on the ground between us.

'I don't care who it is you're writing love-letters to, your whore or Joseph Stalin.' Nickel waved his pistol at the bread. 'But it doesn't matter. If you're lucky, you'll get to hang for this. If you're lucky.'

'No, no. There's - '

'Silence!' he screamed. 'Push the tray towards me.'

I had no choice.

Nickel squatted on his haunches, lifted the tray, tipped the loaves onto the dirt and peeled out a sheet of baking paper from underneath. Handling it as if he'd found the Shroud of Turin, he examined both sides, then held up to the light, but could see no writing, not even a watermark.

Undeterred, he pulled another sheet, and another, until the metal tray flashed white in the sunlight.

He went through the entire van, ripping open every box, flinging every cake and cream puff onto the growing pile, scouring every inch of cardboard, but of course, there was nothing to see. The Ghetto's messages were written on tiny scraps of paper encased within the hollowed-out loaves now buried at the bottom of the pile.

***

Meanwhile, Julius Ritter forged the work-orders that the Chaze took to his parties and nightclubs as proof of Camp Moda's continued need for expansion. His superiors didn't need much prompting. If the Ghetto contained the highest concentration of Jews, it stood to reason the highest concentration of shoemakers were also to be found within its walls. Jewish craftsmen were skilled, and better than anything, they'd work for soup. The Chaze was given permission to take as many as he could find.

It took less than four weeks from establishing contact with the kashariyot to putting a rescue plan in place, but on this occasion the Chaze had no idea how little time we had. The first Ghetto Aktion took place against both I and II on October 1st, which, by a startling twist of fate, was the day of Yom Kippur, the Jewish Day of Atonement.

At noon, when the synagogues were full, Germans and Lithuanians under the command of the SS Officer Schweinberger entered Ghetto II, rounded up approximately 1,700 Jews and deported them to Lukiszki. In the afternoon Schweinberger turned to the Judenrat of Ghetto I and demanded 1,000 Jews by 7:30 that evening. Residents found by the Jewish Police to be lacking work-cards were arrested, transferred into German custody and deported. Of all the horrors, one story about an old Jewish teacher forced to dig a ditch stood out. The SS pushed pork into his mouth while he worked. The teacher spit it out. They kept pushing it in, and he kept spitting it out and fighting them. Another SS man took pictures of how they forced a Jew to eat pork on Yom Kippur. Finally the Germans lost patience and shot him and clamped the sausage between his teeth like a cigar.

9

The shock-waves of the strike and its timing reverberated around Camp Moda for days. Many of my fellow prisoners had regarded the Ghetto as a place of safety and refuge, an opportunity for Jews to live amongst their own, free from abuse and persecution. Instead of words of consolation, all I could offer was silence. I alone knew what fate awaited the deported.

The Chaze sunk into a deeper depression than August, and disappeared for three days straight on 'official leave'. Not even Julius Ritter knew where he spent them. But he returned sharp and slimmer, with a new determination, and the Council of Four pledged to press ahead with our original plan as quickly as possible. The Yom Kippur sweeps were extensive, but not exhaustive. There were still prisoners trapped in the Ghetto without work-orders, but we knew for certain that they would be taken next. A new list was drawn up in consultation with the Akiva leaders, and Oswald Zgismond started preparing the stables to house another sixty workers.

Renewing the wining, dining and outright bribing of his friends at Gestapo HQ, the Chaze was able to find out the date of the next scheduled Aktion: October 16th. Another Jewish holiday, Sukkot, or the Feast of Tabernacles. This was no coincidence. Every time we thought we understood the depths of the Nazi's depravity, they found new ways to surprise us. Unfortunately, the Jewish calendar has an awful lot of holidays.

For once, we were ready.

On October 13th, Herr Ritter and the Chaze left the camp in an armoured truck bound for Wilno. According to sixty-four year old Rose Ziekel, when my two friends jumped out inside Ghetto II and started hunting for the names on their list, they were more fearsome than any Gestapo. People were terrified, and fled screaming.

Only later did Rose realise that the screams were the Chaze's necessary alibi. Any reputation he'd acquired in the SS for being soft on Jews was shed that day.

Amongst all the bluster and panic, eighty-seven prisoners were shoved into the truck and brought back to Moda, twenty-seven more than the approved list of 'Specialist Artisans' provided for. What none of the watching gate-soldiers saw during the melee, was the Chaze's revolver fall from of his holster, to be snatched from the gutter by a young woman who may or may not have been kashariyot X. The Council of Four had taken no official decision on arming the Ghetto, and I could see no good coming from it. But whether by design or chance, the next stage of the struggle had begun.

After the success of the first rescue, we redoubled our efforts for a second. The tactic of scheduling Aktions for Jewish holiday worked to our advantage: we always knew when the next one was coming. Following on from the Succott, the Shemini Atzeret was celebrated between October 16th and 17th outside the Land of Israel. It only took the Chaze a few days to discover that the Nazis planned to mark the occasion with the total liquidation of Ghetto II.

Ritter fabricated new orders, Zgismond oversaw the building of another consignment of bunk-beds, and I took particular care when unloading the baker's next batch of loaves.

On the afternoon of October 15th, the Chaze and Ritter drove through the Ghetto gates to find the streets full of people, owners of work-passes frantically registering, while whoever could do so tried to hide, to bury themselves in a basement or attic, and hope to wait out the groups of Lithuanians roving from house to house. The Aktion had already begun.

One young boy concealed himself in a warehouse above a closed-up staircase in the courtyard of Shali 4, entering via a hole in the wall of the bordering top floor apartment. Many groups of people with bundles gathered there, sneaking along like shadows by candlelight around the cold, dank, walls. The whole hide-out was filled with a restless murmuring. An imprisoned mass of people. Everyone began to settle down in the corners, on the stairs.

They were like animals surrounded by the hunter. The hunter on all sides: beneath then, above them, from the sides. Broken locks snap, doors creak, axes, saws. The boy felt the enemy under the boards on which he was standing. The light of an electric bulb seeped through the cracks. They pounded, tore, broke. Soon the attack was heard from another side. Suddenly, somewhere upstairs, a girl burst into tears. A groan broke forth. They were lost. A desperate attempt to shove sugar into the girl's mouth was of no avail. They stopped up the child's mouth with pillows. The mother of the child was weeping. People shouted in wild terror that the child should be strangled. The child was shouting more loudly, the Lithuanians pounding more strongly against the walls.

When the fist broke through, it was Herr Ritter's.

'You are safe now,' he said, smiling through the hole in the plaster. 'Come with us and you will live.'

Fifty of them did.

But three thousand did not.

Very quickly, our operation became victim of its own success, if you can forgive use of such a word within this context. The camp's population had doubled in a month. Apart from the overcrowding, which was a blessed relief for the rescued, compared with what they'd known, there was another problem: the inhabitants of Ghetto II were no craftsmen, and struggled to hold a tool without slicing open a finger. We had to keep this from the SS, and to work twice as hard ourselves, to cover the short-fall. Pockets of resentment grew amongst established Moda prisoners, but most understood, accepting the sacrifice with great magnanimity. But it was clear that we could take no more.

With half the Ghetto already gone, the remaining resistance was preparing for imminent liquidation. Their messages demanded weapons, and only weapons. Incredibly only one gun existed anywhere within the walls, the Chaze's single snub-nosed revolver, passing from each would-be-fighting unit like an icon. More were needed, they pled, and urgently. Guns, ammunition, explosives.

Within our Council of Four, I alone expressed

reservations, and requested time to consider the ramifications. What had guns ever solved? Arming the Ghetto was an act of collective suicide. If the authorities discovered the plan, it would be suppressed in an instant, and followed by swingeing retaliations, inside the Ghetto and out. Even if guns managed to find a way in, there was no hope of a tiny band of prisoners fighting off the might of the German army. The venture was doomed, whichever way you looked at it. But the Council took a vote, and the result was 3-1 in favour. I was told that preparations would commence, and I was welcome to rejoin if my conscience would allow.

For three days and three nights, I wrestled with the decision. Was my reluctance to engage in armed struggle - even from a distance - proof of my essential weakness as a man? For two years I had taken the coward's way out, scuttling from hole to hole, only to end up in a labour camp.

If not now, when?

But the risks to the Ghetto, and to the Chaze, seemed too great. I wanted to continue helping as many prisoners as possible, not endanger the last few who remained.

I realised we had no alternative. It was guns, or nothing. I could not stand by and watch.

Even the rest of the Council agreed that acquiring weapons from the camp was fraught with hazard, and would endanger our own people. The Chaze was convinced he could acquire a small arsenal from Gestapo HQ, where he still enjoyed unrestricted access.

The baker was approached to smuggle a crate into the canteen, but refused to take more than scraps of paper. A second large delivery truck brought vegetables to the camp from a nearby farm at six in the morning, three times a week, Monday, Wednesday and Friday. I cautiously kept an eye on security measures, and was surprised at the laxity. The soldiers gave a cursory inspection inside, but nothing thorough. The underneath of the vehicle was not checked at all, and there was enough room between the fuel tank and the exhaust to wedge a large suitcase. But it was moot: the farm driver turned out to be a young Lithuanian nationalist, clearly in awe of the SS. He would not help us.

Finally we arrived at an idea that was as inspired as it was dangerous: the Chaze would open an expansion of Moda inside the Ghetto. Even in its depleted form, Wilno I still had dozens of workshops employing hundreds of Jews. Most of it was self-cannibalising: carpentry workshops producing new furniture from the timber taken from Jewish homes, fur workshops making new coats from confiscated garments. But new goods were still being churned out: everything from marmalade, to carpets and sausages. Everything apart from luxury leather. The Chaze believed he had spotted a gap in the market.

If the Chaze convinced his superiors that the Ghetto could make as much money for the SS as Moda, the inhabitants would be reclassified as essential to the war effort, thereby guaranteeing the Ghetto's survival, which was my overriding concern. But we would also have what the rest of the Council of Four craved, a legitimate pipeline into Wilno I for moving more than just leather. The Chaze commenced his petitioning with more bribery and nights away in the city, restaurants and women and wine. He needed influential friends, and they were not hard to come by.

By the third week of October, Moda's expansion had been authorised, premises secured within the Ghetto and artisans recruited.

On Tuesday October 21st, Ritter and The Chaze left Moda to deliver a truck full of cordovan leather hides ready to be cut.

When we went to bed that night, the truck had still not returned.

Neither man was seen at breakfast next morning.

Outside on the Appelplatz, there was a new Kapo doing the head-count. I knew then that we were finished: the Chaze and Julius Ritter had been caught, their duplicity uncovered. Oswald Zgismond had been arrested. A rumour murmured up and down the lines that he was already under interrogation. It was only a matter of time before the SS came for me. The guards barked their orders as harshly as the night of Ronen Kesselman's execution.

People started stepping away from me as if I was contaminated, an Untouchable.

I remained standing after roll call, waiting for the clap of the iron bracelets.

'What are you waiting for?' the guard shouted. 'Return to work.'

I ran into the factory and hid behind the door. After the last soldier left the Appelplatz, I slipped back out and rummaged through the bins and found a good length of leather strap, strong enough to bear my weight. There was nothing left at Moda for me now.

I marched slowly passed the flagpole towards the back of the canteen, with the confidence of a man reporting for duty.

It was 6.10 a.m.

The Lithuanian farmer had delivered his vegetables and was enjoying a cigarette with one of the soldiers outside his truck. They were talking about an amateur football game, a Munich derby.

I dropped onto my knees and padded across the tarmac until I was under the front bumper. Turning onto my back, I pushed myself under the length of the vehicle and found the gap between the fuel tank and the exhaust. First I tied the leather round my ankles, then raised my knees and tied the strap to the metal, pulling it tight and hoisting my shoes against the undercarriage. I levered my torso up, pressed my chest against the chassis, and found a way to grip the metal that didn't serrate my fingertips. The snug intersection of man and machine, I was invisible. I hoped.

The driver finished his cigarette, bid the soldier goodbye and climbed up behind the wheel.

The engine shook into life above me and a great cough rattled through the exhaust next to my head, exploding like a gun-shot in the pipe. Within seconds I was engulfed in thick fumes, but when the truck started rolling, the breeze cleared the worst of it from my face.

We crawled around the courtyard, through the Appelplatz, past the flagpole and gallows, down the long slope to the gate, finally picking up speed, stones pinging off my back.

Stopped again at the gates, the final inspection. The

truck's rear doors creaked open, German soldiers jumping up, the hunter on all sides. Thumps of boots above, inches from my nose, separated by a thin layer of rusting aluminium. Stomping up to the driver's cabin, back down to the rear. Boots jumped down, the doors slammed shut.

Two knocks on the side panel.

'All clear!'

'Thanks... See you tomorrow.'

The truck shook as the driver pushed up into first gear.

The Moda gates swung shut behind us.

Picking up momentum, the flat-bed jumped and rattled over the forest road as the driver flew from second to third gear and a rip of cobalt sky opened up above.

I needed to get as far away from Moda as I could in the shortest possible time, but gripping the chassis was like squeezing razor-blades. My fingers marinated in their own blood.

The truck slowed down again, grinding back through the gears. Deep inside the forest now: no more blue skies, no open road. My world narrowed to one blind bend after another, at five miles an hour.

I worked my left foot free from the leather strap and jabbed the boot heel at the other bind until it broke. As my legs dropped, I unpeeled my fingers from the chassis, blew a goodbye kiss to the razor-blades and fell, twisting in the short drop, taking the full force of the tarmac with my shoulder. Boots last to hit the ground, I sucked myself into a foetal ball as the tyres rolled by, gusting my shaved head.

When the truck disappeared around the next bend, I bumped out of the road into the ditch, landing in a trough of fallen leaves.

Face down, I inhaled the freedom of the forest floor, the dust and bugs and grit.

10

The last of the morning's stars glinted like pin pricks in the sky.

Low in the east, a pale October sun was beginning its lazy climb. Poland - my sister and mother – was at my back, south-west. Easy enough to navigate on a clear morning: all I had to do was follow the sun.

I turned round and gazed into the forest, a fortress of oak and lime, bog alder and hornbeam. Noble and wise, their boughs would protect me. The foliage was thick at the side of the road, forming an arch above my head.

I ducked through and ran towards the tree's knotted arms.

The solitary house appeared from behind a row of silver birch just after noon.

I dropped to my knees, burying myself in the long grass.

Five minutes passed, in frozen observation.

Ten, then twenty.

No hand pushed open the house's black shutters, no smoke leaked from the chimney. Nobody stepped out the door and nobody returned. Before me, the grass shimmered proudly in the field, undisturbed by foot traffic. I judged the property to be abandoned.

From the outside, it was a dirty little Lithuanian hovel. The tar roof was pocked with holes. The lime that held the stones together was crumbling to dust. A drain pipe peeled away from one corner.. The narrow door dangled askance, moored by a single hinge. Under my hand, its damp wood was soft as fungal flesh. The door yawned open, spilling darkness. Outside, the morning was warming up and autumn bright. There was little incentive to shut the day out but I craved five minutes respite on a wooden seat uncrowded by horned beetles.

I stepped inside.

The crooked door let in little of the day. The window was

warped shut. The walls were black with smoke. I was standing in the middle of the only room, that much I could see. Coal husks warmed the grate, and pools of grease solidified on the brickwork. Somebody had been here, last night or perhaps as recently as this morning. I moistened a fingertip and zig-zagged my initials on the wall, blood on soot.

There was one shelf above a table, both empty, two frail wooden chairs and a bench long enough to stretch my spine and raise my injured foot. The room grew lighter as my eyes adjusted to the gloom. Opposite my head in the far corner, I could make out a shadowed square much like a cushion on the floor.

I pushed myself off the bench to investigate and found something even better than a cushion: a pile of neatly folded clothes. Olive green shirt, sturdy black woollen trousers and a pair of thick socks.

I shed my prison uniform, climbed into my new costume and stole out.

I didn't rest again until late that afternoon, by which time I was well and truly lost. Perhaps an hour of silvery light remained, but the evening chill was already descending.

I stopped at an immense stand of deadwood decomposing into the forest floor, the closest thing to a shelter I'd seen since the hovel. Moss and wildflowers covered the trunks, voles scampered amongst them while a host of woodpeckers flitted in and out, drumming the dusk. There were so many species thriving under the criss-crossed stumps, I believed the stand could take one more. I cleared an oblong allotment of branches from the ground and settled down under a crude wigwam, curling myself like a dog in a basket.

After an hour of fitful dozing, I was awoken by the sound of footsteps disturbing the leaves to my left. I held my breath as the unseen presence picked a way through. The forest was reduced to shadows, and I had hidden myself well amongst the trunks. A dog could have sniffed me out for sport, but there was no panting or excitable canine yelps.

I closed my eyes to sharpen my other senses, but now I was fully alert, I could hear nothing at all.

I was about to exhale a long sigh when the pounding of feet close by kicked up a dry dust-cloud rustle. Then, a second of silence as the feet left the air, followed by a soft hiss not unlike the flight of an arrow. The bough behind me groaned and collapsed as a pair of legs vaulted over. If I had not let out the most almighty shriek, the fellow would have landed on my head.

To my immense relief, the intruder was as startled as I was, and thrashed around on the ground until his shock had spent itself. In the half-light, I could see he was no German: stick-thin and wearing nothing but rags. The feet that had almost cracked my skull were wrapped in filthy, bloodied bandages.

'It's alright.' I raised my hands to show I was unarmed. 'I mean you no harm.'

The lad was long-haired and bearded like Victor of Aveyron, The Wolf Boy. The skin on his cheeks and forehead was smooth and prone to spotting. Like Victor, he was barely a man. I estimated his age as no more than half my forty years. I wondered how long he had been living out here.

'Who are you?' he said, squinting through his tangled fringe.

'One who travels the same path as you,' I assured him. 'I've come from a camp.'

'The family camp?'

I wondered if he meant Moda, and if so, whether news had spread of the Chaze's capture and my breakout.

I said, 'What family camp?'

'In the forest, five miles from here,' Viktor said. 'A hundred people, those who cannot fight. Women, children, the sick.'

'They live in the trees?'

'They have everything. Shabbat, holidays, prayer, marriage, old-timers gathering round campfires.'

'You've seen it?'

He nodded. 'They wouldn't let me stay.'

'Why not?'

'Because I was alone. They didn't trust me.'

'But aren't you... young enough?' I didn't want to offend

him by calling him a child. But that's what he was, I could see now, an adolescent. How could any so-called family camp have sent him packing in those rags?

'We could go back in the morning,' he said. 'Tell them we're brothers.'

'We don't look like brothers.'

'That's true. What camp are you from?'

'An SS camp. Forced labour.'

'Around here?'

'I've been running all day.'

'You're in pretty good shape for a prisoner.'

'We were lucky there, for a while.'

'What does that mean?'

'The conditions were quite decent.'

'So why leave?'

I thought about how or where to begin. 'It's a long story.'

'You got a weapon?'

'I told you, I mean you no harm.'

'I didn't ask what you told me. You got a gun or not?'

'No.'

'You didn't kill anyone?'

'Of course not.'

'There are partisans close, but they won't take a man if he don't have a weapon. If we got but one gun between us...'

'Looks like we're out of luck, then,' I said. 'My name's Jozef.'

He grunted; I did not hear a name.

'You hungry?'

'A little,' I said.

Victor's hand disappeared behind a fold in his rags and came out with a long, spindly carrot, which he tossed into my lap. I could see the carrot had been freshly scavenged. A clod of damp earth crumpled under my fingers. I bit the tip and chewed, sucking down the sweet juice, then chomped the rest of it in four quick bites.

'There's more where that came from,' Victor said.

'More is good,' I managed between mouthfuls.

'Berries, nuts, mushrooms, the whole heavenly table. We'll do alright, me and you. It's not safe to stay here.'

'I thought the partisans were on our side.'

'Where there are partisans, there are Germans hunting them. You stay if you want.'

'Are you with anybody?'

'A few friends. We have a place, a couple of miles from here.'

'What kind of place?'

'It's like a cave.'

My face must have failed to light up with glee, because he added, 'Well hidden. Warm. Now the summer's over it gets pretty nippy out here at night.'

I considered Victor' offer. On my first day I had not fared too badly by myself. I'd managed to find clothes, and a shelter, although not one I wanted to linger in a minute longer than strictly necessary. But now the October night was drawing in, I'd chosen a stand of deadwood as my bedroom. Victor's carrot was the first thing I'd eaten since breakfast.

I wasn't sure what he had seen in me that raised my stock from useless pacifist to desirable cave-dwelling companion in less than five minutes, or why he looked so thin if the forest floor catered such a feast. I decided not to care. I was simply grateful to have found an ally. It was a long time since I'd spent a day with nothing but my own skin for company, and I'd forgotten how to get by.

I followed through a labyrinthine darkness punctuated only by the occasional shard of moonlight through the trees. Along the way, my guide doled out another couple of carrots, mere appetizers for the banquet to come.

After twenty minutes of hard trekking, Victor stopped at an oak as broad as a house and circled the trunk on his hands and knees. I thought he might urinate like a dog.

Thankfully, he didn't cock his hind leg, but instead extended a thin hand to the bark and peeled off a clump of dark green vegetation, holding it up before my eyes.

'Moss only grows on the north side, out of the sunlight.' Victor pointed to a path through the trees. 'Just checking we're going the right direction before we fill up.'

'Fill up on what?' Pointing at the moss between his

fingers, I said, 'I hope that's not your heavenly table.'

Victor stepped back to reveal an enormous growth of fungus, some as thick as standing stones, thriving in the cool damp of the oak's permanent shade.

'First course, wild mushrooms with basil,' he announced with a sweep. 'See those leaves twined around the stalks? Tuck in. I'll try and find us some garlic next time.'

I joined Victor crouching at the fringed giants, found a sprig of green, plucked a handful of leaves and let the sweet tang of peppery mint melt onto my tongue. Less certain of the fungus, I gripped a white slab and broke off a corner. Firm and fleshy, it smelled of fried mushroom and when I chomped a hole through the cap, tasted pleasantly meaty.

There was enough here to feed a family for a week, and as Victor had said, it was just the beginning. Impressed with his survival skills, I felt the need to offer something in return as we ate.

But all I had was the story of what had happened at Camp Moda. In between mouthfuls, I wiped juice from my chin and asked if Victor was interested in hearing it.

He said, 'Did you break out?'

'I suppose so.'

'By yourself?' I tried not to feel insulted by his phrasing. 'Course I bloody want to hear about it.'

I took a deep sigh. This was the first time Camp Moda had become a story to tell. Before now, as recently as twelve hours ago, Moda had been my all-consuming world. I had stopped believing in the possibility of life beyond its borders. The realisation that every act of salvation the Chaze had wrought was condemned to the past and would not – could not – be repeated, hit me for the first time, and it hit me hard.

Julius Ritter, Oswald Zgismond. My friends were dead, or as good as. Only I had survived.

More immediately, I could not decide where to begin my tale. Reels of memories of a summer of war looped behind my eyes, and left me queasy. From the night those first bombs fell, everything had happened so quickly.

Suddenly I was quite tired. The day's travels must have caught up with me. Fed by my new protector, I was set to curl up and sleep, and already felt quite dreamy, as if my mind had surrendered before my body. A build-up of air announced itself in my stomach; I grimaced at my body's unseemly expulsion.

Something was very wrong.

I glanced down at the crumbs of mushroom cap on my shirt.

***

I awoke from terrible dreams of blindness, unable to open my eyes. The lids were gummed together with a crust of glue. I pulled a bare hand from the rough blanket and rubbed the seam of dried rheum until sleep-dust crumbled and ticked down my nose like ants. My eye-lashes wrenched apart, hair by tiny hair, but still I could not see. Fingers clenching into a fist, I flung out my hand and struck a piece of wood thirty inches from my face. It had the contours of a cage. A spray of earth sifted from the gaps between the planks and rained coolly on my chest. I jerked. The spasm rocked my head, left it shaking at the end of my neck like a bomb, I feared it would explode. But the sensation subsided, leaving ashes of my brain, baked in an oven of bone. I tried calling out but my throat was raw, ripped apart, as if I'd gargled with ground glass. The bitter citric tang of vomit tickled the back of my throat. Guiding my hand down the curving wall of wood, I stopped as the heel of my palm hit soil and dragged a path back towards my desiccated head, stopping at the hem of a second blanket that had been placed underneath my back. I crooked my arm at the elbow, pinched wool near my ears and rubbed, the woollen rustle as loud as a monsoon. In straightening my arm, the wrist collided with an object at my side - something smooth and heavy, with a handle - knocked it over, splash, glug. A wetness seeped under my shoulder, blooming from the blanket. I scrambled my fingers in order to save what was left of the water, but the cup had all but emptied. The remaining dregs barely wet my lips. Unthinking, I hurled the mug against the walls, bunched a handful of wet blanket and stuffed it in my mouth, sucking and chewing until

I was swallowing my own saliva.

I lay back on the earth, settling into the head-shaped groove, utterly spent.

***

Maddening grey slithers began to appear between the planks at my feet. At first I thought the light was an illusion wrought by my fevered brain, but the splinters widened, and became so bright I had to avert my eyes. Outside, dawn was breaking. When I squinted again, I could make out the outline of a doorway in the cage, two metal hinges glinting on the left length of the panel.

No sooner had I scrambled to investigate than the gruff barking of a dog came sliding down a slope towards me, commandeered by its master's voice. I stiffened. Victor had said nothing about having a dog. Indeed, there were times last night when I thought he might have been raised by one.

I must have fallen ill after his mushrooms, and passed out on the forest floor. Victor had been sitting next to me the whole time I gorged; he made no attempt to stop me from eating anything dangerous. Now here I was. Poisoned and trapped in some kind of cave or cell. Stripped naked, for the sake of a few clothes.

Why hadn't he killed me? Why nurse me back to life with water and blankets?

There was only one possibility: he wanted me alive. For what ends, I could not – I would not – conceive.

If there was a way in to Victor's cave, there had to be a way out, even if it meant heaving away a boulder. I pushed up onto my shaking hands and knees. The 'cave' had the proportions of an upended bath tub, barely big enough to turn myself around. I lunged in circles, a dog chasing its tail, butting the walls, finding nothing but the suffocating contours of my own cage.

Sweat-soaked, hyper-ventilating, I collapsed to the ground. My frantic efforts had twisted the blankets to one side. I lay on bare earth, slick shoulders collecting grit.

The sound of man and animal picked up as they drew

closer. I withdrew into the rear of the cave and squat on my haunches, ready to pounce, the last futile act of a particularly futile life.

A tall shadow blackened the centre of the door as the dog yapped excitedly, scenting blood.

A key scraped a padlock. The shadow dropped to the ground. A heavy deadbolt clunked.

The shadow returned to full height, a second bolt drew back at chest level.

'Wake him up, Polo,' said a Lithuanian voice, and a snuffling beast pushed through the door, breaking open my darkness with a dazzling vision of canine boisterousness.

The dog's tail thumped from side to side as she snaked towards me, throwing her paws on my shoulders and daubing my nose and lips with a greasy tongue. I fell back against the back wall, coughing and spluttering.

The man clicked his tongue; the dog scuttled back to his heels, whining. Her master crouched down to my level in the doorway, a silhouette against the sun. Beyond him, a dirt track, leading up to a well-tended vegetable garden.

I focussed on the man's face, craggy and drawn, with a pair of thick, raised eyebrows. He wore a neat, pointed beard and a mass of slicked back curls, glossy and black.

'If you're contagious, you better hope the dog don't catch it.' He had switched now to halting German.

'Water,' I gasped. 'Water.'

He looked down and raised the mug I'd flung in anger to his knee. It balanced there as he retrieved a canteen from deep inside his suit-coat and poured. He put the mug back down on the floor between us, and pushed it towards me.

I crawled to it and drank; he refilled and pushed it back. The middle fingers of his hand were crowded with jewelled stones, red, white and green. I noticed the same arrangement on his right hand, resting on his knee.

'Thank-you,' I said.

With an extravagant flourish, he said, 'Bitte sehr, mein herr.'

'You don't have to – I'm not German.' I spoke now in Lithuanian. 'Victor?'

He bared his teeth in a grimace. 'Who the fuck is Victor?'

'The boy who... The boy I was with.'

'You were alone when I found you. When Polo found you.' The man patted the dog's head next to his shin. I could see now that her chops were grey and grizzled. Two minutes ago, she'd been as excitable as a pup.

'Where?'

'Not far from here, near the stream where I fish. What were you doing, spying on me?'

'I was lost. I think I was poisoned.'

'By this Victor, you're telling me?'

I nodded.

'Poisoned how?'

'In the forest.'

'Berries?'

'Mushrooms.'

'You're lucky to have survived. Jewish?'

I nodded. 'I was a prisoner – '

'Enough. I don't need to hear all that. You rest. I'll be back later with some soup.'

'But - '

'Yes?'

There was nothing meaningful I could think to ask, but I wasn't yet ready for the man to leave.

'I am Jozef. Jozef Siegler, from Wilno.'

'Welcome to my kennel, Jozef Siegler. You may call me Mr. Poplowski.'

'I hope I will not bring you trouble.'

'So,' the man said, giving a curt bow. 'Sleep. You're perfectly safe.'

When I awoke again, I could smell smoke.

My worst fears were confirmed when I blinked open my eyes to the orange glow in the corner of the kennel.

But the flame was confined to the wick of a candle, and behind it, resting against the wall, was Mr. Poplowski, the dog's head pillowed on one thigh, an open book resting on the other. The doorway was no longer visible, the night a seam of coal beyond the planks.

Mr. Poplowksi was a small man. The restrictive proportions of the kennel fit him perfectly. Engrossed in his pages, Mr. Poplowski had not noticed me stir: I lay perfectly still, watching him read. He wore the same dark suit, with only a rather grubby vest underneath. I couldn't remember if he was earlier wearing a shirt or not. Complementing the six rings on his fingers was a crossed amulet around his neck, embedded with a large ruby. When Mr. Poplowski came to the end of his page, he glanced down at the candle, and then, as if sensing my wakened presence, over to the bed of blankets.

'The golem awakens,' he said.

'How long have you been there?'

'Is my presence unsettling for you?'

'Not at all.'

'I've brought books – you might be an educated man yet. Books and,' he made a motion with his eyes like he was casting out a line, 'food.'

I followed his gaze across the kennel to the side of my bed, where there was fish soup in a bowl with a spouted lip for drinking.

'Bread,' Mr. Poplowski said. 'On the other side.'

To my right, a plate of soft white slices with the crust removed.

I wiped my slobbering lips with the back of my hand.

'My brother's recipe,' he said. 'Spiny little perch hardly do it justice. I did the best I could with my knife, but... careful of the bones.'

I placed the bowl at my lips and tilted, straining the liquid through my teeth. It was still warm, a garlicky broth thick with soft flakes of white meat.

'It's wonderful.'

'Your belly's bigger than your eyes. Half now, half later. You're still sick.'

I tried to work out how long I'd been down here. From dark to light to dark again. 'I must have slept for a whole day.'

'Try multiplying that by three.'

'Three days?'

'If I wanted to wait on somebody as long as this, I'd have got married.'

I was speechless. Three days since my flight from Camp Moda? Impossible. Without wishing to be crude, there was no physical evidence of a prolonged stay. Urine may have seeped into the earth but its distinctive odour would have lingered. Yet the kennel floor was dry and the air smelled of nothing except hot wax and fish soup.

'I'm aware my manner is brusque, in case you were moved to point it out.'

'If brusqueness is the price for saving a man's life,' I said, 'I gladly accept.'

'It was your fair hair that gave me pause. I thought you might me German.'

'All that glisters is not gold,' I said.

'*Merchant of Venice.*' Mr. Poplowski snapped his jewelled fingers. 'A scholar after all. There are educated Germans too, so they tell me, I knew you were not one of them. Do you know how?'

With the air of a pontificating rabbi, Mr. Poplowski raised his index finger in front of his nose. 'Only a Jew awakens in a cage and accepts the terms of his incarceration without so much as a whimper.'

'We've had a lot of practice.'

He quoted Shylock's Act III soliloquy in reply. 'If you poison us, do we not die?'

'And if you wrong us,' I concluded, 'do we not revenge'

'Bravo.' He clapped his leg in half-hearted applause. 'I have the *Collected Works* back in my library, but for tonight I settled on something a little less... intellectual.' He held aloft the book's scarlet jacket from his thigh.

'*The Phantom of the Opera*,' I said, reading the embossed gold.

'You've read it?'

'I've always been meaning to.'

'You should,' Mr. Poplowski said. 'How about Ambrose Bierce, leaning against the wall?'

There was a second booked propped up behind him. Abrose Bierce was a minor American author who had caused a sensation a quarter of a century ago, when he'd vanished without trace while touring battlegrounds in Mexico.

I said, '*The Devil's Dictionary*?'

'*An Occurrence at Owl Creek Bridge*. A tale from a very different war.'

The American Civil War, in fact. The short story commences with the narrator Peyton Farquhar about to be hanged by Unionists for sedition, but the rope snaps and he plunges to freedom in the eponymous water below the bridge to make his escape. It is only with the very last lines of the tale that the reader discover the rope never snapped at all. The flight along the river was nothing more than Farquhar's dying meditation.

The story seemed doubly ghoulish to me now, given my current predicament. But it could have been worse. An evident student of the Gothic, my captor might have reappeared with a copy of Edgar Allen Poe's *Premature Burial*.

'A morbid choice of reading matter, now that I think of it,' Mr. Poplowski said, as if my thoughts had been projected on the kennel wall. 'There's quite a library in the cottage if you'd care to name your author of choice.'

'Perhaps tomorrow.'

'As you wish.'

Mr. Poplowski roused his dog, tucked the two books into his suit pockets and collected my dish and plate.

'It was delicious,' I said.

'I expect you'll be wanting toast and tea for breakfast.'

'I don't want to put you out,' I said. 'Any more than I already have.'

'Come on, Polo, let's leave him be. Do you want the candle?'

'Take it. I may knock it over in my sleep.'

'We'll talk more in the morning, you can't stay cooped up here forever.'

In the last few minutes of our conversation, I had become filled with a creeping dread. Alone in darkness once more, it bloomed. I imagined the fish soup in my stomach, fermenting alongside the remains of the fungus. Had I fallen prey to Victor's poisoning trick all over again? Who in their right minds feeds a sick man fish soup? I became convinced the two were father and son, that Mr. Poplowski had returned to finishing what the boy could not. After all, the forests of middle Europe are rife with legends of bloodthirsty dynasties like Vlad the Impaler and his descendants, who put Hitler's Reich to shame...

In such a state, I passed the night. Terrified to let each breath go, lest it proved my last.

Dawn lit up the gaps between the planks once again, and found me alive.

I had survived the night, of course. Mr. Poplowski had not poisoned the fish soup. If I was to continue surviving outside the camp, I'd have to get used to accepting the kindness of strangers. This would be a challenge in itself. Any new situation or encounter, especially with a non-Jew, was fraught with danger.

Mr. Poplowski returned as promised with a heavy ivory tray. After I'd playfully wrestled Polo to the ground, her master served tea and toast, remarking how much stronger I appeared in daylight. We ate from porcelain plates and drank from dainty cups - the height of sophistication, for two men and a dog penned together in a hole in the ground. After breakfast, Mr. Poplowski produced a satin handkerchief from his suit-coat (no shirt, vest only) and loudly blew his nose before announcing, 'I have a confession to make.'

He removed a cream envelope from his chest pocket and tapped it against his fingers as he spoke.

'After finding you, I wrote to my brother Anton, requesting advice. He is a practical man with a young family in Poland and a small dairy farm. His reply came first thing.'

'I see.'

'You were very ill when I found you. I began to entertain certain notions of companionship, of which an old man must be disabused. You cannot live indefinitely underground like a mole. And I realise now you would not be safe in my cottage.'

'Safe from whom?'

'I have acquired a reputation in these parts as a... a hermit. A man so intolerant of others he once threw a chap into the stream for the crime of inadvertently blocking his path.'

I was not surprised by this disclosure, although I kept my

opinion to myself.

'To suddenly start playing host to a mysterious stranger summoned from the depths of the forest... Too many questions would be asked. I'd be unable to provide satisfactory answers.'

'I do not wish to cause any trouble.'

'With Anton, the very opposite would be true.'

'With Anton?'

'You would be an invaluable extra pair of hands.'

I wrinkled my eyes, assessing what I'd heard. 'Are you proposing I work on your brother's farm?'

He nodded. 'Anton is setting out later today. He will arrive by nightfall.'

'He's coming here?'

'In order to speak in person, yes. We will have dinner together, the three of us. Providing you are amenable, you could accompany Anton home in the morning.'

Events were moving far too quickly. I did not know what to say.

'Unlike here,' Mr. Poplowski continued, filling the gap, 'your presence on the farm will go completely unnoticed. Casual labourers are two-a-penny in Lublin, or they used to be, before the war. You would be just another transient farm hand, as anonymous as you wished. In exchange for your work, you would enjoy food and shelter, a new life, a new freedom...'

I had stopped listening.

Mr. Poplowski didn't know it, be he had uttered the magic word: Lublin.

The city was on the other side of the Polish border, almost halfway between Wilno and Cracow, where Shoshana had last been bound.

I told Mr. Poplowski I would meet his brother, and was prepared to discuss the venture that evening. But it was already a mere formality. My mind was made up: the two of us would leave for his farm in the morning.

If Anton's promise proved true, I would stay long enough to repay my debt and recover my strength.

If not, I was in Poland, less than two hundred miles from

my family.

Later that afternoon I was invited up to the cottage in order to clean and groom myself for dinner.

The cottage's warren-like interior did little to dissuade me from the notion that its owner was regarded as a hermit. Each room was dimmer and dustier than the last, untroubled by such niceties as electricity or plumbing, but insulated from floor to ceiling with several decades worth of curled newspaper. I bathed at the back in water from a heated cauldron and dressed in one of my host's black and white striped suits.

After shaving, I joined him in the 'library' – rather a grand word for such a shelf-less cell, although well served in terms of the sheer number of books. Undaunted by its general disarray, Mr. Poplowski had what appeared to be his own homespun version of the Dewey Decimal Classification, and knew the location of just about every book we mentioned in our wide-ranging discussion. After my recent privations, the afternoon's wait was most pleasing. I was reminded of that first halcyon summer in Wilno with Shoshana and Herman Glik, and my daily sojourns to the Strashum Library where I first encountered Abba Kovner, cigarette clamped between lips, hovering over an antique Talmud.

Anton Poplowski arrived on a well-cared for horse and cart shortly before dusk.

Facially, he bore his brother's dark, leonine features - the slicked back helmet of black hair, the raised eyebrows that met in the middle, a reflection of that drooping moustache – but there the similarity ended. Whereas my host exuded a saturnine glower, the farmer was a convivial, hale and hearty fellow it was impossible to dislike. In turn, I felt Anton warm to me in a manner his brother had not. It was agreed before the serving of dinner's first dish that the two of us would leave for Lublin early in the morning.

Since our deal had concluded so prematurely, conversation inevitably turned to other matters, namely the subject of my fateful delivery into the brothers' lives. They deserved to know the truth, and I was sure I could trust them.

Even so, I relayed my story in reverse, starting four days previously, when Mr. Popolowski stumbled upon my naked body in a pool of vomit beside his brook, proceeding to my encounter with Victor, my brief and felonious stay at the dilapidated hovel (a partisan safe-house, I learned) and concluding with the revelation of Camp Moda, the minor role I had played in the Chaze's subterfuge and my final escape. It is fair to say my tale was received with an astonishment bordering on the incredulous.

Several cognacs were dispatched, in quick succession. Mr. Poplowski prided himself on his knowledge of the woods, and had believed the cable-works factory to be still abandoned. He knew nothing of its current incarnation at the hands of the SS.

The brothers had assumed I was an escapee of Nazi custody, but of an even more heinous kind than the one I had endured. From the extent of my physical degradation that Tuesday morning, Mr. Poplowski was convinced that that I had somehow crawled out of the execution pits of Ponary.

It was my turn to be dumbfounded.

Having read the Operational Situation Reports copied by the Chaze - the Gestapo's infernal murder tallies where every pound of flesh was assiduously accounted for - I could not believe anybody had survived.

Yet I was wrong.

According to my host, three people had already dug themselves out through the mountain of corpses under which they were buried. Last Saturday evening, a woman called Sara Menkes clawed herself free of the grave the Germans had left her in, their bullet having only grazed her ear. Traumatised, covered in her friends' and family's blood, Sara Menkes stumbled through the forest and collapsed at a partisan camp, perhaps the same one from which Victor claimed to have been excluded.

Shortly after I had made myself comfortable for the night on the front room couch (out of the kennel at last), Anton returned, a candle shadow announcing his presence down the staircase. I assumed he had left his jacket or reading spectacles at the dinner table, and bid him proceed without concern for my disturbance.

'Actually, it was you I was hoping to speak to.'

I sat up against the arm-rest. 'I hope I haven't said anything to cause offence.'

'Not at all, quite the opposite. It's just that I've – well. I've had an idea.'

'Go on.'

'A proposition, if you will. I thought you might want to sleep on it, rather than being ambushed first thing in the morning. Please don't take this the wrong way, but I... that is to say... Well. The thing is, you don't look very Jewish.'

'I assure you I am no impostor.'

'Nobody is suggesting that. Until the war ends, and that day it is surely coming, I was going to propose... Well. What would you think about no longer openly advertising the fact that you're Jewish?'

Advertising? I was aghast. I tried to keep my countenance free of offence, but he must have read my disappointment, for he added, 'Amongst friends, of course, you should never feel the need to conceal yourself. But unfortunately friends are presently few and far between.'

Very quietly I asked, 'Is this proposal a condition of coming to work on your farm?'

'Not at all. We have several real Jews who hide with us, and will always take more. You wouldn't have to live like they do, is what I'm trying to say.'

'And how do they live?'

'In constant fear, Jozef. In hiding. With your looks and build, you could pretend to be a good strapping German, and nobody would be any the wiser.'

'I see.'

'Of course, the choice is entirely yours. Perhaps the idea is a stupid one. I am quite drunk, after all.'

'As am I. Forgive my temper. I am sure you meant well.'

'Sensitivity has never been my strong point. I should have thought more carefully. Whatever you decide, you will be safe as our guest, I give you my word.'

Nothing was said of the matter next morning. In fact, nothing was said at all. We ate in brusque silence.

After breakfast, we worked up a sweat loading the horse's wagon with firewood from another of Mr. Poplowski's kennels, in case the Germans stopped us. It was a rare farmer to venture from one country to the next in search of fallen branches, but Anton's alibi was better than nothing, and dry wood a useful bartering commodity as winter approached.

When the wagon was piled high, the two brothers stiffly bid each other goodbye, no love lost or indeed gained during their brief reunion. I thanked my host for saving my life, a fact he swatted away like a troublesome fly. Nevertheless, I succeeded in shaking the man's hand, then fought off Polo's slathering embrace one final time. Mr. Popolowski led the dog round the back of his cottage, leaving Anton and I alone.

I cleared my throat. 'I've thought about what you said last night.'

'You can spare me the lecture. I know it was crass.'

'Not at all. You were right.'

'I'm sorry?'

It was not as if Anton's proposition was entirely new to me. During the evening of my snatching in Wilno, the kindly processing officer at Lukiskes prison had professed astonishment at my fair features and the proficiency of my spoken German. Later that same night, my cell-mate Ronen Kesselman had suspected me of being an undercover Gestapo spy, placed there to lure a confession. Now, for the third time in as many months, my looks had been called into question.

In the cold light of day, I knew Anton was right.

I had not been blessed with a superfluity of gifts. To fail to take advantage of the one I had - my ability to disguise my true identity with relative ease - was more than foolish, it was potentially fatal.

'I accept your proposition,' I told Anton. 'From this point forward, I will not admit to being a Jew.'

A flock of geese honked from the woods, in seeming mockery.

'If... If you're sure.'

I ignored the geese. 'Quite sure. Were it not for your

brother's cognac, I believe I would have come to my senses far quicker.'

'Well, I must say, that is a relief.'

'A relief for whom?'

'For us both.' Anton fastened the catch at the back of the wagon. 'I was just about to ask you to hop under the wood pile. You can ride up front with me now.'

South of the forest at the tiny village of Kushna, our conversation turned to the particulars of my new identity. Anton's wife came from Hambug; he proposed that for the duration of my stay, I was to claim to be her city cousin, Damian Plotz. I confessed that I knew the Hamburg area well, having worked in Kiel for the best part of a decade.

'As a shoe-maker?'

'In my former life I was a university professor.'

'Good God. That won't do at all. A German academic grubbing in the fields of Poland – who'd believe that? No, no, you have always been a cobbler. Easier that way. I'm sure Hana can provide the name of a Hamburg shop owner who'll confirm your employment, should it come to that.'

'Thank-you.'

'The most successful lies are always sprinkled with just the right amount of truth. The trick is, knowing how much.' After a thoughtful moment of silence, Anton added, 'Kiel, eh? I wasn't so wide of the mark after all. We must take that as a good omen.' He dropped his voice as if the Gestapo might be hiding in the hedgerows. 'What about your family, where are they?'

'My mother and sister were living in Cracow during the invasion. I haven't heard from them since.'

'You're not alone on that front.'

'It is they who are alone. My father never returned from fighting in Siberia when I was a child.'

Anton did not need to reply. We both knew how hard it was for families to get by, even before the war. Without a male bread-winner, the task was often insurmountable. Fortunately the Sieglers had a secret weapon in our midst: Shoshana.

'You should know that I have pledged to find them,' I said. 'After I have worked to repay my debt to your family, I must be on my way to mine.'

'You have no debt to repay, Jozef. If you want to be on your way tomorrow, it will be with my blessing.'

11

Anton was true to his word. Even so, I ended up staying in Lublin many weeks longer than I'd anticipated. When I eventually left, it was dressed from head to toe in the uniform of my enemy, an SS Oberführer called Harry Mohnke.

This book is an attempt to record the chain of events that led to that singular incident coming to pass. At the time, I was convinced that I had no choice. Having already adopted one false identity, I found it remarkably easy to assume a second. But first I would like to express my gratitude to my new Polish hosts, and to say a word as to their own struggles.

The newly christened Damian Plotz arrived at the farm shortly before 11.00pm that Monday, greeted by his cousin, Hanna, and her three delightful daughters, drowsy from their unusually late night. The middle girl Barbora had agreed to forsake her room to bunk with Radka, the youngest, kindly vacating a bed for me. For the duration of my stay, not one of the girls remarked on the indignity of having a Jew sleep between their sheets.

Indeed, with the sole exception of one night in the barn, surrounded by the reek of gasoline, nobody ever referred to me as anything other than 'Cousin', 'Dami' or 'Mr. Plotz', although there were certain undeniable signs that the eldest daughter Eva suspected –and, if I may be so bold – yearned that I was not a blood relative. Perhaps the younger girls had never been told the truth about who I was or where I'd come from. Whatever the family knew, they were so convincing that at times I forgot any of us were acting. I suppose that was the point. If the Gestapo ever found me, everybody would be put to death as punishment, even the children.

The house I was welcomed into was large and clean and untroubled by twentieth-century fads of convenience. Little had changed since it was built some eighty years previously, by Anton's great grandfather. Downstairs was still lit with oil lamps, candles for the bedrooms. One sink under the kitchen window for washing up, washing clothes, and washing ourselves. The lower half of the kitchen window was patterned with clouded glass so people walking along the garden path would not glimpse anything untoward. The Popolowskis were fortunate to have a water tap over the sink. Most of the villagers still used a well. The toilet was a wooden hut at the bottom of the garden between two pine trees. To go, one sat on a wooden plank with a round hole and a bucket underneath. Back in the house, Sunday night was bath night – I had missed it by a day, and would have to wait a week for the next. I resolved to leave for Cracow the following Monday, clean and presentable for the family I still hoped to find.

On my first morning, Anton awoke me at dawn to fetch the cows and help with milking in the barn. High on his tractor, we set out across the fields into a white October sun, tracked by meadowlarks and the prancing family hound. The beautiful and obedient sheepdog Persha was supposed to drive the cows, but her mastery of the creatures did not extend to Fresians. She was no good with the sheep, either, I was soon to learn. The Poplowskis were sentimentalists, and could not bear to let dear Persha go. In addition to the cows and sheep, the farm had a few pigs, some sheep, a lot of hens, a varying population of cats, and two Jewish brothers stashed in a bunker under the floor of the milking barn.

In the excitement of arriving, I had forgotten about the 'real Jews' who also shared my new home. It was only when, after the last udder had been squeezed and Anton sent the grumpy Fresian on its way, that my host took a broom, swept a patch of straw from the floor, then bent down, sprung a padlock and opened a trap door. He lowered a pail containing a freshly-baked loaf and a bottle of water, and thirty seconds later, hauled it back up empty, closed the door, covered it with straw and set the milking stool over the top.

I accompanied Anton everywhere those first couple of days, eager to help, whether it was feeding the fowls and collecting eggs, repairing the battered ploughs or rescuing a sheep that had fallen into a bog at the bottom of the hill and was unable to right itself. I have never slept so well as those nights, such was the wearying physical exertion of the day-lit hours. The farmer's life was something completely new to me. I began the week marvelling at my host's kinship with the wild creatures on his land, his knowledge and poetic commentaries on the weather, the wide blue skies, the brilliant sunshine, the changing winds and panoramic views. But it didn't take long to see the harsh reality behind the bucolic charm.

The first storm of the season came that Wednesday afternoon, as unannounced as a knock at a darkened front door. 'It will be like this until the spring now,' Anton cautioned that evening as we warmed our bones at the hearth. Such ill-timed raids of wind and rain could spoil a hay crop in minutes or strip the head of ripening grain. And then, at the height of summer, there was always the threat of drought to rob the corn harvest. Not only were farmers at the mercy of an unforgiving Nature, but they had to contend with the constant threat of low prices, sickness, poor medical care, accidents and of course, the new and ever-growing encroachment of the Nazis.

The process of Germanization had been underway for two years by this point, resettling ethnic Aryans from the far-flung Baltics in houses and farms in the occupied territories. Starting with the displacement of 'foreigners' in the Danzig corridor in 1939, hundreds of thousands of families like Anton's had been expelled without warning, losing everything they owned. Many elderly and children had died en route or in makeshift transit camps like Potulice or Smukal or Torun. Finally this year, after Hitler's vainglorious invasion of the Soviet Union, resettlement plans had been scaled back; the trains were now more urgently needed to transport soldiers and supplies to the Eastern Front. But the threat to Anton's livelihood remained. There were fates to rival expulsion.

A friend in Lublin had recently had his dairy farm declared as essential to the War Effort. Under close SS supervision, the farmer's family had to toil for a week building and installing a mechanized milking station to fulfil the greedy new quota. Instead of feeding his children, the farmer was now catering for the German army. Anton had survived untouched thus far because he had cultivated good relationships with the head of the Belorussian gendarmerie, a heart-broken man whose wife had been deported by the Russians. In her absence the Belorussian had developed a deep fondness for Anton's bracing pear brandy.

If the work was hard for the men, it was doubly so for Hanna and Eva, who put in the longest hours of us all. When their morning chores were complete, mother and daughter set to work in the fields, and if by any miracle there was no planting or tilling to be done that day, they tended to the garden. The vegetable patch was a vital part of the farm's production, saving money on the food budget and sustaining through times when income from crops or livestock was low. When the storm came that Wednesday, Eva retreated inside to make her own soap and used a broomstick handle to fish laundry out of a scalding hot tub into the wringer.

To this back-breaking litany of labour, one more burden had recently been added: the daily supervision of her younger sisters. Radka and Barbora's school had closed down over the summer, and was forbidden from re-opening. According to Nazi doctrine, the Slavic people did not need or deserve education. Limited elementary-level schooling was in place in some areas, where children were taught in non-Polish languages like German, or, if there were no teachers available, Russian. South of Lublin, there was nothing.

So the children stayed home, adding to their older sister's woes. Where was the mother of the family to be found, you ask? It was not that my cousin Hanna was neglectful – far from it. Onto the mother's shoulders fell the unenviable task of feeding the family and all the extra field-hands who trooped down from the village, depositing children of their own into Eva's custody. Hanna spent afternoons preparing elaborate recipes passed down from her grandmother on a tiny wooden stove upon which I would have struggled to poach an egg. The woman was a veritable conjuror of culinary delights. I had not eaten so well since I left home, forsaking my own mother's cooking. A typical meal at the farm might have consisted of liver and caramelised onions, ham and cherries, carrots with apricots, creamed cabbage and gooseberry pie for dessert, all of it cultivated within a stone's throw of the kitchen occluded window.

The oldest daughter Eva did the best she could to keep the dispossessed brood entertained, but at eighteen years old, she had barely said goodbye to her own childhood, and was already working all hours God sent to merely keep the farm afloat from one day to the next. Now, with Barbora, Radka and the assorted waifs and strays from the village, there were often as many as ten miniature mischief-makers cartwheeling through the cluttered rooms, too young to be put to work and too old to be left unattended. Taking pity on Eva, I helped out where I could. But my own time was limited to the occasional sketching lesson after dinner when the girls had settled down, and in truth, such was their prodigy with pencils, it often felt like they were instructing me. Thankfully, my decade lecturing at the University of Kiel had not been in vain, and I knew my way around a bedtime story better than most.

After we bid the girls goodnight, Eva and I would linger in the corridor outside their room, enjoying a few minutes of each other's company before returning downstairs. I had taken to dropping certain improvisations into my bedtime stories, invoking Lubka the village seamstress's habitual malapropisms, or describing the three little pigs in a manner that evoked a trio of Eva's least favourite pint-sized charges from the village. It was a long time since either of us had anything to laugh at, and I was flattered by Eva's attentions. But she was my host's daughter, and less than half my age. I was not about to bring the house into ill-repute. However, I freely confess that my thoughts often lacked purity.

On Friday a magnificent threshing machine arrived from a neighbouring farm, and brought with it a succession of excitable older boys from the village, although they remained outside with us and did not trouble Eva's crèche. I observed the annual tradition from Anton's side:

First the corn sheaves were taken from the ricks and put into the threshing drum which separated the straw from the grain and chaff. I was amused to watch the village boys gather round the machine, armed with heavy sticks. Amused until the first startled rodent poked its head out from the nest it had made in the rick, only to be greeted by a large, oafish-looking boy who pointed and yelled, 'Jew!' Another boy swung his club through the air and mashed the mouse into a pancake of quivering pulp.

'Jew!'

Bang.

'Jew!'

Bang.

The process of spotting and clubbing was repeated until the grass at our feet was stained red. Anton watched on with a look of grim forbearance. I understood that he was in no position to chastise the spotters for their 'sport', lest his own sympathies be called into question.

When the second rick was loaded into the machine, I announced that Eva had requested my assistance with the canning of peaches for winter, and fled inside.

The house's younger children were forbidden from participating in such blood sports. But this didn't stop them from clustering round the parlour window, intently spectating. One enterprising jug-ear was running a book on how many 'Jews' would be splattered from each rick. The winner received a choice of Eva's coloured crayons in payment. Condoning the corruption of childhood through gambling did not sit well with my conscience, but on the other hand, I had rarely seen the brood in such a state of mesmerised transcendence. Eva was enjoying a rare pot of tea at the kitchen table. I did not wish to encroach on her solitude, but she insisted on offering me a cup as I passed.

'You look like you could do with one,' she said. 'Are you coming down with something?'

'I feel somewhat soothed by your company.'

'Then you must sit a while.'

'I believe I can manage that.'

'Good.'

I helped myself to fresh cream and filled my cup with brown tea. Stirring in sugar-cubes, I lost myself in the dissipating swirl, and was startled to feel my fingers being gently squeezed. Eva patted the back of my hand and then withdrew, folding her arm primly on the table.

'You were supervising the threshing machine, weren't you?'

'There was little supervision required,' I said. 'Everybody seemed to know exactly what to do.'

'It's wicked,' she said, 'how our children are steeped in hatred from such an age. I myself will take no part in it. I won't even touch the corn anymore.'

'Boys will be boys,' I offered glumly. 'It is the same where I come from.'

'Didn't we all used to get along, once upon a time?'

'In the Book of Genesis, perhaps,' I allowed. 'My parents remember the pogroms of last century, and that was under the Russians.'

'It's a contagion. Sometimes I think the whole continent's lost its mind.'

'For each who acts that way, there are others who behave decently. Where there is life, there is hope.'

'You obviously don't know Lublin.'

'Can it be so bad?'

Eva averted my gaze. 'Father hasn't told you.'

I considered my words carefully. 'I have seen the floor of the milking barn, if that is what you speak of.'

'Those two poor souls are all that's left.'

'There were more?'

'This was always a Jewish village, until last summer. All the shopkeepers, artisans and tailors – gone. Overnight.'

'To the labour camps?'

'The lucky ones. Less than three weeks after the Germans arrived, our mayor and the village gendarmerie ordered all Jews to be rounded up. They were divided into groups and the elderly ones were taken to a barn that had been cleared for the purpose, clubbed to death then thrown into a pit in the field.'

Later that afternoon as dusk turned to dark, I returned from a long walk around the farm's perimeter, ostensibly to check on the cows. I could hear the family preparing for dinner as I approached the house, and saw Anton's boots neatly arranged on the back step.

Before I could join the family, there came a furtive rustling from inside the milking barn. I stopped, suspecting thievery. But here was nothing much to steal, except for the two brothers hidden in the bunker. I crept back to the barn, saw a lamp extinguish through a gap in the wood, and stopped on the other side of the door.

Flattening myself against the wall, I watched Anton emerge from the house, wearing his cardigan and slippers, every inch the hard-pressed farmer who had thought the day's chores done, only to remember one more. At the end of his arm swung a large metal can. I wondered what kind of work would not wait until morning. I was about to step out and ask when my host stopped five metres in front of the barn doors, unscrewed the cap, lifted the can and doused the earth with clear liquid. In this manner, he began retreating to the corner, splashing a trail along the base of the far wall, receding into the night. But the smell he left behind was unmistakable: gasoline.

For some unearthly reason he was going to burn his Jews alive!

With two minutes before Anton completed his circuit and threw a flame to his handiwork, I ran inside the barn and pulled the doors shut with a soft click, entombing myself in its depthless black. I could not risk lighting the lamp. Racing to the centre of the floor, I clattered into the milking stool, hoofed away swathes of straw and groped around on my hands and knees until I found the handle, and the solid nugget of metal that encased it. I pulled with all my might but of course it was no good: the padlock would not budge.

The trapdoor opened less than an inch. If I had a crowbar, I could pry it until the hinges ripped asunder. But I had no crowbar. All I could see was the silhouette of a pitch-fork resting against the far wall. I was contemplating using it to try and stab my way through the trap when the barn door creaked open.

'Is somebody in here?' Anton hissed, pallid in the moonlight. 'Cousin Dani, is that you?'

'Give me the key to the padlock,' I said. 'Or else burn the

three of us together.'

'Have you lost your mind? God damn it.' In all my hours at Anton's side, I had not once heard him curse. 'Will you get out here so we can please talk.'

'You may speak to us all if you have anything to say.'

The two prisoners beneath my feet had not made a sound thus far.

Anton replied with a vigorous shake of the head that I now understand as an expression of sheer exasperation. Wide-eyed and mute, he jabbed a finger to the ground I stood on, then brought both hands up to the side of his head, placing the palms flat across his ears.

'This is ridiculous,' he said, after his gestures failed to elicit my response. 'Close the door when you decide you've had enough.'

And with that, he withdrew.

I waited for the shake of his match-box, the rasping pull across the sandpaper, the sizzle of sulphur, the shower of sparks and detonating whoosh as the trail of gas lit up like a landing strip. But none of it materialised. Instead, I heard the farmhouse door open across the yard and Persha welcome her master back with an excited yelp.

After a further minute, I began to feel a little foolish. I had no idea what I'd witnessed, but it was no longer looking like a prelude to a torching. Rather sheepishly, I left the barn and trod the familiar path to the farmhouse back door.

Anton was at the kitchen sink, scrubbing his hands with soap. I called my greetings to the dinner table about to begin their prayers and joined father at the taps.

'Evening cousin,' he said, as if we had not spoken for several hours.

'Good evening.'

'I'll be damned if I can get this stink off.' He raised a knuckle to his nose, sniffed, winced, then plunged his hand back into the water.

I nodded dumbly, an act that required no guile on my behalf.

Leaning into my shoulder, Anton spoke so as to not disturb the prayers. 'Had a tip-off the Gestapo are in the area, looking for Jews. Gasoline's about the only thing that throws their bloodhounds off the scent. Right.' Satisfied with his hand's cleanliness at last, he dried himself on the towel and stepped away from the sink. 'All yours.'

The farm was on tenterhooks for the next two days, but the Gestapo did not come.

By Saturday night, the immediate threat was deemed to have passed. Anton and family decided to keep up appearances by going into the village that evening, where they would enjoy a simple meal at Petr's Inn and, if a musician happened to be passing through, the girls could dance the polka.

In truth, Saturday night was to be my farewell party. Upon completing a week's work, I had informed my host that I would be commencing my trek south on Monday. If I didn't leave before the savage Polish winter bit, I believed I might have stayed in Lublin for the duration, so comfortable were the terms of my lodging. But for all Anton and Hana's generosity, they were not my family.

So that evening Dami joined his cousins aboard the horse and cart and we rode the winding lane through a backwater of dilapidated farms and storks nesting on the tops of telephone poles. Watching over us from the small hill was all that remained of the area's Jews, in the sloping cemetery. There were no more bones left to bury.

Through the pine woods on the distant right lay the drab village with a population of two hundred souls. The village had always been divided: Jews traded in the centre while the Poles cleaved to the edges, tilling the land. Now it was all one. The high street where the carpenters, shoemakers and tailors had built their sturdy nests was now home to an incredulity of cuckolds, resettled party-men who could not believe their luck, spilling out of the shabby day-bar as we passed, drunk and vulgar. I had seen the same walrus moustaches and pot-bellies in Wilno. These were men like the friends of Mr. Donelaitis who'd ganged up on Moshe's friends for telling a harmless joke. Except these villagers had driven a whole block of families out of their houses, and beaten the elders to death like rats from the hayrick.

'Gentlemen,' Anton called across the street as we secured the cart.

A few of the drunks removed their hats in honour of our women. Most did not. One large moustachioed man in black holding court inside the bar to a circle of cronies seemed particularly struck by our arrival. I could feel his tracking gaze as we dismounted and shepherded our party onto the pavement, where Anton was approached by a young boy in a grey suit with knee-socks and shiny buckled shoes. After a brief negotiation, a silver zloty was traded hands and in return the boy hopped up behind the horse and crossed his feet on the creature's rump. It was only then that I recognized him as the scrubbed-up Jew-spotter from the day of the threshing machine.

I was left to dwell on this while Anton and Hana exchanged greetings with the proprietor outside the inn. Petr was tall and thin and smelled of rosewater. A crescent of wispy white hair lay over his pink scalp, lifting like a frond in the evening breeze. He dropped to his knee to take Radka and Barbora's hands as receiving royalty. Too old for such blandishment, Eva remained at my side, introducing me after the girls had skipped in to their usual window table.

'Why do you keep this one hidden in Germany?' Petr said, running a sere fingertip over the vein on the back of my hand. 'Such a handsome chap would set village heartbeats fluttering like a fox.'

'That's precisely why we keep him hidden,' Anton said. 'We've got enough work on our hands with the farm!'

'Lublin's loss is truly the turnip's gain,' Petr said, examining my fingertips before releasing them. Despite my change in circumstances since the war, I had developed little in the way of calluses. My hands still bore the suspiciously manicured look of a man who'd spent his life lifting nothing heavier than the pages of a book.

Inside the snug pine inn, Anton and Hanna sat at either end of the window table, with the two young girls between them against the glass, charitably leaving Eva and I the best view, overlooking the high street. Unfortunately, given the bar full of drunk Nazis opposite, I did not relish being a fish in a glass tank. Every time I raised my head, my eyes locked into the gaze of the tall man in black who'd been so preoccupied with our arrival.

The restaurant filled up as I sought solace in my wine. By eight o'clock, all eight tables were replete. In addition to acting as the Maître D, Petr doubled as waiter and bus-boy. For all I knew, when he disappeared into the tiny kitchen, he donned the chef's hat as well. There wasn't another member of staff to be seen. Consequently, we weren't excessively troubled by our host after the initial greeting, although when he did stop at our table between courses, it was behind my chair he invariably lingered.

The evening began pleasantly enough, though was soon tainted as my thoughts turned towards my imminent departure. When I felt tears brimming, I poured another glass of wine, which provided the sweetest of temporary relief. Before too long I was a besotted fool, prone to the most excessive of eye-watering. Another side-effect: the more I imbibed, the more worried I grew of the large man across the street, whose eyes seemed to follow me from wherever he stood, like Fra Pandolf's fabled painting of the doomed Duchess. Every time I glanced out the window, he was watching. Eventually I became so agitated, I confided my fears to Anton.

'Fellow with the ginger moustache in the black suit,' he said without turning to look.

'That's him.'

'Rest assured, cousin, you've got more to worry about from the friendly inn-keep.'

'But who is he?'

'Ilya Legrino. The only man in this village for whom death is a business plan. He owns the funeral parlour. Unfortunately he's also undertaken something of a shine to my eldest daughter.'

Now his attentions made sense, given my proximity to Eva.

'What's so bad about an undertaker?' I said.

'Ilya's a dim-wit of the highest order. And a particularly

stubborn one at that.'

I laughed. 'So you'll be fending him off until the war ends.'

'Salut,' Anton said, raising a mournful glass.

Towards the end of the evening, an accordion player and violinist strolled in off the street, positioned themselves on stools in front of Petr's bar and struck up a lively tune that soon had the families stomping along, fathers punctuating each verse with lusty whoops. After a couple of minutes, Barbora and Radka skipped up and stood in front of the musicians, hands on their hips, swinging back and forth to the rhythm. Petr swooped in from the side and pulled Barbora towards him. With his arm around her small waist, they began waltzing in a circle before he lifted the girl clean off her heels and span round holding her in his arms, depositing her back to her feet with a bow, to great applause. Eva joined them next, standing in front of the younger two with her hand on her hips, sashaying from side to side. I thought Petr might take her for a spin, too. But it was to me that Eva turned, casting a sly look. Before I knew it, I was propelled from my chair and sent stumbling onto the floor. Over my shoulder I saw Anton rocking back, face creased red and white with laughter.

'Pick her up!' a voice yelled, and I found myself doing just that, although not, I fear, as nimbly as my predecessor.

Lifting Eva was the easy part. No sooner was she cradled in my arms did the violinist double his speed, which the guests took as their cue to start drumming on the tables, sending the cutlery chinking against china. Goaded into action by their insistence, I began to turn, shuffling at first, but with a gay Eva urging me on, we were soon whirling like a Viennese carousel. The inn disappeared in a drunken blur as we sailed round and round and I amazed one and all by remaining on my feet and not flinging my cousin's daughter into the shelf of vintage cognac. After setting Eva down, more wine was poured to celebrate our performance, and I gulped down several glasses in quick succession, thirsty from the exertion.

We must have trotted back to the farm on the horse and cart, but for some reason, I have no further recollection of the evening.

I struggled through Sunday morning with the sorest of heads, milked the cows and fed the rest of the animals in a fugue-like trance before scrubbing up at the kitchen sink and donning my host's spare suit for church. The priest's sermon washed over without making much of an impression, much like the cold sink.

That afternoon, Eva helped me pack a bag of provisions for my departure, and we sat on the bed, laughing at our performance of the night before. There was a moment where I thought I might lean forward and cradle her once again in my arms, but I refrained. Leaving the farm was already painful enough; I had no right to complicate it further.

The big tin bath that hung on the garden fence was carried into the kitchen that evening and put in front of the fire. Water was heated in the copper, and transferred by bucket. The children bathed first, youngest to oldest, then Barbora and Radka went straight to bed. Eva took to the water next, adding her coconut shampoo into the soup, followed by her mother and father, and finally myself.

Alone in my room, I made a final tour to ensure all was packed ready for the morning and saw my photograph of Shoshana on the boards between the bottom of my bed and the wardrobe. I bent down to retrieve it. As my fingers grasped the paper, I could have sworn I heard a faint 'snap' in the air, like the firing of a rubber band. A pain flared up the back of my leg, as if the calf muscle had been whipped by the same phantom band. The entire incident was so unremarkable - I had not stumbled on my ankle, or even twisted it. At most, I was suffering from a tweaked muscle.

I retired early to bed, since dawn was to be my departure. But for the first time at the farm, sleep was elusive. I could not find a comfortable groove in the mattress, and twisted this way and that, each turn aggravating the back of my leg, still sore from the tweaking.

After two hours of increasingly sweaty and fretful restlessness, I gave up, lit the candle and heaved the dusty family Bible off the bedside cabinet.

I awoke with the birds, finding myself propped semi-upright against the pillows, the good book open on my chest. I had made it to the furthest reaches of page two.

Within five seconds of regaining consciousness, I became aware of the most abject pain. If the skin of my left shin had been split open and the bone replaced with a red hot poker, I would have not been in more discomfort. Gingerly, like the child who fears a fiend has stolen in under the covers, I grasped the sheet and peeled it back. My shin was intact, but the foot beneath was a purple, swollen monstrosity.

I tried to ignore the transformation, summoning the indomitable spirit of Gregor Samsa. I was lucky to have made it through the night with only a mutated foot – poor Gregor woke up to find his entire body had morphed into a beetle! It was inconceivable I had inflicted this much damage by the mere act of bending down to pick up a photograph. So I simply refused to believe it, despite the overwhelming evidence to the contrary.

The rest of the house was stirring. Children thumped from room to room, Eva softly sang. I imagined her at the mirrored dresser, brushing her coconut hair in its reflection. A wholesome smell of baking arose through the floor from the kitchen. We were to have one last breakfast together, as a family. Anton had offered to drive me the first twenty miles south, but I was determined to make the journey under my own steam. The family had already done so much.

It was time for me to get up. I had trapped a nerve, that was all. Once I was on my feet, I would soon be back to normal. Such was the swelling, it took five minutes to get my shoe on. The mere act of getting onto my feet was trickier still, since the left one was reluctant to bear its share of the burden, firing molten bolts up to the knee in protest. But I succeeded in setting the shoe down, and kept it down. I even managed to hobble a few steps around the bed, and persuaded myself the pain was tolerable. Hoisting a bag as heavy as a wild boar, I backed out of the bedroom, closing the door for the last time.

Downstairs at breakfast, Anton and Hanna were putting a brave front on my departure for the benefit of the girls, who had grown quite fond of their old teacher. I could not respond in like. All my effort was required just to keep the pain from contorting my features that I was quite incapable of a smile. I must have looked aggrieved, as if I was being evicted from the farm against my will. Several times I was told it was not too late to change my mind, but all I could do was nod. Of the bounty of mushrooms and eggs assembled before my eyes, I was able to eat a modestly-heaped triangle of toast. Eva offered to wrap a pastry for the road, but I declined. I couldn't have carried another crumb.

At the vertiginous descent of the front door step, I was so distracted by anguish that I was barely able to mumble my goodbyes. Eva looked as if she was about to grab my arm at one point, but she composed herself and stepped back into the protective fold of her parents. In this most miserable of manners, I departed, every movement an agony.

Only when I heard the door close behind did I abandon my attempts to walk without a limp. The exertion of those thirty seconds had converted the shirt on my back to the consistency of a damp dish-cloth: I was sodden with sweat before even reaching the farmyard barn. But I kept going, unable to believe I had crippled myself picking up a photograph. Once the heart was pumping in the fresh air, I'd feel right as rain.

Consulting Anton's hand-drawn map, I paused against the lane's first telegraph pole, launching a stork into startled flight. I could only marvel at the grace with which it recovered its trajectory, gliding under such steely wings. My own stuttering progress below would resemble a fox that had chewed off its own paw.

Instead of following the village road, Anton's route sent me over cemetery hill. Cursing my ruined foot, I schlepped it up step after step and collapsed at the summit on a plump pillow of grass. The vast southern horizon spread out before me, and behind, the Popolowsky's smoke signal of a chimney beckoned my return. I was defeated, utterly.

Twenty minutes later, I fell through the front door into Hanna's clutch, an incoherent wreck. She led me first to the parlour couch, where my shoe was prised off the bloated appendage. The men later carried me back upstairs to

Barbora's bed, freshly made since my departure. I watched tablets dissolve in water and fell into strange, ecstatic sleep.

Waking intermittently, I refused all offers of medical help, still convinced the swelling would go down of its own accord. But by evening, my entire leg had turned purple, and I relented.

The doctor arrived shortly before midnight. After a thorough examination, he announced that my non-accident of bending down had severed the tendons from my ankle to the knee, and from the ankle to the toes. A clean break of the ankle bone would have resulted in less damage. Alternating cold and heat treatments were to be applied to the afflicted areas, but the real cure was rest.

I was ordered off my feet for fourteen days.

12

For the first forty-eight hours, I wallowed in a stupor of pain-killers. When I could hobble around on a pair of wooden crutches, I made myself useful around the house with chores that could be performed seated, or slumped on the floor. One of the first of these was to clean out the large cupboard under the stairs – more of a spare room than a closet - where I found Anton's set of encyclopaedias languishing under a blanket, two dozen volumes bound in scarlet cloth. Since the invasion, families were only allowed to own books in the German language, so these encyclopaedias had been hidden away.

I have always been powerless to control myself in the presence of a good book. After the cupboard was tidy, I took the first encyclopaedia to the kitchen table, and began to scan through the entries, imagining myself back behind the soft green lamps of the University reading room.

Before long I was joined by Radka and Barbora, enraptured by the sight of a man so brazenly turning Polish pages. Radka was young enough to have never seen an encyclopaedia, and was amazed to discover that it contained the sum of all human knowledge. When I told her the book on the table contained only words beginning with the letter 'A', she begged me for more. But the day was drawing to a close and Anton would be home soon for dinner. I contented the girls with a cautionary explanation of the effects of Absinthe before ending the lesson with a quick recap of the early successes of Emiliano Zapata, a subject I chose to deliberately dampen their curiosity. Quite the opposite, in fact. I was still explaining the ins and outs of the Mexican Revolution when dinner was served, much to their father's bemusement.

Later than evening, I cornered Anton with my crutches, confessed my crimes and advanced a certain proposition of my own. The brief schooling round the kitchen table had rekindled a spark that I had not felt for many years: I yearned to teach again. It was, I argued, the perfect fit. Thanks to Hans

Frank, the Polish lands were being converted into an intellectual wasteland. Barbora and Radka had received no education since June. Their extended summer holiday had turned into a six-month hiatus and there was no end in sight, like most things. Without some form of academic instruction, their intellectual development may never recover. At the moment, through no fault of their own, the girls were driving their sister and mother to distraction.

Anton was initially reluctant. I was talking about a profession the Nazis honoured by sending educators to the Ghettos, or for immediate execution. Teaching children was no longer a kindness, but an act of war. I reminded him that, should the Gestapo come knocking, we were already in enough trouble. Having a Polish encyclopaedia on the sideboard could hardly make matters worse. Anton had been brave enough to provide a refuge for three of us in or underneath his property. There were few benefits he could receive in return. Why continue to deny his children an education when I was willing and able to provide?'

'School', such as it was, began the next morning.

Eva and I rose early to put together a programme of study: Languages and Mathematics on alternate mornings, followed by History and Geography in the afternoons. Eva was keen to help, and offered to review the girl's written work at the end of the day, to allow me to concentrate on the next.

After breakfast we cleared away plates and cups and wiped the table down ready for work. The girls were delighted to see their school notebooks, which had lain untouched in their satchels since the beginning of the holidays. With one eye on the fields for any sign that the Germans were coming, I began my first 'seminar' in several years.

At Kiel I liked to start the semester with an introduction to Socratic Dialogue. At the farmhouse, it was basic nouns and verbs, which caused me far more difficulty. Neither will I pretend I found the shift from young adults to infants easy in terms of temperament, but the work was stimulating in a way I had not experienced since the days of the Akiva house on Pilies Street. I knew instantly I'd made the right decision.

Keeping the sisters engaged after their initial excitement wore off was a challenge I met with humour and hopefully good grace, although my patience was tested by the girl's third round of uncontrollable giggles. Generally they were grateful students - a courtesy, I gathered, that their previous teacher had not been extended. For the first time since Sunday, I forgot all about my bruised foot, and slept soundly from the minute my head lay across the pillow.

On the second morning we were interrupted by two boys from the village who had come looking to play. Eva announced that both girls were poorly with a bug, and were unlikely to recover anytime soon. But the boys were not to be dissuaded: they returned on the third day with a basket of fruit from their parents, and again on Friday.

Over the course of the weekend, I argued that, should the boys also make the trek on Monday, we might consider asking them to stay. Anton pointed out that the two lads had been amongst the most enthusiastic Jew-spotters at the ritual of the threshing machine. In that case, I told him, they needed an education more than most. Anton ceded way, convinced my mission was an exercise in futility. I would be the first man in Poland to persuade a pair of teenage boys to voluntarily sit a spelling test.

Not only did the boys return on Monday, but they brought three friends. Upon my insistence, Eva swung the front door wide enough to reveal the terrible truth of what was being perpetrated in the kitchen. Such were the initial sneers at our exercise books that I believed Anton was the shrewder judge of character after all. But when the boys understood that the only way to see the girls was around the teacher's table, like the good old days, they grudgingly agreed to join in, 'until we get bored'. They lasted a full day, and came back the following morning with another friend. By the end of that week, there were forty children attending, so many that we had to run separate sessions. Each group met for two-and-a-half hours, with the last children quietly departing in the evening.

The kitchen table could no longer accommodate the new numbers, and I was also worried about its exposed position in the centre of the room. Two seated children could be easily explained; twenty was a different matter entirely. Eva and I prepared a secret classroom in the cupboard under the stairs.

The venture had taken off in ways I had never expected. Now a school was up and running, I was reluctant to walk away from it all, despite the fact I was finally free do so without the aid of crutches. My plan was to train Eva from homework marker to teacher's assistant, to be my eventual replacement. Now that Anton had seen the benefits of home education, he had given Eva his blessing to work alongside me full-time. The two of us became very close, a fact not lost upon some of the older children, but we maintained our professionalism throughout. Day and night, night and day.

Our expansion from a family concern to a fully-fledged village school brought other challenges, in terms of discretion. I feared that the students' parents – many of whom had enthusiastically participated in mass murder at the Nazis' behest – would balk at breaking Hans Frank's ban on Polish education. But in this regard alone, we were aided by the fathers' fervent nationalism. They may have been simple men with violent prejudices, but they were not prepared to stand back and watch their heritage be steamrollered. There were no loose lips to sink our secret ship. Parents didn't talk about neighbours or politics or Germans. Since the murder of the Jews, people didn't talk about anything anymore, Eva explained. The whole community was too stunned by what had been unleashed.

Our students too were natural masters of the cloak-and-dagger. They entered the house from the side door and travelled in small groups or alone. Once inside, I ushered them into the 'classroom' and quietly closed the cupboard door. They carried encyclopaedias tucked deep inside works of German literature so that the soldiers would be convinced they were learning the language of the new Reich. We sat cross-legged on a rug on the floor, Turkish style: there were no desks or furniture that hinted of a school, in case the Germans stormed in. When lessons were over, I would let the children out one by one into the fields, where they came under Anton's watchful eye. They never went down the main lane where German soldiers patrolled, sometimes pausing at

Polish homes and eating their bacon and drinking their beer
and complimenting them for learning German and only
occasionally, if provoked by boredom or beauty, raping their
daughters.

The knock at our house came with the first snow of the
season, in the middle of the night. When I awoke, the curtains
were irradiated by the brightest of white lights. I thought
dawn had broken with a vengeance and Anton was calling for
help with the milking. Stumbling from bed, I looked out the
window on a vista more North Pole than southern Poland, the
covering of snow ghostlier still by the light of a gibbous moon.
I followed a series of freshly dimpled tracks leading off the
main road and my eyes sloped to rest at a sleigh stopped in
front of the barn.

I crept downstairs towards voices, but stopped halfway at
the sight of police trousers and boots on the front door step.
Anton was holding a candle, a coat wrapped over his pyjamas.
Despite the cold air flicking the flame of his wick, he had not
asked the Gendarme to come inside.

'Very sorry to be banging you up in the middle of the
night,' the man said, shaking his plump jowls. 'But I've
received intelligence about your daughters' safety it would be
foolish not to look into.'

'My girls are all tucked up in bed,' Anton said. 'We
appreciate your concern, Master Gendarme, but I'm afraid
you've been misinformed.'

'If the young ones share a room with Eva, they may be in
more danger than you know.'

'Now you're talking in riddles.'

The Belorussian Gendarme inserted a snow-caked foot
into the rapidly closing gap. 'I've had reports Eva has been
giving the other two lessons in Slavic language and history,
which is a serious offence against the Reich.'

'The self-same language you're speaking now, you mean.'

'That is not the point. The law is the law.'

'Reports from who?'

'Not the usual gossip-monger, or I wouldn't be here.' The
Gendarme shook snow off his boot. 'Maybe I'd turn a blind eye

if this nonsense were just within the family. But from what I hear, Eva's got half the boys from the village at it. Secret classroom, notepads, books, the whole works. If you know about this, old friend, now's the time to speak up.'

'Anton knows nothing.' I came down the last two steps into the candlelight. 'It's all my fault.'

'Damien Plotz?' the Gendarme said, unfazed by my appearance.

'At your service. The lessons were all my idea, the cupboard under the stairs, everything.' I turned to Anton. 'I'm sorry, cousin. I just couldn't bear to see the children growing up without an education.'

The Gendarme chuckled. His was a broad, gap-toothed face that in other circumstances could have been regarded as friendly. 'So it's true. I hardly believed it myself.'

'Half true. Eva's involvement is idle gossip, nothing more. I simply offered to keep the children from getting under her feet as she chored. Eva knew nothing of any lessons, and would have thrown me out if she had.'

'My cousin has been invalided these past few weeks, with too much time on his hands,' Anton said. 'I'd thought the injury was to his ankle, but evidently it was his head we should've had examined.'

'And what a head it must be,' the Gendarme said. 'To plunder so many languages while the rest of us can only manage one. You also know German, I take it?'

'Naturally. Hamburg is my home.'

'You won't mind if I verify that while I'm here. Identification papers, please, Herr Plotz.'

I did not know what to say. Anton had talked about getting me forged papers in the city, but the venture had so far come to nothing.

'Lost,' he said. 'Unfortunately he got a little drunk at Petr's Inn and misplaced his wallet.'

'Making quite the fool of himself with the general cavorting, so I heard.'

I confessed to my crimes against the polka, for I could hardly have worsened my plight.

'Oh well,' the Gendarme said. 'I'll just have to take him, as is.'

Anton said, 'You're taking him?'

'If what cousin Dani says is true, Eva will be able to remain here with her sisters. Unless you want me to take them all, of course, for a speedier exoneration?'

'Eva is innocent of all charges,' I said. 'Just as I am guilty.'

'Good man,' the Gendarme said. 'You'll go a long way. Now go and wrap up nice and warm, it's bitter out.'

And that was how it happened. What could I do? If I made any attempt to shimmy down the drainpipe, the girls would be taken in my place. So I dressed for my punishment, in the shabbiest clothes available. At least I would spare Anton the loss of a good suit.

A studied calm settled over me in those final few minutes. Perhaps prompted by the snow's vivid gleam at the window, I believed I had been granted a rare moment of insight. I had been on the run since leaving Kiel in the winter of 1938. Soon I would be at rest. All things considered, I had been shielded from many of the horrors visited upon my people. My experience was largely a closeted one. Even now, as the sands of time were running out, my disguise as a German meant that I was treated with a remarkable degree of civility. I could ask for nothing more.

When I descended the stairs five minutes later, all the Popolowskis were clustered in the kitchen, sobbing. Only our embraces spoke as I passed from one to the other, until I came to Eva's shoulders, last and for the longest. 'Be strong for me,' I breathed into her coconut hair. 'You are the glue that binds this house together.'

The Gendarme's hand steered me out the door into the harsh lunar glare. Where the sleigh had looked empty, there now sat a large SS officer holding the huskies' reins. I supposed I was to be transferred into his custody, where the civility would end. As we approached, the Gendarme opened the side latch, bundled me in to the front seat next to the German, and then squeezed in at my side, his fleshy thigh on quite intimate terms with my own as he squirmed to close the door. He introduced the German as Untersturmführer Amon Göth, a name I had not heard before.

'Well,' the Gendarme prompted with a dig to the ribs, displeased at my silence. 'Convey to my colleague the excellent news.'

'Y-yes,' I stammered. 'Umm... what news?'

The Gendarme sighed, and proceeded to explain in a sing-song voice as if talking to a dim-witted child. 'Your name would be a good place to start. That you are the man we've been looking for. That you speak fluent Polish and Belorussian in addition to German, and that you are a resident of Hamburg.'

I understood from this that the Gendarme spoke little German himself, and that I was expected to translate news of my own capture. Having little choice in the matter, I obliged. Göth continued to stare at his dogs as I spoke, his head jerking curtly at my qualifications. I finished to the sound of the wind sculpting snowdrifts, and was prompted again by the irritated voice on my right.

'And that it is an honour to ride in the Untersturmführer's cabin.'

Once delivered, my translation had the intended effect of spurring Göth into action. He tugged his reins and the huskies began transcribing a wide arc through the snow that led us back onto the main village road.

As we left Anton's property, I noticed two enormous sleighs fall in some twenty yards at our rear, empty with only six policemen between them. Even so, I wondered why such a show of force was needed to arrest one teacher.

The three sleighs continued to plough snow; twenty minutes became thirty and thirty became forty. On the hill tops, the temperature plummeted. When Göth stopped under a tree to urinate, the Gendarme reached behind and retrieved two blankets, one of which he placed on the driver's seat and the second over his own knees.

'We'll get you one later,' he said to me. 'Finest hand-woven woollen throw. Jewish specialty of the region.'

The further we travelled, the more relentlessly the German drove his dogs. A tense expectancy gripped our cabin as the two men studied the lunar landscape. I couldn't understand what they were waiting for. If they were going to execute me, one frozen hillside was as good as any other. The policemen behind us wouldn't even need to dig a hole. I would lie entombed within the drift until the first thaw of spring. In my last allotment of time, my thoughts turned to the identity of Eva's betrayer, the Gendarme's source. How strange that somebody had implicated Anton's own flesh and blood, his eldest daughter no less, in place of Cousin Dami. I could only imagine that somebody had heard how close the two of us had become, and wished to render us apart. Had heard, or perhaps seen, from the vantage point of a bar-stool opposite Petr's Inn on a Saturday evening several weeks ago. Ilya Legrino, the only man in the village for whom death was a business plan. Why would Eva's suitor turn denouncer? Love during wartime was a dark and twisted flower. Anton had told me of a couple in Lublin who had hidden a Jew in their attic. Alone in the house all day, the wife and the Jew fell in love. The woman betrayed her own husband to the Germans. The Gestapo arrived, took her husband away, killed him, and she lived with the Jew. That weekend, the Jew had a heart attack.

13

The wooden synagogue grew out of the distant village like a mountain. Constructed on a square plan, its stepped pyramidal roof was unmistakable to my well-trained eye, and to Amon Göth, who stood erect over the reins as we surfed the final mile. His blanket fell to the floor as he rose. I did not offer to pick it up.

Our dogs skidded to a halt by the synagogue steps but the other two sleighs raced along the sides and stopped at the back. I heard the six policemen crunch down and disappear into the loose settlement of houses. Lights went on in bedroom windows, shouts cried out, and there were several loud crashes. The policemen went from door to door, rousting inhabitants.

Several minutes later, they returned to parade a column of sixteen dazed souls in nightgowns and long-johns: three children, a few young adults, and the rest adults of my age and older. One dignified grandmother wore nothing but a prayer shawl draped around her bony shoulders. While the ragged band passed our sleigh, I studied each face for signs of familiarity, but found none.

There was some misunderstanding, I wanted to tell the Gendarme. These people were innocent. They had nothing to do with my teaching.

The policemen herded them up the steps into the synagogue. When the prisoners were browbeaten into silence inside, we followed Göth out of the sleigh and up into the temple. Pausing at the memorial board, I could see down the aisle to where the villagers stood around the bimah's pedestal in the centre.

Göth strode past them towards the far end and I feared he might deign to address us from the rabbi's seat, but he stopped at the open end of the bimah and produced a black leather notebook from his tunic pocket. Using the eternal light of the menorah, he flicked through the first half of his book until he found an empty page. He wrote the date in a precise, elegant script, November 19th, 1941 and then paused, nodding at me.

'Names,' the Gendarme hissed at my side.

'Damien Plotz.'

'Not you, fool,' the Gendarme said and pointed. 'Them.'

I turned to the nearest Jew and asked his name, which I then repeated to the expectant Göth, who added it to his book. In this manner, I went around the circle, Göth pausing only to clarify the spelling of a particularly troublesome Semitic syllable. The adults in the group appeared relieved by the German's adherence to bureaucratic procedure and proudly offered their names. I, too, started to breathe more deeply between names. This was a registration or census, nothing more. But then I came to the first child, a slip of a girl cleaving to her mother's leg. Instead of recording her name, Göth wrote 'ein Stuck' (one thing). After all Jews except me had been accounted for, I watched Göth tally his column. At the bottom of the page, he wrote, 'Drei Stuck unter sixteen jahr alt'.

Tucking the book back inside his tunic, Göth smiled at me and said, 'As enemy of the Reich, and in accordance with the Führer's will, you are hereby sentenced to death.'

When he turned back to the Jews at the bimah, I understood that the proclamation was not meant for me, but for them. I had been employed for the night as a translator. From the pained expressions on the villagers' faces, they had already understood and did not require my linguistic services. A curly haired youth with a bloody lip who had been staring intently at me for the last minute raised a trembling finger and jabbed it in my direction when I finished.

'Why are you doing this?' he shouted.

Göth ordered the Belorussian to make a final head-count. While he did so, the curly youth continued to drill through to the back of my skull. His quarrel was not with the police, but specifically with me. Somehow he knew I belonged with the others at the bimah.

When the Gendarme was done, Göth removed his book and ensured that the number present corresponded to the written entry. Satisfied, he signalled for the policemen to lead the Jews out to the rear of building, behind where the Torah ark lay.

There was only one-way this was going to end. I had sentenced the villagers to death and now I would be forced to witness their execution. As the Gendarme and I filed out at the rear of the column, I stumbled, held myself against the pulpit and muttered a prayer of strength. If I broke down now, Amon Göth would know the truth about his new translator, and those who had sheltered me would be next for his little black book. With every fibre I could summon, I held myself together and headed towards the door, eyes fixed on the empty balcony above.

Outside, I followed the line down the steps and around the side of vestibule. The snow had blown deep against the wall here, and I made a pantomime of losing my shoe in the drift. The Gendarme shrugged at Schott in apology for my clumsiness. As expected, neither man waited. I collapsed to my knees when they had cleared the far corner, and pressed my fingers to my ears. Muffled, I could still hear the policemen's crude oaths and the terrified cries of the children. From their parents and elders, only silence now. I was sure I heard the Gendarme call out for me, although it might have been the final order, because very soon after a volley of shots rang out. When the firing ceased, I unplugged my fingers and strained my ears against the wind. The children's cries had stopped.

I followed the leaking trails of smoke to the back of the synagogue, but the guns were only resting. The men of the village had been made to watch their loved ones die, a spectacle that had left many of their leggings stained with urine. Women and children first, I thought, the old seafaring command from stories of yore. Black blood pulsed amongst the tangle of sprawled limbs as the policemen picked over the remains, looting jewels and headscarves. At the Gendarme's orders, one of his officers pulled the prayer shawl from the old woman's shoulders, neatly folded the garment in two and handed it to me.

'For the ride home,' the Gendarme said.

When the bodies were plucked clean, the menfolk were forced to heap their wives, children and mothers into one of the waiting vehicles, before receiving a shot to back of the head. They lay where they fell, friends and family slumped together, a sleigh of broken dolls.

14

In every life there are events that redraw the contours of one's sense of existence. Afterward, all is lost. The past becomes inaccessible, like an island at full tide. For me, the cut off point was the night of November 19th, 1941. I had encountered death before, in the guise of Ronan Kesselman's hanging for attempted escape. I had read the Chaze's purloined reports about the pits at Ponary, but that was a distinctively Lithuanian phenomenon, I had told myself, particular to a certain time and place. But to spend a night participating, however tangentially, in the mass slaughter of innocent civilians was an encounter to rupture the soul.

I do not remember the sleigh ride home, nor the jokes I translated between Göth and the Belorussian, giddy as schoolboys after the night's successful liquidation. The other two vehicles did not follow behind, nor did I enquire after them.

We returned along a deserted main road, by-passing Anton's village altogether to enter the south-east outskirts of the city of Lublin, where I finally expected to be locked up in a German cell. Instead, we stopped at a crossroad in front of a small train station.

'Gentlemen,' Göth said. 'Until the morning.'

'Goodnight, sir.' The Belorussian gestured for me to translate. 'I take it you were satisfied with my guards.'

Göth sniffed and dabbed a white handkerchief to his nose. 'They served their purpose.'

The Gendarme stepped out onto the snowy road and stood there holding the cabin door open. I was also expected to disembark. With his other hand, he pointed out a large house on the opposite corner, a civilian home with a wall and a flower garden.

Göth pulled on his reigns and the sleigh resumed its glide into the city. After watching him disappear, I turned to study the house that the Gendarme was walking towards, digging keys from his pocket.

'You'll do mostly interpreting for the Untersturmführer,' he said. 'In the evenings, you'll teach me to speak the language. Unfortunately it's impossible for a man of my background to advance up the ladder without adequate German.'

He stopped at his gate, waiting for me to catch up.

Against every instinct, my feet started delivering me to the pavement.

'The job includes room and board.' The Gendarme's purple nose twitched to emphasize my good fortune. 'Better for a city man like you than being stuck out in the fields. We make a good team, you and I.'

I watched from the porch as he turned the living room lights on, including a decorative vine of tiny swastika emblazoned-bulbs along the windowsill and a garish glowing Bible tableaux on the kitchen archway. Only when I followed inside did I recognize the scene as the Nativity, Mary, Joseph and the baby Jesus surrounded by a menagerie of farmyard animals with eyes that burnt red as coals.

Mein Host banged about from cupboard to drawer in the kitchen, maintaining a line of babbling small talk that thankfully required little input from myself. I stood rooted to a thick Oriental rug before the coffee table. Compared to the Christmas decorations, the rest of the living room was sober and would have verged on tasteful were it not for the sheer amount of paintings and ornaments crammed onto the shelves and sideboard, enough to stock an antique shop.

'Sit, sit.' The gendarme brushed past with a tray on which he had arranged two opened bottles of beer and a bowl of pickled gherkins. Relaxing into a winged armchair, he placed the tray on the coffee table and span it like a roulette wheel until a beer bottle rattled at my knee.

'It's late,' I said, although technically it was early.

'Just one, a toast.'

'I can hardly keep my eyes open. If tomorrow is my first day on the job, I need to make a good impression. I hope you will not think me ungrateful.'

'Pah.' He waved a dismissive hand, quick to disguise his

widowers's loneliness. 'Please, go. I prefer drinking alone if you want to know the truth. Away and get your beauty sleep. I'll show you up.'

The spare room was bare, but spotlessly clean. Bed, chair, wardrobe, portrait of Adolf Hitler on the wall.

Thankfully, my host did not linger. I waited by the door until I heard the stairs creak under his stockinged feet, then backed onto the mattress and slumped against the wall, my head coming to rest against the clammy paint. I removed the grandmother's prayer shawl I'd been given and cradled it in my lap. Reaching to the head of the bed, I shook the plump pillow out its case, bunched the cotton sleeve into a gag, clamped it between my teeth and began to cough hot, tearless jags that tore my gut to shreds.

Two hours later, I rose and silently crept down stairs. The Genadarme was already up, eating porridge in the kitchen in his underpants and sock-garters.

I glanced around the kitchen. A police uniform hung in a clear plastic bag from the back door handle. Eight beer bottles from last night drained next to the sink.

'I only eat oatmeal, Monday to Friday,' the Gendarme said. 'Need anything else for breakfast, put in an order with the butcher. We'll divvy up the bills at the end of the week.'

'Oatmeal's fine.'

'Grab a bowl. I'll give you the low-down.'

There was a whole shelf of bowls next to the fridge, from what looked like a dozen different fine porcelain collections. Not one of them matched. It was like the extravagant mix of paintings and figurines in the living room. I realised with a terrible shudder that almost everything the Gendarme owned had once belonged to the Jews he'd liquidated.

'Not that hungry, to be honest,' I said. 'Do you have coffee?'

'Don't drink the stuff. There might be some knocking around.'

I found it in a cupboard caked with flour from a split bag, tiny little termites ticking over the white dunes. Camp Coffee, in a bottle, gummed to the shelf on a sticky black ring.

The Gendarme didn't possess a kettle, so I set a heavy pan to boil on the stove. I spurned the offer of a chair and leant against the worktop, professing a bad back. My new employer began explaining the various organisational hierarchies of the new Poland, and my place amongst them.

My duties as an interpreter would be split between the Belorussian and German police stations. I had already met Amon Göth. Under his administration, the gendarmerie had two areas of duty. The first was the standard fare of day-to-day policing: preserving peace amongst the locals; resolving social and familial quarrels; investigating fraud and theft and assault.

'Our and bread and butter,' the Gendarme said. 'Or it used to be, before the war.'

As a representative of the Belorussian police, I would naturally wear the uniform. The Gendarme had picked up two white shirts from the dry-cleaners yesterday; I might as well have one now, since we were about the same proportions around the neck and chest.

'Most of your language skills will be used on what the Germans call Political Matters.'

'I'm no politician,' I said.

'Don't worry. We get to root out all the undesirables, most of them foreign but a few homegrown. The agitators, partisans, Communists, Soviet co-workers, sympathisers, anyone who's even suspected of anti-Nazi moves.'

'Root out?'

He twinkled before saying, 'Conveying *executive measures.*'

'Right.'

'And then of course, the Aktions.'

'Like last night.'

'The Jews are dug in all over the place, but we're flushing them out, one nest at a time.'

'Are there many?'

'Göth has drawn up a new list. You alright with that kind of fieldwork? The last interpreter was a sensitive lad. We worked out a little deal, to spare him. There's ways I could protect you - '

'I just want to make sure I'm well rested next time,' I said. 'I'm sorry if I gave a bad impression.'

He shrugged magnanimously. 'Partly my fault. I'll try and give you fair warning next time.'

A plan was already forming in my head. If I had access to the list of villages, I could get a message out and warn the inhabitants what was coming. That might be a tall order: it didn't sound like the Gendarme himself knew the location of the Aktions much in advance. The Belorussian police were second tier, not particularly trusted by the Germans.

'That's all you need to know for now,' the Gendarme said, placing his empty bowl in the sink. 'The rest you'll pick up on the job.'

He unhooked his shirt from the door handle, went upstairs, returned five minutes later in full dress, turned off the stove I was still waiting at and set the saucepan aside. The water had yet to boil, my measure of Camp Coffee congealing at the bottom of the mug.

Outside, a thaw was underway. Early morning traffic had rendered the immaculate snowfall drear and grey slush. We tramped along the road, passed a tobacconists and a dry-cleaners on the corner of a dark alley. The Belorussian police headquarters was less than a mile away, but we only got as far as the shops before coming to a stop.

The level-crossing barrier was down. Angry, hooting traffic snarled up behind a throng of commuters in hats and long coats at the barrier. An immense, apparently endless Deutsche Reichsbahn train press-ganged into military evacuation was stranded at the platform, soldiers leaning out the carriage windows, smoking, singing songs. Banners unfurled along the roof swore a variety of inventive deaths to the Russians. The lower ranking passenger locomotive had been shunted onto the side tracks while the transporter was being repaired.

'It's been stuck there for forty-five minutes,' a businessman blustered as we shouldered up to the barrier. 'Broken rear axle, apparently. How long do these things take to get fixed?'

'Does this look like a train driver's uniform?' the Gendarme bristled, thumbing his chest. 'Make way, make way, police coming through.'

I followed him across to the station on the other side of the road, where a larger crowd had gathered. A cordon of German soldiers were guarding the station doors, preventing access. Behind them, the ticket hall was deserted. While the train was being repaired, the station facilities were reserved exclusively for the SS, en route to the Eastern Front. Regular commuters had been escorted outside to make way. Fairly smarting from the eviction, factory and office workers united in complaint. Children snaked through the dense forest of limbs, making mischief from their elder's woes. I felt a questing tug at my hip pocket and span round, ready to pounce, but the youngster had disappeared. Somewhere behind us, a woman shrieked. Bedlam was on the verge of breaking loose. I watched as the Gendarme raised an arm and waved for me.

'Damien. Herr Plotz. Here!'

I had indeed become separated from my new employer in the melee. But I was standing behind him, not in front. Granted, the face the Gendarme was currently beseeching did bear a certain resemblance to my own, but the body shielded from view belonged to a sturdy SS officer. As soon as the Gendarme thrust a hand on that studded epaulette, he realised his mistake.

'Please. I'm sorry -'

But without a translator, he was unable to explain himself, resorting to childish mime. I hung back, watching him squirm before that mighty officer, who did not appreciate being manhandled.

'My God, you're a police man, too,' the German raged, taking in the Belorussian's uniform. 'Captain's stripes, you can't even speak the language. No wonder this country's so absolutely fucked.'

'Very sorry - '

'Ten engineers dicking around and not one of them knows what to do! We've been on the rails for a day with no problems at all. Then we get to Poland and boom, the whole world grinds to a fucking halt! The payphone's out of order. The tobacconist doesn't even sell Nordlands! Then I come out here and get an earful from this rabble, a bloody disgrace after all we've done for them. If you don't get your people under control, Captain, I will.'

I could stand by no longer. I stepped forward and offered my services. After I'd translated the officer's rant, the Gendarme put a whistle to his lips to quell the crowd, then stopped and pulled me close.

'Tell him they might have some Nordlands next to the dry-cleaners.'

I pointed out the Tabak sign across the road. The SS officer made off without uttering another word, hurling himself forward like a ball-player in a scrum.

When the crowd closed again behind us, the Gendarme was standing next to a group of workers in gas company caps and overalls. The shortest, meanest-looking one crossed his arms high up on his chest and said, 'If they pay you enough to take that crap, I'm in the wrong job.'

His friends concurred, lowing like cattle.

'You saw his rank,' the Gendarme said. 'What was I supposed to do?'

One of the men made a crude suggestion and the others laughed, then formed a circle and began muttering. A loose bag underneath the Gendarme's left eye twitched as if a fly was trapped beneath the skin. He was spared further embarrassment when another spat erupted further down the line. An ejected commuter was frantically pointing across the No Man's Land of concrete into the station restaurant.

Few of us saw the outrage with our own eyes. But word spread like fire over harvest stubble. Two of the elite SS, after finishing their complimentary breakfast of bread and sausage, had enticed a couple of younger waitresses out from behind the grill. Proprietorial arms around thin shoulders, the officers paraded the women past the tables at the window, in full view of the evicted Poles, right through the length of the restaurant into the men's bathroom, from where they had not returned.

As I strained to see into the restaurant for myself, an

object whistled over my head. A plate-glass window detonated behind the cordon of soldiers at the entrance. Thinking the explosion had come from within, the soldiers span round, and a second rock landed between a set of German shoulder blades. Ten inches south of denting the back of his skull. All around me, Poles were on their knees, tearing up the ground for rubble.

'There's a phone in the dry-cleaners.' The Gendarme scanned for reinforcements but found only myself. 'Call the station before we're mopping up a bloodbath.'

Rifles volleyed as I barged through the mob to the level-crossing. I froze mid-stride, cringing. A flurry of shots and then no more. Silence. The Germans had fired over the protesters' heads to restore order. No more missiles rained down on their cordon. An uneasy truce seemed to hold.

I hopped the barrier and sprinted up the street towards the shops by the Gendarme's house. Hurtling from the other direction, two young Poles swerved around me, one of them dropping an object that bounced into the gutter. I called out but they didn't hear me and didn't stop. In the road I kicked through slush, unearthing the leather wallet they had dropped. Turned inside out, and picked clean of cash. All that remained in the wallet was a Waffen-SS identification card. It belonged to the officer the Gendarme had just upset, Oberführer Harry Mohnke. I recognised the raging face from his photograph.

I span round to face the narrow alley next to the dry-cleaners. A pair of black leather boots splayed out from behind a dumpster bin. I announced myself as the Gendarme's translator. No answer. Nobody else was watching us. All eyes were on the siege on the other side of the road. I crept into the gloomy alleyway and peered around the dry-cleaner's bin.

Oberführer Mohnke lay propped against the wall, ambushed before he could buy his Nordlands. One of the two fleeing youths had probably been hiding where I stood now, at the alley's entrance; his accomplice had pushed the German in. They'd fought. Mohnke's had fallen backward, or been pushed. His tunic was torn open, one missing button, his cap dislodged. The flattened back of his head was glued to the wall with a paste of blood and brain.

Gagging, I stumbled away, turning towards the light. Over the stalled traffic, I could hear the futile piping of the Gendarme's whistle in front of the train station. I looked back at the gleaming insignia of a senior SS colonel's grey-green tunic, the pair of oak leaves on his silver braided collar, and that German jaw that had been only ten minutes ago been mistaken for my own.

Hiding behind the dumpster, I kicked off my shoes off and yanked my trousers down around my ankles. In my underpants, I tugged Mohnke's boots from his legs, unbuckled his belt, grabbed hold of the flared fabric at his hips and pulled, exposing two pale white thighs, a scarred knee and a pair of sturdy shins. The pulped remains of his head came unstuck from the wall, chin flopped down and rested against his breastbone. I pulled on the man's trousers and boots, but spent the next five minutes trying to stuff his feet into my shoes, which were a size smaller.

Centauroid, half-man, half-beast, I rose to finish my transformation. I wrenched my white shirt open without popping any buttons and unfastened the man's tunic. Extricating first his left arm then his right, I slipped the jacket from his back and peeled off his white vest, slick with sweat. Of all the man's noxious garments, it was that damp vest I could not stand to feel against my chest. I twisted it into a rag and buried it in the dumpster. His tunic fitted me well enough, a little long in the arms and a touch short at the back.

Not bad. Not perfect, but it would do.

Almost.

The only distinguishing features were Mohnke's nose and mouth: fleshier and closer together than my own. What a shame it was the back of the German's head his attackers had caved in and not the front. For this deception to work, I had no choice but to alter his appearance, with only the bluntest of surgical instruments at my disposal.

Gripping his lapels, I pulled the body forward until it was facing the corner of the dumpster. Then I reared back on my right foot, placed my left one squarely behind his head and stomped. The first kick met some resistance. I stomped again, bone and cartilage crunching underfoot. The third time, the centre of Oberführer Harry Mohnke's face split around the perpendicular steel edge like a watermelon under a machete. I left him embedded there, pausing only to retrieve the old woman's prayer shawl I had dropped.

Back out on the street, I tugged my zip as if emerging from a sly urination, for the benefit of any curious on-lookers. A factory whistle blew, high and lonesome. The pavement in front of the shops was busy with the hustle of early morning workers. Nobody paid me much notice. If you saw the SS, you put your head down and kept moving. Vehicles were still stopped at the level-crossing but drivers had turned their engines back on, and not in wishful thinking. The whistle was not from any factory. Straddling the tracks, the troop transporter train was puffing steam into the cold air. The engineers had finally fixed the problem; the train was ready to leave.

The quickest way out of the Gendarme's purview was on that train. All I had to do was get to Lublin Main. I would determine the rest from there.

Resisting the temptation to goose-step in my new boots, I cut between bumpers and hurried across the road. The cordon of soldiers was gone from the front of the station. A weary porter was brushing up a mound of broken glass at the windows. I hurried past him into the building. No inspector asked to see my ticket. The restaurant was starting to fill back up, a queue already forming at the counter. I followed the signs out past the Waiting Room.

The first platform was empty.

While I crossed the footbridge to the other side, the Lublin locomotive let out another long mournful whistle beneath my feet. At the far end of the track, the chimney pumped a dark plume that spiralled to a taper. Men skidded along the platform and dived into open carriages, officers at the front in first-class, soldiers at the rear.

About to descend the final flight of stairs, I paused as heavy bootsteps clanged across the walkway behind me. Somebody shouted, 'Hey, wait!'

I could do nothing but flatten myself against the wall as

the soldiers raced past, shoving each other and giggling. One of them called out, 'Stop that train!'

I followed them down through a fog of hissing steam on the platform to the rear of the train, as far from the officers' quarters as I could get. In Second Class I stood less chance of being recognized. Or not being recognized - whichever was worse. With the engine goading the wheel pistons into motion, I gripped the handles of the last open carriage and hurled myself in.

The lion's den resembled a debauched Kiel dormitory after finals, except my enemy wore Wehrmacht uniforms not waistcoats and blazers. Almost all were drunk. A few soldiers had passed out, stripped naked, dead to the world. The rest had been enjoying the stations' facilities while the train was fixed and had scrambled back as the whistle blew. I found myself squashed on a corner bench with a group sharing a bottle of vodka. Red-nosed and emboldened, the lad at my elbow turned with a wink and ventured, 'Checking up on us, sir?'

'Something like that,' I said.

'Where are your men?'

I pointed vaguely to the snaking carriages ahead, but the lad mistook my gesture and placed the vodka in my hand, closing my fingers gently around the bottle.

His friends cheered when I took a swig.

'Thanks, I said, gulping. 'Needed that.'

Handing it back, I closed my eyes, savouring the spirit's deep, intestinal glow.

I sat wedged against the wall in darkness as the train left the station and chugged towards Lublin Main. When I was certain the soldiers had forgotten about me, I allowed my hand to roam the pockets of my new uniform, taking an inventory.

One box of Nordland cigarettes, unopened, and a smooth, silver lighter heavy as a pebble.

The salvaged wallet, empty except for Harry Mohnke's identification card.

My prayer shawl. That was it for the trousers.

I loosened a button on the tunic and dug inside the breast pocket, where a square of paper rustled, and something hard dug into my skin when I pressed, brass shell-casing or a pen lid,. The object was concealed in an envelope, but there was a second letter behind it that I unfolded first, since it was already open.

A military form, authorising fifty-four hours of Compassionate Leave for Oberführer Harry Mohnke to attend his brother's funeral in the family home of Dahme, near the Polish border. Today was the second of a four-day pass.

The envelope contained a long door key and the transferred title deeds of an apartment in Cracow on the corner of Traugutta and Dabrowskiego that had belonged to Erich Mohnke, the deceased brother.

I knew the area well.

Podgorze was just outside the Jewish Ghetto, less than three miles from where my mother and sister had lived, their last known place of residence.

15

Five hours and three kilometres later, I arrived at Cracow Glowny. Or Hauptbanhof Krakau, as the proliferation of scarlet and black drapes now proclaimed. The station had been Nazified; I knew the feeling.

Navigating the busiest transportation hub in the administrative capital of occupied Poland was not the smartest move for a Jew in a murdered SS officer's uniform, but now I was here, I had no choice but to keep moving.

Summoning Mohnke's arrogance at Lublin, I barreled through the crowd towards the exit and set off south towards Podgorze on foot.

High above the banks of the Vistula, Wawel castle was now called Krakauer Burg, the entrance's bronze likeness of Taduesz Kosciusko on rearing horseback replaced by Governor Hans Frank's huge black Cadillac. Not even a German car for this stalwart of National Socialism! The pretender-King and his Queen Beatrice rode around like movie stars. Meanwhile, Polish civilians were banned from visiting their ancestral seat of the castle now, except for construction workers and cleaners.

At the northern edge of Old Town, the Battle of Grunwald, that great turning point of medieval history when Poles and Lithuanians united to defeat the Teutonic Knights of 1410 was no longer commemorated by an enormous plinth. Five hundred and twenty-nine years later, the Knights roared back, riding Panzer tanks, obliterating all trace of Polish independence. My mother's last letter had warned of the rampant destruction of the city's monuments, but I was still shocked.

After Grunwald and Wawel, it had been Adam Mickiewicz's turn. What had a Romantic poet ever done to the Nazis? German police cordoned off his monument at noon on 17th August, 1940 in the Rynek, the Old Market Square and the vandals moved in with scaffold and tools. They set about tearing off the allegorical figures from Mickiewicz's feet, as if Motherland, Science, Courage and Poetry were street sluts to be whipped. Grown men cried out in the gathered crowd, amateur photographers were beaten and arrested. Many of the assembled citizens did not know Adam Mickiewicz from the Old Testament Adam, but they came to understand the poet that day, after he was toppled. In being struck down, Mickiewicz became more powerful than the Germans could ever imagine. Within forty-eight hours, black market photos of his falling monument were selling quicker than cigarettes. Two years later, one solitary soldier had been posted in Adolf Hitler Platz to keep dissenters from turning the spot into a shrine. He saluted as I strode past. A few seconds later, I realised he was saluting me.

While Johann Goethe's Faust had once professed a desire to reroute the Rhine to encircle Wittenberg, the Nazis had been as yet unable to alter the flow of the Vistula, which still snaked around Kazimierz as lazily as I remembered.

The island's Jews were gone, unceremoniously dumped in a Ghetto across the river.

Erich Mohnke's apartment was situated in a leafy Podgorze neighbourhood just north-east of the Ghetto, a stone's throw from its prison walls. For now, I tried not to think of the squalor and misery within, lest the mask slip and my emotions betray me.

There were many more German soldiers on patrol south of the river than the isolated clusters I'd glimpsed in Old Town. After the shock of seeing streets full of uniforms, I became appreciative of the camouflage they provided. Who would notice one more SS? Thankfully, no-one did. Head held high, I crossed the road to Traugutta Street, the corner of Dabrowskiego.

I had survived my first hour in the city.

Stopping opposite 65, I turned out the envelope from my pocket and studied the apartment's transfer deeds. I ruled out the possibility that Harry Mohnke's brother was married or had children. Any beneficiaries would have inherited the property, not his brother. But that did not necessarily mean

Erich lived alone.

According to the paperwork, the apartment was number 3E. I scanned the brick wall up to the third balcony. A good sign: the curtains were drawn. No lights on.

I crossed the road and unlocked the front door. The lobby was dank and musty. To my right was a wall of labelled letter-slots. 'Mohnke, Erich' was not hard to find: his was the only slot bulging with mail. I removed several weeks' worth of envelopes.

There was an elevator, but I didn't relish being stuck inside the cage with a curious busy-body. The staircase was at the rear. What I could not see from the letter-racks was the proximity of the janitor's kitchen, tucked away behind the stairwell. I hurried past the open door, but it was too late. A chair squeaked on linoleum and the ancient janitor was hobbling towards me, a rolled newspaper clutched in his liver-spotted hand.

'Hey, stop there!' Dim eyes focused on my uniform, the stripes on my shoulder. His glower lifted like a summer fog. 'Oh, please forgive me. Heil Hitler. How can I help you, sir?'

I stepped towards him, palm extended. 'Harry Mohnke.'

'Harry?' His hand went limp in mine.

'Erich's brother.'

'I was so sorry to hear the news.'

'You must be Mr...?' I wagged a finger next to my head.

'Escherich, Bela Escherich.'

'That's right. Erich mentioned your name.'

'Your brother was a hero, Oberführer Mohnke. Those Warsaw Ghetto rats should be exterminated. Instead they talk about sending them to Madagascar.'

'Thank-you. We are all very proud of Erich. The funeral was most... touching.'

'There have been so many sacrifices of late.'

'We are gaining ground,' I said. 'There is a real momentum. I predict our victory early next year.'

'I didn't mean to suggest your brother's death was in vain - '

'Of course not. Forgive me, I am quite shattered.'

'Please.' Escherich pointed his newspaper to the stairs.

I turned away, then stopped. 'No visitors I should know about, I trust?'

'Everything's just as it was, sir.'

'Good. And not that I'm expecting anybody, but I would appreciate keeping my arrival quiet, until tomorrow at least.'

He tapped the side of his nose and grinned. 'In that case, for the sake of appearances, you may wish to leave a few letters in Erich's rack.'

I peeled off a handful and handed them over.

'May I ask how long you intend to stay, sir?'

'Tomorrow.'

'Probably for the best.'

'No,' I said. 'We'll talk about my plans tomorrow.'

'Oh. Yes.'

'Good night, Bela.'

The third floor hallway reeked of boiled cabbage, peppered with the tang of fresh vomit. There was a bundled bed-sheet outside the door of my neighbour's apartment, upon which a note had been pinned: APOLOGIES FOR THE SMELL – SICK CHILD. PLEASE STAY AWAY. I kicked the sheet along to the end of the corridor and left it outside my door, to deter well-wishers.

I knocked, loud enough to raise an army. The only sense of movement I was aware of came from behind me. My neighbour was at the peephole, studying the back of my head. Resisting every urge to spin and glare, I guided the trembling key into the lock and turned.

The hallway was hot and narrow, two doorways in the opposite wall and a further two at each end, front and back. All were shut, except for the kitchen, where the door-panel had been removed from the hinges. It was a sad, otherwise unventilated space with only one worktop and no table.

Next door was a tiny bathroom, where a man could urinate, shave and fill the tub without breaking into a stretch.

The back room contained Erich's bed, desk and wardrobe. A spare uniform hung from the pole, a few tailored shirts and ties, a smart grey suit, two pairs of shoes underneath. The shelf above the clothes held a brown leather suitcase. I was about to place the old lady's prayer shawl inside when I stopped. I cursed my lack of foresight.

What if Harry Mohnke had luggage on his train? For a two day visit, he must have taken a case. But then failed to collect it at Lublin. The porters would have found a bag by now. It could be gathering dust in the Lost Property office. Worst case scenario, if Harry used luggage labels, an enterprising porter had already alerted the authorities.

I found a telephone in the front room, dialed the operator and asked to be connected to Lublin Hauptbanhof, where I gave my rank and explained my forgetfulness, blaming it on the preoccupied state following my brother's funeral. The clerk was most sympathetic, but didn't know anything about a case. He promised to call me back as soon as possible.

I could do nothing except to tremble and perspire. Even controlling my breath proved gruelling, and I feared I might pass out. Eventually I managed to persuade my lungs to inflate beyond the dimensions of a pea, and the dizziness passed. My new life – if that's what this turned out to be – would be fraught with fear from one minute to the next. If I could not learn to live with it, I may as well end it now.

Thirty minutes later the telephone rang, startling me from silent contemplation. It was the clerk: Harry's suitcase had been handed in to Lost Property.

'That's excellent news,' I sighed, and surely never had a man sounded more relieved.

'There's just one slight problem, Oberführer. According to the label, the final destination was not Cracow.'

'You're right. I forgot to write a new one after the funeral.'

'I hope you forgive the intrusion, Oberführer, but for the sake of security, I must ask you to confirm the original destination on that label.'

'Of course,' I said, playing for time. I had forgotten the name of the city where they'd buried Erich Mohnke. All I could think of was that it began with D.

Dornburg, Dornstadt, Dornstetten...

'The name of the city, sir?'

'Oh, right, yes. You need to hear it from me, don't you.' Dresden, Dachau, Dortmund. 'I was waiting to hear hear it from you.'

'The other way round would be preferable.'

'Otherwise I could have confirmed anything you said.'

'Exactly. To make sure your suitcase doesn't get into the wrong - '

'Dahme.'

'I'm sorry?'

'My brother was buried in Dahme.'

A pause.

'Thank-you very much, sir. Your case will be on the first train to Cracow tomorrow morning. Can I assist you with anything else?'

I curled into Erich Monhke's bed and slept the sleep of the dead.

The next morning, I decided to return to Izaaka Street as Jozef Siegler and seek out any original neighbours who had known my family. It was six months since Shoshana had taken my mother to a friendly farm outside Cracow, from where they had hoped to leave for Palestine. She hadn't revealed the name of the village in her letter, for obvious reasons. I had no way of knowing if they were still holed up in the countryside, if they had managed to escape, or if their plan – like so many others - had failed.

I left Harry Mohnke's uniform in the wardrobe and dressed in cotton shirt and woollen trousers. For the first time in daylight, I opened the bedroom curtains to assess the lay of the land. At the foot of the building was a maze of vegetable gardens, sheds and workshops. The area was bordered by an empty plot of land on one side and across Tragutta Street by a new-looking wall that extended in both directions at a length of several metres, and didn't seem to be guarding much except a nest of grim tenements, crooked as tombstones. When I followed the barricade round to the east as far as I could, I saw the curious sight of a large concrete gate in the middle of the wall, through which a rail train emerged, loaded with glum passengers.

I had inherited a room with a prime view of the Jewish Ghetto. Izaaka could wait another hour.

The janitor was changing the light-bulb on a tottering

ladder when I got downstairs. I stood gripping the side-rail as he worked.

'I trust you found the sleep you were looking for, Mr. Mohnke.'

'It was a little odd lying in my brother's bed, but tiredness soon got the better of me.'

'In that respect, I envy you. The older I get, the more tired I become, but now I can't sleep. God's nothing if not a joker.'

'I was looking at the allotments under the bedroom window. Did Erich have a plot?'

'Not much of a green-fingers, your brother. He couldn't even keep a spider plant. I ended up adopting it myself.'

'That sounds like Erich. Do you mind if I take a look?'

'At his plant?'

'The allotments,' I said.

With a final twist, the light-bulb flickered, casting Escherich's gaunt face a sickly yellow. 'Follow me.'

Outside it was bitterly cold in the shadow of the tenement. The gardens were well-tended and generously proportioned, but little grew in winter apart from onions and lettuce. I pretended to study the soil until I heard the janitor close the door behind me, then I began searching for the path that would deliver me onto Tragutta, twisting and turning past shed and green-house until the Ghetto suddenly reared into view across the street.

The wall rose three metres high and was topped elegantly with curved panels which bore a striking resemblance to matzevahs, Jewish tombstones. Most of the buildings behind it were already dilapidated before the war, and chronic overcrowding had only hastened their decline. All windows that faced outward to Tragutta were boarded up to prevent contact with the Aryan world. The air that did manage to escape over the wall reeked of sewage and clogged water closets. Lines of scrubbed clothes and sheets hung stiffly between balconies, garments frosted overnight. I grabbed a wheelbarrow from outside the nearest shed and trundled out to the pavement.

I met three young soldiers in the empty lot of land next to my apartment block, smoking and stamping the ground while two suited Jews attempted to dig trenches with long handled hoes. The older prisoner wore a tall, dented hat and long black beard that obscured the worst of his shame like a scarf, and had paused momentarily to watch my approach.

'Need any work doing round here?' one of the soldiers shouted in Polish when he saw me. 'We've got Jews to do the heavy lifting now.'

I stopped, set the barrow down, slapped my head as if cursing my memory, turned round and trundled back the way I'd come. The soldiers were having too much fun with their prisoner to follow me.

The Ghetto gate through which I'd seen the tram emerging was two blocks in the other direction, and heavily guarded by soldiers and the Polish Blue Police. I had no wish to risk any further contact, so stopped again at the allotments and gazed up at a soot-stained block of flats that soared high above the wall. The windows facing me were bricked up, but there was a side block that intersected, and these windows had been left untouched.

As I stood watching, a figure approached the top floor window and flung the pane open. The red-armband of a black SS sleeve appeared momentarily. A shouting match began inside the room, as if a tug of war had broken loose. A female voice protested, 'No, give him to me!' Seconds later, a bundled ball sailed out the window. The blanket whipped back in the breeze to reveal what looked at first like a pink doll. Before I realised what I was looking at, the bundle plummeted beneath the wall out of sight. The crunch of impact on the courtyard was drowned out by the screams of the baby's mother above, who was in turn silenced by a single gun-shot.

When I threaded my way back through the maze of gardens, I heard the janitor calling for me. I was in no mood for small talk, but there was no way of avoiding him.

'Thank heavens I found you,' Escherich said, visibly flustered. 'You've got a visitor.'

'What happened to telling nobody I was here?'

'I didn't, I swear. They know everything.'

'Who are you talking about?'

'The big boss. Oberführer Scherner. SS and Polizeiführer for the whole of Cracow. He's waiting inside.'

'For me?'

'I'm pretty sure he hasn't come for your brother's spider plant.'

I found myself being ushered back towards the lobby. The Oberführer was standing at the letter-slots with his hands crossed at his back, gazing out onto the busy street. His Mercedes was idling at the kerb, the chauffeur tapping the wheel. I coughed as I approached.

'Harry,' he said, turning round and removing his cap to reveal a broad glistening dome. The man's neck strained at his white collar while he squinted compassionately behind thick spectacles. His face was red, snub-nosed and bloated, quite ugly, and could have been mistaken at a distance for a bank-robber with a stocking pulled over his head.

'Dear boy, I'm so sorry I couldn't be at the funeral.'

I knew then that any bond that existed between Scherner and Erich Mohnke was not shared with the brother; this was the first time they – that is to say, we - had met.

We shook hands. The handsome jacket was tight around his chest, reinforced with a black belt across his solidly substantial gut. He was perhaps fifty years of age.

'Your father told me you were in town.'

So Scherer knew my father, and had spoken to him as recently as yesterday. Like the suitcase left on the train, the thought that I might have parents to contend with had never crossed my mind. The sheer lunatic scale and folly of my endeavour was only now dawning on me.

'Is my timing inconvenient?' A small tip of tongue dabbed the Oberführer's wet lips. 'Depending how long you're here for, I could always try and reschedule.'

'Not at all. This is... quite the unexpected honour. Please, you must come up.'

He pushed the cuff back from his left wrist and squinted at his watch. 'If you're sure.'

'It's the least I can do.' I steered Scherner towards the elevator. 'Tell me. Have you visited Erich before?'

'Ashamed to say I haven't. Yourself?'

I remembered Anton Poplowski's words: the most successful lies are always sprinkled with just the right amount of truth. The trick is, knowing how much.

'Before the war, I was in Cracow many times.'

'Always meant to stop by and see Erich, you know how it is,' he puffed, breathless from crossing the lobby. 'I can't quite believe he's gone.'

'We're all in a state of shock.'

I closed the scissor-gate. The elevator delivered us to the third floor. My neighbour in 3B had not ventured outside their door yet, and the soiled bed-sheet still languished outside my apartment.

'Sick Child,' the Oberführer said, backing away as he read the note. 'I'm sorry to hear that. Erich never mentioned you had children. Or that he was an uncle...'

'The sheet's not mine,' I said. 'I'll have a word later with the bitch next door about the merits of diligent border-control.'

'Or we pay her a visit while I'm still here,' he leered. 'I do love a spot of aggro in the morning, gets the heart pumping.'

'Very kind,' I said. 'But I should try and stay on relatively good terms with the neighbours.'

Inside, I stepped into the kitchen, immediately filling the pokey space to capacity. The Oberführer waited in the hallway.

'I only arrived late last night,' I called, grateful for the distraction of having to legitimately hunt for cups and saucers. 'This may take some - '

The first cupboard I opened above the sink was well stocked with tea, coffee, powdered milk and a metal espresso pot.

'Voila,' I heard from the hallway.

I set the pot to boil above the flame and rinsed out a couple of cups that had collected a thin film of dust. There were no more chores to make myself busy with.

'This isn't a half bad place, you know.' Scherer had begun to pad about in the corridor. 'Kitchen's a bit limited, but I don't imagine your brother spent a lot of time at the stove.'

'Frying an egg was Erich's limit. Let's go through to the

front room. All mod cons there. He's even got a couple of chairs.'

I showed Scherner to the sofa and doubled back across the room to take the armchair. As I passed the telephone table, I noticed the folded prayer shawl I had left when I rang Lublin train station last night. I stopped and straightened the edges like a lace doily, then placed the telephone on top of it. Only the tassels showed around the base. Scherer hadn't appeared to notice.

'How was the reception?' he said after I pulled my chair towards the sofa and sat down.

'I don't know,' I said evenly. 'I haven't used it yet.'

Behind their lenses, his eyes narrowed in confusion. I understood at once my mistake.

'You were talking about the funeral,' I said. 'That was embarrassing.'

'I spoke to your father on Monday, briefly, to offer my support.'

'He never mentioned it.'

'Coming after your dear mother, it's been the most abject year. How did Otto seem at the service?'

'Dignified, unlike myself. I sat through the whole thing in a trance, like it was happening to somebody else. Hardly even remember the hymns.'

'Often the way with these rituals. I suspect the real grieving has yet to start.'

'I keep asking myself, why Erich and not me? I'm sure father thinks the same. My brother was a real hero.'

Scherer set his boots apart and leant forward, gripping his knees. 'Your contribution to the administration is invaluable. There's more to war than guts and glamour. Men of your father's generation can't always find the words to express their pride, but that doesn't mean they don't feel it. If anybody should bear the blame for what happened to your brother, you may look no further than myself.'

'In what possible respect?'

'It was Erich who requested transfer to Warsaw, to be nearer your father. But I was the one who approved it.'

'You had no way of knowing. The Warsaw Ghetto is not

your responsibility.'

'Those JFO sons of bitches wouldn't have infiltrated if it was. Now, let's hear no more of this nonsense. The telecommunication work you're doing in the East is absolutely vital, Harry. Captain Muller's been singing your praises.'

'You've spoken to him?'

'I've seen a lot of men in your shoes, unfortunately, friends and brothers of the recently deceased. It's not easy for those left behind. They nearly always start thinking the same thing, that they've got something to prove, and I tell you, it's a death sentence. I want you to promise you're not going to take any risks when you go back – Russia's deadly enough and it's going to get worse before it gets better - '

'I'm not - '

'I haven't finished yet. I don't know all that happened between you and your father, and it's not my place to speculate, but I know how fond he is of you. If he lost another son now... well, I dread to think.'

The espresso pot began to spit in the kitchen.

'Lecture over,' Scherner said, and leant back in the sofa. 'We'll have our coffee and then you'll be rid of me.'

At the worktop, I assembled the tray, coffee and cups, sugar and powdered milk. An opportunity was opening up before me, the beginnings of a plan I had not dreamed imaginable. If I found the correct words for the Oberführer, I would be in a position to help the last remaining Jews of Cracow.

If not, I would be lucky to join them.

'Afraid all I could find was powdered milk.' I set the tray down on the table in front of the sofa. 'It's Klim though, none of that Polish rubbish.'

'Black as Himmler's heart for me.' Scherner stirred a cube into his cup and tapped the spoon against the rim before returning it to the saucer. 'Apologies if I overstepped. Your father and I go a long way back, and I feel a sense of responsibility.'

'Not at all. In fact, your words chimed with something I had been thinking myself.'

He sipped, his tongue dabbing those fleshy lips.

'The dilemma is about returning to the east, as you intimated. Rest assured, thoughts of bravery are the very last thing on my mind. The truth is, I wonder if I'm ready to go back.'

'Not a problem. What did they give you, a four-day pass?'

I nodded, recalling the paperwork in Harry's pocket. 'Today is the last.'

'Leave it with me. What do you need? A week? Two?'

'I'm not sure...'

Scherer set his cup down on its saucer. 'Given what your family has endured, it would be not unreasonable for the Reich to provide alternative deployment, should you so wish. There are a number of possibilities closer to Dahme, for example, were you so minded.'

'That's very considerate of you. But there is something else I must do first.'

'You have a specific location in mind?'

'I do. What would you say to my staying right here, in Cracow?'

'Excellent choice, naturally. As administrative capital, you'd be hard-pressed to find better opportunities. I know for a fact the Telpod factory on Lipowa is about to undergo a massive expansion, and we need good men in liaison.'

'Actually, I was thinking of right here.' I turned and pointed down the hallway towards the wall on Tragutta Street. 'Or rather, there.'

'The Ghetto?'

For the first time in the visit, Scherer smiled, splitting his bloated face like a knife. 'I'm not sure what your father would say about that.'

'If I choose to honour my brother's death by working to strengthen Ghetto security, I know I will have my father's blessings. To continue Erich's work in the city he loved. I can think of no nobler calling.'

'You've given the matter some thought, I see.'

'In truth I have entertained little else.'

'I suppose I'd be able to keep an eye on you. Ghetto work is a fairly rough guard detail. It's a lot more hands on, Harry, than repairing telephone lines.'

'When it comes to crushing Jewish resistance, who has greater motivation than my own?'

'Motivation isn't everything. And what do we do with you when it's crushed?'

'They'll always be more Jews.'

'I wouldn't be so sure about that,' Scherer said. 'You graduated Jünkerschule?'

Luckily I had memorized the details on Mohnke's ID card.

'Of course. Bad Tölz, 1937.'

'37. First year in-take.'

I smirked. 'First and best.'

'You certainly have the necessary self-belief, I'll give you that.'

'Is that a yes?'

'Not to mention the bloody-mindedness.'

Scherer drained his coffee and tilted the grounds in the bottom of the cup, divining my future.

'Alright, Harry. You've clearly got your heart set on this, and I don't want to be the one to stand in your way. I think we can work something out. It'll be subject to approval of course, like all Ghetto details.'

'Thank-you, Oberführer. I won't let you down.'

'Not that I put any stock in superstition, but the timing is quite fortuitous. A few of us are having a little informal get-together tonight. Wine, women, a crap game or two. Willie Kunde will be there, the Ghetto commander. I could make the introductions.'

I grimaced. 'I don't want to appear ungrateful but perhaps I could join you another time? I haven't had a chance to sort through my brother's belongings yet.'

'Of course, too soon. I thought it might be.'

'Not at all. I'm keen to begin my new duties without delay. Work is one of few comforts at a time like this. I was due to report back to Captain Muller tomorrow, as you know. Perhaps Commander Kunde would be able to receive me then instead?'

'I'm sure he'll find your zeal as heartening as I do. I'll tell him tonight. Shall we say 9.00 o'clock tomorrow at

Jozefinska?'

'Jozefinska,' I repeated. 'Inside the Ghetto?'

'And I'll let Muller know he'll be needing a new engineer.' He gave me a card from his wallet. 'Any problems, day or night. Call me.'

After returning the Oberführer to his Mercedes, I didn't know whether to throw up in the gutter or punch the air. The adrenaline wore off before I was back inside my apartment, replaced by dread.

I was not a deceitful man by nature – or perhaps I should say I did not like to think of myself as one - but a master of masquerade I had to become. One mistake, one slip of the tongue, and the show was over, with no chance of a reprieve.

How did an actor go about preparing for a new role? I had no idea, but there was surely a lot of hard work behind the scenes before the drama began. Not just the parameters of one invented life to learn and inhabit, but a whole network of connections to memorize, familial and social, domestic and professional. As if this wasn't complicated enough, my new life was not invented; it already belonged to somebody else. There was no room for artistic license when playing Harry Mohnke, no scope for improvisation. I had to know every single detail of the man's life.

I found a pad of hotel stationary in the front room sideboard and sat down to record all I could remember:

Harry Mohnke: difficult relationship with father. Black sheep of family?

Telecoms engineer, Eastern Front

Captain Muller, superior officer

Erich Monhnke stationed in Cracow

Left this year to be closer family home, in Berg, north-east Germany

Not good with house plants

Didn't cook

Killed last week in/around Warsaw Ghetto, attacked by Jewish Fighting Orgnaisation.

Father Gert. Friends with Scherer

As I struggled to recall more, I began to feel I was being watched. I put it down initially to a heightened state of paranoia, but the suspicion became so oppressive I had to jump up and look out the window. The Mercedes was gone, of course. No pairs of binoculars were trained on my apartment from the opposite rooftops.

Walking back, I noticed for the first time the painting on the living room wall above where I'd been sitting: a gloomy rendering of Jesus Christ's betrayal and seizure by Roman soldiers. Up close, I could see Christ's hands clasped before him in weary resignation, his head averted. His hooded eyes looked down at my empty chair as if to say, Judas.

It was too much to bear; the painting would have to go.

I gripped the frame just below the top corners and lifted it from the hook. Concealed behind, embedded in the wall, was a black and gold safety deposit box. I pulled the door, but of course it was locked, and needed a combination.

The only number I could think Erich might have used was his apartment's telephone line. I tried it, several times, forward and back, before giving up on the safe and rehanging the picture over it. I bumped my chair further along the wall, out of Christ's sight.

Two hours of frantically ransacking the rooms failed to turn up the combination. I was obsessed. At the start of the day, I didn't even know there was a safe. Now I could think of nothing else. What did he keep in there?

At noon I stopped, exhausted, close to fainting.

There was half a loaf in the kitchen, mottled with blue mould. I discarded the bread, chewed the crust and chased it down with bites from a liquefying onion. The food was better in prison.

Wrapping myself up in Erich's raincoat, I left the appartment, braced for the blast across the Vistula. There was one more act of cultural desecration that I hadn't witnessed on my tour last night.

In one of my mother's last letters, she dubbed the German

actions against her adopted city as The War Against Statues.

Dear Mother, statues were only the beginning.

The grocery store on Izaaka Street abandoned by my family when they fled to the countryside was now called 'Schmidts'. Mr. Zygot's workshop next door had been re-annexed and was now a florist's kiosk. A swastika replaced the Star of David my mother had been forced to display in her shop window.

I could not bring myself to browse inside.

16

Next morning, I found a box of brushes under Erich's sink and buffed my boots until they sparkled.

I ironed stiff creases into my dress trousers and pressed a clean shirt from the wardrobe.

I polished the insignia on my tunic and picked lint from the sleeves.

Finally, examining myself in the mirror with a grim smirk of satisfaction, I was ready.

Leaving through the front entrance, I doubled back on Tragutta to Dabrowskiego in case the soldiers were still humiliating ditch-diggers out back. I approached the Ghetto from the Lworska gate, which seemed to be guarded by at least three separate authorities. German sentries with ferocious Dobermans, Polish Blue Police and a strange hybrid I did not recognize, three young men wearing street jackets and trousers, but matching berets with yellow ribbons. When a stoop-shouldered member turned to salute me, I saw Star of David bands around their arms.

Ordnungsdienst.

There had been rumours of a Jewish Police in the Wilno Ghetto, but this was first time I had seen them. It was Gestapo custom to appoint a few able-bodied Jewish men as wardens of their fellow prisoners, like the Kapo system at Camp Moda. For an extra ration of bread, they would implement Nazi rules, report violations, and generally become the eyes and ears of the Gestapo. The youngest of the yellow berets at the Lworska gate even sported an adulatory stripe of moustache under his nostrils.

The open wound of the Ghetto oozed before me, teeming with rats and misery. I had never seen so many people standing idly in the mire, freezing - very possibly - to death. Endless crowds in every dreary direction, bodies ejected from over-stuffed apartments with nowhere to go.

I stepped back to the gate. 'Place is a damned zoo.' When he didn't reply, I said, 'Commander Kunde's office on Jozefinska?'

'This is Jozefinska,' a German sentry nodded, pointing to the grim thoroughfare from which I'd retreated. 'Number 37 down there on the left.'

If a musician were tasked with scoring a tour of Dante's underworld, he could have done worse than wander two hundred metres along Jozefinska for inspiration: gun-shots, dogs barking, children wailing, the amplified stomp through glassless windows of boots on stairways, doors ripped from hinges, the constant call-and-response of German yelling and Yiddish screaming, interspersed with the occasional futile moan.

Strewn in the middle of the street, a pile of suitcases, handbags, bundles and an over-turned baby carriage. I wondered why nobody was picking them up. For scrap, if nothing more. A scrawny three-legged dog pawed the foothills, and arched its spine in electric fright when the mound began to shift. I checked my tunic pocket for one of Erich's biscuits, crouched in the gutter and called the mutt over. It gently nuzzled the shortcake out of my palm, then bit my wrist and bolted.

From a high balcony, an old woman let loose a rasping cackle at my expense.

At least I'd made somebody's day.

Two, if we count the dog.

Outside number 37, a pimply Jew, peacocking in his beret and yellow ribbon, pushed an old man against the wall and tore his overcoat open to reveal nothing but a threadbare vest.

The boy reared back and dug his thumbs under his Sam Browne belt. 'Don't come the innocent old coot with me. I know your type. If you ain't got the goods on you, they're buried nearby.'

The old man hung his head and sighed. 'Shame on your family, Shmiel. Such effrontery from a good Yiddische bocher.' Looking up, he scowled into the boy's face. 'That I must stand to witness such cheek, such chutzpah!'

'You don't have to stand,' the boy said, 'Not if you you don't want to.' He swung his knee into the man's groin and left him doubled up on the pavement.

The ground floor was filled with SS and Gestapo officers, NCOs and adjutants, not a Jewish yellow-beret in sight.

Past a steep staircase, the open room was sectioned into six pairs of clustered desks at which soldiers pounded typewriters and shouted into telephones. The left wall was covered with maps of the Ghetto and the right one was lined with filing cabinets, perhaps two dozen of them. Inches above our heads, the low ceiling bounced and shook as if hosting a training session for Olympic trampolinists. My arrival went unnoticed amidst the din. I circumnavigated the maze of tables until I came to a waiting area of empty chairs next to a lone filing cabinets and a swastika flag by the far window, and I sat.

If Oberführer Scherner had attended his party last night, then Commander Kunde would be expecting me. If for any reason the two had not spoken, I was going to have to find Kunde by myself.

I breathed deeply and focussed on the telephone conversation taking place at the nearest desk. The officer had a long, slightly crooked nose and a narrow mouth that puckered into a bored smile as he raised his eyes at me while he listened.

After a lengthy bout of silence, he spoke again into the black receiver, 'Fair enough, but that's Lublin. I don't see what it's got to do with us.'

Lublin.

My ears burnt like two electric coils at the city's mention.

'Do we have a name?' The officer stopped smiling, made a note, then lay the phone on his desk and got up and walked towards me, stopping at the filing cabinets. He dropped to one knee to search the bottom drawer. Seizing a manila folder, he returned to his desk, and picked up the phone. The thudding on the ceiling was now so violent that a fine rain of plaster had begun to sift down, and the officer had to shout to make his connection heard.

'Gusta Tova Draenger?' He extracted a letter from the fat manila folder and scanned its contents.

'You're right, the bitch was definitely one of ours. Or she was.'

A pause.

'According to this, she and her husband managed to get out the Residential District two days ago. A group calling themselves the Jewish Self-Help Society wrote to Chief Muller, asking for permission to set up a farm in Kopaliny.'

Another pause as he traced a finger down the letter.

'I quote, 'to study agriculture in readiness for immigration to the Land of Israel.'

Mocking laughter ensued.

The crooked-nosed officer said, 'You'd have to ask Muller's office that. To keep up the hope? Maybe it's better to have troublemakers outside the District than in. Tents and pissing and all that - '

The thumping suddenly stopped upstairs, and the office fell silent. A great screeching as furniture was dragged across the floorboards over our heads, then a series of grunts before a glass window smashed. I whipped round just in time to see a wooden chair plummet past and splinter on the cobbled courtyard behind me.

Then a typist resumed his clatter and slowly the office volume levels cranked back up to just short of where they were before the disturbance.

Returning the telephone to his ear, the officer said, 'Your Lublin station man didn't say anything more, I suppose?'

Lublin station.

A chameleon, my face blended right in with the red flag next to the window.

'All right.' The crooked-nosed officer scribbled on the letter. 'We'll add Kopaliny to the list. Thanks for letting us know.'

When he replaced the receiver, he looked up and said, 'How can I help you, Oberführer?'

'Harry Mohnke,' I said. 'Transferring in.'

'Oberführer Mohnke, of course. My commiserations for

your brother.'

'Are you Commander Kunde?'

'Me? No, no. The higher-ups are... well, they're higher up, aren't they.' He smiled and pointed at the ceiling. 'The Hauptsturmführer's office is on the first floor. I'm August Brühl. Department of Civil Affairs.'

We shook hands across his desk.

'Good to meet you,' I said. 'Is it all Civil Affairs down here?'

He began pointing off the other five sections. 'There's Bookkeeping, Intelligence, Archives, Vehicles and Statistics.'

'And did you know my brother?'

'Unfortunately not. Erich was based at Pomorska.' He looked embarrassed to have no further consolation to offer. 'Let me take you on up to the Hauptsturmführer.'

As we rose, two yellow berets crossed the courtyard behind me, approached the wall and bent down to retrieve the defenestrated sticks of furniture. A chicken wandered across the cobbles and stopped to peck. When the Jewish Policemen came back up into view, Brühl and I saw they were clutching not the remains of a chair, but of the chair's former occupant.

The woman – little more than ripped skin and bloodied bones – still out-weighed her wooden seat and must have hit the ground first.

'Who's that?' I asked.

'Just an old seamstress.'

'A trouble-maker?'

'Loitering during work hours.'

I sat back down rather too quickly.

Brühl said, 'Kunde's actually in quite a good mood for this time of the morning.'

'Even so, I am a little early.' This wasn't true: my watch revealed it was already ten past nine. 'Perhaps that telephone call of yours was fairly urgent business? Don't mind me if you want to get back to it.'

'I believe it might have been.' Brühl looked down at his file. 'Perhaps I should file a brief report.'

When Brühl had loaded a sheet of paper into his typewriter, I stretched my legs out, crossed my ankles and manufactured a yawn. 'Trouble at Lublin? Sorry, couldn't help overhearing.'

'There was, two days ago.'

Clack clack clack.

'Sabotage?'

'A police translator was attacked.'

Good God – I was right. They were already onto me.

'At the train station?'

'Outside.'

'Jews?'

'A gang of Poles. Five gas-workers. They were involved in an altercation with the Belorussian Gendarme, ten minutes previously.'

Clack clack clack.

'Previous to what?'

'The Belorussian's translator being found with his head caved in.'

'Ah,' I said. 'And the Poles?'

Clack clack clack.

'Executed yesterday. All except one. Houses seized by the Haupttreuhandstelle Ost. '

The four syllables knocked against the bars of my heart, one for every dead Pole.

Ex/e/cu/ted.

In switching clothes with Harry Mohnke, I had already caused the deaths of four men, guilty of no more serious crime than letting off steam to a pompous Gendarme.

I wanted to stop listening.

I wanted to crawl away and wait out the rest of the war in Mr. Popolowsky's hole in the ground.

'Let me guess,' I said eventually. 'At his hour of need, this wretched Pole suddenly remembers a piece of vital intelligence that might just save his life.'

'Claims he knows a young Jewess in Cracow.'

'Course he does.' I nodded, squinting. 'This Tova Draenger creature?'

Clack, clack, clack.

'Apparently she's a kashariyot.'

Brühl had used the old Hebrew word for connector, which

I pretended not to understand.

'A Communist spy,' he explained. 'Pretty young things who slip in and out the zoo gates, delivering weapons and whatnot. Most of them look about as Jewish as Marika Rokk. Tova Gusta Draenger would have been the perfect candidate.' Brühl held up a photo of a striking beauty with her hair piled high in a ribbon. 'Except...'

'She's not in the Ghetto – I mean the District – anymore.'

I managed to correct myself, remembering the German's fondness for euphemisms.

'As of last week, she's a farmer in Kopaliny,' he said. 'Who knows, maybe they are just planting cabbages out there.'

Brühl pounded the last few keys, pulled his report from the carriage roller and lay the page on top of the folder for the ink to dry.

'Finished,' he said. 'Ready to go?'

'You stay. I've already taken up too much of your time.'

I weaved unmolested through the various crowded desks - Bookkeeping, Intelligence, Archives, Vehicles and Statistics – to the steep staircase by the front door. I was now twenty minutes late. It would have been far saner to keep walking, out onto Jozefinska, to slink back through the Lworksa gate and return to Erich Mohnke's apartment. Perhaps a day would pass before Scherer or Kunde sent somebody to check up on me. Time enough to dispose of the uniform and get out of the city. But what would happen to the prisoners of the Ghetto then? I had already abandoned one family; I would not do so again.

I gripped the slippery bannister and hauled myself up the narrow steps. Approaching the midway point where the stairs changed direction, a door slammed shut on the first floor and what sounded like a beer barrel began to crash through the building, once again causing a fine rain of plaster to sift from the cracks above my head. I stopped on the small platform halfway down and waited for the beer barrel to reveal itself as an enormous pair of jackbooted shins. They lunged down the last few steps, delivering me face to face with a broad and ruddy Aryan colossus.

We tried to pass each other on the cramped landing like feinting boxers. It was only when I stopped to flatten myself against the wall for the German to pass that his sharp blue eyes came into focus through fronds of blonde lashes.

'So the Lesser Spotted Mohnke does exist after all.' The colossus crushed my fingers in his palm, a punishment for my lazy time-keeping.

'Hauptsturmführer Kunde.'

'I was beginning to think you'd gone back to Russia.'

'Please forgive my tardiness, sir. Sorting through my brother's possessions, I'm ashamed to say I lost track of time.'

He relinquished his grip. It would appear that Erich Mohnke's death was still a valid currency.

'You're here now, that's what matters.' Kunde slapped a pair of white cloth gloves against his wrist. 'Unfortunately, I have to go out. Let's talk on the way.' His powerful arm steered me back round to the stairs I'd ascended. 'After you.'

I skidded down the steep steps quicker than the angle strictly allowed, compelled by the juggernaut at my back.

When we reached the bottom, Kunde gripped my elbow before I could open the front door. 'I'd better introduce you to Civil Affairs first, or Brühl will throw a tantrum.'

Kunde had started out across the office floor when I said, 'Not necessary, sir. We have already met.'

Instead of turning, he stood quite still. Seconds came and went. From the way his chin twitched on his bull-neck, I knew exactly what Kunde was thinking.

How exactly had the Lesser Spotted Mohnke found time to gossip with a bloody clerk on the opposite side of the room if he was already running twenty minutes late to meet me?

It was a good question.

A better one: with so many enormous lies to worry about, why did I keep tripping myself up in the trivial ones?

'I'm glad you two have already been acquainted,' Kunde said finally.

I held the front door open and followed him out onto Jozefinska.

'My brother worked at Pomorska,' I said, hurrying to keep abreast. We headed north, into the grey heart of the Ghetto.

'But Erich and I often talked about the Residential District - how effectively it was managed. He was full of admiration for your men, Hauptsturmführer. I can see why. It really is an honour to work for you. Thank-you for agreeing to have me, at such short notice.'

'To be honest, it's good timing. We took on another six informants last week. Brühl needs all the help he can get. The Lesser Spotted Mohnke will certainly earn his keep.'

'The Department of Civil Affairs?'

'Good title, yes? Took a long time to come up with something so meaningless.'

'What's the nature of the work?'

'Think of it as a Snitch's Paradise. Your King Rat is Symche Spira, a carpenter turned Ordnungsdienst, until last week when Pomorska saw fit to promote him again. Promised to make old Spira police chief of Tel Aviv in return, when we take the city. You'll find him at the wireless every morning now, cheering on the over-nights from North Africa. Talk about geese voting for Christmas.'

'Symche Spira,' I marvelled, hoping the Hassidic syllables didn't sound too smooth in my mouth. 'He sounds like a cartoon character.'

'Wait till you see him,' Kunde laughed. 'Strutting the streets like a South Sea Republic despot, more gold on his cap than the Vatican. A thoroughly venal and uneducated specimen, obsessed only with power and status. The most dreadful Jew you can imagine - an absolute gift for us. Old Spria's handpicked a team of rats, men and women who'll sell out their own grandmother for a shekel. They monitor unsatisfactory residents, plots of seditious affairs. Spira reports to Karl Brandt across the river, and Brühl in the Residential District. Brühl and now you. The security of the District is in your hands, Mohnke. I know how seriously you'll take that obligation.'

'Nothing is more important to me, sir.'

We turned right on Solna Targowa and doubled back past the rear of the police station and the courtyard where I'd seen the chair fall out of Kunde's office window. A soldier was doing a bad job of reversing an olive platform truck out of the service entrance onto the street, its tyres chafing against the kerb like folded party balloons. The recently defenestrated seamstress's bare ankles rolled against the truck's taut canopy.

'Thirty streets, three-hundred-and-twenty residential buildings, and three-thousand–one-hundred-and-sixteen rooms,' Kunde waved expansively. 'One apartment allocated to every four Jewish families, but even with such generous provision, many newcomers find themselves standing on the streets.'

'That seems to be the most popular occupation,' I said. 'Do any of them have jobs?'

'The lucky ones. About 60% still work outside the walls, which they're going to have to plug next year.'

'The walls have gaps?'

'No. At least, not unless the Lesser Spotted Mohnke knows something I don't.'

'You said they're going to have plug the walls?'

'They're going to have to plug the jobs. And sooner rather than later.'

I didn't understand what this meant. The Jews weren't going anywhere. That was the entire point of a Ghetto.

Solna Targova had delivered us on onto the square of Zgody Square, the Ghetto's only open space.

'We're about to meet the one Pole crazy enough to live and work here. Tadeusz Pankiewicz. That's his shop.'

Kunde pointed to a double-fronted corner store at the far end of the square, behind a crowd of young men who dispersed when they saw us. As we got closer, the Polish word Apteka assembled over the doorway.

'A pharmacist?' I said.

'A dispenser of health and happiness, indeed. Rather ironic, no, after this month's clarification from Berlin.'

'What clarification, sir?'

'That's the spirit.' Kunde tapped his nose. 'The Jewish question. You catch on quick, Mohnke.' He dropped his voice to a stage whisper, 'Old Tadeusz serves his purpose, keeping up morale, lending an illusion of permanence. Christ, we've spoiled the Jews rotten when you think about it. Their own pharmacy, hospital, café and cabaret... even had a stand up comedy show for a while. If they think 1941 has been funny, wait till they catch wind of 1942.'

The corners of my mouth furrowed in grimace and grin. What was this clarification? And what was going to happen next year? The only Jewish question I knew was what to do with us now that mass immigration was off the table. Julian Scherner had made a comment about an eventual end to resistance, and now this. I had to find out the truth, because my fears were at that moment ripped from the apocalyptic pages of H.G. Wells. The Germans were a cultured people, not crazed Invaders from Mars.

We had arrived at our destination: Apteka Pod Orlem.

Pharmacy Under the Eagle.

I remembered Shoshana telling me about an old-world druggist she'd visited in Podgorze named after the white-plumed Polish national symbol. Now the shop laboured under a very different bird of prey, the Imperial Eagle of the Third Reich.

Kunde pushed in, letting the door fall against my forearm, and immediately began haranguing the white-coated proprietor on the whereabouts and well-being of an undisclosed female, who was, I supposed, the object of our visit.

Rigidly perpendicular at his counter while the Hauptsturmführer jabbed, the pharmacist quietly closed his till and met Kunde's ranting with an impressively stony face. Magister Pankiewicz was an unassuming man in his early forties, marked by large deep eyes and a drooping black bow-tie. There was something about his posture – all backbone, that impassive gaze - that reminded me of a young Buster Keaton.

Above the odd couple, a wooden spread eagle clasped an ornamental clock, wing tips flanked by a framed certificate on one side and a fairy-tale poster for Soneryl sleeping tablets on the other. A wall of shelves stretched up impossibly high, alternating displays of tall blue and white porcelain jars and wide necked bottles with glass stoppers, labelled in Latin with names like Podophyllin, Ferri Sulph. Exs., Calcii Hypophosph. Below the counter, a few hundred fragile drawers, varnished as a doll's house, hid their pharmacopoeia of ancient remedies.

I loitered at the rear, superfluous, thrust back in time to my parents' grocery store in the Carpathians. There was a long table with two mixing bowls and a pestle and mortar at which I could almost see my mother grinding horseradish roots. Mahogany cabinets towered from dark wooden floorboards, while the far wall was leavened by only the odd stripe of sickly green paint between cupboards. It was a small room, fastidiously cluttered and lit powerfully from brass ceiling lamps. But I had seen enough of the Ghetto to know there was no wattage of bulb capable of dispelling the all-pervasive gloom.

'Of course you can see her,' Pankiewicz was saying. 'But you must remain calm, Hauptsturmführer.'

'I. Am. Perfectly. Calm.'

'And no more shouting, please. The girl's half-terrified already. And that's not in anybody's interest.'

'She's here?'

'I thought it prudent to invite her, yes.'

'Why on earth didn't you tell me?'

'It wasn't for lack of trying,' Pankewicz said. 'If you'd like to come this way.' Unhasping the hinge beside the till, he lifted the counter upright for Kunde to enter. The two men walked past the crowded shelves and disappeared into the pharmacist's office in the corner, leaving me alone.

I stepped up to the counter to try and listen. The only sounds were the ticking of the clock under the eagle and the standard shouts from the streets. The office was well sound-proofed, or Kunde was keeping good on his word to control that temper. It was impressive to see how the pharmacist had stood up to the most senior Nazi in the Ghetto, the degree of power that white coat conferred. I could not imagine Kunde being spoken to in such tones by anybody at 37 Jozefinska.

I backed away, pulled up a stool at the long table and idly examined the instruments. The mixing bowls were spotlessly clean, the marble mortar and pestle unblemished. I wondered whether any of the massed ranks of jars and bottles were in use, or if they were all for display only, like the Jewish Police sign outside the building where old babushkas were flung to their deaths for taking unsanctioned breaks.

I laid the pestle on the table, but it rolled rather quickly off the edge and I had to dive to catch it, at which moment Pankewicz' office door opened and a young brunette emerged wiping a thermometer on her striped smock. She was smiling shyly to herself, but her face wiped blank when she looked up and saw me crouched at the table cradling the pestle.

'It was going to fall,' I said.

'They are not toys to play with.'

'I know. I apologise.'

The assistant performed a curdled curtsey and made her way down the length of the counter, as far away from me as possible. I watched her busy herself making preparations from the tiny drawers. She was no older than the undergraduates I had known at Kiel, in a former life. Once upon a time, we would have worked and laughed together as student and professor. Now, I was the enemy. If Tadeus Pankewicz was the only Pole who lived in the Ghetto, then his staff had to live outside. Which meant the pretty young woman doing her best to ignore me came and went past the soldiers at the gates on a daily basis.

'My name's Harry, by the way.'

'Helena.' She spoke without looking up from her work.

'You might have guessed it's my first day in the Residential District.'

'Welcome, then, if welcome is the word.'

I coughed, clearing my throat like a love-struck chump. I had never been any good at chatting to women I considered attractive, even without the yolk of an SS collar around my neck.

I said, 'I'm not really sure what I'm doing here, to be honest.'

Finally, Helena's sweet eyes flickered up to meet mine.

'At the pharmacy, I mean.'

Before I could work myself up to ask more, the bell rang above the front door and a smart, rotund gentleman carrying a sturdy brown bag bustled in, expelling a puff of a breath. Despite his severe grey parted hair and tweed suit, the man's thick eyebrows bestowed the air of a nascent adolescent. He looked straight through me but his eyes glittered when they alighted on Helena at the far end of the counter.

'Miss Krywaniuk,' he said, smiling. 'I came as soon as I heard.'

'Good morning, Dr. Zurowski.'

'Oberführer Mohnke,' I said, inserting myself between the two. As I reached out to shake the doctor's hand, I realised I was still gripping the pestle.

He stared at it briefly, nose twitching, then returned his attention to Helena Krywaniuk.

'Is everybody here?'

'They're waiting for you, Doctor.'

'Then I shall not tarry. Oh. While I remember.' He raised his bag and held it to his stomach. 'I have the Boric acid you requested.'

'Very good. I was just making the tincture.'

Zurowski set his leather bag down next to the till, rummaged through to the bottom and removed two bottles of thick black liquid that Helena carefully walked back to her work station. The doctor closed his bag, lifted the hinged countertop, squeezed through the opening and let himself into the pharmacist's office. In the few seconds the door was ajar, I saw Kunde pacing the floor, hands clasped at his back. The door closed. I turned, frowned to Helena, but she was bent beneath the counter, busy with her black bottles. I sidewalked a few steps towards her and she rose, pinching her smock at the waist.

'Busy day,' I said.

'They all are.'

'Is it usual to treat sick patients on the premises? There is a hospital, I understand.'

'Forgive me, I don't know the details.'

'Yet you came out with a thermometer - '

The door opened again. Hauptsturmführer Kunde's flushed face poked out and whistled for me. His obedient dog, I trotted the length of the counter.

'This is going to take a while.' He handed over a slip of paper. 'Go back to the station, give this to Brühl and the two of you get over to Kazimierz sharpish to convey an executive measure.'

Conveying executive measures. The Belorussian Police Chief had used the same phrase to describe the massacre outside the synagogue.

I turned the slip over. A single name was scrawled on the other side, above an address: Marek Ringelblum, seventeen Szeroka Street.

'A Jew,' I said. 'Outside the Residential District?'

'Last known hiding place. The bastard's going by the name Jaroslav Filov, but I've got it on very good authority he's JFO.'

The Jewish Fighting Organisation. If I went with Brühl, Marek Ringelblum would be captured, tortured for the names of his associates, then killed. If I went alone, there was a chance I could spare him.

'Sir, if I may. The Kacick Street gate is on the other side of Zgody Square. I could be over the Slaskich Bridge in five minutes – it would take me twice that to return to Jozefinska.'

'This is true.'

'Should I go directly to Szeroka then, or to Brühl?'

'That depends.'

'On?'

'Were you in the habit or querying senior officers' commands in the East?'

'No, sir.'

'Just here, then. Funny Scherer never mentioned that.'

'Forgive me. After what happened to my brother in Warsaw, I don't want these JFO bastards slipping away.'

'Hands On Harry, eh?' As a nickname, it was better than the Lesser Spotted Mohnke. 'You'd better be off then. Just don't screw this up.'

I bowed and hurried out the front door, feeling the glare of Helena Krywaniuk's sweet, baleful eyes between my shoulder blades.

One day, when this was all over, I would come back and tell her the truth. Until then, there was nothing I could say – to anybody – not if I wanted to preserve my cover. I couldn't even tell the man I was racing to rescue.

It would be hard enough to let Marek Ringelblum go

without making him suspicious, never mind confiding that I was a Jew who had infiltrated Willie Kunde's inner sanctum. Word of even a slightly sympathetic SS officer would spread round the Ghetto quicker than Typhus.

There was a very good chance I wouldn't get to exchange a word with Ringelblum. If he was a vigilant member of the JFO and saw an SS officer pounding the door, it could be Harry Mohnke who ended up dead.

And this time with no hope of an Act Two.

A ring of maple trees stood at the northern end of Szeroka Street, its crooked roof-line presiding over a row of quaint merchant houses. I knew the area well. My mother's old shop was less than a mile away, on the other side of the Remuh synagogue, in what used to be the heart of the Jewish Quarter.

17 Szeroka was an abandoned bakery called Pivorski. The plate-glass door and windows were whitewashed and plastered with dusty sheets of newspaper. There was no way to see inside, or for anybody to see out.

I stepped back to the pavement and studied the prescription slip. I needed an excuse, something to blame for the blunder I was about to make. Kunde's handwriting was a densely slanted Gothic marvel, the crossed seven in '17' resembling a miniature swastika. Depending on your perspective, however, it could also be mistaken for the number 4.

I turned round and scanned the terrace on the other side of the street. Even house numbers: 18 directly opposite, 16 on the right, 14 about two hundred metres away.

I grabbed Pivorkski's padlocked handles, rattled the door in its frame, then pounded on the glass.

I hissed in Yiddish, 'They're coming for you. Run now, out the back.'

Then I crossed the cobbled street and slowly approached number 14, studying my piece of paper.

Rapturous shouting from within the house – I had to knock twice before I got a response. This was good. No way they would have heard my noise a minute ago.

A bald man with a scabby red nose and scalp opened the door, saying, 'Come on in, join the party - '

Glassy eyed at eleven o'clock in the morning, he stopped when he saw my uniform. The silver drinks tray he was holding started to slide.

'Don't tell me the neighbours have complained - '

He was cut off by an impromptu round of cheering from a room off the hallway.

'Oberführer Harry Mohnke,' I said. 'Department of Civil Affairs. Papers, please.'

The schnapps bottle and tumblers slid back across the tray as the bald man's other hand fumbled into his back pocket for his wallet, which had got snagged in the fabric.

'We're good Volklistes here, officer, as you can see.' He produced a pink coloured Personal Identity Card, triple stamped by the Third Reich.

A chant broke out behind the door: 'Sieg Heil! Sieg Heil!'

The photograph in the top right corner showed a thoughtful looking younger version of the bearer, before his face became ravaged with dermatitis. I barely glanced at his details.

I said, 'Do you know anybody who goes by the name of Jaroslav Filov?'

'Never heard it before. Why?'

Before I could answer, a chubby youngster in a Wehrmacht uniform came prancing into the hallway. 'Look, Dad, they've got pictures and everything - '

Like his father before him, the soldier stopped in his tracks when he saw me on the doorstep.

'Pictures of what?' I said.

The young soldier raised a limp newspaper from his thigh. 'The Americans.'

A small headline announced the declaration of war against the USA, but the page was subsumed by an enormous photograph of Hitler receiving salutes from the Reichstag, the Führer anointed like Christ by the emanating rays of a white supernova behind the stage.

'Father,' the soldier said. 'What's happening?'

'I'm not sure. Do you know anybody called – what was it – Jaroslav Filo?'

'Filov,' I corrected.

'No,' the son frowned, and pushed a hand through a thick sprouting of dry hair. 'I don't think so. Why?'

'There's been some kind of misunderstanding,' I said. 'Could I please have a drink?'

The old man poured me a measure of peppermint schnapps.

Emboldened by my gulp, I said, 'I have come directly from the SS command post inside the Residential District.' I rubbed the back of my hand across my lips. 'We have just received intelligence that suggests a Jewish terrorist, a member of the Jewish Fighting Organisation, was holed up inside your house. Obviously I see now that that is... unlikely. But the information was delivered to me personally by my commander, Hauptsturmführer Wilhelm Kunde.'

I held up the prescription slip for their inspection. The father was perhaps too drunk to notice, but the son squinted his fat face at the number and said, 'Hang on. That says 17, not 14.'

'What?'

'Pivorskis,' he said to his father. 'It's been empty for months now.'

I returned the glass to the tray. 'I apologise for the intrusion - '

'Lads,' the youngster shouted into the hallway. 'Get your guns. We're going on a Jew hunt.'

I tried to protest, but it was too late. Whooping like a Red Indian, he pushed past me and tore across the cobbles in his stockinged feet. Another two soldiers ran out the house before I could recover my balance.

'Don't you worry, Oberführer,' the father said. 'My boys will get your man.'

That's exactly what I was afraid of. By the time I caught up, one of them had already put a brick through the Pivorksi window and another was picking jagged shards out of the hole. When the gap was big enough, I followed them through.

The small bakers was deserted. I squeezed past the brick ovens at the other end of the counter, the long handled peels and paddles gathering dust against the wall. Opposite the kiln was a fire escape that the soldiers had missed.

The door was open.

I quickly stepped out, heard a manic dog barking across the yards, jumped back in and pulled the door shut. The pungent smell of old flour was already furring my nasal cavities and I thought I was going to be sick.

'Jackpot,' the chubby soldier called. 'Come have a look.'

In the white-tiled back room, arranged between enormous bowls where the Pivorskis used to mix their dough, the soldiers had discovered an entire JFO forgery workshop.

Propped on plastic orange crates was a blackened tray of purloined Nazi stamps and a typewriter. Behind them, three cartons of blank ration books and piles of just about every identification paper known to man: student cards, boy scout cards, social security cards, driving licences, fines, certificates of employment and university diplomas. Hundreds of them. There was even a small roller-printing machine in the corner that I originally mistook for a pastry press.

I returned to the father's house with the youngest Mochowitz soldier-son in order to put in a call to Jozefinska. This provided a brief moment of embarrassment, as I did not know the telephone number. Recalling Anton's sage advice once more, I explained that it was my first day on the job.

Fortunately the operator was able to connect my call to the station; I made a note of the number for future reference. Hauptsturmführer Kunde had not yet returned but I was transferred to his adjutant Rottenführer Ritschak. I explained that Kunde had given Marek Ringelblum's name and address at the pharmacy, told him what I found and requested a truck to 17 Szeroka.

While I was waiting, Mochowitz senior offered another schnapps to toast our success.

'I'm not sure my superior will see it that way,' I said after putting the phone down. 'I had an executive measure for Marek Ringelblum, not just his workshop.'

'That haul will lead to the capture of a dozen Marek Ringelblums,' Mochowitz said, his scabby nose glowing purple. 'Not bad for your first morning, I'd say.'

The truck delivered the contents of the workshop back to 37 Jozefinksa shortly after twelve noon. I unloaded the tray of stamps while two SS soldiers grappled with the orange crates and followed me in through the station's front entrance.

It took a few seconds for the desk officers to look up from their work, but when they did, they greeted us like returning heroes. A ripple of applause broke out from the Vehicles and Statistics departments at the front, and before long the entire office was on its feet, NCOs and adjutants rushing to relieve our burdens, stacking the evidence on a desk that Augustus Brühl cleared opposite his at the far windows. Even the one-armed Rottenführer Ritschak joined us from the first floor to ferry a carton of ration books.

'Anybody would think you're trying to show me up,' Brühl said, then grinned lopsidedly and shook my hand. 'Congratulations. I've moved once in three hours to go to the bathroom and Harry Mohnke's cracked a JFO forgery ring.'

'Beginner's luck.' I slumped into my new seat. 'It's all downhill from here.'

'Bullshit. And I thought I might be onto something with this Kopaliny business.' Brühl pulled his own seat round to my side and sat down so close his knees pressed into my thigh. 'So what happened? The last I saw, you were running up the street after Kunde.'

I told the short version of the discovery on Szeroka Street, omitting my 'confusion' over the two addresses. Brühl explained that I should start work on the resulting reconnaissance. He was aware of Harry Mohnke's previous experience as an SS telecoms engineer, and ascertained that I might not be familiar with investigative protocol. I asked for a brief refresher.

'Obviously the first job's to check archives to see if Marek Ringelblum already has a file, or any known associates. Then it's a case of going through every sheet of paper with a fine-tooth comb. It looks like Ringelblum took his little black book with him, but if he ran in a hurry, there's a good chance he left something behind. Names, addresses, contacts. Christ, we'll even put his doodles under a microscope. You know about indented writing? If he wrote something on top of another piece of paper, the other piece might contain an impression. The printing press will be turned over to the Pomorska, but they'll need you as liaison. Whose office were the stamps taken from? Ditto the cartons of ration books. Who works there, who had access? Pretty Jewish secretaries, printers' assistants, cleaners? Then there's your own paperwork, the report you'll have to submit, in duplicate. One more thing. If good luck comes in threes, you should buy a lottery ticket tonight. And remember who told you.'

'I always remember my friends,' I said. 'What's my second piece of good luck?'

'Your luggage turned up.'

'My what?'

Brühl pointed under the desk. Standing upright was a canvas suitcase with leather corner protectors, stencilled with Harry Mohnke's initial. It looked intact, apart from a long stain like a map of Italy down the front.

'Turns out the Hauptbanhof lost your address, but they got in touch with Pormorska and found out you were stationed here. Voila. A porter brought it over a few minutes ago.'

'Thank God.'

'Lost for forty-eight hours, that's got to be a record, even for Deutsche Rail. You must have given up hope.'

I toed the case affectionately with my boot. 'The thought had crossed my mind.'

'How'd you forget it then?'

I recalled the scene I'd faced with the Belorussian Gendarme outside the train station. Impossible to believe it was only two days ago.

'It was chaos. We were held up for hours - broken rear axle, apparently.'

'At Lublin, right?'

So Brühl knew. There was no point in denying it.

'Everybody got off to use the station facilities. Then there was a huge pile on when they finally got the train going. All mixed up together, soldiers and officers. I thought somebody had walked off with my case my mistake, but I guess not.'

'Cheer up, old boy.'

'Cheer up? Have you seen the size of that stain?'

'I did, yes. I thought it might be an old one.'

'Please. You think I'd have taken a bag like that to my brother's funeral? My guess, some soldier's jar of home-made pickled cabbage exploded in the racks.'

'Why don't you call Left Luggage and complain? They have a duty of care. You might get something back.'

The last thing I needed was to spend any more time talking about what happened at Lublin train station two days ago.

'It's thick canvas,' I said. 'I'm sure my clothes will be fine.'

***

Quite late in the day I realised Wilhelm Kunde had not returned. I couldn't say why, but his absence disturbed me. There was something about our visit to the pharmacist that didn't quite ring true.

I casually asked Brühl if he knew if Kunde was alright, but my colleague did not share my concern. The Hauptsturmführer's comings and goings were notorious. Several times a week he could be expected not to return to Jozefinska after lunch. This was now a whole day, but since nobody else was worried, I kept quiet.

The office was almost empty when Brühl tucked his chair under his desk and offered to buy me a drink to celebrate the Department of Civil Affair's first major breakthrough. Caught off-guard, I did not get my rejection in quickly enough.

'There's a great dive bar I know just north of Rynek Square,' he said, warming to his theme. 'Michael's Cave. Fashionable young crowd, students and the odd trendy professor, but it should be quiet this time of day.'

'The place on Tomasza Street,' I said. 'Isn't that a jazz club?'

Negro music was banned from radio broadcast and the last jazz cellar I frequented in Kiel had closed down in 1937.

'They might play the odd subhuman African standard in the evening,' Brühl said, buttoning up his jacket with long slender fingers. 'I'm sure we can find an oompah band if that's more your style.'

'You'll have to find out my style another night, I'm afraid. I'm not lugging this filthy old suitcase all over town and back.'

'We'll get a cab. Could even drop it at yours first.'

'I can't. Erich's girlfriend is popping round later. There's some jewellery and clothes she needs to pick up.'

'That doesn't sound like a lot of fun. Another night then. Don't work too hard.'

I didn't. Five minutes after Brühl left, I followed suit out onto a dark and grey Jozefinska.

I could look no Jew in the eye. Here I was, taking my suitcase home to a nice warm apartment, while their luggage was piled in the street like trash.

Back through the Lworska gate, I passed a group of bricklayers packing up their barrels as a beautiful, well-dressed young Jewish woman headed towards them, returning from a job outside the Ghetto. One of the lucky ones. Perhaps a secretary in a Government office from where Marek Ringelblum's stamps or ration books had gone missing. Thanks to my exploits, she might return tomorrow to find the Gestapo waiting at her desk.

First she had to navigate the No Man's Land of a pavement of Polish builders. I braced myself for their abuse, but it was a feminine yelp that pierced the air. I span round. One of the men had pulled a stick of quicklime from his barrel and was flicking hot white streaks at the woman's shoulders. Quicklime burnt her hair, her shoulders, her pretty neck and face while the bricklayers stood laughing.

I strode back and gave the woman my handkerchief to wipe the caustic from her skin.

'This Jewess is a commodity in the war effort,' I shouted to the thug with the white stick. 'You've just defaced essential property of the Reich. I ought to report you for treason.'

I waited, fuming, while the woman hurried under the gate and showed her Arbeitsamt pass to the soldiers on guard. She was safe, for now.

I made it back to my apartment without being spotted by Bela Escherich and locked my door. If there were planks and a hammer, I believed I would have nailed myself in.

After changing out of the uniform, I sat down briefly in the living room and gazed at the square of white paint left by the Judas painting and the safety deposit box it had concealed.

Ten minutes later, I took Harry Mohnke's suitcase into his brother's bedroom and opened it on the mattress. The contents had not been marked by whatever stained the front; at least I'd been right about that. In fact, his things were in pristine condition, barely even creased.

A clean white shirt.

A pair of silk pyjamas.

Socks and shorts.

A wash-bag containing razor and toothbrush.

That was it – the standard weekend-away bag. Nothing to help me flesh out the character of the man whose identity I had assumed.

Lifting the case up onto the wardrobe, I stopped when I noticed a bulge in the lid pocket. Back down on the bed, I unzipped the pouch.

Harry Mohnke's leather address book, each entry filed alphabetically. Fourteen names, friends and family, mostly in and around Dahme, a few further afield.

The good news was that Harry had no-one in Cracow who would be tracking him down. If his contacts book was as fastidious as the rest of his suitcase, there wasn't a single soul in the city who knew him. Now his brother was dead, there were no other siblings. Which just left the father. From the way Julian Scherer spoke, the two weren't particularly close. Presumably they had met at Erich's funeral. With any luck, the father would not be communicating any time soon. Harry certainly wouldn't be.

The address book contained one loose sheet behind the back cover, a brief, prophetic note from the dead brother:

If anything happens to me, look behind the Caravaggio.
6-5-1-2-6-9
E.

There it was, finally. The combination.

Inside the safe, arranged in bundles the size of house-bricks, was over six thousand Reichsmarks in crisp five denomination banknotes.

I went to bed early, too early for sleep. Lying in darkness, my mind spiralled through the day's events, reshaping conspiracy from confusion.

Wilhelm Kunde's failure to return to Jozefinska still troubled me, as did the episode at the pharmacy. The more I thought about it, the more it felt like I'd wandered into a scene from a French farce. The secretive examinations in Tadeusz Pankiewicz' back room, the snooty assistant, the mysterious doctor with his imposing eyebrows. Although I had been the one to suggest going alone to Szeroka Street, it was almost as if Kunde had ordained it, by shepherding me out of the station in the first place, cutting me off from Augustus Brühl, the only colleague who could have helped. Was Kunde testing me? To see what Julian Scherer's much vaulted family friend was capable of? If so, had I passed?

Then there was the unexpected arrival of my suitcase. Brühl hadn't said anything, but he must have worked out I was at Lublin train station on the same day the Gendarme's translator was found murdered. If he ever saw a photograph of Damien Plotz, my little adventure was over.

I needed to befriend Brühl, to keep him close. Maybe I should have gone to the jazz cellar after all.

I knew I wasn't going to fall asleep tonight without a stiff drink inside me. Mr. Mochowitz' glass of cheap liquor had settled my nerves that morning. After forty-three years, I had finally developed a taste for alcohol. A war will do that, I suppose.

I dressed in civilian clothes, took down the Caravaggio, opened the safe, peeled off a handful of five Reichsmark notes and went out into a blizzard to buy two bottles of peppermint schnapps.

18

Next morning I was summoned to Kunde's office. The one-armed Rottenführer Rausch was typing in the corner and the Hauptsturmführer was at the ledge, slotting a replacement window pane into place. Job done, he took off his white gloves and tossed them out into the courtyard. Instead of falling, they knotted together at the thumbs and floated away over the roof of the detention centre like a bird.

'I hear congratulations are in order.' Kunde walked round and sat at his desk. Cautiously I approached, remaining on my feet.

'Thank-you, sir.'

Clack.

Clack.

Clack.

'Shame Ringelblum got away though. I know for a fact he was there earlier that morning.' Kunde turned his attention to the paperwork on his desk and I thought I was dismissed.

'I'm just going through your report,' he said. 'Very thorough. Only one thing I want to get straight, in terms of the order of events. Mochowitz came out onto the street and offered use of his telephone after you'd gained access to the bakery?'

'Yes, sir. I wouldn't have had much need of his phone before.'

'No, no,' Kunde murmured. 'I see that.' Dabbing his finger, he turned to the next page. 'Except I called Mr. Mochowitz last night, to offer my personal commendation.'

I cleared my throat. 'Did you, sir?'

Clack.

Clack.

Clack.

'He said the first he knew what was going on was when you were outside number 17, rattling the doors and shouting. Apparently you didn't gain access to the shop then, but crossed the road and knocked on Moschowitz' door, pretending to be looking for the Jew - '

'Look, Wili, I have money.'

'I'm sorry?'

'Lots of money.' I reached inside my jacket and yanked out a chain of banknotes like a magician pulling an endless silk streamer.

Knock.

Knock.

Knock.

I opened my eyes.

Half slumped on Erich Mohnke's couch in t-shirt and shorts, my right shoulder on the floor and the side of my face gummed to the carpet with drool. One empty bottle of schnapps on the table. I must have fallen into a stupor before starting the second. According to my watch, it was quarter-past eight in the morning.

Knock. Knock. Knock.

Somebody was banging on the apartment door.

I lurched across the room fearing I was about to be sick. Ordering my stomach to stand down, I peered through the spy-hole in the hallway. A small man in a Gestapo-like overcoat and large trilby hat gaped back at me.

I opened the door.

'Mr. Mohnke?' he said, removing his hat. The top half of the man's head appeared much too large for the rest of his boyish face, certainly too wide to be adequately covered by the few wisps of blonde hair vainly layered across the scalp.

'Harry Mohnke,' I said.

'Forgive me for disturbing you so early, but I wanted to introduce myself. I'm often away on business. We're neighbours. I live opposite. Your brother was a good man. You must be very proud of him.'

'Yes,' I said, offering my hand. 'I am.'

'Rudolf Ditzen. If there's anything I can do, please let me know. I'm not home that much, but you can always leave a note, or let Mr. Escherich know.'

'Thank-you,' I said. 'And what is it you do, Mr. Ditzen?'

'Industrial surveyor.'

'Right.' I had no idea what that entailed. 'I appreciate your kindness, I really do.'

I kept a grin plastered across my jaw until Rudolf Ditzen disappeared down the corridor to the stairwell.

Twenty minutes later, clutching the unopened bottle of schnapps in a checked cloth bag, I was out on the street.

Instead of doubling back on Tragutta towards the Lworska gate, I followed the Ghetto wall round on Kacik where the snow was deeper and crossed the river on the Slaskich Bridge. I strode north through my mother's old neighbourhood, forking right at the Remah synagogue for Szeroka Street.

Mochowitz answered his door in a dressing gown as purple as the scab on his nose.

'Oberführer Mohnke,' he said. 'Not more Jews in the neighbourhood, I trust?'

'We must always be vigilant,' I said. 'But no, none that I'm aware of. I wanted to thank-you again for your family's assistance. As I mentioned, it was my first day in the Ghetto, and I earned quite a few plaudits for my discovery. To a large degree, I owe that to you, and your continuing discretion. If my oversight with the addresses should ever come to light, my reputation would, I'm afraid, suffer... quite dramatic consequences.'

'It is a pleasure to be of assistance. Trust me, it's my boys who feel like heroes. They'll be dining out on the story for months.'

'Well, this little aperitif is a token of my gratitude.' I removed the gift from the bag and presented it as ceremoniously as one can a bottle of peppermint schnapps.

'Humbled, sir. Touched and humbled.'

'And should you or your family ever need a well placed associate within the SS,' I continued. 'Please call me at Jozefinska Street. I even know the telephone number now.'

I gave Mochowitz a slip of paper with my contact details.

'Very kind.'

'Heil Hitler.'

Half a dozen Ordnungsdienst men were assembling for roll call outside the station when I arrived. Their senior officer inspected the line, fussing over buttons and belts. Although not wearing his infamous white admiralty jacket – perhaps it would have rendered him invisible in the snow - the tiny figure of Symche Spira was unmistakable. Struggling under heavy grey coat and cavalry breeches, he looked like a child let loose in his father's wardrobe. The eyebrows, glasses, nose and moustache could have been styled on Groucho Marx. Spira stopped halfway down the line and tutted at a crooked cap. He reached his spindly arms up to straighten the man's brim, while the officer beneath grimaced and the square-jawed bruiser next in line closed his eyes and sighed in grim forbearance.

A black limousine pulled up on the dot of nine o'clock. Hauptsturmführer Kunde swung out and crunched across the pavement, ignoring the salutes of the ODs and giving myself only the most cursory of nods. Inside the building, he made straight for the bolt-hole on the first floor and would not be sighted again for the rest of the morning.

Augustus Brühl was typing a letter at his desk at the far end of the office. Noticing his empty cup, I offered to fetch drinks and returned with two strong black coffees.

'So did you get to hear any subhuman African standards?' I asked.

'No. Had an early night. You?'

'Same.'

'How about the borscht juice?'

'Sorry?'

'Or was it pickled cabbage.'

'I have no idea what you're talking about.'

Brühl stopped typing and made a show of folding the piece of paper down over the carriage roller in order for an obstructed view across the desk.

'Your suitcase,' he said. 'Any stains?'

'Ah, right. No, all good. I told you, thick canvas.'

'Glad to hear it. Erich's girlfriend?'

'Yes, she popped round.' I shrugged stoically. 'That's the

last of his stuff gone now.'

And the last time I could use sorting through Erich's belongings as any kind of excuse, I realised.

'Things will get easier,' Brühl said, letting the sheet of paper spring back behind the carriage. 'With time.'

All in all, it was an encouraging start to the day. Kunde was back in the building and wasn't about to summon me upstairs for a dressing down anytime soon. If he had already forgotten about Szeroka Street, that was absolutely fine with me. Brühl appeared not to have any lingering suspicions about the nature of my stop-over at Lublin station either. The only person who'd spent the night obsessing about all of it was me. Here at Jozefiniska, it was business as usual.

Which provided me with a different set of challenges: I didn't know what 'normal' was. I was flattered that Brühl thought enough of my abilities to let me get on with the work single-handedly, but it would have been helpful to know that work actually entailed.

The Marek Ringelblum case had already run its course. We'd searched through every scrap of paper yesterday; there was nothing to follow up, never mind anything for me to conceal. The Gestapo had come over night and taken the printing press back to Pomorska. At some point I could expect to be called upon, as liaison, but until then, I had to find a way to occupy myself.

All I could come up with was sorting through the contents of my new desk. The furniture had obviously belonged to somebody else before me – I didn't like to think about their fate. In the more hopeful fantasy, my predecessor was dismissed for failing to keep the desk drawers tidy. Things were certainly a mess down there, a dusty, ink-stained mess strewn with loose drawing pins and stray staples.

I wondered if it was possible to waste an entire week pretending to be busy. Why not? Certain teachers I knew at Kiel had made careers of it.

With roll call over, Symche Spira came in hopping from foot to foot to advise us of a 'red hot' lead from an informant. Brühl laced his fingers behind his head and leant back, crossing his boots on the slats of an empty seat. I got up and pulled another chair from the waiting area by the window.

'Sit down,' I told Spira. 'You're giving me motion sickness.'

'Thank-you, sir. But I prefer to stand. Bad back. The doctor said - '

Brühl rolled his eyes. 'Get to it.'

Spira removed his cap. I half expected his glasses-and-nose ensemble to come away with it.

A Jewish high school beauty called Anna Salit had got herself mixed up with Rudolf Korner, assistant chief of Cracow Gestapo. In exchange for her protection, the girl had allowed herself to be 'turned out' as an informant. Thanks to her looks and intelligence, Salit became one of the most feared Jew-hunters in the city. No shelter, bunker or safe-house was safe from her reaches. One of her favourite tricks was to swaddle a doll in a baby carriage and wait around in playgrounds, eavesdropping on Polish mothers. In this way she heard from a neighbour of a spinster called Danuta Jagiellon who was hiding a Jewish lover by the name of Moses Montefiore. Salit followed the neighbour home to the Rondo Mogilskie area and had just this minute supplied the address to Spira, who was barely able to contain his glee.

'That's it?' Brühl said. 'One measly Jew? Hardly seems worth my while.'

'Jagiellon's a rich cabaret singer. If we play her right,' Spira paused, leaning in and shaking, for some inexplicable reason, a pair of imaginary maracas. 'The bitch might turn out to be a golden goo-oo-oose.'

'Alright,' he sighed wearily. 'I'll add her to the list.'

When Spira left, Brühl jumped up to use the bathroom, telling me to check the Registry. 'If Montefiore's got family, we might be able to squeeze them too.'

I suspected the lover's name was an Akiva alias. I'd once taught a short course on nineteenth century London and knew that the original Moses Montefiore was a Sherriff of the city, and something of a Jewish activist, in his own way. At a banker's dinner party, an anti-Semitic nobleman whom Montefiore was seated opposite recounted his recent travels to Japan, where 'they have neither pigs nor Jews.' 'In that case, you and I should go back,' Montefiore replied. 'So it will have a sample of each.'

The only Registry I knew was the one where I'd searched for Marek Ringelblum. I was on my knees checking for non-existent Montefiores when my colleague came back from the bathroom, buttoning his overcoat.

'Have you already checked the Registry then?'

'Which one?'

'The whole District.' He turned and pointed to the wall under the staircase. 'Eight filing cabinets, every single animal in the zoo, all seventeen-thousand of them, alphabetically indexed.'

I should have thought of this before. Everybody had to be accounted for, even the Jews. It was the German way. To think I hadn't looked yet. Who else could be in those drawers? The last I'd heard from Shoshana, she'd taken my mother and sister to live in the countryside. But that was six months ago, an eternity during war. They could be anywhere now, including right underneath my nose.

I crossed the room and overshot the cabinet labelled 'M, N & O', stopping instead at its neighbour, 'S, T & U', where I would find any imprisoned Sieglers. I opened the top drawer and flicked through the name cards, starting with Sachs and getting as far as Scholem when Brühl approached, pointing to the cabinet on my left.

'Montefiore begins with M,' he said.

I knocked my head. 'Stupid me. I was looking for Salit.'

Outside, the snow was so heavy it was quicker to walk across the river to the Old

Town. We headed north into the Ghetto, crowds parting to let us pass. A sullen young man in a shop doorway removed his cap and stood watching us go, clenching and unclenching fists at his thighs. A gaunt woman lay twisted against the wall, starving to death before my eyes. Such thick, dark locks and the olive skin of an Italian movie star. She looked to be in her early twenties, with the body of an animate corpse. How did a young woman end up like this? Brühl picked a path over her withered legs and said, 'Even crocodiles look after each other better than this lot.'

We turned right on Solna Targowa to cut across Zgody Square. I realised I had made the same journey yesterday, at almost the same time.

'Are you sure Kunde's happy with me?' I said. 'He brushed past earlier with a face like thunder.'

'I wouldn't take it personally. It's not you.'

'What is it then?'

'I don't like gossip. I leave that to Vehicles and Statistics.'

'You don't talk much to anyone, I've noticed that.'

'It's difficult for... men like me,' Brühl said. 'I'm not the social type. The office have all been together since March, when the Zoo was established. Civil Affairs is new.'

'How long have you been here?'

'When was Monday? You lose track of time in this place. Since then, anyway.'

'You only started a day before me? I thought you were part of the furniture.'

'I've known the Hauptsturmführer for two years, on and off. When I heard they were giving Spira a spin, I jumped at the chance. Came over from the Governor General's castle.'

'Because you like dealing with informants?'

Brühl smiled. 'Because I like working in a gold-mine. Haupttreuhandstelle Ost take the lion's share when it comes to Aryanising enemy property, but we do alright. Enough to keep a chap in cognac and cologne anyway. And Kunde's a decent boss, which is rare enough. Rottenführer Rausch, upstairs? Not the smartest tool in the box. The Hauptsturmführer keeps him on as adjutant – a one-handed typist. That's loyalty. And now there's you.'

'Me? I don't think Kunde had much choice in the matter.'

'Don't be cryptic, Harry, it doesn't suit.'

'What are you getting at?' I stopped and looked over my shoulder. 'I'd rather this didn't get out, at the station. Is it alright if we keep it just between you and me?'

'Absolutely.'

'My father's close friends with Oberführer Scherner.'

A beat passed, marked by a whistle. 'Talk about friends in

high places.'

'As Erich's little brother, I've lived my whole life under a shadow. Now I'm finally out of it, I don't want people thinking I got special favours. That sounds callous, but I don't mean it.'

'I understand.'

'Let's just say an arrangement was made, and I got lucky.'

'Good for you. Seriously. Make the most of it. The gold-mine's open for another few months yet.'

I nodded, unsure what he meant.

'Your old man and Scherner, eh, you dark horse. How do they knew each other?'

For once, I was all out of lies. A picture of Rudolf Ditzen in his large hat and coat floated into my mind.

'They were neighbours.'

'In - where was it - Dahme?'

I nodded, desperate to bring this strand of the conversation to an end. We had reached Zgody Square. On the other side of the square, a short queue stretched out the pharmacy door, the Ghetto's older residents leaning on their sticks.

'Look here,' I said. 'If Kunde's in any kind of trouble, you would let me know.'

'In trouble?'

'If he's unwell. You said we might only have a few months left...'

'God, no. Kunde's not going anywhere. Strong as an ox, that man. That's his problem, really. An excess.'

'Of?'

'Vitality.'

'Now you're being cryptic,' I said.

'Let's just say, the Hauptsturmführer's not the one in trouble. He's the one who got somebody else in trouble. Why do you think Dr. Eyebrows was summoned?'

'I have no idea.'

'Come on Harry, use your imagination. Back room job. Hot towels, coathanger...'

Brühl mouthed the three syllables, for we were approaching the pharmacy corner.

Abortion.

'Who's Kunde been schtupping?' I said. 'Not a Jew?'

But my companion would not be drawn.

The elderly couple outside braced themselves as we passed. Doubled over on two scythe-like sticks, the man cursed a greeting, ragged white beard fringing his coat like a ruff. The woman clasped his arm with an arthritic claw and turned to watch us go. Her tiny skull rustled in its headscarf like an Egyptian relic.

Rondo Mogilskie was a quiet suburb on the north-east of the old town, but it wasn't promising. The apartments might have been considered chic at the turn of the century, but the buildings had not aged well. We stood on Jozefa Brodowicza looking up to Danuta Jagiellon's sixth floor.

I said, 'Damn that Spira for sending us on a wild goose chase.'

'In the folk tale, the goose is well hidden, otherwise somebody else would have found it first.'

'Good point.'

'The youngest brother discovers the goose that lays the golden egg in the roots of an old oak tree.'

'You're confusing your versions,' I said. 'That's the Grimm Brothers. It's the feathers which are golden, not the eggs. After the brother, the whole village tries plucking the bird, but they all get stuck fast, a whole line, glued to each other.'

'Hang on. There are two golden geese stories?'

'Both end badly,' I said. 'The other one's English, but don't hold that against it. The English goose lived in a nice barn, with a greedy farmer. He wanted her to lay two eggs a day instead of one. When she said she couldn't, the farmer killed her.'

'English folk tale logic,' Brühl scoffed. 'Declare war on Hitler one minute, let us walk all over Poland the next.'

The apartment door was opened by a woman in her seventies, possibly the same age as the wizened babushka outside the pharmacy, but there the similarities ended. Bright yellow hair cascaded on her shoulders and taut silver blouse. A chain of belts encircled her hips, hoisting a white leather skirt above her knees. Barefoot, varnished toenails, one ankle bracelet.

'Frau Jagiello?' She nodded, rolling her lips together. Her mouth was painted like a clown's, a ring of red from the nostrils to the chin the only sign that something was amiss.

I enquired if her daughter was at home.

'There are absolutely no children allowed in these rooms, young man. I believe they are reared next door, however.'

'It's a Danuta Jagiellon we are looking for,' I said. 'Could that be you, Fräulein?'

Brühl brushed past without awaiting an answer. I swept my hand through the air and followed Frau Jagiello inside.

The living room was as garish as its owner, but of considerably more value to a man like August Brühl. His eyes swept like klieg lights over the gilt-edged mirrors and gold drapes. There were no newspapers, no mess, no dirt – no sign of a masculine presence in the room for at least forty years. Frau Jagiellon showed us to a pair of brocaded chairs beside a vase while she seated herself in a leopard-skin throne by the fireplace.

'I don't wish to alarm you,' I began while Brühl continued his shameless inventory. 'But we're investigating reports of Jewish bandits holed up on the sixth floor. Have you noticed any suspicious activity?'

'I wouldn't know, my dear. I haven't been outside for years.'

'Are you alone here?'

'I am alone, but I am not lonely. I feed my mind on the finest diet of dramatic Scandinavian compositions. Ibsen and Strindberg are my companions in dotage.'

'That's heartening to know,' I said. 'But presumably they don't bring the groceries.'

'I have a house-maid once a week, for milk and whiskey -
'

'I'm sorry,' Brühl said, hopping to his feet. 'May I use the bathroom?'

Frau Jagiellon looked from him to me and back again. She might have been old, but she was as a shrewd as a serpent. 'Down the corridor, last door on the left.'

Alone, I continued. 'And you receive no other visits or gentleman callers?'

'You are the first contender for the sobriquet in many months.'

'And how about neighbours. You mentioned a family with children next door?'

'I hear their racket from time to time, but that's - '

When I was sure Brühl was out of ear-shot, I sprang off the seat and kneeled at the old lady's side, taking her jewelled fingers in mine. 'Please, Frau Jagiellon, we haven't much time. I want to help you. Tell me where Montefiore is.'

'What are you doing?' She pulled her trembling hand away. 'Get off me!'

'Not everyone in this uniform means to do you harm. But you have to tell me the truth.'

'I am telling you the truth. How dare you suggest otherwise! What is this, some kind of trick?"

'I'm not a Nazi,' I said. 'I'm - '

A piercing whistle rang out from the hallway. The old lady gasped and gripped my wrist as Brühl shouted, 'Harry. Get down here. I've found our man.'

Frau Jagiellion's head bowed. A small voice croaked, 'What will to happen to me now?'

'I don't know.' Whispering, I rose to my feet and backed away. I tried to help. I'm sorry.'

Three doors were open off the main corridor. I guessed Brühl had nosed into each one. I paused at the first, the dining room. Wood stove and stone sink, low-hanging chandelier over the table, four empty chairs.

Next door, a luxurious dressing table held hairbrushes, perfumes, and candles. Books and newspapers lined the bedroom shelves. The bed's coverlet was tossed back, revealing nothing but empty space between the mattress and the carpet.

I found Brühl crouching in the corner of the second bedroom. He was alone, except for two dolls propped against the wainscoting, a grinning Mickey Mouse and a pig in a red bow-tie, and the full-size stuffed ostrich towering above, its beak pointing to the window. I approached the bizarre menagerie, stopping when I saw the wooden cot my colleague was squatting over.

Without turning round, he said, 'Say hello to Moses.'

Squirming contentedly behind its bars, a naked infant squeezed Augustus Brühl's index finger. The covenant of circumcision had already been performed between its plump thighs.

I might have muttered, 'Jesus Christ.'

'Good old Symche Spira. He always delivers the goods. Come over here, will you, keep this chap quiet.'

Brühl stood; we swapped places. The baby reached for my finger. How easily its affections were transferred.

Brühl said, 'Don't these Poles realise we're trying to save their wretched country?'

'What on earth are we going to do with the old dear? She can't go back to the station.'

'Why not?'

'She's Polish.' I waited a second but Brühl's furrowed brow only deepened. 'It's a Jewish Ghetto.'

'The cells are full of Poles. They're incorrigible, I told you. Trespassing, smuggling, looting. We only bother arresting Jews if they've got money - '

Frau Jagiellion appeared in the doorway, clawing the rings from her fingers. 'Take them all,' she said. 'I wouldn't last a day in prison.'

I turned back to the cot, leaving Brühl to collect his bounty.

I was staring at the baby's gurning face - the left eye creasing shut while the other rolled like a marble, the way its button nose lifted up to one side, curling the lips like a fortune-telling fish – when a pistol exploded behind us.

Frau Jagiellion remained on her feet for a second, swaying, then fell against the door-frame. A bone snapped as she went down, possibly her hip. Not that it mattered. A hole had opened up in the middle of her forehead from which a thick line of blood tracked like lipstick.

Replacing his pistol in its holster, Brühl looked at me and said, 'She was right about one thing. They'd have eaten her alive in prison.'

Moses' face contorted into a tight purple bud then opened into a howl. I tried feeding my fingers into its mouth like a pacifier, but it almost choked.

I managed to say, 'What about the baby?'

'Honestly, Harry. What kind of monster do you think I am?' Brühl tumbled a handful of rings into his tunic pocket. 'Killing babies? Not my style at all. That's why I brought you.'

I had resigned myself to committing heinous acts in order to preserve my identity, but this... It was out of the question. I gripped the bars as if I might lift the cot up, infant and all, and crash it down on my colleague's head.

'For God's sake.' Brühl stepped up so close behind me I felt his chest against my back. He gently squeezed my shoulders. 'I was joking. Babies have a habit of soiling themselves on me – you carry it. Come on, let's get out of here. HTO will be here any minute. We'll let them clean up.'

19

With Moses Montefiore wrapped in a nest of blankets, we trudged back through the slush to Podgorze. Rocked by motion and cocooned against my chest, the baby slept. Brühl tried engaging me in conversation about the collected worth of Frau Jagiello's apartment, and what amount her rings might be pawned for. My muted responses conveyed what I hoped passed as aloofness, and he soon stopped. We walked the rest of the way in silence.

Just outside the Ghetto, on Kacik Street, a detachment of elderly male prisoners who must have been standing around the streets with no jobs to go to found themselves shoveling snow to clear a path for Wilhelm Kunde's limousine. The rear window cracked down and his white-gloved fingers beckoned through the gap and beckoned us.

'I'll see you back at the office,' Brühl said.

'What do I do with baby?'

But Brühl was already climbing into the back of Kunde's limo and did not supply an answer.

If the prisoners had been able to work faster, if we'd met the Hauptsturmführer's procession earlier, I might have been able to spare Moses from his fate. But the guards at the Kacik Street gate had already seen me. An SS officer cradling a swaddled baby was not a sight they were likely to forget.

I had no choice but to carry Moses into the Ghetto, enduring their stares with a mirthless grin.

Dr. Fischer at the Jozefinska hospital could not accept the child and directed me further down the street to the House of Orphans at number 14. A softly-spoken old man called Dawid Kurzmann, Director of Religious Matters, received the baby with warmth, but warned that the orphanage was already stretched beyond capacity. They only managed to limp along thanks to donations from the Ghetto's inhabitants. A mentally disabled boy named Juliusz Propst had been successfully transferred to a specialist institution in Iwonicz in 1940, only to be returned to the orphanage this summer, in accordance with German policy. And only last week - before my time, I pointed out – Kurzmann had been forced to accept a group of ten children from a Cathlolic nursery outside the Ghetto walls, on Koletek Street. Although uncircumcised and well versed in the catechisms, SS Obersturmbannführer Pavlu had insisted they were Jewish. Unsurprisingly, the new group were finding it difficult to adjust.

I realised I had listened too sympathetically to Dawid Kurzmann's complaints.

'You'll have no worries with this one,' I grinned, extricating my finger from the baby's hot fist. 'With a name like Moses, he'll fit right in.'

20

Even after doubling my dosage of schnapps to two bottles that night, I resurfaced from dreamless depths at four in the morning, my mind churning. It was fair to say the new job was not working out as hoped.

In three days, what had I accomplished?

Closed down a Jewish forgery workshop, confiscated the equipment, failed to stop an elderly Polish partisan from being executed, rescued a baby from a life of pampered safety and delivered it to an over-stretched orphanage in the Ghetto. It was difficult to see how a real SS officer could have acted much worse.

Was I supposed to spend the rest of the war at the beck and call of Jews like Symche Spira and Anna Salit? Scurrying over the city to carry out their dirty work? The worst of it was, I couldn't even bring myself to dislike them. The informers were doing what it took to survive. I had come back to Cracow to help the wretched, withered roots of humanity starving to death on the pavement, those who could not help themselves. The old man and woman queuing outside the pharmacy. The children. My own mother and sister, wherever they were.

I took another fifty Reichmark from behind the Caravaggio and found the only baker in Podgorze open at 5 AM. Filling my pockets with pastries, crepes and onion cakes, I ventured back to Lworska. There were only two guards at the gate at this time of morning, and no dogs. I passed through clutching my overcoat to stop the bread rolls from banging against my thighs.

As I'd hoped, the streets were empty. Even the Ghetto had to sleep. I retraced my steps from yesterday, heading briskly towards Solna Targowa.

The gaunt woman was still twisted against the wall under a stiff blanket, her hair and lashes rimed with frost. I broke off a chunk of plain white roll and held it to her lips until she bit.

Too weak to chew, she let the bread dissolve on her tongue and grunted for another. I fed her this way until a door banged in the street. Placing two more bread rolls under her blanket, I hurried away.

I did not have to search too hard for more in need. There were a dozen unfortunates sleeping rough on the main thoroughfares, propped up in doorways and alcoves.

Where I heard the disconsolate wails of children through tenement windows, I posted pastries through their letter boxes.

My tour brought me back onto Jozefinska. The House of Orphans was locked, but I succeeded in raising its director, Anna Feuerstein. I introduced myself and explained that I had delivered Moses Montefiore into her care yesterday.

'If you're here to interrogate the lad, Oberführer, you'll have to come back in about eighteen months. He should be able to manage 'Yes' and 'No' by then.'

'It's my job to keep an accurate tally of population numbers for the Registry,' I told her. 'May I assume the boy has survived his first night?'

'You may.'

'Thank-you.' I nodded, turned to leave, then stopped, patting my coat for the last of the onion cakes. I handed Director Feurstein the greasy bag. 'A little stale, but I'm sure your children aren't fussy.'

At 6.40 AM, I was the first German to arrive at the station. There was a skeleton crew of Jewish Police guarding the cells in the courtyard, but otherwise I was alone. I made straight for Wilhelm Kunde's office and knocked, but of course there was no answer. The door was locked. My guess was that Rottenführer Ritschak had the only spare key. I snooped around the secretaries' desks in the corridor, but there were no important documents to discover.

Downstairs, an officer from Vehicles and Statistics had arrived and was busy making coffee. I declined his offer of a cup and headed to my desk, but noticed Symche Spira at the back wall, a set of headphones clamped over his head in place of the usual peaked cap. Jerusalem's next Chief of Police, catching up on the overnight reports from North Africa. I doubled back to the wall of filing cabinets containing the Ghetto Registry.

After twenty minutes of searching, I was able to state categorically that as of Friday December 18th, 1942, there were no female Sieglers living anywhere within the Ghetto walls. I didn't know whether or not to celebrate. I crossed over to the wall of maps on the other side of the office.

Shoshana's last letter had been franked in the town of Novy Sacz, about 60 km south-east of Cracow. She had not disclosed the farm's address, which had been sensible at the time, but infuriating six months later. I found Novy Sacz on the map and made a crude sketch of the surrounding locale, including the names of the eight closest villages. With a vehicle, I would be able to get round them all in a day. It was a start. As I was slipping the sketch into my pocket, a whiff of cologne announced a presence at my back.

I turned and flinched: Augustus Brühl standing very close, practically leering into my face.

'Good God, you frightened me.'

'Cursed with fleet feet, my mother was a ballerina. Which worm are you looking for?'

'Which what?'

'The early bird and all that. I thought I was getting a good start on the day. What unearthly time did you get in?'

'Couldn't sleep. Been here a couple of hours now.'

'Progress?'

'Not so much. I'm still getting to know the lay of the land.' I leant away from him and tapped the edge of the map.

'Literally.' Brühl put an arm around my shoulder and turned to study the terrain. 'Beautiful countryside outside the city, if you get the chance. Eagle-nest castles, the Tatra mountains, Zakopane town...' His other hand flicked from attraction to attraction. 'We should go for a spa one weekend.'

I thought about the risk, in terms of public nudity. Like Moses Montefiore, I too had been circumcised. 'I suffer from quite bad eczema, so maybe not such a good idea.'

'Healing waters, what could be better?'

'I'm talking about the risk to other bathers. My skin is

prone to... quite significant flaking.'

'Ja, enough! That sounds ghastly.' Brühl's face contorted into a rictus, then brightened as his finger trailed up the main road north of Cracow. 'Remember that business in Lublin?'

I frowned, staring at the city on the map, trying not to fixate on the convergence of railway lines.

Brühl continued. 'Police interpreter with his head caved in?'

'Oh, yes, right. Gang of Poles arrested.'

'One of them gave Gusta Draenger's name, in Kopaliny.'

'That's right. Turns out his story was full of shit. The Hauptsturmführer and I took a ride out to the Draenger's farm yesterday afternoon. Nothing doing but a bunch of snooty Zionists pretending to be farmers. They really are learning how to plough the Holy Land.'

'You left them to it?'

'What's another few months, in the grand scheme of things?'

Later that day, when I had some time to myself, I pulled Gusta Draenger's file from the Registry. She wasn't living in the Ghetto anymore, but the Nazis had compiled more information on her and the husband than just about anybody else.

Gusta and Shimshon Draenger were first identified as troublemakers when they met in the Akiva youth movement as teenagers. The story of idealist young lovers was a familiar one to me. I had seen the same in Vilno with Vita Kempner and Abba Kovner, and, to a lesser extent, my own sister and Herman Glik.

Gusta went on to become one of Akiva Cracow's most active members, committed to educational work, first as a group leader and later as a member of the movement's central committee in Poland. At the same time, she wrote for and edited the youth newspaper, *Zeirim*, and kept the movement's records in the city.

Following the invasion of September 1939, Shimshon Draenger was arrested by the Gestapo for having edited Akiva's main paper, *Divrei Akiva*, which had published articles by Irene Harand, an Austrian Catholic who had founded an anti-Nazi organisation called The Jewish Defence Movement. Gusta, by this point was engaged to Shimshon, asked for permission to go with her husband to the Troppau concentration camp near Opava in the Sudeten Mountains.

At the beginning of 1940, an enormous bribe obtained their release, but the couple were placed under surveillance, obligated to report to the Gestapo three times a week and to sever all relations with their comrades and younger members of the movement. Reports show however that they continued to meet in secret at various informal House Committees.

Gusta and Shimshon married in the spring of 1940. So strong was their love that Gusta could not bear to part from her husband. On three separate occasions she gave herself up to the Gestapo upon discovering they had arrested Shimshon, even though she was not wanted herself. In May 1941, she had followed him into the Ghetto. Now husband and wife were out, tilling the fields and dreaming of the Holy Land.

I found the letter that the Jewish Self-Help Society had sent from an office in Nowy Wisnicz to Chief Muller, requesting 'approval for a series of courses to be offered for the purpose of retraining the Jewish youth' and 'permission to establish a farm in Kopaliny'. The letter was dated Saturday 12th December, the very day I left Lublin with the Gendarme.

I took this coincidence as a sign that our paths were destined to cross. But the Draengers were not my immediate concern; they had escaped the walls of the Ghetto. There had to be an element of a resistance left behind. I was determined to find it and establish contact.

I went back to the Gestapo surveillance reports of 1940, cross-referencing the Draengers' young Akiva associates with the contents of the Registry. Of the twenty-three names, only one was listed as a resident: Syzmek Lustgarden. He was never personally under surveillance and was now just one name amongst seventeen-thousand. Syzmek's file was minimal. Born on April 4th 1921, currently residing in an apartment at 13 Jozefinska, a stone's throw from the police station.

Slight though the information was, there was another

coincidence. Syzmek lived next door to the House of Orphans, number 14. I had passed his building only a few hours previously. Twice in two days, in fact. Although my pulse raced at this, I tried not to read too much into the proximity. After all, the Nazis had taken the population of an entire metropolis and condensed it into one tiny suburb. The Ghetto Jews lived in a city of doll-houses.

***

I walked past number 13 on three separate occasions that afternoon, and stayed behind after the rest of the office had gone home. When Rottenführer Ritschak left at seven, I positioned myself at the first floor window. Syzmek's building was on the opposite side of Jozefinska, about a hundred yards to the left. The terraces were three stories high, and Syzmek lived on the top floor, which was divided into as many as five rooms. I had no way of knowing which was Syzmek's. But it didn't matter. Eventually that night I saw enough to know that my intuition had paid off.

The crowded street began to thin out after eight o'clock, when it was too bleak for anybody but the most resilient or destitute. Shortly before nine, a group of four young men broke the curfew of cold, walking past the police station from the direction of the Lworska end. They crossed the road a little further up, and disappeared inside number 13. Within five minutes they were followed by another group, two men and three women. A little later, a third group approached from Solna Targowa. I was too far away to distinguish their gender, but I counted another four people enter the building.

By a quarter-past eight, Syzmek Lustgarden's building had absorbed a total of fourteen additional bodies. They were assembling to celebrate the onset of the Sabbath, taking their seats at the festive table covered with white cloth and candles, as we had done on Pilies Street.

This was it. I had found the headquarters of Akiva's Youth Movement.

21

There was a letter for Harry Mohnke in the mail-box when I arrived home, the first piece of mail since my arrival in the city.

The envelope was handwritten, and franked far away in the north-east of the country, in Neustadt, the nearest large town to Dahme.

Dear Son,

I've thought long and hard about what you said at St. Mary's chapel.

I'm glad we had a chance to talk after the service. If your brother's death has brought the two of us back to our senses, then, well, that's something. What I'm trying to say is, I would like to accept your invitation.

I intend to travel to Cracow on December 24th, and will leave on the morning of the 26th. If you could recommend a suitable hotel somewhere near your apartment, I will make the necessary arrangements.

Yours,

Papi

22

I'll say this for Otto Mohnke's letter: having seven days before I was compelled to leave the city to become a fugitive certainly focussed the mind. There were two things I had to do before I fled.

Most difficult was to make contact with Syzmek Lustgarden. The convenient way was to send a letter of explanation to apartment 13. But Syzmek could dismiss a letter as a hoax, or a honey trap. There was also the fear that a piece of paper could fall into the wrong hands. There was only one alternative: we had to speak face to face.

But first, I had to discover what exactly it was the Nazis were planning for next year. Scherer and Kunde both mentioned the Jews were running out of time. Augustus Brühl told me that the Ghetto 'gold-mine' was only open for another few months. Yesterday he'd repeated the phrase, when he spoke of closing down Kopaliny: What's another few months, in the grand scheme of things?

The morning after Otto Mohnke's letter arrived, I told Brühl it had been a hard week and I was ready to take him up on his offer of a drink. We agreed to go to Michael's Cave straight after work.

As we left the station at 5 o'clock, Brühl told me he needed the bathroom. He'd catch me up. I stepped out onto Jozefinska and began to dawdle towards the Lworska gate. The street on Saturday was the quietest I had seen it in the daytime. Religious services were forbidden in the Ghetto. I wondered how many secret Sabbath ceremonies were being held behind closed doors, in cellars, attics and back rooms like number 13, while others stood guard.

Brühl caught up with me at the end of the street, reeking of cologne, his short dark hair slicked back with water. He slapped my back and removed his wallet from his trousers.

'Those rings pawned for two thousand Marks,' he said,

fanning a bunch of banknotes. There was a young Jewish couple up ahead, embracing against a doorway, but otherwise our side of the street was empty.

'Put it away,' I said.

'Take your share.'

'Not here. It looks cheap.'

'A thousand Marks not good enough for you.'

'It looks grubby, handing over money in the street. Something Jews would do.'

'Fair enough.' Brühl put his wallet away. 'I just don't want you to think I'm stiffing you.'

'I don't.'

'Kunde couldn't be happier, you know that. Jagiellon's apartment made him very rich, Scherer too.'

'I can't claim much credit for that. Right place, right time.'

'You're my good luck charm anyway.'

The two Jews stepped apart as we passed, the man tipping the brim of his hat and burying his black beard in the crook of his shoulder. At that moment, I knew I had seen them before.

They were certainly not in the flushes of youth. Husband and wife might now sport heads that glistened like Russian crude oil, but there was no doubting they were the same wizened couple I'd passed yesterday on the steps of the pharmacy. I stopped and marvelled at their rejuvenation.

***

Several blurred hours later, Brühl was drunk enough for me to safely ask my question without raising suspicion. Not that the first part of the evening had been a waste of time. It was good that Brühl had warmed to me so quickly; we were laughing and banging the table like freshman undergraduates at the end of the first week of studies.

The only people making more noise in the cave than us was a party of Polish businessman, bluff red-faced types in three-piece suits. One of the most jovial and handsome men paid a fleeting visit on his way to the bathroom; Brühl introduced him as Oskar Schindler, a sound Party man with friends in high places who owned the Ghetto's metal-work factory, Emalia. Pots and pans, but a gold-mine all the same.

With a succession of Red Barons in his hand, Brühl felt comfortable in broaching the subject of my brother's death, and I was more than happy to oblige. When I described the manner of Erich's murder in the Warsaw Ghetto, beaten to death by the animals of the Jewish Fighting Organisation, it was as if our dark corner of the cellar was illuminated by a light-bulb flickering over my colleague's head.

'That's why you wanted to work here,' he said. 'I get it now.'

I shrugged.

'It was never anything to do with the money.'

Brühl was mortified by his earlier attempts to press the banknotes into my hands. I told him not to be stupid, that the largesse of the District Jews was a distinct bonus. I accepted my share of the pawn money as proof.

After talk of my family, conversation turned inevitably to his. One older sister, mother and father. The classic German set up. I asked if he was seeing them next weekend, over Christmas.

'No. For the first time in my life, I'm going to be spending the holiday alone.' He beamed. 'And you know what? I simply cannot wait.'

It turned out that his sister was also at war, mainly with her husband but also her two children, another boy and girl, and anybody else who crossed her path. According to Brühl, Emmy Koch was an overbearing tyrant, who never regarded a family get-together as a success unless she had ruined it for all involved. Brühl recounted a particularly gruesome drive they undertook to Hildesheim last year, where he was seated up front between the long-suffering husband at the wheel and the sniping wife in the passenger seat. Literally stuck in the middle of their argument for a grand total of seven hours, there and back. Never again, Brühl vowed. Hence the fact he was actually looking forward to Christmas for once.

I asked how he'd managed to extricate himself.

'I just told her. That's it, sis,' I said. 'I'm out.'

'Impressive. And how did she take it, with a slap?'

'Well, when I say I told her...'

'You mean?'
'I wrote a letter.'
'Coward,' I laughed.

***

'So look.' The time was finally right. Much longer and I risked blacking out and not being able to remember anything I heard. All that lined my stomach was a couple of plates of herring and sauce that the club's owner had brought over. What's going to happen next year?'

'With any luck they'll get a divorce. Emmy might be happier.'

'No, I mean, here. The war.'

'Oh, easy. We win.'

Bottles were ceremonially raised and clinked.

'But how? We haven't managed to finish off the Jews yet, and they're not even armed.'

'Don't you worry about the Jews, my friend. Matters are in hand.'

'That's what I keep hearing. Just a few more months. Their time will come. It sounds like a lot of hot air to me. Is there anything more than talk?'

'It is talk, yes. But that's a strategic decision. If you catch my meaning.'

'Not really.'

'It has been *decided*.'

'I see. Very grand. What has?'

'Hinrich Lohse was in Berlin last month, right, with the Minister for Eastern Territories. Lohse was asking the same thing, the same thing we've all been asking.'

'And?'

'Eastern Territorories told him. Clarification of the Jewish question has been achieved through, and I quote, verbal discussions. Further queries should be directed to local SS authorities.'

I dashed my bottle against the table. 'Achieved through verbal discussions. What the hell does that mean?'

'No paperwork, for one thing, which'll save your fingers

some typing.' When that didn't have the intended cheering effect, Brühl said, 'Don't you see, we've been given carte blanch. They're leaving it to the SS.'

'I suppose that's a step in the right direction.'

'You bet it is. Kunde's already started drawing up the plans. The District needs to keep a slimmed down workforce, a few healthy youngsters. Everyone else is expendable. The infants, the elderly, the idiots. We start draining the swamp next year.'

'To where?'

He winked. 'Why do you think we're not leaving a paper-trail?'

I sobered up pretty quickly after that and called an end to the evening after a respectable period had elapsed. When it came to settling the bill, the giant, white-haired owner told us there was no need. Oskar Schindler had already paid.

***

Arriving back at the apartment sometime after eleven, I ran through the key facts that Brühl had divulged. It didn't take long, for there were hardly any. As evidence of a pogrom to end all pogroms, his admission was frustratingly opaque.

But that was only half of it.

Far more chilling was what Brühl had left unsaid, the awful winking implications. I questioned whether my addled mind had filled in the gaps correctly, as their author had intended, or whether I simply heard my own fears echo in the silence.

I wrote his words down at the living room table and passed out.

23

That Sunday morning, my breakfast reading consisted of *Der Stürmer* newspaper and the following list of statements I'd recorded from Augustus:

It has been decided.
Clarification of the Jewish question has been achieved through verbal discussions.
Further querries should be directed to local SS authorities.
We've been given carte blanche.
They're leaving it up to the SS.
We start shipping them out.
Why do you think we're not leaving a paper-trail?

I should have known what the Nazis were planning. I'd read the Gestapo's own Situation Reports about mass executions at Ponary, and witnessed for myself the 'liquidation' of an entire village under the supervision of Amon Göth. These were not the isolated acts of bloodthirsty rogues, but the opening salvos of a coordinated spree. Hitler was letting loose his hounds of hell, for whom a continent's worth of Jews had been systematically starved, exhausted and penned up in Ghettos.

How could I contemplate fleeing Cracow now? The only good to come out of last night was that I didn't have to. Thanks to Augustus' sister, I had a way out. All I had to do was write Otto a letter. The German way.

With no shops open on a Sunday, the only typewriter was on on my desk at Jozefinska. I donned my uniform and left.

Save for a Jewish Policeman guarding the cells, the office was deserted. I sat down and typed Otto Mohnke's address onto a blank envelope, then fed a blank sheet into the carriage roller.

Dear Father,

Erich's death has shaken me to the core. These last few weeks in Cracow have been unbearable, and I am only now beginning to put my life back together. I know the same is true of you.

It is with this in mind that I'm afraid I must ask you to postpone your Christmas visit. Please don't think ill of me. I meant what I said last week about wanting to patch things up with you. I thought I was ready, but the sad truth is, I am not. Next week is just too early. I fear that may do our relationship more harm than good.

Although I know this will be painful for you to read, I hope that you will respect my wishes and refrain from contacting me until I am feeling stronger.

So I will wish you a Merry Christmas, and hope that we both enjoy a much better New Year than 1941.

Your son,

H.

24

On Monday I was directed to accompany Symche Spira to the Rekawka Street apartment of an OD officer suspected of mutiny. The two men had been feuding last week over a percentage of a bribe that had failed to find its way into Spira's back pocket, the customary flow of direction in the Ghetto.

In revenge, Chief Spira had appointed the officer, a dim-witted but strapping soul by the name of Manny Jagur, to lead the execution of two Polish youths who had slaughtered a German horse and attempted to sell its meat on the black market. They were due to be hanged outside the Jozefinska cells first thing that morning, but Jagur had not reported for duty. His fellow officers claimed he was refusing to carry out the sentence, and had spent all weekend bragging that he'd tell Spira where he could put his 2 ½ %.

When we eventually broke into the apartment, we found Jagur dangling from a brass fixture above the toilet, a knotted bed-sheet throttling his neck, eyes distended.

I left Spira to supervise the body's removal.

To cleanse myself before returning to the station, I made a lone pilgrimage to the two outposts of Ghetto resistance. Not having met Syzmek Lustgarden, I had no way of knowing if he was one of the young men passing in and out of number 13 Jozefinska. It didn't matter. For now, it was enough to know that Akiva was flourishing.

In Zgody Square, the pavement outside The Pharmacy Under the Eagle still served as a meeting point for a large group of men and women. I kept to the shadows of Solna Targowa and tried to overhear their conversation, but the wind was blowing in the wrong direction.

As one of the only Poles with unrestricted access to the Ghetto, Dr. Zubrowksi was ideally placed as a conduit to the outside world. It was a miracle to be blessed not only with such a man of medicine, but one with the aptitude and willingness to put his own life at risk. The doctor was smuggling in bottles of hair-dye for the older residents, to make themselves look less 'expendable'. Whether he was operating with or without Tadeus Panciewicz' consent, I could not say.

***

A black Mercedes limousine was parked outside number 37. The registration plate told me it was not Wilhelm Kunde's usual car, but I failed to heed the warning.

Inside, the station was in immaculate order but as empty as the Marie Celeste, all chairs neatly tucked under desks and not a slip of paper out of place. In the middle of the wall of maps, a giant poster of Odin as Santa Claus now hung, the great-bearded God in a wide-brimmed African colony hat, whipping a white stead and carrying a sack full of gifts. A Chritmas tree stood under the stairs, the star at its top replaced with a Sig rune. Swastika baubles nestled in the branches like hand grenades. From the first floor, Kunde's gramophone record blared out nationalist marching hymns:

> The flag on high! The ranks tightly closed!
> The SA marches with quiet, steady step.
> Comrades shot by the Red Front and reactionaries
> March in spirit within our ranks.
> Comrades shot by the Red Front and reactionaries
> March in spirit within our ranks.

As I wandered in a daze towards my desk, I saw the combined workforce of Intelligence, Archives, Vehicles and Statistics assembled in the courtyard outside the cells. Glass flutes raised, they faced the gallows at the far brick wall. On the platform, two small figures slouched, hooded, cowering under nooses. A modest sprig of holly adorned the trestle. Changed into full admiralty whites, Symche Spira was seated at a brass lectern at the condemned men's side. I was surprised he had made it back so quickly; my pilgrimage had taken longer than I thought.

I had no choice now but to step out and join the madness. I shuffled round the back of the crowd towards the lone figure of Augustus Brühl, glum under a jaunty paper hat.

'Grab a glass.' He pointed to a table of refreshments in the corner. 'Any excuse to get shit-faced before noon. Even an office party. *Especially* an office party.'

'I'll pass,' I said. 'I'm still hungover from Saturday night.'

'Northern cissy. Where have you been anyway?'

'Stopped off at the pharmacy for some morphine.' My fingers found the lining of my empty pocket. 'Want one?'

'I'll save that for later. You missed the grand entrance.'

'What do you mean?'

Lifting his chin, Brühl squinted at the balcony above our heads where an unseen hand lifted the needle from the grooves. The strident brass had blown its last fanfare.

Symche Spira took this as his cue, rose to his lectern and proceeded to read the sentence of the two Polish horse-slaughterers. The ceremony continued until Manny Jagur's replacement placed the noose of the hanging rope over both boys and crossed the gallows platform to the tall wooden handle that would release the trap doors. After a final nod from Spira, the hangman closed his right hand on the lever and gave it a quick jerk. The floor under the first boy dropped away and almost instantaneously his spinal cord ripped apart with a sickening crunch. His feet twitched a couple of times and the air thickened with the smell of his loosened bowels and bladder.

The hangman kicked the wooden lever loose and quickly reset it to trigger the second platform. Again, he jerked back on the lever, the floor fell away and the boy dropped. This time there was no accompanying snap as the noose shifted sideways and the momentum failed to break the neck. The boy jerked his legs and twisted his arms, his body spiraling on the end of the rope. A muffled gurgling emanated from his hood as the boy slowly choked on his blood. After what seemed like an eternity, he finally stilled and was silent.

I closed my eyes to observe the Kadish and to remember Ronan Kessselman, whose death still haunted my dreams. But the *Horst Wessel* song started to thunder out from the gramophone. Even in the sanctity of my own head, there was nowhere to hide.

'Three hangings in one day, that's a record,' Brühl elbowed me in the ribs. 'I said you were my lucky mascot.'

'Three?'

'Manny Jagur, you dope fiend.'

'Oh, yes. Him.'

'Good old Manny, what a way to go. That's how we should do the job-lot next year, none of this gallows business. Stand them all on the seat of a giant crapper.'

'What? Who?'

'The Jews. Cut out the middle-man. One flush and they're straight down the sewers.'

'A crapper?'

'Manny Jagur, remember. Christ, Harry, hope you've saved some of that morphine for me.'

'Mohnke!'

I wheeled round, but the voice was coming from above. Wilhelm Kunde was leaning against the balcony rail, grinning behind a fat cigar. 'There's somebody I want you to meet.'

I stepped back for a better view and squinted up.

The balcony was crowded with VIPs in uniform and civilian dress. I saw the bloated, snub-nosed face of SS and Polizeiführer Julian Scherer but it was the soles of a particular pair of height-adjusted Adelaide brogues poking over the balcony's edge that I fixated upon, because I was the one who had stitched them.

'Allow me to introduce Reich Commissar of the Ostland region, his eminence Hinrich Lohse.' The flushed baby face of the Fat Führer appeared above the shoes. Kunde prompted, 'If you recall, these are the two men who found the Jagiello apartment.'

'Yes, yes,' Lohse said, beaming down at us. 'Sterling work. Those goods will fetch a fortune at auction; the War Effort depends on men like you, Oberführer Brühl.'

Brühl thrust his champagne flute at me and saluted. 'Heil Hitler!'

I heard Kunde whisper my name into the Commissar's ear. Lohse pushed his thick spectacles against his eyes and said, 'Yes, Harry Mohnke. Haven't we met before?'

Before I could answer, Kunde said, 'You saw his brother's photo, sir. Erich was killed in Warsaw.'

'Jewish terrorists. That's right. Scherer's tight with the father.'

I nodded. 'Yes, sir.'

Polizeiführer Scherer stepped up to the railing at mention of his name and raised his hand. 'Harry.'

'Sir.'

'Your father called me last week with the news.' Scherer winked. 'Good man, very wise.'

He was talking about father's letter. My reply wouldn't yet have reached Dahme.

'We're fortunate to have you, Oberführer,' Lohse said. 'Enjoy the celebrations'. He signalled for the party to move back into Kunde's office.

***

Back in the apartment, I was overcome by thoughts of my own mortality. The line I walked was high and thin, with no safety net to break my fall.

If Hinrich Lohse had recognized me, it would have been my body twitching at the end of that noose, after the torturer had earned his keep. I was no fortress of silence. Sooner or later I would have surrendered the names of Dr. Zubrowksi and Syzmek Lustgarten. At least my body would just be tossed in a simple unmarked hole in the ground at the end of the day, which was no more than I deserved.

But if I died of a heart attack in my bed, I would be afforded the 'honour' of an SS funeral and buried in a Nazi grave next to Erich Monhnke. This would be unbearable, as far as eternities went. I decided to leave a message in Yiddish about my person, and finally settled on a needle and thread as the safest means of inscription.

But Erich possessed no sewing box, and we were well past the hour when I might have gone out and purchased one. It became imperative that I did not set out the next day without this proof of identity stitched into my vest. The only neighbour

I could think of to impose upon was Rudolf Ditzen, across the hallway.

I could see a light on through his keyhole, but my raps went unanswered. It was late – perhaps Ditzen had fallen asleep with his lamps on. I gave one more half-hearted knock, and was surprised to hear the rustle of a bolt being drawn back on the other side.

Ditzen in darkness had something of the mole about him. Pink button nose, big flat dome of scalp, tiny eyes squinting at the hallway bulb. For some reason he had turned off his own lights – behind him, the electric cord still swung at the side of his mirror. The other doors behind him were closed to preserve the warmth.

'Mr. Mohnke,' he said after thirty seconds of quite exquisitely painful silence. 'Is everything alright?'

'Apologies for the late hour, Ditzen. I'm trying to find a damned needle. I don't suppose I could borrow one?'

'A needle?' He tapped the inside of his arm, near the elbow.

'A needle and a reel of cotton.'

'Yes, right. I think I have some. One minute.'

He closed his door and left me standing in the corridor. Less than a minute later, he returned with a small piece of cardboard wrapped with thread and studded with two needles.

'Perfect,' I said.

'Keep it.'

'Very kind. Darning my - '

'Goodnight,' he said, closing the door before I could finish.

'Socks.' The bolt drew back in place. 'Goodnight.'

25

I waited long into Tuesday afternoon for one of Symche Spira's informants to come to the Department of Civil Affairs with news of a lucrative lead. A Polish factory worker outside the Ghetto was rumoured to be forging employment permits for pretty young Jewesses, who he proceeded to offer as escort girls to his clients. While August Brühl was taking down details, I gathered up the Syzmek Lustgarden file I'd been studying, walked over to my colleague and placed it next to his paperwork.

Brühl checked the name and frowned. 'Who's he?'

'An old Akiva contact of Gusta Tova Draenger.'

He opened the file and dangled the single sheet. 'Not much here. What do you know?'

'Two years ago they were all under Gestapo surveillance. And now he's squeaky clean? I don't believe it. So I did some asking around.'

'You were here all day Sunday, putting me to shame again.'

This was true. Hungover from our Michael's Cave rendezvous, I'd spent the next day smuggling food from Erich's kitchen into the Ghetto, and dropping it in the streets.

'These Jews are dogs,' I said, avoiding the eyes of the informant. 'It takes them a while to get used to a new master, that's all. Now they talk to me.'

'Dr. Doolittle.'

'Something like that.'

'And what do they say?'

'That Lustgarden's up to his old tricks, running an evening prayer group out of his apartment. I'm going to pay him a visit.'

'Why not do it tonight and catch a full haul?'

'I thought about that. But if I get to him by himself, there's always the chance I can turn him.'

Brühl flashed a grin at the informant. 'See this? Only been

here a week and already he's thinking like one of you. You can tell Spira his days are numbered.'

'So do you want to come? It's only down the street.' I pretended to throw a punch. 'One, two, we work him over like Frau Jagiello.'

But as I'd hoped, the organiser of illicit prayer meetings proved no contest for the cocktail of bribery and sexual exploitation that Brühl had just been served. He declined.

As I moved to retrieve Lustgarden's file, Brühl's long cold fingers stopped the back of my hand. Lowering his voice, he said, 'Go easy, alright?'

'On Lustgarden?'

'On yourself.' I tried wriggling my hand free, but Brühl clamped tighter. 'You looked shattered yesterday, and I don't just mean the black mollies. Pace yourself.'

For the benefit of both our reputations, I pounded ferociously on Lustgarten's door and when the father answered, snarled at him to fetch his son and leave us.

The younger Lustgarten darted across the hallway into the kitchen, where I heard a woman I took to be his mother plead to be able to stay and watch her stew. The son calmly insisted she go next door, promising he would not let the pot burn.

I stood loudly cursing in the corridor while the elders left, mother shouting instructions about when to add the beans as father pulled her away. They disappeared through a neighbour's slitted door.

I marched into the vacated hallway and made sure Lustgarten and I were alone. One water closet, a bedroom with three matresses, living room with a window that opened onto a dank well-shaft in the centre of the block and a tiny cluttered kitchen at the back that made Erich Mohnke's look imperious. True to his word, Szymek Lustgarten leaned against the stove, ankles crossed, an open book in one hand and a long wooden spoon in the other.

A pair of thick dark eyebrows raised on his forehead as I approached the doorway, the only sign that being paid a house visit by the SS spoiled his day. With slicked back hair and collar wide open over the lapels, Lustgarten looked more like a Hollywood idol than a Hebrew scholar.

I picked my way past the pots and pans stacked on the floor and stopped at the sink, where I removed my cap and said, still in German, 'Do you speak Yiddish?'

'I do.'

'Say something.'

'Why?'

'Humour me.'

Turning back to the pages of his book, he said, in exaggerated, cartoon Yiddish, 'I'm not your talking monkey.'

'Very good,' I replied, in the same tongue. 'Now I want you to put the book down and give me your full attention.'

Lustgarten obligingly put the paperback onto a crowded plate shelf above his head and dangled the spoon like a hypnotist's pendulum. 'Permission to keep stirring, Oberführer? My mother's very insistent.'

'Jewish mothers, I know them well'. I removed my jacket and hung it from the door handle. When I started unfastening my cuffs, Lustgarten said, 'Sorry for the heat – air conditionning's on the blink. Maybe you could send somebody round?'

I placed a finger to my lips, then opened my shirt buttons, pulled it off and draped the garment over the jacket.

Finally, I reached behind my shoulders and lifted the cotton vest over my head. I folded it into a square in my hands until the stitching was clearly visible next to the label, then passed the vest to Lustgarten.

'*My name is Jozef Siegler,*' he read, cradling the fabric. '*25/03/1901. I am a Jew.* Where did you get this? Why are you wearing it?'

'In case I am discovered.'

'Discovered?'

'May I?' Lustgarten returned the vest and I started putting my clothes back on, talking as I dressed.

'I'm not Oberführer Mohnke, I'm Jozef Siegler. My family lived in Cracow before the war, in Kazimierz. They had a grocery store on Izaaka. I worked in Germany in the 30s, until things got too bad. Then with my sister, I joined Akiva. This was in Wilno. We were smuggling Jews across the border, but the Nazis invaded there too. I was arrested, my sister fled. Three months ago I broke out of a labour camp near Ponary, and found shelter with two brothers, first in Lithuania and then in Poland. I was able to pass as a member of the family, as a Pole. I used to be a teacher, I was good at languages. So I became known as Damian Plotz. Word of my arrival spread. After a month in the village, the Belorussian Chief of Police came to the house. He needed a translator, at short notice. For the sake of the family, I could not refuse. It was awful, the things I witnessed that night. I knew I had to do something, to try and help. I agreed to work for the police full-time, in Lublin. On the way, there was a fight outside the train station and the Belorussian Chief and I became separated. I found an SS officer murdered in an alleyway. His name was Harry Mohnke. It was uncanny, we looked like brothers. I took it as a sign. I put on his uniform, and left him wearing my clothes. Damian Plotz was dead. Mohnke was coming back from his brother's funeral, another SS, killed in Warsaw, and was on the way to Cracow, where the brother kept an apartment. I found letters in his pocket, legal papers and a key - '

I stopped, distracted by the engorged flame at the stove, now feeding on the end of Lustgarten's wooden spoon. The ladle was already blackened and trailing smoke. Lustgarten snapped out of his trance, flung the spoon to the floor and stamped out the fire. He blew out the stove and set the pot on the side to cool.

Composure regained, he turned to me and said, 'Are you finished?'

'Almost. I decided to come back to Cracow to look for my family, but then I managed to get Mohnke assigned to the Ghetto. To the station at Jozefinska, the Department of Civil Affairs. It was the best place to be. That was two weeks ago.'

'And what do you want me me to do?'

'Do you believe me?'

'Why have you come here?' He pointed to the floor. 'I mean, to me.'

'Because you know Gusta Tova Draenger.'

At mention of her name, his whole attitude changed.

'You know Gusta?'

'Not personally,' I said. 'Not yet. I came because you're Akiva.'

'How do you know that?'

'The SS knows everything.' I smiled. 'Well, almost everything. I read your file. I want to help.'

'I can just see you lighting Sabbath candles in your lederhosen.'

'You must be able to see what I can do.'

'I can see that you're saving your own skin, and that's fine. If I had those big blue eyes of yours, I'd probably do the same - actually, no. Even if I had a face like Gerhard Bartels, I don't have the chutzpah to do what you're doing.'

'You're already doing it,' I said. 'Last Saturday I watched more than half a dozen men and women troop up your stairs here. That's nowhere near enough, but it's a start. Think of what we could do together.'

'The start of what?'

'Resistance. An army.'

'Those men and women are boys and girls, only a couple of years younger than me. They're not soldiers, they're scouts. With the schools closed, education is our only fight. Reading and worship. If you were Akiva, you'd know that.'

'I joined Akiva in 1941, with my sister. We worked on Operation Punsk, transferring orphans across the Lithuanian border. When that became impossible, we ran a youth house on Pilies Street, in Vilno old town. I was like you then, a scholar. I used to spend my afternoons in the Strashum Library, studying ancient texts, and telling my students about them in the evenings. My sister Shoshana, she was the fighter. A couple of her friends came to see me one night, Vitka Kempner and Abba Kovner. We had a discussion in a kitchen much like this. They pleaded for me to join them, made wild prophecies about Europe becoming a burial pit for the Jews if we stood by, but I refused. Six months later, December 1941, the Akiva secretariat brought a young boy from Cracow to tell us a story. The man was Joziek Rudashevski, the boy was Jacob Shmiel. Jacob had witnessed the first SS purge on Kazimierz, the raiding party for furs and jewels. For an encore, the Einsatzgruppe locked a group of men in the Stara Boznica synagogue and burnt it down.'

'I remember.'

'Still I would not be persuaded to take up arms. Shoshana left that night, to join the struggle. I haven't seen her since.'

'Well there's no Shoshana Siegler here, if that's who you're looking for.'

'Don't make the same mistake as I did.'

'Look, if you want to play cloak-and-dagger, that's up to you, my friend. But I won't be putting Akiva at risk. Even if the whole Ghetto rose up en masse, we'd be crushed in minutes.'

'So what do you propose?'

'Those raids you mentioned, burning the synagogues. That all stopped when the Germans set up the Ghetto. It's not perfect, but times are tough. The world's at war in case you haven't noticed. We keep our heads down and we get by. Now if you'll excuse me, the stew's ready and my parents are hungry.'

26

I left my apartment in the usual manner on the morning of Thursday December 23ʳᵈ, eschewing the elevator to walk the four flights to the ground floor. As I approached the penultimate stairwell, I passed an envelope propped against the windowsill.

A plain postcard on closer inspection, the address side left blank.

When I turned it over, thirteen shots of pure adrenaline surged into my heart:

Polish people wake up! Why suffer war and death for the Hitler
plutocracy?

The handwriting was precise, each letter scratched in the blocky style of the signwriter.

It wasn't from Akiva; Syzmek Lustgarten didn't know where I lived.

As I wiped my fingerprints prior to replacing it on the sill, a middle-aged woman appeared at the top of the flight of stairs, smart in mauve hat and coat, a handbag plumb at her wrist.

'Halt!' I shouted in Polish, although she was walking towards me and not away. 'Identify yourself.'

'Magda Pryzotsky, apartment 21.'

'What are you doing?'

'I'm on my way to the National Bank. I work as a teller. Is everything alright?'

'Did you just pass anybody suspicious?'

'You're the first person I've seen. What's happened? May I approach?'

Magda Pryzotsky and I had never met. Our morning routines deviated by that all-important factor of three minutes. But now she had seen me, with the postcard.

'Please,' I said, softening my stance. 'Come down.'

When she joined me on the landing, I held up the postcard. 'I found it here. Two minutes ago.'

Trembling, she accepted the card and turned it over. As red as my face turned, hers blanched white. She pushed it back at me.

'Whoever would leave such a thing?'

'That's what I intend to find out. They've written their own death warrant for sure. Oberführer Mohnke, I live on the fourth floor. I help oversee the Jewish Residential District.'

'I've heard. Your poor brother. So sad.'

'Terrorists have got their tendrils into all corners of the Reich,' I said. 'Even this apartment block. Can you think of anybody here with a grievance? Anybody particularly angry or upset?'

'I wouldn't know. We all keep to ourselves. Whatever would have happened if you hadn't been here to find it?'

'What would you have done, Mrs Pryzotzky, if I'd taken the elevator instead of walking this morning?'

'I'd go straight to Escherich,' she said, and when I raised my eyebrows, added, 'And then contact the police.'

'Very good. If everybody is as patriotic as you, this Communist won't have any place to hide.'

27

On the evening of the December 24th, I gave in to Augustus Brühl's requests and agreed to join him for another festive drink at Michael's Cave. Abruptly cutting short our last rendezvous had failed to rule me out as a drinking partner. In truth, I don't think Brühl had anybody else. We were as lonely as each other. He even suggested that, as two unencumbered bachelors, we celebrate the 25th together, at his apartment. The works: roast goose, gingerbread cookies, Bach's *Christmas Oratorio*. Thankfully I was quick-witted enough to recall Otto Mohnke's letter. I told him my father was coming to town, and the two of us did not get on, like his sister. As much as misery loves company, I would spare Brühl on this occasion. He understood perfectly.

'Happy families are all alike,' I quoted, 'but every unhappy family is unhappy in its own way.'

'Dostoevsky,' Brühl said.

'Tolstoy,' I corrected.

'Smart-ass,' he said. 'Let's get blotto.' He began roaring with mock belligerence, 'Down with a Christ who allows himself to be crucified! The German God cannot be a suffering God! He is a God of power and strength!

It was going to be a long night

No jazz band but a string quartet playing carols when we arrived at the cellar. Soothing enough, until I realised it wasn't just the musicians who had been replaced:

Silent night, Holy night,
All is calm, all is bright.
Only the Chancellor stays on guard
Germany's future to watch and to ward,
Guiding our nation aright.

Drinks ordered, we speculated on how the rest of the

office might be celebrating the holiday. Wilhelm Kunde was a dedicated practitioner of Paganism, I learned. It was on his orders, the poster of Odin as Santa Claus was hung on the map wall, and the Sig rune placed atop the Christmas tree. Kunde had also petitioned Hans Frank to restore the date of celebrations to the winter solstice, but that was beyond even the purview of the General Government. Brühl swore that the Hauptsturmführer's friends spent the night of the 21st atop the mountain in Zakopane, cavorting with torches while their families gathered round a bonfire in the town below, although I suspected my leg was being pulled at this point.

'Hey, talking about Christmas,' Brühl said, interrupting himself. 'Remember baby Moses?'

'I'm pretty sure you've got your Old Testament wrong there, my friend. Moses was the bearer of the Ten Commandants.'

'And the Exodus, delivering the Israelites from slavery,' Brühl said. 'The Moses I'm talking about marched himself right back into it. Or you did, I should say. Moses Montefiore.'

'The little sack of shit I carried from Jagiello's?' I recalled how we'd left each other on the street. 'You went off with Kunde. What was I to do? I dumped him at the House of Orphans.'

'I know, because that's where you thought he belonged. His mother, apparently, thinks otherwise.'

'What mother?'

'I was talking to old man Kurzamnn today. Turns out mama Montefiore is one of our Jews. Sent her precious boy to stay with Polish partisans in March, to spare him from the District. Now he's back, right in time for the fireworks. I tell you - a Christmas miracle!'

I tried not to slump.

Our beers arrived and Brühl proposed a toast to Moses' short life. From the strained grin on my face, he realised that for once his clowning had gone too far.

'I wouldn't let it spoil your evening.' He leant back and rested a boot on his knee. 'Montefiore's a Schindler-Jew.'

'I don't speak Yiddish,' I said glumly. 'So I don't know what that means.'

'Oskar Schindler, remember, paid our tab last week? Owns the Emalia factory, enamel and ammunition. Guards his workers like gold-dust. Little Moses' mother works there. The baby's probably better off at Emalia than he was with Jagiello.'

The way he spoke of Schindler's protection made me think of Camp Moda, and the Chaze. There were other good men and women out there, I had to believe it was true. Emalia, the Pharmacy, and now my own apartment block, if the postcard could be believed. We didn't know each other, and it was probably too dangerous to ever meet. But it was enough just to know they existed.

'Hello, Michael.' The white-haired owner was collecting glasses from a table behind us when Brühl called him over. Pointing to a side alcove behind a velvet curtain, he asked, 'You haven't got Herr Schindler stashed in there, have you?'

'No, sir. Tonight is the Mayor and the Chamber of Commerce. Herr Schindler is in Paris for the holiday, I believe.'

'Lucky bastard.'

As the owner bowed, I placed a hand on his forearm. 'Tell me, is your name really Michael?'

'It is. Friends call me Michas.'

'And do you know the Rock of Gibraltar?'

Widening his eyes at me in exasperation, Brühl said, 'You'll have to excuse my friend, he doesn't get out much.'

Michael smiled. 'Situated off the coast of Spain?'

'The very same. Owned by the British.'

'I've seen it in the atlas,' the owner said. 'But it's one of the many countries I have never been to, and don't suppose I ever will.'

'And this bar's got no connection?'

'Seeming as the bar is mine, sir, no, neither of us do.'

'Amazing. There's a network of limestone hollows within the Rock, and the biggest one is called Michael's Cave.' The owner looked decidedly nonplussed at my revelation, and really who could blame the poor man. 'It's a synchronicity, that's all. A coincidence.'

'I understand.'

After our host had taken his leave, Brühl said, 'Harry, you are a complete one-off.'

'It's perfectly true. The name comes from a grotto in Italy where the archangel Michael is said to have appeared.'

'I don't doubt it. How does a telecoms engineer know all this stuff?'

'I used to be a teacher,' I confessed. 'In another life.'

'My God, they let you loose in a classroom? Poor children.'

I shifted, my seat suddenly as unforgiving as concrete. How sad that I now felt more uncomfortable trapped in the truth than a lie. Another life indeed.

'The University of Kassel,' I said.

The substitution was inspired. If Brühl ever thought to check up, I had dealt myself an ace, in terms of plausible deniability. Kassel? No no. I was at the University of Kiel.

'What was your subject?'

'Humanism and Civil Society. A hot-bed of Marxism back then, as you can imagine. I annoyed most of my colleagues by attending the Militant League for German Culture conference in 1933, and said goodbye to the rest when I joined the SS a year later.' I grinned. 'If they could see me now.'

'I can't believe you never told me. I studied Literature at Wittenberg.' He beamed as if the act conferred brotherhood upon us.

'But not *Anna Karenina*.'

The joke sailed over his head like the Hindenburg. He said, 'I was a total book-worm, before the Cleansing. But one never really stops being a student. What did you teach?'

'Plenty of texts that have gone up in flames since. Heinrich Heine was a favourite, before his Jewishness... became unavoidable. I do think his early poetry is rather sublime.'

'I may still have a volume,' Brühl whispered. 'How decadent we are. My tastes were always more... Anglo-Saxon in nature. Victorian Gothic in particular. *Dr. Jekyll and Mr. Hyde*?'

'Wonderful novel. Man as Divided Self. Very Nitzchean.'

'My tutor said it was about alcoholism, the gentleman who transforms into a monster after supping his vile brew.' We knocked our bottles together. Cheers.'

'Faust's pact with the devil.'

'Another professor with ideas above his station.'

'Oscar Wilde,' I said. *'The Portrait of Dorian Grey*. More split personalities.'

'The sodomite?' Brühl said. 'Steady the buffs, Harry. Even I have limits.'

28

I spent the morning of the 25th smuggling what little happiness I could into the Ghetto. City shops were bare in the run up to Christmas while Herman Göring ensured German shelves groaned with food and consumer goods sacked from the Ostland. But with careful purchasing throughout the week, I managed to replenish my supplies. Children's gifts were harder to come by. Chocolate SS soldiers, toy tanks, fighter planes and machine guns were all that was left unsold in this year of years. A few boiled sweets was the best I could offer the orphans.

Filling my pockets with cartons and bags and tins, I trafficked the contraband from my apartment and through the Lworksa entrance. For once, the streets were deserted, making my food-drops easier to make. On crowded mornings I had learned to disguise my intentions under a snarling façade, screaming abuse at an unsuspecting prisoner one minute, then disappearing round the nearest corner and leaving two eggs propped against the wall. It didn't matter if the residents came to detest Oberführer Harry Monke. In fact, as long as it perpetuated my cover, I positively encouraged it. But today I had the streets to myself.

Hanukkah celebrations could no longer be conducted amongst festive crowds, publicly displaying their joy. Tenement window sills might have been denuded of burning candles, but parties and prayers and speeches and jokes were being held in nearly every courtyard and back room; today, even in rooms which faced the street. With only a skeleton crew of Jewish Police on patrol, nobody was likely to be arrested for lighting a menorah. Like Augustus Brühl, even the OD had limits.

I spent the morning of the 25th caring for one extended family. When my cupboards were empty, it was time to start searching for the real thing.

Equipped with a bag containing a peasant's outfit and the

crude sketch of Novy Sacz as my only map, I climbed aboard a V3000 truck from in the Jozefinska workshop and drove it out the courtyard. The glum posse of Blues at Lworska were the only guards to see me leave. Should my actions be questioned when the station reopened tomorrow, I had an answer prepared: my crotchety father was visiting, and demanded to be taken for a tour of the countryside after lunch. Having no vehicle of my own, I took the liberty of borrowing one. Surely the Germany army could not begrudge Julian Scherer's family friend, not on Christmas Day.

The drive south took a little over an hour in light traffic and snow. By twelve noon I was approaching Novy Sacz. Knowing nothing of the area, I stopped at a swastika-festooned hotel on the outskirts of town and interrupted lunch to enquire about the size of nearby villages, and their Jewish populations. The staff could not have been more helpful. I left with a ranked list of ten, six of which tallied with the names I had already ear-marked as Shoshana's possible destinations.

On the eastern side of Novy Sacz, Logi was a prosperous satellite community to an aircraft factory commandeered by the Nazis. The Jews were allowed to remain exclusively on the four tidy streets that bordered the market square, as quiet today as the Ghetto. I headed towards the two towers of the modern synagogue and parked between the public baths and the kosher abattoir, both of which were closed for the day. It was the perfect place to change clothes.

Appearing in full SS regalia to Syzmek Lustgarten was a mistake I woud not make again. Despite the embroidered vest and my well-practised spiel, he had never accepted me. I'd left his apartment with nothing. I could not risk such a failure when it came to my own mother and sister. If there was information about their whereabouts, it would be passed on to Jozef Siegler, not Harry Mohnke. I shed his skin behind the truck and pulled on the ragged shirt and trousers I'd brought from the Ghetto.

After knocking on a few doors on Nowy Rynek, I was directed across the square to Waska Street, to the house of Ester Bram, who had arrived with her son earlier this year from Cracow. Alas, the names of my sister and mother meant nothing to them, but Mrs. Bram insisted I stay for a cup of hot milk.

Born in Logi, my host had returned home at the start of the year, when the Germans were trying to make Cracow free of Jews rather than imprisoning them behind walls. Anybody with friends or relatives in the surrounding District was encouraged to flee. They were even allowed to purchase one-way train tickets, a mode of transport otherwise forbidden to them. Although the move was an upset, eleven months later, Mrs. Bram was glad she'd made it. Life was simple but comfortable. Mother and son both found work at the aircraft factory, she a clerk, he an engineer, and the German bosses weren't so bad, when you got used to them. Every now and then, news reached the village about detention camps being built in different parts of the country, but Logi was safe. The Germans needed skilled labour. After half an hour, I too was lulled by the warmth of the fire and the general atmosphere of security. I could have stayed all afternoon, the rest of the war. But I knew the Brams were mistaken. The Germans wanted to create an illusion of peace and quiet, in order to execute their plans with the minimum amount of resistance. There were more than enough Aryan engineers to go round. I said my goodbyes and wished mother and son a happy new year, which was all they wanted to hear.

As I suspected, life was very different in the impoverished villages west of Novy Sacz. The second one on my list was suffering a Typhus epidemic. My truck was stopped at a Red Cross blockade on the outskirts of Swinecze before I had a chance to change out of Harry Mohnke's uniform. The health inspector explained that a doctor from Dusseldorf was fighting the outbreak and had imposed a temporary ban on traffic in and out of the village. The sick Jews had been quarantined in a building situated amongst Christian homes, which had provoked much restlessness from the neighbours, inflaming an already volatile situation. The inspector was sure the travel ban could be lifted for the military, but it would have to be cleared by the doctor first. I had no wish to divert the medic's energies but at the same time, I couldn't leave without making sure my own family were not amongst the afflicted. I wrote a brief message which the inspector had delivered. Forty minutes passed while I waited in the truck, playing noughts and crosses on the back of the vehicle log book. When a reply came back, I could scarcely believe my eyes.

The doctor had heard about a Cracovian mother and daughter on the other side of the river Dunajec. The tiny farming village of Paskow was ninth on my list, thirty miles east of Swinecze. While this was enough to excite me, it was the second sentence that converted me into a stuttering fool. The daughter was rumoured to be a courier for the Jewish underground. That had to be Shoshana! I will endeavour to wire ahead, the doctor's note finished, so the authorities may detain her on your behalf.

It is safe to say I had never driven so recklessly in my life.

Afternoon had dissolved into evening by this point, and the only lamps in the darkness were the V3000's. In the end, all my slips and slides and near-misses with stray cows in the middle of the road were for nought.

When I arrived, Paskow was a ghost village. The Jews had fled, and it had nothing to do with the doctor wiring ahead. Paskow didn't have a pair of tin cans or length of string left, never mind a radio set. Windows were smashed, doors kicked in, empty homes ransacked by mobs. Outside the barns and cattle corrals, all that remained were a few split sacks of salt and flour.

I found an elderly man at prayer in the ruins of one shack, too diminished in body and mind to leave. He offered no reaction to my SS uniform, and invited me to observe the lighting of the third Hanukkah candle and to join his blessing, that a miracle would descend on the entire House of Israel, as in days of old.

The ceremony over, he told me what had happened. On December 21st, the residents of nearby Zagory had been ordered to get ready for transfer to the Gorlice Ghetto. They had obligingly made their preparations, loading food and cases onto wagons. But on the 22nd, every man, woman and child was taken to ready-dug pits, ordered to undress and executed. The same day and at the same time as the Jews of Jod, the Jews of Kislowszczyzna and its neighbouring small yishuvim were killed – all in all over 500 Jews. Two days ago, when news reached Paskow, the population scrambled into the night, spilling east towards the Ukranian border. Not one of them had been heard of since.

Crushed by the vicissitudes of hope and despair, I drove back to Cracow in a trance. To this day I can recall nothing of the ninety mile journey.

It was one in the morning when I arrived at the Ghetto; eight hours until I was due back at my desk. The gate guards were too drunk to speak as I passed and there was nobody in the workshop to see me return the truck. At least I had managed to get out and back without arousing suspicion. Next time, I would need considerably longer than a day. Crossing into the Ukraine was not a decision for my current state of mind. I could barely keep my eyes open as I stumbled home to Tragutta.

Such was my desire to collapse into bed that I almost walked straight past the mail-boxes in the lobby. Christmas Day had come and gone and there was still no indication how Otto Mohnke had taken his sole-surviving son's rejection. I back-tracked to my mail-box in case correspondance had arrived in my absence.

One parcel wrapped in bright red paper, no label, hand delivered. Somebody had been intending to give it to me in person, but found the apartment empty. From the way the gift flexed between my fingers, I knew it was a book. I tore it open in the lobby, unable to wait for the privacy of my hallway.

The volume was yellowed and well-thumbed and I knew before I inspected the cover what it was and who it was from: *The Lyrical Ballads of Heinrich Heine*. A handwritten inscription adorned the front page:

'You were right. They are rather sublime. Seasons Greetings, your friend Augustus.'

29

Given all that happened yesterday, I was content to be leaving the apartment only five minutes late for the first day back at work. The chill I'd caught changing Harry Mohnke's uniform behind the kosher abattoir had blossomed into a full-blown cold, which slowed my pre-coffee shaving. I had to keep pausing not only to wipe the bathroom mirror but the tip of my own nose.

There was one consolation to being five minutes behind schedule. It further reduced the chances of meeting Magda Pryzotsky again, the woman who'd seen me with the postcard. I'm sure we were both relieved about that.

Approaching the Lworska gate, I was hailed by Augustus Brühl, normally parking his car when I arrived at the station. Today he looked like he had walked the five miles from Kleparz. Walked or ran. Between the sweat on his face and and the snow-stains on his trousers, the man was drenched. I waited for him to catch up.

'Harry, I'm going to tell you something now, and I want you to promise you'll listen very carefully,' he commanded, catching his breath. I wondered what on earth he was going to say.

'Under no circumstances must you ever, ever think of buying a DKW.'

I coughed. The cold had worked its way down to my chest.

'Nothing but trouble that car. I leave it in the garage for one day – one day - and she's as dead as a doornail this morning. And that's after the 300 Marks I've already spent this year on a new carburettor...'

I let him vent as we entered the Ghetto. Car-talk had never been one of my specialties.

'Anyway,' he said, his own battery finally running flat. 'How was your Christmas?'

We crossed onto Jozefinska, where the wrenching struggle for survival was starting up after the briefest of respite. Queues were already forming outside the shops, which would not open for another hour. Old people leaning on sticks, cripples in carts, babies at their mothers' breasts. The rest without faces, backs curved, heads hanging low. A cavalcade of poverty.

'Strained,' I said.

'Your father?'

'As predicted. Look, thank-you so much for the - for that book. Very thoughtful of you.'

'Pah. It was only gathering dust in my cupboard.' He swatted my gratitude away like a cloud of flies. 'You two were out late last night.' Since there was no question, I didn't risk a reply. 'I waited until evening, but you weren't back.'

Still no question, but my silence was becoming conspicuous.

'We went for a drive,' I said. 'To get out of the house. Ended up getting lost, which led to more arguments. But at least we changed the scenery.'

'It was dark by three in the afternoon,' he said. 'You couldn't have seen much. I didn't know you had a car.'

'I don't,' I said, and suffered a coughing fit, doubled over on the pavement, hand clutching my mouth. The line outside the baker's regarded my condition with sly bemusement.

'OK, Harry?'

I span my finger like a clock, waiting for the fit to pass. When it did, I wheezed, 'Don't tell anyone, but I borrowed a truck from the workshop.'

'Why would I tell anyone?'

'You wouldn't.'

I coughed again. The line shuffled aside to make way for my spluttering. A tall, angular woman who'd been eyeing me hissed a stream of Yiddsh invective as I passed, and her companion snickered. I didn't know either of them. The thin woman shook her curls and spat in the gutter.

I was reasonably sure she'd told me, 'Abi gezunt dos leben ken men zikh ale mol nemen.'

Which translated as, Stay healthy, so you can kill yourself later.

'My Yiddish is a bit rusty.' Brühl had stopped walking

again. 'But I don't think she wished us Seasons Greetings. Harry, for Christ's sake. She spat at you.'

'She did, didn't she?' My voice was far away and dreamy, as if I was observing from a distance. 'I thought I imagined it.'

'Want me to improve the bitch's manners while you catch your breath?'

'No thanks. I'll handle it.'

In the Nazi rulebook, there was only one penalty for such a brazen display.

I found myself unholstering my pistol and slowly turning round to face the woman. The rest of the line shrank back against the baker's window. A young man at the end started pleading with Brühl for mercy, but I could only watch my plucky assailant straighten her brittle shoulders and stare right back into my eyes.

What else could I do, but walk up to her and stop an arm's length away, my right hand raising my pistol, the end of the barrel finding the middle of the woman's forehead.

In Yiddish, I whispered, 'God forgive me.'

Using my other hand, I pulled back the safety catch.

'Harry.' I jerked round. Brühl said, 'It's Devorah Montefiore.'

I knew the name, but I couldn't place it.

'Mother Moses, your Schindler-Jew,' he said. 'Come on, it's not worth the hassle. Oskar'll have our guts for lederhosen.'

He pulled my arm down and prised the pistol out of my grip. I stared at my empty fingers, twitching as if charged with an electric current.

30

Marooned between Christmas and New Year, the next week in the office was the most quiet I had ever known in the Ghetto, or ever would. Most of the Germans were hungover from nightly festivities to which I was thankfully not invited. They spent the mornings cloistered behind newspapers, emitting a variety of toxic gasses. Lunches were an extended boozy affair, cold cuts, cheese and beer served from crates in the courtyard. Kunde's collection of seasonal records was on heavy rotation but the man himself rarely deigned to put in an appearance. Symche Spira's team of informants had also taken the week off, or else had no fresh leads to report. Outside the station, the Jews and Poles were behaving themselves. There was no crime to speak of, no smuggling or attempted escapes. I'm ashamed to say I was bored. It got to the point where I actually looked forward to a coughing fit as a source of entertainment and exercise.

When our telephone rang that wet Wednesday afternoon, Augustus Brühl and I locked horns to answer it. He got to the receiver first and I went back to the cartoon of Hitler I was perpetrating against Wehrmach-issued stationary, a doodle masquerading as sabotage, or the other way round. I was vaguely aware from the way Brühl loaded his typewriter that the caller wished to give a statement, but I was more interested in perfecting the Führer's savage slash of hair. It was only when Brühl checked the spelling of the caller's name that I stopped scratching in order to listen.

'P-R-Z-O-T-Z-K-Y,' he repeated between striking the keys.

'Initial, M, for Magda.'

Clack clack clack.

'Apartment 28, Tragutta 9.'

Clack clack clack.

'I know the area well,' he said, somehow keeping his eyes from mine. I admired the restraint. 'It's just around the corner.'

This was the moment in the interview when Mrs. Przotzky named me as the person who'd found the postcard. I suspected as much, because it was here that Brühl stopped repeating her words out loud while he typed. I didn't need to hear the rest of the story to realise I was its main protagonist.

'This is extremely helpful information,' Brühl said, when the statement was finished. 'You may rest assured we will proceed in the strictest confidence. Good day to you.'

He replaced the receiver, removed the form from his typewriter, stamped it with a seal from his ink tray and waved the paper, blowing it gently. When it was dry, he got up from his desk, walked round to mine and set the report down on the pile of paper under which I'd buried my cartoon. I glanced at the subject line and saw my address.

'Ah, yes,' I said. 'The postcard woman.

Brühl deflated. 'You mean you know about it?'

'Of course.'

I scanned through the first part detailing our encounter at the window sill.

'So it's all on the level?'

'Seems to be.'

It was the second half of Mrs. Przotzky's statement that caught me by surprise:

Hauptsturmführer Mohnke asked if I knew anybody with a motive or a grievance. I didn't at the time. But I was talking to the janitor over Christmas, and he happened to mention a couple who live on the top floor. Their son was a Volkliste, fighting in Russia. He was killed during the summer in the Battle of Rostov. His mother and father took the news very badly, and have since had a few arguments with other tenants. Apparently the parents threw a party when General von Schobert crashed his aircraft in a Russian minefield last month. The General was their son's commander.

'Von Schobert's death,' I said. 'She never mentioned that to me.'

'Claims she only found out recently.'

I nodded. 'Seems pretty cut-and-dry to me, in terms of means and motive. What's the problem? Better late than never.'

'Jesus, Harry. Have you no idea how serious this is?'

I counted off the offences on my fingers. 'Subversion of the war effort, undermining military morale, sedition and defeatism. Is that about right? Oh, and punishable by the guillotine.'

'It's your own apartment block.'

'I can hardly be held be responsible for that. I only moved in last month.'

'Why didn't you say anything?'

'It's outside the walls, not a District matter. We've got enough on our plates, I didn't want to bother you.'

'I'm not talking about me,' Brühl said. 'Why would you sit on something like this?'

I shifted in my seat. Sit on it?'

'There's no report, man. No investigation. Przotzky's had to follow the damn thing up herself.'

'No investigation?'

'This was almost a week ago. The Gestapo don't bloody stop for Christmas! What on earth were you thinking of?'

I hunched forward, pressed my fingertips to the corners of my eyes and raked them down the sides of my nose to my lips. I sniffed disconsolately and said, 'I must be losing my mind.'

'Oh, Harry. Those damn pills.'

'I filed a report. I know I did.'

Brühl pulled up a chair and sat down at my side, knees pressing into my thighs.

'Alright, look. This is how we play it. You've only just moved here. You've had a devastating loss. Your brother's a war hero - '

'I *am* losing my mind!'

'Steady. We're going for the sympathy vote, not the loony bin.'

I grabbed the handle underneath my desk, yanked the drawer out and rifled through the stack of paper until I found the Photostat I was looking for.

'I knew it.'

I handed the flimsy copy to Brühl.

'What's this?'

'My report. I wrote it up immediately after I found the postcard, December 23rd.'

Brühl gazed from the sheet to me and back again. 'So the Gestapo did already know?'

'I sent it over to Pomorska Street that afternoon. I remember putting it in the mail-bag, along with the card.'

This was partly true. I had filled out a report about finding the postcard when I arrived at Jozefinska, and I did make a Photostat, but the original never found its way to HQ. I burnt it that night in my fireplace. The card, however, didn't come with me to the station in the first place. After Mrs. Pryzotsky left, I ran back upstairs and locked it in the safe, behind the Caravaggio.

***

Hans Frank threw an enormous party at the castle that New Year's Eve to raise money for the Winter Aid, the Nazi charity charged with helping impoverished Germans stock up with fuel. The bash promised gallivanting of a more refined nature than Kunde's Solstice rituals: waltzing to the likes of the Blue Danube and the Fledermaus overture.

I didn't know the first step of a waltz, which was a problem, since dance lessons were a mandatory element of the Jünkerschule training that Harry Mohnke had undertaken. Fortunately, I saw an easy way out, and for once it required little in the way of subterfuge. In the days leading up to the 31st, I made a very public display of my coughing fits, ensuring each one was louder and a more-sustained production than the last. At one point, I got so carrried away that telephone conversations in the vicinity had to be suspended until my attack ceased. When I announced my withdrawal from the party that morning, it was met with a general sense of relief. Even August Brühl didn't seek to change my mind.

Several months later, in the rural idyll of Kopaliny, I was to learn of a momentous New Year's Eve gathering that took place a thousand kilometres away in Lithuania, hosted by a brave poet I had once met and scorned, Abba Kovner, gaunt and heavy-lidded at the tender age of twenty-three.

Life had not improved for the Jews of Wilno since my departure. Word from survivors of the Ponary massacres had begun to slip through the gaps in the Ghetto walls, but, much like Syzmek Lustgarten, the prisoners of Wilno were still not ready to believe the truth. Only a handful listened. But this handful decided to act. Amongst these committed crusaders, December was a month of intense debate. The most pressing dilemna was whether to remain in Wilno or attempt to join comrades in the larger Ghettos of Bialystock or Warsaw, or flee into the forests. Abba Kovner argued to stay. Fighting was his passion, and he dreamed of uniting the Ghetto to join him. To this end, he sought to organise a mass meeting with all the various youth organisations in attendance. A date was chosen, December 31st, a day of so many social gatherings that one more might go unnoticed by the ever-vigilant Nazis. So it came to pass.

That evening, a hundred and fifty young men and women came together in a public soup kitchen on Strazuna Street. Abba Kovner called the meeting to order and read the speech he had been working on for many days and nights, a call to arms that remains amongst the finest achievements of his verse:

Let us not go like sheep to the slaughter, Jewish youth!

Do not trust those who are trying to deceive you. Out of 80,000 Jews of the Jerusalem of Lithuania, only 20,000 remain. In front of your eyes our parents, our brothers and our sisters are being torn away from us. Where are the hundreds of men who were snatched away for labour by the Lithuanian kidnappers? Where are those naked women who were taken away on the horror-night of the provocation? Where are those Jews of the Day of Atonement? And where are our brothers of the second Ghetto? Anyone who is taken out through the gates of the Ghetto, will never return. All roads of the Ghetto lead to Ponary, and Ponary means death.

They have all been shot there. Hitler plans to destroy all the Jews of Europe, and the Jews of Lithuania have been chosen as the first in line.

We will not be led like sheep to the slaughter!

True, we are weak and defenceless, but the only reply to the murderer is revolt!

Brothers! Better to fall as free fighters than to live by the mercy of the murderers.

Arise! Arise with your last breath!

Kovner finished to thundering silence.

But the words had lit a fire. Seconds later, the group broke out in spirited song. In Wilno at least, the revolution had begun.

31

'Gentlemen, it's starting.'

With those words, Wilhelm Kunde proclaimed the commencement of the programme that would bring about the annihilation of the Polish Jewry. Of course, there was no mention of genocide in his address. To hear Kunde speak, it was all a matter of streamlining the administration: effective immediately, twenty-nine villages in the vicinity of the city were to be amalgamated into a region known as 'Greater Cracow'. The villages had been selected because they contained high numbers of Jews who'd found shelter during the previous year's expulsions. Henceforth, all Jews residing in 'Greater Cracow' were required to relocate into our Residential District on the morning of January 23rd.

While Kunde droned on, I recalled the villagers of Zogory, who'd received a similar edict about the Gorlice Ghetto, only to be taken out into the fields, ordered to undress and lay face down in a muddy mass grave. The Jews of Jajsi who were told they'd be moving into the Braslaw Ghetto, the Jews of Slobodka to Braslaw and the Opsa Jews to Vidz. The last stage of resettlement was death.

It was January 3rd 1942.

Had my family scrambled towards the Ukranian border with the other residents of Paskow, they might be safe. But if Shoshana decided to try and join up with the residents of a larger Ghetto, as suggested in Vilno, she would be heading into the firing line.

Kopaliny was spared from the original twenty-nine villages. If Akiva were organising resistance from the farm, I needed to warn them. Even if the Draengers were only learning how to plough for the Holy Land, they deserved to know the truth. The weight of evidence was now overwhelming. Ponary, Brühl's warning about the coming fireworks, the old man of Paskow, and the so-called 'expansion' of Greater Cracow.

If the Jews think 41 has been funny, wait till they catch wind of 42.

I wrote to Gusta and Shimshon that evening, laying everything bare, and offering my help. For return correspondence, I used an alias and an apartment number on the non-existent sixth floor of the Tragutta block. Immediately after posting the letter, I sought out janitor Escherich and explained that Pomorska HQ was running a covert military-intelligence operation in his building. Any mail that arrived for the alias I'd chosen (Mordka Zygot) should immediately be given over. I knew Escherich would cooperate. He was still shaken from the postcard incident.

An Inspector Schmidt of the Gestapo had last week taken away Mr. and Mrs. Nowak, the grieving parents from the top floor, on suspicion of undermining military morale. Although Magda Przyotsky was directly responsible for their arrest, it was I who had failed to save them. It was a very long night following their disappearance.

Nobody in the building, least of all myself, was prepared for what happened next.

Three days later, Mr. and Mrs. Nowak returned home, pale and diminished, but otherwise unscathed. Extensive interrogation and handwriting tests had cleared them both of involvement.

The postcard writer was still at large.

***

Augustus Brühl and I were reassigned from the Department of Civil Affairs in order to help oversee the new resettlement policy. I saw this as demotion and was worried we had fallen out of favour. To have a seditious propagandist living in my apartment block was hardly a ringing endorsement, although I was never personally under suspicion. The Gestapo accepted I had filed my report, and sanctioned a delivery boy as a result. Brühl's fall from grace was more troubling. He had committed no faux pas, but since the start of the new year, the rift had widened between him and the rest of the station. Clusters of men always seemed to be mocking him for some indiscretion, but fell silent when I approached, or their conversations changed tact with a beguiling ease. Perhaps it was all in my mind. Our new job was only a temporary one, Wilhelm Kunde explained with a dry chuckle. We would be soon back to doing what we did best, flushing out Symche Spira's gold-bricking rats.

The first task was to visit the twenty-nine villages to announce the imminent changes in status. We travelled together in Brühl's DKW rather than splitting the load, in case of hostile reactions. Amazingly, there were none. A few grumbles was the worst of it. There'd been a new measure or directive against the Jews every week for two years now, and they had survived. Why should this one be any different? If Augustus Brühl hadn't been at my side, I could have given them a few reasons.

Twenty-nine times I steeled my heart against the villagers' weary acceptance, and the prospect of finding my own family crowding the market square. If Shoshana saw me goose-stepping out, she would have understood. If my mother saw me in Nazi uniform, she was likely to drop dead of shock.

Twenty-nine times I prepared for the worst, and twenty-nine times I survived.

But what next? Were Brühl and I set to be mere messengers? Or would we be sent for the 23rd to oversee the digging of the pits, and the final relocation? We were 'friendly faces', best placed to provide a reassuring continuity when the villagers began to suspect they were never going to see the Ghetto.

32

In the end, all were spared, and none were.

Brühl and I had orders to remain at Jozefinska on the 23rd, 'resettlement day'. I prayed all night for the souls of the soon-to-be departed, and again before I left the apartment.

I wasn't expecting any immediate panic within the Ghetto. News of the massacres would take days to seep through the walls. If Syzmek Lustgarden's response was anything to go by, people would largely be deaf to the chatter. Who could blame them. It profits the Death Row inmate little to learn of his neighbour's execution.

So sunk in disconsolation was I that morning, crossing the groundfloor lobby, I almost failed to notice the postcard pinned to the centre of Bela Escherich's noticeboard, petalled by his usual array of housekeeping reminders.

The Führer has no wife,
The butcher has no sow,
The baker has no dough!

That is the Third Reich. Hitler's might before right will
bring us no peace!
Down with Hitler's crew.

I read it twice, then hurried towards the front door. This time, nobody saw me.

Another card, on this day of days.

As I stepped out onto the street, I thought back to when I found the first card, the day before Christmas Eve.

Good God - that had been December 23rd.

Here we were again, exactly a month later, to the day. What on earth did it mean?

I turned left on Tragutta and walked north, into rising river mist. At the end of the street, a low-sided army truck passed slowly on intersecting Kacik, its cargo obscured behind taut canvas and poles. An officer I didn't recognize was hunched in the cabin at the steering wheel, cranking his neck. I watched the truck trundle by. At its rear, great folds of the green cover had been lifted up, and a herd of dark bearded faces in caps and scarves stared out, gripping the poles like prison bars. Jews.

No deportations from the Ghetto were scheduled for today. So where were the Jews going, and on who's orders?

I ran towards the Kacik junction. The truck-driver had found the small pedestrian gate next to the Rynek market square, and was attempting to negotiate through his window with the Blue Police on guard. Eventually, the driver turned off the engine, got out, walked round the side of the truck and opened the back doors. The peasants helped each other down with cases and bags and filed through the narrow squeeze-point into the Rynek.

The prisoners weren't being taken away; they were arriving.

A breeze funneled off the river, bringing with it the rumour of a distant roar, car horns and cheers, a rally or procession. I followed the tram-line away from the wall towards the water's edge.

Traffic was backed up on the two bridges, all the way in to Kazimierz, solid lines of army trucks nose to tail, loaded with peasants. Twenty-nine villages' worth, a people in mandatory exodus. The road-sides lined with Polish commuters, cheering goodbye to the Jews. The trucks were moving, slowly. They bumped off the bridge at Podgorze and snaked around the far end of the wall to the main gate. For once, the Germans had to be taken at their word. Resettlement meant just that.

I was in Vilno on 20th March 1941, the day the Cracow Ghetto was opened, but this must have been what it looked like. Hundreds of Jews arriving with knapsacks, cases, boxes and bundles. All streaming into the gloomiest, grimiest quarter of the city, a place with no sewers and paved with cobblestones. The mud in the streets splashed as people walked, tripping on the uneven pavement, dropping clothes and other possessions into the sticky black mud. Their meagre property lay trampled, crushed, covered with dirt.

Waves of people, one after another. Mentally ill people with ghoulish eyes and uncontrollable limbs, sick people pulled on droshkeys, and a great unmediated mass of men and women, tall and short, attractive and ugly, strong and frail, stooped and trudging under the weight of their luggage. Animals of all sizes, brushes, bowls, irons, pillows, pots and pans, cutlery, possessions beyond number.

And leaning out of tenement windows, aghast, the Ghetto's original ghosts. Apartments were already full to bursting. Where were these peasants meant to go?

In the course of a single day, the population grew by more than two thousand people.

***

At the start of the next week, on the coldest day of the new year, two SD and one SIPO trucks drove into the Ghetto, shrilling through loudspeakers strapped to their roofs that the city captain had ordered all Jews to give up their furs. An infestation of lice from the recently arrived country cousins was claimed as pretext, expertly salting the wounds of resentment. All garments must be handed over.

Obersturmführer Koerner, Obersturmführer Heinemayer and Unterstrumführer Vollbrecht commandeered a former schoolhouse on Limanowskiego Street. The collection began immediately. On a day that saw the temperature plummet to minus ten degrees, Jews in flimsy cloth coats queued for hours to rid themselves of thick warm furs. One helpful soul, in addition to handing over his wife's blue fox pelt, brought news from his tenement that a neighbour had been seen cutting a coat into ribbons rather than surrendering it. A pack of German dogs soon dragged the trouble-maker out of his cellar, where he was burying the pieces. Soldiers pushed him through the streets to Limanowskiego, where they shot him in the face. He landed in a pile of coats spilling out the schoolhouse doors. Snowflakes started to fall, first pirouetting through the air, then covering all in a thin white layer, like an embalmer's sheet.

In total, the Fur Aktion yielded twenty-three men's fur coats, a hundred and thirteen ladies' fur coats, three hundred and fifty-eight men's coats fur linings, fourteen silver fox pelts, a hundred and forty-four red fox pelts, five hundred and fifty-three hand-warmers, four thousand nine hundred and seventy-two fur collars, four hundred and fifty-eight assorted pelts, two hundred and eighty-one sheepskin coats.

Two thousand four hundred and eighty-three receipts were issued.

33

As promised by Wilhelm Kunde, August Brühl and I were soon back to doing what we did best in the Department of Civil Affairs. Symche Spira's networks of spies set about drawing up lists of those suspected of withholding furs. They were brought to Jozefinska and beaten until they revealed the hiding place. Work was suspended one February morning by Rottenführer Ritschak's announcement that all staff were required to report to the Jewish Hospital for a health inspection.

The office let out a groan at this, which I thought churlish. With a Typhus epidemic running rampant, it was better to be safe than sorry.

Even in its impoverished state, the Ghetto hospital was a wonderful sanctuary of order and cleanliness to all prisoners who visited. Nobody had to lie on the floor, as they did elsewhere. There were beds, clean sheets, and food. The clinic was open twenty-four hours a day. A committee of three doctors could release workers for reasons of illness. Hundreds of people sought appointments everyday, mostly in the evening when they returned from work. The Ghetto hospital had general practitioners, specialists, dentists, laboratories including an X-ray department and, until last week's decree forbidding births, its own children's ward.

Today the third floor gynaecology department was given over for the check up all German and Polish authorities who policed the Ghetto. It was only when I entered the ward that I realised the inspection had nothing to do with Typhus. Infectious diseases of a very different nature were the order of the day. The poster on the wall was my first clue: a chorus line of blonde beauties receding into the distance, tight black dresses accentuating their curves and – leaving little to the imagination – the intersecting Vs of their crutches. A red banner above their blonde heads proclaimed '98% OF ALL PROCURABLE WOMEN HAVE VENEREAL DISEASE'.

Being circumcised, I lived in constant fear of public nudity, avoiding all baths and swimming pools and only urinating in closed lavatory stalls, or else walking back out if the closet was occupied. My colleagues must have thought me the most constipated man in the Reich. It made no difference to Germans whether a chap had lost his foreskin for religious reasons or an accident, or because of a congenital or acquired phimosis. Anyone lacking a foreskin was immediately under suspicion. So-called 'circumcison reversal' was a burgeoning field, although most of the specialists were charlatans. I knew an eminent plastic surgeon in Wilno who had supposedly taught Moshe and some of the other Pilies Street boys to lengthen their foreskins by sleeping with a bottle of water attached to themselves, gradually increasing the volume night by night. The surgeon claimed the method had helped Jews avoid persecution in Roman times. Too squeamish to hang a bottle, I tried gingerly pulling on mine for a week to reverse the Mohle's handiwork, unsurprisingly to no avail. Now after several years of successful concealment, I had walked straight into what the other officers were calling a Troddelappel – a Prick Parade.

The corridor was teeming with gate guards, German soldiers and Polish Blue Police, stripped to the waist except for ID tags and caps, mired three deep against the wall while I scrambled after Augustus Brühl towards a hand-painted 'Officer's Area' sign at the far end.

'I haven't a drop of juice left for myself,' one irate solider shouted. 'And you pecker-checkers expect me to have anything left for a whore!'

Another insisted, 'You ought to be over on the Eastern Front, they're crazy about Russian brothels!'

The doctors gave as good as they got, especially if anyone didn't have his works ready in time. At the inspection area, a soldier dropped his trousers in a slouching doctor's face, impassive behind tortoise shell spectacles. The doctor flicked a lazy cigarette at the man's groin and sneered, 'Pull that foreskin back further, man! Should come easily to the likes of you!'

We left the scrum behind for the more sedate atmosphere

of the Officer's waiting room, but we weren't exempt from examination. The only exit was via the doctor's consulting room, guarded by a stern nurse outside who was collecting my colleague's identity cards. Once ticked off on her list, the men sat down on a pair of long benches against the wall. When they saw myself and Augustus Brühl enter the room, three men on the second bench got up and squeezed onto the end of the first. Brühl's unpopularity had plummeted since the new year, and it was contagious.

What the hell was I going to do?

Pretend to have a heart attack and get carried away on a gurney? The way my chest was banging, I might not even need to fake it.

I handed our ID cards to the nurse and joined Brühl on the empty bench. My one ally, the only person who might have helped me, and he was the least popular officer in the Ghetto. I had hitched my wagon to the wrong star. Brühl was continuing to haemorrhage friends and I was no closer to finding out why. Something had happened over the Christmas holiday. Had the Gestapo found out that he had given me a banned book? I shivered and moaned. The Prick Parade was of much more immediate concern.

'What's up with you?' he said.

'I think I'm coming down with something.'

'Well, you're in the right place.' His eyes drifted up to the yellow Syphillis poster on the opposite wall. 'Or possibly not.'

'Thanks for that.'

He nodded to the slogan on the poster, a German officer straightening his tie at the sight of a shapely woman leaning against a street corner. 'Self-control is self-preservation, Harry, remember that.'

Before I could reply, the nurse took her next card and called my name.

I don't remember my companion wishing me good luck, or the long walk past the crowded bench to the nurse's desk.

The door to the consultation room clicked shut behind me. The doctor was grotesque, eyes and lips squeezed shut by drapes of purple fat. A round chin studded his jaw like a roast apple. He wagged two bejewelled fingers for me to approach.

'Trousers.'

'How would you like me to save you the bother?'

'I'm paid to bother.'

'Not enough, I bet. It's not pretty down there. The dreaded drips and sores.'

'Let's see what's going on.'

'I'm already taking sulfa drugs and penicillin, from the Pharamacy Under The Eagle. Kunde's man sorted me out. Oberführer Scherer and I were hoping to keep a lid on this.'

'Pity you hadn't taken your own advice. Put a helmet on next time you see action.'

'I will, don't worry. Look, the men out there don't like me too much. They think I'm a stickler for the rules, and I suppose I am. Most of them.'

I took out my wallet.

'If word gets out that I've got the clap, I'd never hear the end of it.' I counted off five of Erich Monhnke's hundred Reich Mark notes onto the doctor's desk. 'You'd be doing us all a huge favour to keep this off the record.'

'I suppose there's no point in needlessly disrupting morale,' the doctor said, covering the money with a blank certificate. 'Of course, my nurse is also responsible for the paperwork.'

I doled out three more hundreds. The doctor's fine eyebrows kept arching until another five notes were piled on his desk.

***

Back at the station, another purge was in progress, conducted by the same three men responsible for the Fur Aktion, Koerner, Heinemayer and Vollbrecht of the Political department of the SD and SIPO.

I don't know if the timing was coincidental, or if our medical inspection was ordered to make sure there was no interference from the existing Ghetto security. But once again, Jozefinska has been sidelined.

One hundred and forty prominent Jews, mostly intellectuals, had been arrested while I was stuck in the Prick

Parade. They were now crammed into our cells. Deportation was scheduled to a new camp I had not heard of before, called Auschwitz.

34

SD and SIPO visits to the Ghetto became increasingly common after that, and arrests of Jews a daily occurrence. A pattern quickly established itself. Individuals were taken to our prison and transferred in small groups to Auschwitz. Before the end of the week, the station received a batch of telegrams addressed to the families of the first wave of deportees. Each hand-written message was a variation on a very limited theme:

Husband/brother/son died in the concentration camp Auschwitz. The Komendant.

In the beginning it was accepted that relatives had died of natural causes. But the deportations continued, and for each one, a telegram followed a few days later. A ripple of alarm began to wind its way through the crowded streets, and would not be quietened. The days of wilful ignorance were over.

At first, I thought the endless telegrams were an administrative blunder, some young clerk failing to realise all these notifications going to the same Ghetto. But I quickly realised the authorities just didn't care. Sooner or later, every last Jew would end somewhere like Auschwitz. The last stage of resettlement was always death. Sometimes it just took a while.

It was during this period I received a rare letter. I was accosted by Escherich, hobbling out of his kitchen as I returned home. The square of bright paint under the stairwell where his noticeboard once hung was now covered with a print of Wilheln Sauter's Eternal Soldier. Following January's postcard, the janitor had spent the day in Pomorska at Gestapo HQ, put up in what he described as more of a hotel room than a cell. Inspector Schmidt told him the quietude was to help 'give him space' to recall valuable information. Whether it succeeded or not, I can not say. But the next morning, Escherich was back at his kitchen table.

'Come here,' he closed the kitchen door behind me. He lifted a spitting egg pan from the stove, set it on a trivet, then reached up to a shelf of mason jars and removed a white envelope.

'It came today,' he said. 'Mordka Zygot, just like you said. Sixth floor and everything. Should I tell Inspector Schmidt?'

'On no account,' I said, a little too abruptly. 'That is, I'd like to surprise him myself.'

'You think this Donelaitis is the postcard writer?'

'I'm afraid I'm not at liberty to disclose details in such a sensitive case.'

'Sounds Lithuanian to me. Never trusted them.'

'Very wise.'

'No Lithuanians registered here, I checked.'

'If he's a tenant, he would have assumed a different identity,' I said. 'Or she.'

'What do I do next?'

'Nothing. You've done all that was required.'

'Will there be more letters?'

'I hope so. If there are, do exactly as today.'

'Should I call you at the stationhouse? It's been sat here on my shelf for a whole day.'

'Better to let me know in person,' I said. 'Anybody could be listening to a telephone line.'

'Spies?'

Turning to leave, I nodded. 'Dangerous times.'

As I opened the janitor's door, Rudolf Ditzen was standing on the threshold, overcoat draped over his elbow, hand raised, ready to knock. He frowned when he saw me blocking his way, that expansive brow rippling like the Sahara.

'Oberführer Mohnke.'

'Ditzen.'

I folded my hands behind my back, concealing the envelope I hoped he hadn't seen. Unfortunately the Janitor interpreted this as some kind of sign. I felt his rasping breath at my shoulder.

Escherich shifted into place at my side. 'Not expecting any post were you, Ditzen?'

My soul groaned.

'No special deliveries I should keep an eye out for?'

'Chance would be a fine thing,' Ditzen said. 'It's been a while since anybody sent me a parcel. No, I'm afraid it's my water pipe. I don't know if they froze again last night but I couldn't get anything out of it this morning. Had to leave without even brushing my teeth.'

'Nobody else has had a problem.'

'It must be just mine then. The same thing happened last year, or the year before.'

'Which taps are you talking about?'

'Gentlemen.' Turning sideways, I put my palms to excuse myself. 'I'll leave you to it.' I slipped between them out the door.

I made it to the third floor landing when I heard Ditzen puffing up the steps behind me.

'Here, what did he mean about special deliveries?'

I'd already started up the third flight and didn't stop.

'We've had another postcard, haven't we?'

I made an exaggerated show of glancing up and down the stairwell before continuing in a hushed voice. 'Don't take it to heart, Escherich probably mixed you up with somebody else. He's going through a rough patch.'

'A new card would spoil the pattern. It's the tenth today. The last two appeared on the twenty-third.'

'I don't know anything more about these cards than you, Ditzen. The Gestapo are handling the investigation, I work in the Ghetto. I don't interfere with their work, and vice versa.'

'The whole thing's got me on edge.'

'As are we all. But I think the less we talk about it, the better. Otherwise we're falling right into their hands.'

'Yes, alright. I should be grateful, really, having you as a neighbour.'

For the second time in five minutes, I wished Ditzen a good evening, and hurried into my apartment. Safe behind my locked door, I tore open the letter from Kopaliny.

35

Justyna commends you for preserving the sacred flame of resistance and prays that throughout this bleak winter you will continue to feed it with the live coals of your heart!

Sequestered as Justyna and XXXX are in their rural tranquillity, she wants you to know that the group will never lose touch with what is happening. They know that the mass killings you witnessed outside Lublin are spreading. Thanks to fearless couriers within the Jewish Quarter of Cracow, Justyna has learned this week of the deportations aktiza and subsequent murders in the death-camp of Auschwitz. In XXXX and XXXX, the movement has lost two towers of strength who were expected to contribute significantly. Cut is the branch that might have grown full straight. Several important leaders remain in the Jewish Quarter, including XXXX, who confessed he once turned you away. He hopes you can return, to receive the welcome you are due. One knock on his door - then two - then another single knock.

This is a time of great and necessary momentum. Despite the most vicious setbacks, the organisation is flourishing. As of January 21ˢᵗ, the United Partisan Organisation was formed in the nerve centre of the Wilno. Their moto: We will not allow them to take us like beasts to the slaughter. It was believed to be the first movement of its kind, and has already spawned others, in Gebultow, in Warsaw, in Hipnitz. The commander in Wilno is known to you, Sacred Flame, and regards your position as one of great strategic importance. He asks that that you do not judge XXXX too harshly, and reminds that once upon a time, you too were slow to heed the call to action.

Be that as it may. Deep in every heart, bringing us ever closer together, lay the yearning for vengeance, vengeance for our families taken to the death camps, for the wrongs and sufferings we ourselves had borne.

Sparks are now ready to ignite in every country. If a fire can be lit in one, the flames will sweep across Europe. You are one link in a chain of fire that will cleanse the world. You can only get rid of this evil by digging it out at the roots. Justyna promises that soon her agricultural tools will be gone from her shoulders, replaced with weapons to hurl into the fury of battle at your side. Her hands, once caked in fertile loam, will soon be soaked in blood.

36

That Sabbath I was shattered, having spent the day smuggling food into the Ghetto. I was dozing on the sofa when the knock came on my door. Nobody apart from Rudolf Ditzen bothered me of an evening, and tonight I was in no mood to listen to his theories about the phantom postcards. I lay there waiting for him to cross back to his apartment, but the knocking grew louder. After thirty seconds, it stopped. Ditzen must have got the message.

Padding across the carpet to turn out the light in case he returned, I saw a white square of paper on the carpet next to my boots. It had been pushed underneath the door.

I raced up, yanked the handle and peered round the frame. No sign of Ditzen. But at the other end of the corridor, a tall figure in a leather jacket and cream chequered trousers was about to descend the stairs.

I called out; he stopped.

'Harry,' Augustus Brühl cried, squinting into the darkness. 'I'd given up on you.'

I bent down to grab the paper, a stiff white envelope, sealed, blank. No address, no message. But there was something inside, stiff like a card.

Brühl was walking towards me. 'Be a sport, hand it over.'

'Someone slipped it under my door.'

He unfurled his long fingers. 'Don't make me beg.'

'It's yours?'

'I wrote a note, in case you were out.' He plucked the envelope out of my hand. I watched it disappear inside his jacket.

'A note about what?'

'Oh for goodness sake, would it hurt you to act like a human being just once in a while. Invite me in. You're outrageously sober for a Saturday night.'

'I was asleep.'

He loomed up close and stared into my eyes, breathing

whiskey fumes. 'Let's do something about that.'

I closed the door and followed him into the kitchen, where Brühl was slamming open my empty cupboards. I'd never seen him out of his uniform. Perhaps this was how the bright young things dressed nowadays. The leather jacket was crude enough, something a factory worker would wear, but it clashed so terribly with the plaid pants. I thought he was wearing a stocking over half his head, until he turned round, dangling a solitary teabag. It was a knitted hat, pulled down over one ear like a fascinator.

'Don't say this is all you've got to drink?'

'Forgot to go shopping,' I said. 'I think there's some of Erich's corn brandy left in the fridge.'

'Who's this Erich all of a sudden?'

'My brother,' I said. 'You know, the dead one?'

'Ouch. I deserved that.'

I found the brandy lolling at the back of the fridge in a pool of salad juice. The fat bottle was glazed red, a bratwurst with a diagonal white label at the top like the eye of Cyclops.

'Juckemoller,' I said, setting it down on the counter. 'Any good?'

'With a beer we could have boilermakers.'

'If we had a beer.'

'A Von Collins, then.'

'What's that?'

'Cocktail. Lemon juice and sugar.'

'I'll try. Fancy some cold cuts?'

'Good sport, wouldn't mind a peck. I'm going to give myself the grand tour.'

'Go ahead.'

Using a wooden chopping board as a tray, I assembled a bowl of sugar, the lemon and sausage, a chef's knife, glasses and Juckemoller and carried them through to the living room.

Brühl was leaning on the edge of the table, admiring the Caravaggio.

'Haven't seen this beauty since I was at university,' he said. 'We took Fine Art in the first year.'

'It's Erich's.'

I directed him to the armchair in the corner and took the

sofa opposite, placing the tray on the table between us. Leaning forward, I poured two measures of brandy, stirred in a couple of spoonfulls of sugar, chopped the lemon and squeezed the juice.

I passed him a glass and a coaster. 'Never made a Von Collins before. Don't be too harsh.'

'As if I would. Thanks.'

'Cheers.'

He took a sip, smiled and leant back against the cushion, contemplating the painting again.

'Do you know the story?'

'Jesus and Judas?'

'They say Hitler has the original stashed at the top of Berchtesgarden. Which is odd, when you think about it.'

'I suppose so.'

'The style's so... modern. For the Führer. Doesn't really fit with the style. Approved Art and all that nonsense.'

I nodded.

'Caravaggio paints like Americans shoot crime films,' he said, warming to his theme. 'Gritty, here and now. Bible scenes from the street, the gutter. None of the bright classical sheen of a Raphael or a Michaelangelo.'

'If you say so.'

I took the knife, cut some salami and pushed the board across to Brühl.

'The faces in the crowd were all real people.' He tossed back a slice and talked while he chewed. 'Caravaggio's friends and lovers. That Roman solider and the chap with his hand up on the left.' He swallowed the last of the meat and clicked his tongue. 'Was that beef salami?'

I nodded again.

He continued. 'The same people crop up in most of Caravaggio's paintings. The scum of the city – rogues, whores, rent boys.'

'When I meet the Führer, I'll be sure to warn him.'

'Imagine. All that degeneracy, hiding in plain sight.'

Blanching, I managed to squeeze out a yawn.

'I'm boring you with all my art history talk.'

'Not at all,' I said. 'I'm exhausted.'

'What have you been doing all day?'

'Working. I can't keep up with all these arrests the SIPO keep making.'

'Harry.'

'I have no private life, it's sad.'

'Now we both know that's not true.'

'You flatter me.'

To keep busy, I leaned forward to cut more salami. I focussed on the knife until my hand stopped shaking.

Brühl said, 'I stopped by at Jozefinska this afternoon. I left my gloves there. Didn't see you though.'

'I went for a wander.'

'Like you did Christmas Day when I also missed you?'

'That was different. I had my father in tow.'

'Come off it. We both know what you were really up to then.'

'Getting lost in a blizzard, as I recall.'

I pushed the salami board across the table, but Brühl raised his glass instead.

'I know about the pecker-checker at the hospital, too. Another fine story.'

I left Brühl's slice untouched, but cut another for myself.

'Oh Harry. It all makes sense now.' He lifted the glass to his lips. 'I should have known, the first day I set eyes on you.'

The coaster had become stuck to the bottom, and fell off as it attained height, bouncing to his thigh and onto the carpet. He leaned over to pick it up, offering the bare nape of his neck.

***

After scrubbing myself clean of blood, I found Julian Scherer's card and called him at home. His wife answered.

'We must have you over for dinner one of these days,' she said.

'Very kind.'

A piano was playing in the background. It stopped, then Scherer picked up the receiver.

'Harry, I wondered how you were getting on.'

'There's been an accident.'

'Christ, not Otto?'

'No, father's fine. I didn't know who else to call.'

'What's happened?'

'I think it's better if you could come over, sir.'

Twenty-five minutes later, Scherer's Mercedes pulled up to the curb. He had driven himself, as I requested. No chauffeur. I met him outside the elevator. Short-sleeved shirt and cotton trousers and odd socks, I remember that when he took of his shoes. One blue, the other green. He looked healthier in loose-fitting clothes, less like a heart attack waiting to happen. Which was encouraging, for both of us.

We stopped in my hallway, before going further in.

'He was already drunk when he turned up,' I said. 'I gave him brandy, which didn't help.'

'Who are we talking about, son?'

I opened the living room door. Augustus Brühl was sprawled in the middle of the floor on an island of sticky red newspaper.

I remember my hands tightening around the knife handle, lifting it back over my head and plunging down into the bare nape of his neck. Hitting spinal cord, the blade skidded into his carotid artery, spraying wet heat across my chin. Brühl sunk to his knees, gurgling, and fell chest first into the table, which collapsed under his weight. I ran to the kitchen and returned with an armful of newspaper to soak up the blood. He drowned in it, eventually. It takes a very long time for a man to die.

'It was horrible,' I said. 'He tried to kiss me. We fought, I grabbed the knife.'

'Good for you. The hell is he wearing? Jesus, what a disgrace.'

'What am I going to do?'

'Nothing.' A small tip of tongue dabbed Scherer's wet lips. 'Go out for a drink. When you get back, all of this will be gone.'

'Thank-you.'

'ID.'

'Sorry?'

'Have you got his ID?'

357

'I haven't touched him.'

Scherer slid his shoes off, approached the body and patted down the pockets of the leather jacket. He pulled out a wallet and the white envelope Brühl had slipped under the door.

'Know anything about this?'

'No.'

He inserted a finger and sliced it open. Inside was a hand-drawn picture of a heart, pierced with an arrow. Scherer opened it and read the inscription. 'Dear Harry, Be My Valentine.'

'Valentine?' I said.

'The dirty bastard. It's a stupid American tradition. February 14th.' Scherer's face soured. 'Lover's Day.'

'Good God.'

'Don't worry, you're not the first.'

'I feel sick.'

'He tried this on at New Year's Eve, at the damned castle. They found him in a lavatory cubicle with one of the waiters. Absolutely no shame. Telephone?'

Behind me, he called a man called Muller, gave my address and hung up.

'It's Saturday night, you're out having fun. Stop off at a few bars, make conversation. Go back to some girl's place and screw her brains out for all I care. Tomorrow's a new day.'

***

When I came home at midnight, it was like nothing had ever happened.

Scherer's men had even taken the broken sticks of coffee table and scrubbed the living room carpet.

37

At work the next day, I sat opposite an empty desk. Nobody asked me where Brühl was. I don't think anybody cared.

Two Gestapo inspectors arrived after lunch, and went straight on up to Wilhelm Kunde. They stayed for no more than ten minutes. Rottenführer Ritschak telephoned immediately afer they left and summoned me to the office. It was the only other time I'd been there since my first day.

A brewery driver had discovered Augustus Brühl's body behind the notorious Michael's Cave nightclub in the town centre. His throat had been cut, but the weapon was not found. From Brühl's clothing, leather jacket and a woman's hat and trousers, he had been consorting with homosexuals. He had brought disgrace upon the regiment. I was to be in charge of training his replacement in the department for Civil Affairs. Our Spokesman for Jewish Matters, Untersturmführer Karl Mende, would begin his new duties in the morning.

At least now Brühl's death was public knowledge, I didn't have to hide my shock. There was little sympathy from the rest of the office. Mende stopped by with his ever-present copy of Der Stürmer to size up his new desk, but offered no words of condolence. He ordered two Jewish ODs to take Brühl's chair out to the courtyard, where it was chopped up for firewood. Mende was an overweight man slightly older than myself, with a face only a mother could love, always puckered, and permanent bags under his eyes. His right eye was smaller than his left, or else he kept it in a permanent squint, as if straining to see. After Brühl, and possibly myself, Mende was the least popular man in the office.

I moped around for another couple of hours and left early. Before I went, I took a blank ledger from my desk drawer and, making sure nobody was watching, tucked it into my satchel.

***

The study of language ruled my life before the war began, but I'd barely looked at a book since, much less composed anything more substantial than a short letter. I hated words because I'd seen how the Nazis employed them as a cover for evil, and was guilty of doing so myself. I despised words for they could never hope to express the emotion tormenting my people. And yet, my desire to write was now as strong as the revulsion I felt.

It had taken the death of one man to bring me to this, and a Nazi at that. Like them, I had murdered in cold blood. I could never forgive myself.

The war had taken everything. Words were now all I had left.

I sat in the armchair with the ledger on my lap, staring at the first blank page. It was less terrifying than looking at the recently scrubbed carpet at my feet.

Where should I begin?

In Vilno?

In Kiel?

The foothills of the Carpathian Mountains, where I first came into consciousness, aged four?

I decided to start at the very beginning, the earliest memories passed down to me, my mother's childhood in the Pale of Russia at the tail-end of the nineteenth century.

When Elena was one year old, rioters drove her family out of their home village. The government blamed the Jews themselves for exploiting the masses, who were now - quite justifiably - fighting back. The following year, Jews were officially forbidden from settling in any rural areas, or from buying property.

When Elena Shapiro was three, thousands of illegal Jews were rounded up by the police and expelled...

38

At the beginning of March 1942 all Jews were ordered to appear at the Judenrat office for registration, where they were issued with special identity cards. It was The Department of Civil Affairs' task to review the daily lists with Symche Spira's informants, cross-referencing each name for known associates of Jewish criminals, updating our records accordingly.

Each day brought approximately five hundred new names. On average, I processed four-fifths of them, while Karl Mende might have put his newspaper down for long enough to do a hundred. If Mende had been as dedicated to his job as he was to Der Stürmer's back pages, we would have finished the job in half the time. His inefficiency was an office joke. Mende was typical of the Nazis I'd seen rise to prominence: starting as an unknown groom in Köln, he'd gone on to achieve a modicum of success as a jockey, where he'd fallen under the patronage of Werner Rahm, a horse fancier and old comrade of Heinrich Himmler. Because of that, Mende was now unassailable. He often met Rahm in town for lunch, which meant he'd be gone for the rest of the day. These appointments were the highlight of my week.

To give the man his due, Mende wasn't just lazy, but brilliantly imaginative in his work avoidance. Often he'd toss a whole ream of Judenrat forms my way, because 'the letters were too small'. Most Fridays he'd put his feet up, claiming to have forgotten his reading glasses, then hide behind his newspaper for the rest of the day. The chutzpah, as my mother would say.

One afternoon he came back from lunch pushing a handcuffed Jewish boy he'd caught climbing through a hole in the wall with a bag of potatoes. Mende dumped the boy at my desk, told me to do the paperwork, then lurched away to the bathroom. Five minutes later, when I was leading the boy to the cells, we passed Mende in the courtyard, tossing grain to the chickens and clucking like an imbecile.

***

The investigation into Augustus Brühl's death was officially closed. Julian Scherer telephoned one evening while I was writing the story of Shoshana's Magic Bell and how she lost her eye in our parents' grocery store. A Polish waiter at Krakauer Burg castle had been charged with Brühl's death after the murder weapon was found in a 'trophy drawer' in the kitchens, covered in dried blood. The waiter was hanged at dawn that morning. To save the regiment from further embarrassment, the details would not be reported, but Scherer wanted to put my mind at ease.

'It's over,' he said.

I tried to sound grateful for the fact that an indiscrete New Year's Eve dalliance in the castle bathrooms had led to an innocent Pole's death.

'Your father's told me about the letter you sent last year,' Scherer said. 'I don't use the word lightly, but the man is heart-broken.'

'As am I. It's a wretched situation.'

'You had your reasons, I know, and it's not for me to judge. But for the love of God, Harry, don't leave things like this.'

'I won't.'

'If you want me to broker peace - '

'I'll do it.'

'You'll call him ?'

'I will.'

'I believe you owe me, Harry. Do this, and we're even.'

***

On February 23rd, a third postcard arrived.

Eluding capture had boosted the Phantom's confidence. This time he left his handiwork outside the apartment block, pinned to the tram-stop timetable on the corner of Tragutta and Wielicka:

Free Press!
Continue with the Nazi system and the common soldier
Hitler and his gang will plunge us into the abyss!
This Hitler Göring Himmler Goebbels gang is for Poland
only a death chamber!

Inspector Schmidt returned that night with a team of twenty Gestapo men. They swept the building, interviewing each tenant, myself included, and took handwriting samples.

***

At the end of February, Rottenführer Ritschak announced that all staff were to be inspected again for sexually-transmitted diseases. The tests, I learned, would be monthly affairs. The Jewish Hospital had been used since the Ghetto opened, and the SS loathed it.

Today, however, Ritschak crowed, the authorities were pleased to announce a significant change in policy. Following questions about the Jewish Hospital's suitability for SS officers, a more accommodating centre had been selected. The Eagle Pharmacy was closing for the rest of the day, and the Jozefinska staff were cordially invited to make our way to Rynek square, at our own convenience, where tea and biscuits would be served. The city's Chief Medical Officer himself would be supervising proceedings. Ritschak was keen to point out that although Hauptsturmführer Kunde had listened to his men, in terms of environmental concerns, inspections were still mandatory. Failure to report before the end of the day would be considered a gross breach of responsibility, and swift disciplinary action would follow.

I wasn't surprised that Mende left for his appointment while Ritscak was still climbing back upstairs, nor that my work-shy colleague still hadn't returned by mid-afternoon. When the clock struck five o'clock, I could put it off no more. I took one final look around the office.

After my last scare at the Jewish Hospital, I made sure to always leave the apartment with sufficient bribery funds, and had still barely put a dent in Erich Mohnke's cash reserves. I prayed that the Chief Medical Officer was as grasping a man as his grotesque predecessor. If I did happen to meet the world's first incorruptible Nazi, there was no Plan B.

The usual crowd of desperate humanity milled around in front of the Pharmacy's closed doors. The surly youths made no attempt to move aside, and for once I ignored their mulishness. Germans still acted civilly within the shop, as if they too yearned an escape from the barbarity outside.

Magister Pankiewicz and Helena Krywaniuk were laughing behind the counter, but promptly stopped when I entered. Stony-faced, Pankiewicz consulted his list. As hoped, I was the last of the Jozefinska officers to present myself. The consultation room was empty. Miss Krywaniuk would show me through.

I was about to enquire as to the Chief Medical Officer's temperament, when Dr Ludwik Zurowksi opened the door behind the counter, he of the snug tweed suit and preternaturally black eyebrows.

'I thought I heard voices,' Zurowski said, making little snapping jaws of his hands. He smiled blankly at me, no recognition.

'Oberführer Mohnke is the final appointment,' Miss Krywaniuk said. 'Would you like me to assist?'

'I'll be fine, thank-you.' Zurowski held the door open for me. 'Oberführer Mohnke, after you.'

I smelled coffee and peppermints on his breath as I brushed past. The room was empty. Zurokski showed me to the bed in the corner, stepped back and pulled the curtain round on its rail, leaving me to undress.

'We've met before,' I said, through the fabric.

'We have?'

I removed my jacket and shirt, draping them over the back of the chair.

'I'm better with names than faces,' Zurowksi said.

I folded my vest carefully and placed it on the bed.

'Very briefly, last year,' I said. 'Here, out front. Wilhelm Kunde's lady-friend.'

'Ah, yes.'

But I could tell he didn't remember me.

I removed my boots, socks, trousers, down to my shorts.

'Are we ready?'

'All set.'

Zurowksi pulled back the curtain and chuckled when he saw me sitting on the side of the bed, stripped to my underwear. 'Very thorough. Unfortunately it's just the shorts that need to come off.'

He perched on the edge of the chair and leaned forward expectantly. I rose and dropped the elasticated waist to my knees.

After a minute of gentle lifting and prodding, he said, 'Unless I'm very much mistaken, your foreskin has been removed.'

'Masel tov.'

He gave another uncertain chuckle.

I pulled my shorts up and sat back on the bed.

'The circumcision was quite a while ago, I'd hazard. Accident? Infection? It all looks very clean.'

'Would you mind locking the door, Dr?'

'Absolute discretion is assured, you needn't worry.'

'The door,' I said. 'Please.'

'Alright. As you wish.'

When he returned, I handed him my folded vest.

'You require a laundry service?' he asked.

'Read it.'

'Read it?'

I pointed to the tiny stitching under the neck.

'*My name is Jozef Siegler,*' Zurowksi intoned reluctantly, as if he was being set up for a cruel joke. '*25/03/1901. I am a Jew.*'

Dropping the vest on the mattress, he said, 'I don't understand.'

'I was circumcised in the Brasov synagogue in Romania on April 2nd when I was eight days old, according to the ceremony of brit milah. After a simple meal of fish and eggs, my foreskin was buried in our garden, under a young juniper tree.'

'A juniper tree?'

'If you want I can recite the rabbi's prayers, but unless

you speak Yiddish, it won't mean much.'

'You can get dressed now.'

'I realise how this looks. I was a prisoner, in Wilno, in a labour camp. I broke out when I learned the truth. The mass executions, the burial pits - '

'The Pharmacy is about to close, Oberführer. In terms of STDs, you have a clean bill of health. That's all I need to know.'

39

By mid-May, the census was nearing completion. Twenty-thousand men, women and children, crammed into sixteen square blocks. The pressure was intolerable, residents clawing chunks out of each other for territory, like rats and foxes. Everybody knew the situation could not endure. The question was, what came next? Five months after Augustus Brühl's promise of racial apocalypse, the Ghetto population was more numerous than ever. It was hard to see this as any kind of victory for the Jews. I couldn't help thinking of the German expression, 'shooting fish in a barrel'.

One upshot of such a regimented and fastidiously documented concentration was that I knew my family had not been dragged back behind the walls. Was I glad? Were they safer inside or out? That depended what kind of night I had. Every morning I rose and scoured the freshly-delivered Judenrat lists, before setting to work archiving for the department.

Towards the end of one such day, I asked Karl Mende for his list, as was my custom, in order to make sure no Sieglers were amongst his paltry contribution. Being a Friday, Mende was at his least productive, barely processing fifty names to my hundred. With undisguised glee, he dumped his in-tray on my desk and went back to the newspaper he'd been scowling at all afternoon, that shriveled right eyeball of his red and angry. Not content with frittering his day away, Mende now tried to distract me from my work. It was like sitting opposite the class clown.

As soon as I began ticking names off his list, Mende started challenging me with tricky crossword clues. I maintained my default position, which was to ignore him. Only once did I rise to the bait.

Rublach Josef M 14/11/1884

'Five across, eight letters: to cut goods from leather.'

I put my pen down. 'What kind of goods?'

'Leather ones.'

'Thanks,' I said. 'Big help. The word is clicking.'

Goldstein Chaim M 20/3/1882

'Nope.'

'Have it your way.'

Burgenblatt Dyna F 10/10/1917

Mende said, 'Actually, it's fleshing.'

'Why ask if you've already got it?'

'I grew up with horses, I should know.'

'That explains a thing or two. Which side of the stable door?'

'What did you say?'

Farbstein Luba F / /1922

I put my pen down again. 'Fleshing is separating the fat from the skin.'

'That's cutting,' Mende said.

I fought the urge to launch my pen as a projectile. 'Clicking is cutting out the pattern, goods from leather. It happens after the flesh has been removed.'

Zygot Mordka M 13/02/1872

I read that last line again.

Zygot Mordka M 13/02/1872

Good God.

Mr. Zygot, the old bachelor who'd lived next to my mother's grocery store on Izaaka Street. It had to be the same man. Neither first nor second name was that common, and the date of birth fit with his age. This was the closest I'd got to my family since Paskow. As of the January resettlement, Mr. Zygot lived right here, in the Ghetto. Apartment 4, 13 Cranach Street. Shoshana might have told him something, a destination, a message to pass on.

I resolved to wait around until the stationhouse was empty, and visit Cranach Street that night. Karl Mende had already gone home for the weekend; I'd been too wrapped up in my discovery to notice.

I carried on working until seven o'clock. On my way out, I passed the waste-paper basket into which Mende had tossed his well-worn copy of Der Stürmer. I wasn't able to resist pulling the newspaper out to check the crossword for five across, still convinced I was right.

I couldn't believe what I saw.

Although Mende had spent the lion's share of the afternoon working on the puzzle, he hadn't written a single word. Instead, each white square was filled with a tiny inked swastika. Even more of a mystery, five across contained three spaces, not eight, and the clue had nothing to do with clicking or indeed fleshing. Leather cutting wasn't mentioned anywhere on the page.

Number 13 was occupied by two families, the Zlatins and the Freilichs. Neither were related to Mr. Zygot. He had been brought up on a stretcher by two members of the Judenrat in January, who informed Mr. Freilich that the apartment was below minium occupancy.

I explained that Zygot's name had been passed to the Department of Civil Affairs by an informant, and that I needed to interview him as a matter of some urgency. Mr. Freilich wished me a wry good luck.

'Is he dead?'

'He should be so lucky.'

'We should be so lucky,' his wife corrected.

There were nominally six people in that modest single room, but the number grew to twenty-six by evening, when the streets emptied. When I entered, it was already well into double figures, the younger children huddled together on the dirty floor. All the furniture had been pushed together at one end of the room, a sideboard and large table around which the adults squeezed, playing cards. Later in the evening, the grown-ups would take turns to sleep sitting up, since there wasn't enough space for everybody to stretch out at once.

I found Mr. Zygot against the far wall. He had shrunk dramatically but I recognized him by the stripe of scarred flesh on the right side of his beard where no bristles grew – as a child, Mordka had fallen face-first into his parents' fireplace. A pillow had been placed under the old man's head, but his neck was twisted, and his head lolled awkwardly against the wood. I crouched next to him, beside a sleeping teenage girl crippled by polio.

Mr. Zygot's eyes were open, but failed to focus when I loomed across his field of vision.

'I am trying to find your old neighbours,' I whispered. 'From the shop on Izaaka Street. You remember Elena Siegler and her daughter. Shoshana Siegler, the girl with one eye. Mr. Zygot?'

Gazing at the ceiling, he mumbled something about a park. There were no green spaces in Kazimierz.

'Do you mean the cemetery?'

He shrugged a little. 'Why do you live in a park?'

'Me? I don't. I'm looking for Elena Siegler.'

'Ah.' The hint of a smile. 'Evidence.'

'Yes. Do you have information?'

'I want to see a better world.'

'You won't get any argument from me there.'

Next to me, the girl started making strange noises in her sleep and kicked my thigh. I shifted closer to Mr. Zygot.

He peered up at me and said, 'The walls are pale violet. The floor is of red tiles. I will make you sketches of the other rooms too one day.'

Mr. Zgoti had nothing for me. His mind had gone.

In a rare act of clemency, the Ghetto had taken his soul, and left a babbling babe in its place.

40

Dr. Zubrowski appeared at the stationhouse four days after my medical, but ventured no further than the front desk. I watched him charm Klaus Rother, our new Spokesman for Jewish Matters, Zubrowksi peering past Rother's bony head, finding me at the back of the office. The doctor's dark eyebrows rose to form a fuzzy question mark and with a slight tug of his jaw, he gestured for me to meet him outside. Zubrowksi and Rother shook hands, and the doctor left. I waited two minutes, then told Mende I was popping out for some fresh air.

I caught up with Zubrowksi at the end of Jozefinska, on the corner of Solna Targowa. After a hearty greeting, the doctor said, 'Keep nodding and smiling as if we're talking about a night at the opera.'

'Anything but Wagner.'

'I owe you an apology, Mr. Siegler. A mutual friend has been in contact, and it would seem I was wrong to doubt you.' He stole a sideways glance my way as we walked towards Zgody Square.

'Do you think it's easy, what I do?'

'Should I have brought flowers? A portable string quartet? I said I'm sorry, let's leave it at that. This isn't a social call. Are you aware of recent developments near Lublin?'

'No.'

Zubrowski looked around to make sure nobody was following. 'A farmer was executed last week following a tip-off he was sheltering Jews in his barn.'

'Oh no,' I groaned.

'Unfortunately, yes. Anton Popolowsky. The SS shot them all. The Jews, the children, everybody. Please, keep smiling, I know it's difficult. But there's worse to come. The local Belorussian Gendarme has since been looking into the death of a certain police translator, Popolowsky's cousin from Hamburg, believed to have been killed six months ago in an unprovoked street fight.'

'Believed to have been?'

'After Popolowsky's arrest, suspicions were raised regarding Damien Plotz's racial purity. Fearing he'd been fooled into hiring a Jew, the Gendarme ordered the translator's body to be exhumed. A colleague of mine performed the autopsy.'

I groaned again. 'What did they find?'

'A tattoo. Here.' Zubrowski pointed to the underside of his left arm, near the pit. 'O RHD minus.'

I repeated the letters, for they meant nothing to me.

Zubrowksi said, 'It's his blood type.'

'Tattooed on his arm?'

'All Waffen-SS are required to wear a Blutgruppentätowierungin in case a transfusion is needed while unconscious.'

'Shit. So the Gendarme knows Plotz was SS. What happens now?'

'Luckily for you, he isn't likely to make this official. Burying one of Hitler's Oberführers by mistake isn't the smartest move a Belorussian could make right now.'

'How did you find out?'

'Your green-fingered guardian angel in Kopaliny. They've got more couriers than the Polish postal service. This little morsel came out of the Lublin Chief Medical Examiner's Office.'

We had come to a stop at the western side of Zgody Square.

'Alright,' I said. 'So what am I supposed to do?'

Zubrowski shrugged. 'On this occasion, I'm just the messenger.'

He opened the door, slipped inside and turned round the sign to 'CLOSED'.

***

Arriving home that night, I cleared the last flight of stairs and paused at the sound of German voices in my corridor, on the other side of the Fire door. Low and muttering, indistinct but unmistakable.

Gestapo.

If I'd taken the elevator that stopped right outside my appartment, the cabin would have served me up like a dumbwaiter to the Maître d'. But I had my own rules. I walked the four flights, as I did every day, no matter how weary. Advantage was mine: the Gestapo knew nothing of my approach. I knew exactly what to do next, to turn and flee. I had rehearsed it so many times that I dreamed only in frantic chase scenes, like the Keystone Cops. So why did I side-step up to the Fire door, cup my eyes and peer through the glass grille?

Two detectives were smoking outside my apartment, backs pressed to the wall, felt hats trapped and tipped above their foreheads. The flash of my face at the glass failed to rouse them.

I ducked back out of sight and flattened my own spine against the cool plaster. I had finally decided to run when a door slammed shut in the corridor. Almost simultaneously, the one I was sheltering next to in the stairwell pushed open. Rudolf Ditzen appeared in the opening, head bowed, arms crossed behind his back. He lurched forward violently as if pushed, and I stood aside.

Ditzen's hands were cuffed in bracelets. Inspector Schmidt followed him out onto the landing.

'Oberführer Mohnke.'

'Inspector.'

I stood holding the door while the two smoking detectives came through, the first one carrying a cardboard box.

'Ditzen was hiding it under the floorboards,' the detective said. 'Tenant below heard him scraping around and reported the noises.'

'Hiding what?'

The detective opened the lid. The box looked empty, until he tilted it into the light. As the shadows receded, I saw a fountain pen and two bottles of ink and a bundle of plain white postcards.

41

By the end of May 1942, I'd filled almost two ledgers' worth, detailing my flight from Kiel to Wilno and Camp Moda, the first fateful donning of Harry Mohnke's uniform, and the consequences of that decision. I wrote every evening from six to nine, fired by caffeine. Most of the work was done in the armchair in the corner of the living room where Augustus Brühl had died. When my back began to ache after longer sessions, I moved onto my bed and wrote propped up against the pillows.

Two ledgers covering the first forty years of my life, locked away in the safe. I would take them out most evenings and re-read a few pages, before continuing with my third, which dealt with life in and around Jozefinska. The autobiography had become a diary, a way to process the daily madness. Most days it was the only intelligent conversation I got.

I'd just finished transcribing the previous day's events. As if Ditzen's arrest wasn't enough to weigh on my conscience, there was Dr. Zurowski's news from Lublin. It had taken a day, but I'd just about talked myself down from a full-scale anxiety attack. The riddle of Damian Plotz's identity wasn't unravelled, I decided, but it had been definitely been tugged at. At least nobody had any idea that Harry Mohnke was part of the knot. A tattooed blood type was all the Gendarme had unearthed, and as Zurowski said, the Belorussian wasn't likely to talk. I'd decided my positon was safe when a barrage of knocks thudded outside. The janitor, probably, come to gossip about Ditzen.

I tucked the ledger under my mattress and went to unlock the door.

'Karl,' I said, utterly stupefied, gripping the door like a plank.

Mende and I barely exchanged pleasantries at Jozefinska and certainly never discussed where I lived, although my address was easy to find, were he so minded. Clutching a brown paper bag, my colleague lifted out two dirty eggs, jiggling them in his palm like a conjuror.

'Straight from Izzie,' he said, his favourite courtyard chicken.

'Thanks... Very kind.'

'Catch, quick.'

He feigned a throw and snickered when I whipped my wrist against the door-frame mid-flinch.

'Take 'em, then.' He dropped the pair into my cupped hands and brushed past me into the hallway with a snide, 'You're welcome.'

I scrambled after him, stopping to set the eggs down on the kitchen worktop. One started rolling towards the edge as I was leaving, but I caught it and nestled them both in a folded dish-cloth.

When I caught up with Mende, he was making himself comfortable in my favourite armchair.

'Enjoy those yolkers,' he said. 'Might be the last you get.'

'Oh.' I took the opposite sofa. 'Do you know something I don't?'

'We've got a fox prowling round the courtyard.'

Wincing, he tugged his pistol free from its holster as if the barrel still burnt against his shirt. Metal clinked on the glass as he set it down on the table.

'Hate foxes. Nasty little diseased vermin. Coming into our house, staking a claim on things what don't belong to him. Can't have that, can we, Harry?' With the usual scowl, he glanced up at the corners of the room behind me. 'Bit pokey, this place.'

'It's snug enough.'

'Just you here?'

'The three of us,' I said.

'Three?'

'What's the expression? Me, myself and I.'

Mende leant over the table and used two fingers like a bat to flick the pistol grip. Hypnotised, I watched the gun spin round on its chamber like a roulette wheel.

'No family?'

'Not in Cracow,' I said. 'My father lives in Dahme. It's not something I like to talk about, but you might have heard the gossip.'

'Bunch of old women,' he said contemptuously.

'Aren't they. My father's old friends with Julian Schermer, that's all. He was here a couple of weeks ago, actually. Schermer, not my father.'

I stopped babbling and drew away from the gun. It had come to a stop, with the barrel pointing directly at my groin. Leaning back on the sofa, that's when I saw it - after Karl Mende, the second most terrifying object in the room: a Jozefinska stationhouse hard-backed ledger under his chair, behind the paper bag.

I was sure I'd locked my journal away after tonight's writing session. But there it was, lying on the carpet.

Did Mende notice it while I was in the kitchen fussing over his eggs? Had he opened it, seen my Hebrew, then pushed it out of sight?

Was I gone long enough for any of that to happen? It had only felt like seconds at the time.

'I got a wife back home,' Mende said. 'Wife and son.'

'Congratulations.'

'You being sarcastic?'

'Not at all. I love children.'

'The boy's eleven. Tomas.'

'Nice name.'

'Doing well at school. Very good with words, the teacher says. Like you, Harry.'

'Me?'

'Don't shit a shitter. You're a smart bloke, nothing to be ashamed of.'

'I suppose not.'

'You used to be a teacher, I heard.'

'Ah, the gossip again.' I wondered what else he'd learned. 'I worked in a university for a while, yes.'

'You worked in one,' he said, curling his lip. 'Sweeping the floors, was it?'

'I was a professor. It was a long time ago. Another life.'

'I know that feeling. I haven't seen Tomas since they opened the Ghetto last March.'

'Where do they live?'

'Köln, unfortunately, with the wife's mother. Bloody British butchers.'

The RAF had been bombing the city for two years now, on an almost weekly basis.

'Tom wrote me his first letter last week.'

'That's great.'

'Want to see it?'

The conversation had taken an odd dreamlike quality.Why did Mende want me to read his son's letter? Perhaps he didn't trust the teacher's praise and wanted a second opinion.

'Sure, why not. Bring it in one day.'

Mende bent down, groped under the seat and come up clutching the ledger. When he opened it, the pages were blank, whereas mine were filled with dense Hebraic script. So we were both stealing office stationery. Me for my memoirs, Mende as some kind of scrapbook for his son.

Flicking through to a folded sheet of cream paper carefully preserved in the centre of the book, he teased it out, pinching the edges like the relics of a saint. He handed me his son's letter.

Tomas' writing was printed rather than cursive, but it was neat, almost obsessively so, with good grammar, save for the occasional lapse in punctuation. The boy was a very articulate eleven year old. His teacher was telling the truth.

I'd scanned as far as the third line when Mende said, 'Speak up.'

'Sorry?'

'Come on, read it out loud.'

'Really?'

'Yeah,' he said, the tone inviting my indulgence. 'I like to pretend I can hear him.'

I knew Mende was lazy, but this made no sense. Surely if he wanted to 'hear' young Tomas, he'd read the letter to himself, rather than suffer my halting tones.

That's when it hit me. The thought tumbled through my mind, falling into place like a deck of riffled playing cards, image after image: Mende's paltry paper-work; the forms he'd dump on me, citing 'tiny' or 'foreign' handwriting; his ever-present copy of *Der Stürmer*, worn – I saw now – as a trusty shield of deflection; the crossword puzzle inked in with nothing but tiny swastikas; the non-existent clue about leather cutting.

Mende couldn't read.

As in, he didn't know how. A fully-functioning illiterate adult. Office-work he somehow bluffed his way through, but a letter from his son was different. That's why he'd sought me out tonight, at home.

'From the beginning, then,' I said.

"Dear Father, I hope you are not alarmed, you should not be, unless you know where one of the Wellington bombers went. I have heard that it caused heavy casualties by the railway yard. But this I know because I saw, and so did everyone else in the house.

'Here is my story: I heard the clock strike 11 o'clock. I was in bed and just going to sleep. Between two 'clock and 2.30 o'clock, Nanna Hannie woke Grandpa Kurt and told him she could hear the guns. Grandpa woke Mother and Mother woke me. We were all awake by now, and started making our way down to the bunker. We saw flashes and then heard 'Bangs' and 'Pops' on the stairs.

'Suddenly a bright yellow light appeared and died down again. 'Oh! It's alright' said Grandpa. 'It's only a star shell'. That light appeared again and Mother, Nanna, Granda and I rushed to the window and looked out and there right above us was the Wellington!

'It had broken in half, and was like this: it was in flames, roaring, and crackling. It went slightly to the right, and crashed down behind the church!! It was about a <u>100 yards</u> away from the house and directly opposite us!!! It nearly burnt itself out, when it was finished by the Fire Brigade.

'I would rather not describe the condition of the crew, of course they were dead - burnt to death. They were roasted, there is absolutely no other word for it. They were brown, like the outside of Roast Beef. One had his legs off at the knees, and you could see the joint! The Wellington was bombed from an aeroplane above, with an incendiary bomb by a Lieutenant

Kleine. We have some relics some wire and steel framework.

The weather is beastly but Auntie and Uncle are jolly people, hoping you are all well, love to all. Your loving son Tomas.

Please don't be alarmed, all is well that ends well (and this did for us). We are all quite safe. Mother will write again soon.'

When I looked up, Mende's mask of indifference had slipped. His right eye, normally aggravated by squinting, was now leaking tears. He rubbed the moisture into the side of his nose and shook his head as if dispelling a bad dream.

'You read beautifully,' he said.

'What a charming boy. I can see how proud you are.'

He cleared his throat in mute agreement.

'Look, while it's still fresh, why don't you write a little reply. It'd make his day.'

'Not tonight,' Mende said. 'Didn't bring my glasses. Maybe when I get home.'

'Come on.' Before he could stop me, I swapped the letter for the ledger on his lap. 'You tell me what you want to say, I'll write it down, then you copy it up when you get back. How's that sound?'

'You sure don't mind?'

'Mind? I'm a professor, remember, or I used to be. A beautiful blank book like this, it's my duty to fill it.'

I found a pen in my shirt pocket, tapped the nib on the first page and said, 'Dear Tomas...'

42

A couple of days later, Mende found me in the bathroom after coffee and asked if I would help with a letter to his wife. He came to my apartment that evening, and the next, wanting to write again to Tomas. Whether out of habit or sheer bloody-mindedness, he never failed to show up without his trusty copy of *Der Stürmer* under his arm. At least I managed to wrest back my favourite chair the second time, by leaving a pair of underpants draped over the back like an anti-macassar when I went to answer the door. Mende took the sofa when he saw them. I regarded this as a minor victory, until he kicked off his boots and socks and lolled about like a seal, rubbing his bare flippers all over the arm-rest.

The following Tuesday he dictated three more communiques, not to family, but old foes who had once wronged him. There was a lot to get off his chest. The cinema projectionist who'd shown the reels of Leni Riefenstahls *Victory of Faith* in the wrong order, the jockey who'd crashed into him on the home straight at the Munich Brown Ribbon and the old school teacher who'd sent Mende out of an examination for tapping the desk, accusing the boy of 'communicating answers in morse code'. Each monologue came out fully-formed; I could tell Mende had been rehearsing all week. He began innocently enough, with a 'You probably remember me from winning the Grand National in 1933' or 'Greetings from Cracow, the Jewel of the Reich, where I have been stationed at the personal request of Governor Hans Frank'. Mende would go on to give his selected career highlights, before ending by settling old grievances, one of which had not been aired for thirty years. These shifts were signposted with a faux-magnaminous 'I forgive you, by the way,' or a 'It was such a long time ago, I hardly remember,' before going on to recount the details with a degree of recall to shame Marcel Proust.

For light relief as I rested my pen, Mende liked to treat me to his opinions of the men we worked with. Becher was a degenerate who kept pair of knickers in his pocket to sniff. Rottenführer Ritschak was an idiot who'd shot off his own arm cleaning his gun. Stape would have gambled his own mother away if she wasn't a toothless old crone. But it was for the Eagle Pharmacy that Mende reserved his most cheerful scorn, specifically Tadeus Pankewicz, the Jew-loving Commie destined for a one-way ticket to camp Belzec.

'But Kunde loves the man,' I protested.

'That whole shop is rotten. What do they expect, allowing Poles in and out the District like that. Notice how the Commie only employs the most beautiful sales-girls. One wink at the gate guards and they're through, no matter what they're carrying. At least half the black market comes through that Pharmacy, maybe more. Not just a few potatoes stashed in handbags either. I heard Irena smuggled grenades stashed in her knickers. She's hot stuff, but, Jesus Christ, imagine dipping your wick into that without knowing it.'

If these rumours came from anybody else, they might have some credence. But if the Gestapo looked into everybody Mende defamed, half of Europe would be under investigation.

'If it's true, it's happening right under Kunde's nose,' I said. 'He trusts Pankiewicz more than our own medics. I've seen it.'

'You didn't see what happened this afternoon.'

'At the stationhouse?'

'The Pharmacy.'

The Hauptsturmführer's stunt was the talk of the Ghetto. He had stopped by the drugstore and ordered Pankiewicz into the office, where he explained they were to play a joke on the two assistants, Irena and Helena. Kunde would cuff the boss, walk him out of the door and then, when they were out of sight, fire his revolver into the air to make the women think Pankiewicz had been executed. He was appalled, but couldn't talk Kunde out of it. In the end, everything went as the German had said, but during the whole ordeal, the pharmacist couldn't shake the feeling that he was being marched to his death.

'That's how much Kunde trusts your friend,' Mende said.

It was true that eyebrows had been raised recently at the amount of medical certificates handed out by the Pharmacy, allowing residents to travel outside the walls to purchase drugs Pankiewicz could not provide. He explained it as an inevitable consequence of January's mass resettlement. The Ghetto population had grown by a factor of two thousand, the Eagle had not. Like all resources, the shop was struggling to cope. The Jozefinska stationhouse certainly understood that feeling. Medical certificates continued to be tolerated.

But last Tuesday, one day before Kunde's stunt, Pankiewicz had stormed through the stationhouse to the courtyard, demanding access to a prisoner in our gaol. A few of us downed tools at the commotion and followed him out. The prisoner in question had been arrested that morning by Karl Mende and myself in connection with an assault on a German soldier. Manni Konigsberg was part of a young Akiva cell, most likely attempting to acquire weapons for the resistance. The soldier was drunk and could remember nothing of the attack, but one of Symche Spira's informants fingered Konigsberg as the ringleader, and I'd been unable to protect him. Now Pankiewicz was trying to intervene.

'The man suffers from a rare blood disorder,' he shouted at Werner Fricke, our gaoler. 'Without an immediate injection of Vitamin B12, he will die in your cells.'

'Saves us a bullet,' Fricke said. 'He's due to be executed in the morning.'

'I will hold you directly responsible for the violation of the 1929 Convention for the Amelioration of the Condition of the Wounded and Sick in Armies in the Field.'

'Armies in the Field, my arse. He's a terrorist coward who put a decent soldier in hospital.'

'And you're putting him in the grave without due process -'

I stepped between the two. 'Look, Fricke, I arrested the bastard. I want to see him rot as much as you. But Pankiewicz has a point. We've got to think how it looks.'

'Fuck how it looks. He's an animal.'

'And a sick animal gets a vet, right? Nobody's talking about rushing him to a private room at the Beelitz-Heilstatten.

If this glorified pill-pusher thinks he can help, let him. But stand in his way and this gets reported, we'll end up with Red Cross stationed here, right inside the District. Do you want to be the one to explain that to the Hauptscharführer ?'

Fricke conceded, Pankewicz administered his vitamins, and Konigsberg was shot at dawn.

**

Mende failed to arrive at my place the next evening, as agreed. Relieved as I was to be spared more of his vengeful letters, I couldn't help but worry. Any unexpected change in routine was alarming, but coming so soon after I'd stood up for Manni Konigsberg, Mende's no-show felt fatal.

He didn't show up at Jozefinska the next morning, either. For the second time in three months, I was left sitting opposite an empty desk. To paraphrase Oscar Wilde, losing one partner may be regarded as a misfortune; losing both looks careless.

Not that any of Mende's colleagues were concerned by his absence. In terms of productivity, he was no great loss. After stewing in cold sweat for as long as I could tolerate, I followed Rottenführer Ritschak out to the courtyard and aksed if he knew what had happened to my colleague.

'He's with the Hauptscharführer.'

I raised my eyes to the balcony. 'In his office?'

'No.' Ritschak awarded me a conspiratorial leer for persistence. 'They've gone to Lublin. Classified meeting. You'll be hearing about it in due course.'

One day later, I was sitting opposite the same empty desk.

Neither man had returned from Lublin.

I tried to construe this as a positive. If the worst had happened, and they'd found out about the Gendarme's translator, and somehow made the connection with Harry Mohnke's broken down train, Kunde would have ordered my immediate detention. He wouldn't stay the night and saunter back a day later.

Although, of course, from his perspective, the situation

was more complicated. My transfer to the Ghetto had been personally authorised by family friend, SS and Polizeiführer Julian Scherer. Kunde couldn't act unilaterally. Too many sensitive conversations had to take place before I could be punished.

Twenty-four hours' worth, perhaps.

I was visited that afternoon by an unemployed accountant called Daniel Dryzin, who claimed to have information about a troublesome folk-singer.

Dryzin was sallow, stocky and short, with a touch of deformity to his thick chest and bow legs. When I invited him to pull up Mende's seat, he was as tall sitting down as he was standing up.

'A folk-singer and a writer,' Dryzin continued. 'His name's Mordecai Gebirtig. His family moved into the District in March. Since then, he's been collecting, composing and performing songs illegally.'

'Is it illegal to sing?'

'His stuff, yes. See for yourself.'

He removed a piece of yellowing paper titled 'Undzer Shtetl Brent! 1936, Pryztyk'.

'Something about *Our Town*,' I said. 'I don't speak Yiddish. Translate.'

'*Our Town is Burning*,' Dryzin said. 'I'll read the last verse. 'It's burning, brothers! Our town is burning! And our salvation depends on you alone. If our town is dear to you, grab the buckets, douse the fire! Show that you know how! Don't stand there, brothers, looking on, with futile, folded arms. Don't stand there, brothers, douse the fire! Our poor village burns!''

'It's a description of a fire,' I said, swallowing my bile. 'I don't see the problem.'

'It was a riot, sir, not a fire. A mob of Poles destroyed Jewish houses and beat them. A shoe-maker had his head split open with his own axe.'

'And how did this song come into your possession?'

'Gerbirtig gave his papers to the daughter of a friend of his, for safe-keeping. My daughter knows his daughter. She was able to take this, as proof.'

'Proof of what?'

'He sings the song at gatherings, secret ones. To incite others. They go wild, clamouring and yelling. It's a rallying call. Don't stand there with futile, folded arms. It's a metaphor, sir, for standing up and taking action against you, against your men.'

'Thank-you for explaining the literary technique, Professor Dryzin. Does it incite you?'

'Me?'

'Yes, when you read it just now. Are you not a Jew? Doesn't it fill you with a righteous fury?'

Dryzin looked appalled. 'No. The only thing it incited me to do was to report it.'

'For which we are all grateful. I shall keep the song.'

'Of course, sir. That's why I brought it.'

I was about to dismiss him when a car blasted its horn outside to clear the road. Through the front door, I saw a black limousine pull up to the kerb. Karl Mende squeezed out the driver's door, walked around the bumper and opened the rear one for Wilhelm Kunde. At the front desk, Klaus Rother saluted as they entered the building. Kunde disappeared immediately up the stairs on the left and Mende walked through the maze of work-stations towards us. He stopped behind me, put his hands on my shoulders and dug his thumbs into the muscle.

'Don't think I'm ungrateful, Harry, but I'm going to have arrest you for bringing the Reich into disrepute.'

His grip tightened.

'Get the fuck out of that seat.'

I stood up, pushing into Mende, who hadn't moved.

'Not you, funny man,' he said. 'I go away for a day and you turn this place into a kibbutz. You, midget: move.'

Dryzin hopped down. I started to sway from side to side while Mende took out a handkerchief and unfolded it over his seat cover.

'What's he got for us then? Better be good.' Mende glanced at Dryzin and I, then scowled at the yellowed sheet of paper on my blotter. He groaned. 'A poem?'

'It's a song,' Dryzin said. 'A protest song, performed right here in the District.'

'That's better.' Mende crossed his boots on the desk and laced his fingers behind his head. 'Keep going.'

Dryzin told the story of Mordecai Gebirtig while I concentrated on slowing down my heartbeat with a series of long, subtle breaths. When he was finished, I asked Mende what he thought we should do.

'Sounds like a job for your pharmacist, Harry.'

'I'm not sure I follow.'

'He's so fond of giving injections, he can rustle up a drop or two of diphtheria.'

'The vaccine?'

'Christ, no. The bacteria.'

Mende clutched a fist to his throat, splayed the fingers in a sudden spasm then moaned as they wilted like dead leaves. I had no idea what this was supposed to mean.

'Paralyze this singer's vocal chords,' he explained. 'That should teach him a lesson. No sense in over-kill, is there?' He grinned at Dryzin. 'Now whistle on out of here, Shorty. Station's closing early.'

The last few Jews scurried towards the exit. Klaus Rother closed and locked the front door behind them, then signalled to an unseen presence at the back of the office. At his gesture, one of the younger officers came in from the courtyard carrying a bucket of iced champagne, followed by two more, while a fourth ferried a crate of glasses. They set up bar on Rother's counter and began de-corking bottles and arranging flutes on silver trays as if drilled in the kitchens of the Hotel Adlon.

Wilhelm Kunde descended the stairs while they poured. He had visited the barber, perhaps as recently as this morning. Hair chiselled into a neat wedge, pushed up at the front and shorn at the sides over those ears, wide as shovels. His freshly-shaved cheeks glistened like apples. Champagne flutes were distributed to our desks as Kunde stood at the counter with his back to us, rehearsing his thoughts.

I wondered what they'd heard at Lublin. Could the Allies have surrendered? It seemed impossible, given the current precarious balance of power. RAF Bomber Command had only just carried out the first 1,000 bomber raid, against Mende's beloved city of Köln. The US naval task force were at that moment heading for midway in preparation for the expected Japanese attack. But on the Eastern Front, the Battle of Kharkov had ended in German victory, with over 230,000 Soviets killed. One thing was certain: the war would end, on a day much like today, and chances were nobody would see it coming.

Glass filled, I joined the rest of the office in standing to receive Kunde's speech.

'As many of you know, I have expressed before my deepest conviction in God. Not the Christian God, but a belief in fate, in the ancient one as I call him – that is the old Germanic word: Wralda.'

Shoulders slumped at this, ever so slightly. Wralda. Was that why we had gathered, to pay respect to some kind of pagan deity? Would Kunde be off to the mountains tonight, gallivanting around his bonfire? Mende too? I wasn't surprised.

'The essence of these megalomaniacs, these Christians who talk of men ruling this world, must stop and be put back in its proper proportion. Man is nothing special at all. He is but a speck on this earth. If a big thunderstorm comes, he can do nothing. He cannot even predict it. He has no idea about the inner workings of a fly, however grotesque. Or how a flower blossoms. They are miracles. Man must once again look with deep reverence into this world. Then he will acquire the right sense of proportion about what is above, and how we are woven into this cycle.

'The time has finally arrived when we will have to deal with this Christianity once and for all. The time has come when we must settle accounts with this greatest of plagues, which has weakened us in every conflict. Mighty as our ancestors were, they lacked the resolve for such decisive action. That burden has now passed down to us, in this eternal chain and sequence.'

The crevice between Kunde's eyes deepened like a scar.

'Yesterday, I attended a briefing by Odilo Globocnik, SS

and Polizeiführer of Lublin District. We have at long last received instruction as to the ways and means of liquidating the Polish Jewry, henceforth to be known as Aktion Reinhard, in honour of its instigator, the Schutzstaffel-Obergruppenführer.

'This process will begin in three days time. Let us drink to mark this most momentous of days in the history of the Germanic Reich.' Kunde raised his champagne flute, lower lip jutting like a stanchion. 'To Wralda.'

***

It was during these preparations that I first learned the name of the Hauptsturmführer of a tough Sonderkommando unit who'd done 'sterling work' for racial purity in the Lublin area and was relocating to Cracow to ensure that June 1st ran smoothly. Mende and I were selected to accompany Wilhelm Kunde on a tour of the Ghetto when our guest arrived. His name? Amon Göth.

I dropped my coffee when I heard that fateful triptych, claiming to have burnt my lips.

For four hours last November, I'd sat with the man's thigh next to mine on the front seat of a sled. Thank God we'd travelled at night, over fields lit by nothing but moonlight. I recalled Göth was suffering from a cricked neck. He couldn't turn round and spent the whole journey staring at the haunches of the pack he drove. But I'll never forget his face in side profile, its rugged aristocracy: the thuggish brow and hooked nose, the long slit of nostril sharp as a papercut, the wedge of grimaced mouth and weak chin. When we reached the synagogue, I'd made myself scarce and kept to the shadows. On the ride home, Göth and the Belorussian celebrated by getting drunk.

It was possible he wouldn't remember the night at all.

But that didn't stop me ransacking Erich Mohnke's bedroom cupboards for a Zeiss Opticians case, and rubbing hemp oil under my nose and shaving eight times in two days to stimulate growth.

I inspected my work in the bathroom that morning. The

results were satisfying; the round spectacles and faint moustache just enough to alter my appearance. There was even a touch of Heinrich Himmler in the reflection, a popular look that season amongst pro-Nazis of a certain age. Every bar in the city had at least one face like mine staring into his dregs.

43

The day started peacefully at Jozefinska. Several times I caught myself day-dreaming that the last six months of relative stability in the Ghetto might last until the Allies won the war. But then a memo crossed my desk stamped with the word 'Reinhard', or I overheard mention of the Lublin troop deployment headed our way.

To put my new disguise to the test, I asked to borrow Mende's newspaper. He tossed it over. After a few seconds of turning pages and squinting, I said, 'I'm sure the damned print gets smaller every week.'

My colleague gave a non-committal grunt. I could have told him I was a Jewish spy and it would have got the same response.

I grandly swept an arm into my jacket pocket, came out with the Zeiss case and hooked the metal arms over my ears as deliberately as a palsied grandfather.

Mende didn't even look up.

I'd been keeping one eye on the front door, but in the end the devil slipped in through the courtyard. Seated opposite me, it was Mende who noticed first, and raised a welcoming arm.

The field-grey shoulder boards of an army Hauptmann swept past my chair, trailing aftershave and cigarette smoke. I watched him receive Mende's effusive handshake. It was as if Wralda himself had descended from the mountaintop.

To my eyes, Amon Göth looked more like an overgrown school-boy than a God in the daylight. Softly-spoken, with gentle eyes, cherubic cheeks and a touch of the sniffles, I found it hard to reconcile his face with the mask of the butcher who'd presided over the slaughter of an entire village. He'd filled out considerably in the past six months, developing a paunch and fleshy jowls. But it was the face I kept coming back to. Large, malleable, fleshy, ears fat as lemons.

'And this is Mohnke,' Mende said. 'The department couldn't function without him. I'm not sure any of us could.'

Göth turned his transparent blue eyes my way. He sniffed, dabbing a tissue to his nose. 'You used to be the professor?'

'That's correct, sir.'

'I don't know how you controlled yourself, all those fine young beauties hanging on your every word.' He gave a shy smile. 'Did you? Control yourself?'

'I'm German,' I said. 'Self-control is my birth-right. Although I might have given myself the one or two nights off.'

'All part of a girl's sentimental education, I'm sure. This place must be a hell of a come down after campus life.'

'I've seen worse, sir. I was in Southern Russia last year.'

'Good God, my sympathies. Everything's relative, eh Professor? The shock-haired Jewish physicist was right about that at least. Russia's not going anywhere unfortunately, but we'll have this place in order before long, I give you my word. Now where can I find your Hauptsturmführer?'

Ten minutes later, the four of us were ready to begin the tour. Since it was a glorious summer afternoon, Kunde had arranged for his open-topped sports car to be waiting outside instead of the usual limousine. The smaller sized vehicle meant the chauffeur wouldn't be accompanying us.

'Mende, you drive,' Kunde said, allocating himself the passenger seat.

I realised this left the two of us in the back. Göth took the nearside seat, so as to better converse with his host, diagonally rather than to the back of Kunde's head. Which left me on Göth's right. It couldn't have worked out any worse. Within minutes of Göth's arrival in Cracow, I was recreating the exact conditions of our sled ride.

Fortunately, Göth was too amused by life in the slums to pay me much attention. We drove the length of Jozefinska, Kunde pointing over his shoulder to the Jewish Hospital and House of Orphans as if ticking off the sights of Rome. At the far end of the street we turned left and doubled back on Limanowskiego, the other main thoroughfare that ran the Ghetto's length. At the gate we followed the southern wall round on Rekawka Street, and finally took the 'scenic' route back, criss-crossing each of the sixteen blocks along the way.

Before we reached the stationhouse, Göth asked me to describe the work of the Department of Civil Affairs. I explained the role of Smyche Spira's Jewish Police, his team of informants, and recapped some of our successes.

'Superb work,' Göth said. 'And you will of course be instrumental in the build-up to tomorrow.'

'We can't wait to get started, sir.'

'In order to ensure the Aktion passes smoothly, the Jews must be led to believe that a large-scale resettlement programme is commencing. You can lay the foundations when we get back. Call in your informants and spread the word.'

'Yes, sir.'

'The Jews will be so desperate to get out of here, they'll believe anything.'

'Where exactly are they going?'

The kindness passed from Göth's face in an instant and those eyes ran cold. Sensing the change in ambience, Kunde twisted round in his seat. The look he gave me made it quite clear that I had not been brought along to question a superior officer's orders.

'That is to say,' I explained. 'To minimise panic, it might help if I could tell the Jews where they were being resettled to... But, as you said, they'll think anywhere is better than this place.'

Göth closed his eyes, settled his chin on his fist and inhaled deeply.

'You're right,' he said eventually. 'Let's tell them the truth. They're going to larger cities in the East, where there's more space and better conditions.'

'Very good, sir. I apologise if I was disrespectful.'

Göth waved a dismissive hand. 'I need to be challenged from time to time, it's good for my constitution. It's funny, you remind me of somebody, Professor. I just can't think who.'

'You may have seen a photograph of Erich Mohnke in the papers last year,' Kunde said. 'Assassinated in Warsaw. Harry's the younger brother.'

'That's it,' Göth crowed. 'Blown up by the JFO. Take your cap off.'

I complied, running a hand through my hair.

'Christ, you're the spitting image. You even wear the same glasses.'

'I'm two inches taller,' I said. 'It's the only way our mother could tell us apart.'

Kunde said, 'The father's old friends with Oberführer Scherer.'

Göth rubbed his nose with the tissue and gave a startled sneezed. 'You know, I think I'm going to like Cracow after all. The four of us must have dinner one night. I throw the most exceptional parties.'

44

Overnight, the Ghetto was surrounded by German police and SS. The Jews were woken at dawn by a chorus of loudspeakers, ordering everybody to report outside: 'This is not a deportation. Repeat, this is not a deportation. You are being resettled for your comfort and convenience.'

It was our job to patrol the streets, make selections and compile the first of many lists. Those employed in factories or workshops were permitted to stay, along with members of their family up to fourteen years of age. These lucky few received my seal of the Polzeifuhrer on their identity cards. All others not in eligible employment were told to collect their valuables and baggage of up to 20kg, and to report to Zgody Square. After barely enough time to pack a hairbrush, let alone kiss loved ones goodbye, the Jewish Police started knocking on doors, pulling those without the proper seals back onto the street and driving them towards the assembly point. Kunde, Göth and an Oberführer I did not know called Otto von Mallotke swept up the rear.

The rest of Jozefinska were dispatched ahead to the Square, where a truck full of small wooden desks and chairs awaited. We unloaded the furniture and set up a neat row opposite the Pharmacy, then made sure each desk was equipped with the correct stamp and ink tray. In an idle moment, I caught myself thinking of June mornings long gone, laying out exam papers in the Great Hall of Kiel before the students arrived.

The square started filling from all directions with a stream of women, children, and elderly. They had reported so often in so many towns and cities, they knew exactly what to do. Everybody moved like clockwork. Lines were formed at the desks, ID cards clutched and ready. While they shuffled forward, I wove in and out, distributing chalk for the labelling of baggage. No need to lug cases around in the heat, everything would be taken on ahead. At the head of the queue,

Jews were greeted by smiling young Germans who praised their good fortune, wished them luck and then stamped their Ghetto permits with the word 'Cancelled'.

A flotilla of horse-drawn wagons entered stage-left, to excited whoops from the children. SS officers tossed them carrots and sugar-cubes to feed the animals, a week's worth of Ghetto rations gobbled up in minutes. Families were invited to sit down in the back of carriages and Karl Mende and I were sent up to the Pharmacy roof with a pair of Zeiss Ikon Contax round our necks to record the moment for posterity. How humane those Germans were, how considerate.

By the time we'd come back down, the Square was a bear-pit. Families were chased down from the wagons by dogs, tumbling on each other as they jumped. Soldiers shouted and forced them up, beating legs, driving the deportees out of the Square en masse. Guns were fired, but the only screams were the incessant yells of the SS. I joined the scramble, scooping up those who had fallen before the pistols picked them off. Looking back over my shoulder for stragglers, the Square was littered with a dozen corpses.

We chased the column north towards the station, where there was a small labour camp for Jews who worked on the railway. 150 of ours were shot en route. The survivors were greeted by a line of prisoners hanging from the footbridge like ghoulish wind-chimes. Hands tied behind their backs, heads bowed from broken necks, they hovered above us, seven souls in ascension.

The soldiers worked in shifts, but I could not stop, not while there were bewildered elderly people to try and reassure, or bereft children looking for somebody to hold their hand, even a German officer. As a result of the first day of Aktion Reinhard, the Ghetto was cut by 7,000. 1,000 of the weakest were killed by Ukranian guards at Plaszow-Prokocim while their friends and family were loaded onto sealed baggage cars.

Amon Göth's superiors were not satisfied with the numbers and on Thursday June 5th, the Ghetto was once again surrounded by SS and Schutzpolizei. Jewish identity cards were re-examined and another 4,000 were rounded up and forced to wait in Zgody Square throughout the hot summer morning. With no escape from the scorching sun, the Jews were left to bake, crying out for water. The concrete was too hot to lie on, so they stood until they could stand no longer.

I arranged for the Pharmacy girls to bring out jugs of water for the Jozefinska officers, making sure there was plenty left over for the Jews. Pankiewicz had marked a tiny X on paper cups containing phenobarbital and codeine, to pacify the wailing children. As I distributed drinks, I chanced upon a strikingly tall mother and baby encircled by a group of friends providing shelter. The mother's neck was emaciated and the bosom to which she clutched her child was shriveled. Half her hair was combed and the rest unkempt, but those tight curls were unmistakable. The last time our paths had crossed, she'd spat at the ground and cursed me. Now she refused my water.

'Don't worry,' I told her. 'I can help.'

The friends closed ranks around her as if I was the devil incarnate. 'Your kind of help we can do without,' said a man with a scar over his eyebrow. 'Leave her be.'

But I could not stand by and watch mother and child dragged kicking and screaming to Plaszow. I found the man in charge of the Aktion, and pointed out his problem.

'That woman is a highly skilled employee at the armaments factory. Herr Schindler will be furious if she is deported.'

Oberführer Mallotke sighed and said, 'Name?'

'Devorah Montefiore.'

Mallotke consulted his clipboard.

'She's on the list,' he said. 'There's nothing I can do.'

'Does it say Essential Worker next to her name? Because that's what she is.'

'It doesn't say anything.'

'Then there's been a mistake. Schindler lost a worker like this on Monday. The man responsible is in Southern Russia now.'

Mallotke processed this information with a curt nod.

'Alright. Let's see what she has to say for herself.'

We marched back to the circle of shade-makers.

'You.' Mallotke singled out the woman in the centre. 'Job?'

'Munitions worker, Deutsche Emalia. I made 45 mm anti-tank shells.'

To Devorah Montefiore I said, 'Don't worry. There's been a misunderstanding. I'm getting you out of here.'

She cried out as Mallotke crossed her name off the list.

'You are free to return to the factory.'

'No, please let us go,' Montefiore cried. 'My boy is sick. He'll die if he stays here.'

What did she think was going to happen? A week of this bloodshed and still the Jews believed in the Promised Land, while their brothers and sisters were thrown on the garbage heap.

Mallotke said, 'It is mandated, essential industrial workers must stay in the District.'

'Then let the baby go without me, I beg you.'

The scarred man quickly put his arms out for the child. 'We'll take him.'

'Children under fourteen are to remain with their parents. We're not operating a crèche. Guards!' Mallotke whistled for two Jewish Policeman. 'Escort this woman and her child back to the Emalia Deutsche factory. They are to arrive safely, or you shall answer to me.'

Her wails haunt me still, the wails of the only woman to be saved.

For all Göth's efforts, several thousand people remained in the Ghetto without the correct seals in their identity cards. Symche Spira's Jewish Police combed the streets, and the informants continued to feed us names.

On Friday June 6th, a new decree was issued. Blue slips were to be stapled to identity cards. From this point forth, only Jewish residents in possession of these Blauschein were entitled to remain within the walls. The entire Ghetto population was ordered to report for further inspection, including those who had already received the seal of the Polzeifuhrer on the subsequent two Aktions. Since no rain had come to wash Zgody Square of its blood, the unfortunates were ordered to assemble in the courtyard of the Optima factory at Wegierska Street.

The courtyard filled up very slowly with those denied permission to remain: the old and the lame, cripples on crutches leading the blind and the mentally ill. Several patients were carried from the hospital and tipped off their gurneys. It took until late Friday afternoon for everybody to be rounded up, at which point the SS and Schutzpolizei went off duty for the weekend.

The Jews were simply left where they lay, with Jozefinska staff expected to guard them in shifts. I did not go home, but stayed in the courtyard, distributing food and drink to the most needy. Many collapsed from exhaustion or fear, and did not move again.

The rest were marched to the railway station first thing on Monday morning.

On Friday June 20th, SS and Polizeiführer Julian Scherner proclaimed an 'amputation' of the Ghetto, reducing to less than a third of a square mile. The south side of Limanowski Street was to be severed from the main body, leaving only the north. Residents of Limanowski, Czarnecki, Benedikt, Kragus and Wegierska streets were given five days to find new living quarters within the curtailed area. This latest Aktion coincided with a new policy for the Jewish Police: if Symche Spira's men failed to deliver a family into the street, their own flesh and blood became forfeit.

The first wave of suicides occurred on Saturday June 21st, while Wilhem Kunde was at the stone circle in Odry for Midsummer Solstice. Inside the Ghetto, the sun had long stopped shining. Escape attempts over the walls became nightly affairs, punishable by a bullet in the back.

As half the Ghetto scrambled to relocate into the other, apartment floors became the hottest black market commodity, snapped up sight-unseen. Bidding wars broke out for cupboards and water closets. Occupancy was limited to one person only – no luggage. Residents of the condemned streets had to leave behind most of their belongings, which sat untouched in vacant buildings. Even gangsters didn't have the energy to steal, or the space to store their loot.

At Jozefinska, additional shifts were required to cope with the upsurge in curfew violations, and I volunteered. I spent my days in the office and the nights patrolling the walls, bringing food in through a hole and spiriting out children in sacks and cardboard boxes, drugged by the Pharmacy to keep them from crying out. When dawn broke at half past four, I would go back to my apartment and sleep for two hours, then return to my desk for the day shift.

News of my commitment eventually reached Julian Scherer, who came over from Pomorska to personally thank me. Shaking the hand that had signed the Aktion to liquidate the Ghetto was the least of my worries. Scherer wanted to nominate my 'bravery before the enemy' with an Order of the Iron Cross, the same award Erich Mohnke had received posthumously. I explained that while I was grateful for the recognition, I could not consider myself a worthy recipient, compared to the sacrifice my brother had made. Scherer reluctantly agreed not to put my name forward. But in return, I had to attend a dinner at his apartment that weekend.

45

Scherer had met me three times by this point, and never when I was wearing my new spectacles or moustache. I didn't take any chances Saturday night, and left both items at home, shaving again for the occasion. In place of the Zeiss case in my trouser pocket, I carried a pack of Nordland cigarettes, Harry Mohnke's brand of choice. Smokers enjoy only one advantage at awkward social occasions: a ready-made excuse to disappear intermittently without appearing rude. Perhaps that's why people take up the habit.

The Oberführer's city residence was a luxurious penthouse apartment in the heart of Kazimierz, with a receptionist on the ground floor. Scherer himself greeted me at the door, a grin threatening to split his face like a ripe tomato. The first of many champagne glasses was thrust into my hand and I was tugged into a grand, open-plan living room that could have housed half the Ghetto. A radio cabinet was playing waltzes at an intrusively loud volume. In the centre of the room on a lionskin rung was a grand piano. To the right a cluster of white leather armchairs and sofas overlooked the city through an open French window, and in the other corner, a cloth-covered table, set - I noted with alarm - for six people and not three.

'Please tell me you didn't invite my father,' I said quietly.

Scherer raised a quivering finger to his lip. 'Oh dear. I thought that's what we agreed...'

'No. We did no such thing. I'm sorry Oberführer, I can't do this.' I started backing away.

'Harry, relax. Of course I didn't invite him. Willi Kunde and Amon Göth are making up the numbers.'

I rubbed the smooth groove above my lip. 'I suppose I can put up with those two bums.'

'Ha!'

Elsa Scherer was a large, softly-spoken woman, placid in nature, and impossible to dislike, despite her choice of husband. The three of us awaited the others on the armchairs, where talk turned to Harry Mohnke's home town of Dahme, his mother and brother's death, and how the family was coping. Frau Scherer didn't seem to know about the estrangement between father and son. The Oberführer steered conversation round to life in Cracow, but his wife possessed a steely persistence beneath her easy-going façade, and wouldn't be dissuaded from her line of questioning.

'And how's Kate managing?' she asked.

My mind went blank. Kate? In all Erich Mohnke's letters and journals, I had never come across the name. There was no sister, so I guessed that Kate was an aunt, or a friend of the mother's.

'Kate's doing much better, thank-you.'

Frau Scherer clapped her hands in glee. 'Is she walking again?'

I found myself nodding along. 'Yes. Yes she is.'

'The poor dear broke her hip skiing in Switzerland,' Elsa reminded her husband. 'The doctors said she'd be bed-bound.'

'Doctors,' Scherer grumbled. 'I think we've all had enough of so-called experts.'

'We must all go and see her. We can take Harry, too. I'm sure Otto would love to meet us.'

The doorbell rang. The rest of the party arrived together. Kunde was accompanied by his glamourous wife Christina, a diminutive blonde with an infectious laugh and a lazy eye, while Amon Göth came alone. Neither man remarked on my lack of moustache, but I took the armchair as far away as possible from Göth, and pushed it back even further out of his sightline. Scherer's two young daughters came out of their bedrooms to perform duos on their accordions, with father accompanying on the piano.

After the girls went to bed, Frau Scherer led the way to the table, directing us to our seats. Host and hostess took either end, with Kunde and Christina between them on one side. That left Göth and I together on the other, as if we were a third couple. I found myself seated once again on his right, this time with no cap, glasses or moustache to hide behind.

Dinner was served 'farmhouse style' by Frau Kruk, an

excellent chef who'd worked for a German nobleman before the war. I was relieved to hear that beef steak followed the starter of white bean soup, and I would not have to eat pork.

During the main course, conversation was stopped by a sombre announcement that came over the radio. The presenter apologised for interrupting programming in the kind of tones reserved for Hitler's death or surrender. But no news bulletin followed, only dead air.

'Thank God we're not in Berlin, Professor,' Göth muttered at my side. 'Out to dinner there, you leave with dessert or spend the night shacked up in the cellar.'

I realised then what was happening: radio silence meant an Allied air-strike over the capital was imminent.

'The Baltic's taking a hammering,' Göth continued. 'Especially Kiel, with the navy and shipbuilding. When was the big one, last April?'

'I'm not sure,' I said. 'I was in Russia.'

'Of course.'

Silence continued to hiss from the cabinet speakers, engulfing the room. We were eventually jolted from reverie by our own localised hostilities, the crack of distant gunfire across the river, from the Ghetto. It was 9.00, the nightly escape attempts were beginning. Frau Scherer flinched at the echoes and pushed her plate of pancake away untouched.

'Compassion is one of my wife's greatest virtues,' Scherer explained from the head of the table. 'It is in fact the main reason I married her.'

'The violence in our Residential District is unforgivable,' Kunde said. 'But a philosophy of racial purity does not allow for niceties. You can rest assured, Frau Scherer, the days of city centre shootings are coming to an end.'

'Heinrich Himmler toured Auschwitz only yesterday,' Scherer said. 'Great things are expected.'

'Belzec, too,' Göth added. 'Total refurbishment. The Professor and I will soon have this unpleasantry off your doorstep, m'am.'

'Let's not talk about it during dinner,' she said.

'Quite right.'

Scherer wiped cream from his mouth with the corner of a

napkin. 'Why are you riding him like that, Amon?'

'I'm not sure what you mean.'

'All this 'Professor' business. Share the joke.'

'I wasn't aware I'd made one, sir.'

'It's a nickname I picked up at Jozefinksa,' I explained, discretely nodding to Göth to let it go. 'I'm what passes as the brains of the department.'

'I would hope so,' Scherer said. 'Compared to Karl Mende.'

Soon after that, a waltz recommenced from the radio. False alarm – Berlin was in the clear for now. Scherer rose to turn up the volume until we could no longer hear the Ghetto and we finished our apple pancakes with something of the earlier bonhomie restored.

'Wonderful meal,' I said. 'Please excuse me for a few minutes.' I tapped a Nordstrom out of its box. 'I prefer not to blow smoke over the table. May I use the balcony?'

'Of course.'

Passing the piano and armchairs, I stepped out the French windows, lit a cigarette under the moon and stood taking in the Cracow skyline, then looked down past my shoes to the street below.

The Nordland had burnt halfway down when the curtain lifted and Amon Göth pressed his face to the glass, hands clutching his cheeks in a parody of *The Scream*.

'Room for two out there?'

'I'm almost finished.'

'Stay a while.'

He lurched up to the railing, banged his knee and cursed. I shouldn't have been surprised how drunk he was. Thanks to me keeping his glass full, Göth had emptied the best part of two bottles of champagne down his throat.

'Smoking alone is such a crime,' he said. 'Everything tastes better with company, even tobacco.'

But the cigarette soon made him glassy eyed and wistful and he appeared to lose himself in the clouds. It would only have taken one shove to send him toppling over the barrier. The street below was empty except for a dog trotting along the opposite pavement. It crossed the road and passed under the building, disappearing from view.

'Why do I get the feeling there's something you're not telling me?' he said. 'Professor.'

'Guilty as charged.'

'So share the joke.'

'For as long as I can remember, I've been the black sheep of the family. My father didn't approve of academics.'

'Your own father didn't know your profession?'

'It seemed easier that way. He thought I was in Kiel for the naval base. I actually did end up there, after Junkeschule. Then Erich died last year and somebody at the funeral let slip we'd met at Graduation. Father's hardly spoken to me since.'

'I fell out with my old man when I joined the Austrian Nazi Party,' Göth said. 'He'd have been delighted with the likes of you.'

'Pity we can't swap. So what's all this I hear about Belzec?' I said. 'Some kind of renovation?'

Göth opened his mouth like a fish. A fleet of smoke rings sailed into the night.

'I get it,' I said. 'No shop talk at the weekend. Ignore me.'

'Have you ever been?'

'To Belzec?'

'It's unrecognizable, I tell you.'

'From what?'

'It looks like a standard transit camp from the outside. Zone 2's screened off by fir branches over a barbed wire fence. The Jews get unloaded in Zone 1. When a train arrives, the Sonderkommandos tells the passengers to get ready for communal showers.'

'They must stink to high heaven by this point.'

'They strip off and run naked along the Tube and before they know it, they're locked in Zone 2, in the chambers. Used to be a home-made job botched together in the barracks, a few planks plugged with sand and rubber. Lots of leaks, usually only one room working at a time. Long queues build-up, people get ansty. Totally unfit for purpose, the whole thing.'

'Leaky showerheads? Sounds like they've got it better than us. Have you ever tried flushing the loo at Jozefinska?'

'You ought to see the new block, Harry, The bunker. It'll

404

be the envy of the industrialised world. Brick and mortar, the size of a football pitch, six chambers, insulated with cement walls. They'll be gassing 1,000 every thirty minutes when it's up and running. And all of it expressly designed to empty our little Ghetto. Quite humbling, when you think about it.'

There'd been rumours of mass executions at the camps before, but since nobody had ever escaped to tell their story, nothing could be proven. We'd seen how the Germans cleared the streets that summer; we were under no illusions. Hundreds shot before the trains were even loaded. What kind of greeting did we think was waiting, behind closed gates.

But this?

Mechanized gas chambers killing 12,000 a day?

Even now, two hours after the conversation, as my hand shakes across the page of my ledger, I cannot believe what I heard.

46

An insecticide manufactured by I.G. Farben and known commercially as Zyklon B was first used to kill 600 Soviet prisoners of war in a makeshift gas chamber in the Auschwitz cellars on September 3rd, 1941. In Poland that summer, five killing centres stood equipped for the most efficient mass murder the world had ever known: Chelmno, Belzec, Sobibor, Treblinka and Auschwitz-Birkenau. Ten months after the first gassing, Reichsführer Himmler spent the weekend in the Silesian countryside, inspecting the camp's ongoing expansion and construction of four large chambers and crematoria. The piece de resistance was Himmler's observation of a successful Sonderaktion from beginning to end. Two convoys of Jews arrived from Holland, were detrained, then gassed in bunker 2, and their bodies removed to be buried in mass graves. The whole process ran without hitch. The very next day, Reichsführer Himmler ordered all Ghettos in the Generalgouvernement to be eliminated by December 31st 1942. Jozefinska received the memo on Sunday July 19th.

The Eagle Pharmacy had not yet opened its doors when I almost broke them down half an hour later. Helena Krywaniuk let me in, her fingers shaking at the latch. Perhaps she thought I'd come to arrest her. Pankiewicz stood ramrod straight at his counter, adjusting weights on his scales and refusing to look up until he'd found the balance.

'I need to see you,' I said. 'In private.'

'What's the matter?' he said when we were inside his office. 'You look awful.'

I told him everything I'd learned about the gas chambers, and steeled myself for his inevitable disbelief.

He cast those deep eyes to the floor and fiddled with his bow-tie.

'We know.'

'What do you mean, you know?'

It turns out somebody had escaped after all. A dentist called Jiri Bachner had been amongst the first deportees from Cracow last month. When his transport reached Belzec, Bachner broke loose from the others and hid in a latrine. He spent two days submerged up to his chin in the excrement pit and broke out of the camp on the third night, stealing past the stack of corpses outside the bunker. A fortnight later, trudging along the train tracks, he made his way back to the Ghetto.

'He came back?' I said. 'Why?'

'The same reason you're here.'

'And that was, what, a whole month ago?'

'The Judenrat didn't want to start a panic, based on one person's story. Bachner's hair had turned completely white and at times he was incoherent. He looked like a madman.'

'So they ignored him?'

'Initially, yes. But Akiva sent a kashariyot to follow the trail of the deportees. They made contact on the Aryan side with a Polish railroad worker familiar with the transport routes. They went together and confirmed what Bachner saw.'

'So now what?'

'The decision's already been made to close the farm at Kopaliny. Gusta and Shimson Dawidson will be leading a return to the Ghetto, to direct operations from here. We have a friendly guard who will open up the gate for them, a good Catholic man, a police sergeant from Vienna. Like you, he left his regiment in the Ukraine to get posted here, to help. He brings food and takes children out, for no bribe. We need you to meet the Dawidsons in Kazimierz and escort them to Zgody Square. If anybody stops you, they are prisoners, under your custody.'

Deportations from Belgium to Auschwitz began on July 22nd.

On the 23rd, Treblinka received its first consignment of Jews from the Warsaw Ghetto into its ten gas chambers, each holding 200 persons. Until Zyklon B could be supplied, Treblinka relied on carbon monoxide pumped in from vehicles outside the chamber. As in pre-crematoria Auschwitz-Birkenau, bodies were disposed of in pits.

So it continued, day by day.

The Dawidsons chose Saturday 25th July to re-enter the Ghetto. Black Sabbath, the saddest Shabbat of the year, when Jews commemorate the destruction of their Holy Land and Temple by the Romans. History was repeating itself, but today the enemy wore steel helmets with lightning bolts not feather-plumed galeas.

At 9.00 o'clock that evening, I approached the designated bench in Kazimierz, a few blocks from my mother's old shop in the heart of what used to be Jewish Cracow. I had last come this way in December, when Kunde dispatched me to bring in Marek Ringelblum from Szeroka Street.

The Dawidsons were sitting next to each other in front of the desecrated tombstones of the Remuh Cemetery. It was a popular spot for young Aryans to be photographed with the ruined synagogue as comical backdrop. Gusta and Shimson looked much like any other couple – his eyebrows a little bushier than the young Poles, perhaps – but what marked them out to me, as promised, were their immaculate overcoats. Given the heat, even at this time of night, most strollers only wore shirts or blouses.

Lingering in the shadows, I watched the Dawidsons' false bonhomie as behind them a couple posed cheek-to-cheek by the torn graveyard wall, the way Gusta threw her head back and laughed along with everybody else when the lovers poked their tongues as the flashbulb popped. On seeing my approach in full SS regalia, the group squealed and called for me to join the portait. I declined, walking briskly along the pavement towards the bench.

Shimson told me not to stop with a terse shake of his head. Had the plan changed? I kept on walking to the corner of Ciemma Street and paused to cross the busy road. The Dawidsons caught up as we waited for a break in the traffic, but stood apart from me, on either side of the lamppost.

Wordlessly, at half a block's remove, they followed me through narrow streets onto the broad Starowilsna Bridge and into Podgorze Island, and from there along the banks of the Vistula to the north-eastern side of the Ghetto. I passed in front of the last tram collecting Aryans at Kacik Street, and when it rumbled away, I thought I had lost them.

Instead, they had metamorphosised. Walking towards me across the tracks were two disheveled Jews with tangled hair, overcoats discarded to reveal Ghetto rags underneath. Shimson even had his own hand-cuffs. He fastened his wrist to his wife's and and passed me the key, but drew his hand away before I could take it.

'I don't have a spare,' he said.

'I'd better not lose it, then.'

'You brought your own gun, at least?'

I nodded.

'Just try not to shoot me in the back.'

Gusta gave him an admonishing tug of his wrist

'It's alright,' I said. 'I've actually never fired a gun before, so it's good advice.'

'This is your Sacred Flame? God help us all.'

'Shimson!'

'New ID for you,' I said. 'With added Blauschein.'

Shimson inspected the cards.

'What's Deutsche Emalia?'

'Metalworks factory. Oskar Schindler's agreed to put you on his books.'

'It's perfect,' Gusta said, putting her card in her purse. 'Excuse my husband. We're just anxious to get inside.'

I pointed my pistol in the direction of the Zgody Square gate and followed an arm's length behind. There were three guards on duty and our friendly Vienese police sergeant could have been any of them. His name had not been revealed to me, and vice versa. I still don't know if the Dawidsons showed their cards to the right guard. But we were nodded through without a single question being asked.

Halfway across the Square, Gusta brought us to an abrupt halt and dropped to her knees. I thought she was overcome with emotion, and I was right, in a sense. Pulling Shimson down with her, Gusta lowered her face and kissed the blood-stained concrete.

'We're home,' she said.

I let Gusta knock on the door of 13 Jozefinska, and

watched from the corridor as Syzmek Lustgarten came out grinning, embracing Gusta first, then Shimson. From the apartment came the sound of an acoustic guitar and singing, and for the sweetest of moments I was transported back to the easy camaraderie of Pilies Street, of nights spent with Moishe and Baruch and the others, Herman Glik and Shoshana. Those days were gone forever.

As I turned to leave, Lustgarten pushed past Shimson and grabbed my wrist, then threw his arms around my shoulders and kissed my ear.

'Come in, come in,' he said. 'Nights like this are few and far between.'

After my last reception, I wasn't expecting this.

'There somewhere else you'd rather be?' Lustgarten said. 'An oompah band maybe?'

'My orders were to see the Dawidsons safely delivered...'

'How do you know they're safe? I might have a bunch of cannibals in there, tearing them limb from limb.' He squeezed my biceps and licked his lips. 'A fine bit of German fleisch on the bones yourself, Mein Herr.'

The humour was intoxicating. I couldn't remember the last time a genuine laugh had troubled my throat.

I followed him in past the kitchen, scene of December's terse exchange, and on into the living room, packed to the rafters with two dozen souls, not a cannibal amongst them. I was the golem risen from the silt of the Vistula, my murky green collar studded with arcane runes. Nobody dove shrieking out the window into the well-shaft when they saw me, although the guitarist in the corner did fumble a chord when he looked up.

A small pale man with coal black hair rose from an armchair and donned glassses to make sure he wasn't hallucinating, then came towards me with his hand raised.

'Dolek Liebskind,' he said as we shook. 'We owe you a huge debt. I don't know how you manage it, day in, day out.'

'I'm not the one in fear of being deported.'

'Not yet,' Shimson said, eyeing me from the opposite chair. He flinched as Gusta swooped towards him, bumped her hip into his elbow and snuggled up to his shoulder on the arm-rest.

The three chairs constituted the Akiva elders, but the term was a relative one. At thirty, Dolek Liebskind was their senior by five years. I was old enough to be the father of many in the room, and the grandfather of some. The only person who made me feel young was the craggy-faced guitarist in the corner. Regardless of age or gender, there was no hierarchy amongst the leaders. Command dove-tailed ceaselessly from one to the other. All decisions were taken collectively, after consultation and conferment. I have tried to record faithfully who said what, but any mistakes in attribution are my own. At times it was like watching a four-headed hydra.

I recognized Liebskind's name from the original Kopaliny letter sent to Chief Muller by the Jewish Self-Help Society, of which Liebskind was supervisor. Shimson had been his close friends for years; they called each other brother. Dolek had spent the spring at Kopaliny, but had been living in the Ghetto since June. How porous those precious German walls were, how wide the gaps between the cement! Dolek Libeskind himself, the thorn in Wilhelm Kunde's side, living in the Ghetto for two months, and even I didn't know. The third chair was taken by Romek Liebowicz, a sleepy-eyed socialist with a broad face shiny as a wax-work.

Around these four, kneeling and cross-legged, their disciples gathered. When Syzmek Lustgarten called them 'kids', he wasn't exaggerating. Most were barely out of their teens. I recognized some as the sons and daughters of deportees, knocked from their parents' arms in Zgody Square by the batons of the Jewish Police. Their belongings were piled up against the walls in bags and boxes, everything the children could carry. They'd lost families and homes this summer, before Lustgarten provided a refuge. I took my place amongst them, by Gusta's chair. She was talking to a group of kasharyots, trading tales of close shaves and lucky escapes. It turned out the Dawidsons had been dodging police all afternoon. When two officers boarded an Aryan-only bus outside the city, Gusta had the window open and was ready to jump. But it turned out the only crime the cops were interested in was a broken rear headlamp.

The loud laughter of the kashariyots almost masked their fear. A young nurse called Halina Rubinek who'd served as a courier in Warsaw told how she'd avoided certain death on Zelazna Street when stopped by a patrol to have her bag checked. She threw the sack open with a flourish and began juggling potatoes. A gendarme even joined in on the act and grabbed a handful of spuds, his fingers stopping just short of the bullets buried beneath.

Adina Meed had slept with a gentile watchman in order to gain access to his factory window. Afterwards, they smuggled out a carton of dynamite, having to quickly break it down into smaller packs to pass it through the grille. The big, burly watchman shook like a blade of grass in a gale as he worked. When finished, he mopped the sweat form his brow and thanked Adina for curing him. She asked what he meant by cured. 'I'm sworn off pussy for life'.

After a few more minutes, Dolek Liebeskind called the meeting to order. He produced a tattered copy of *Oyf Der Vakh*, the underground Yiddish newspaper from the Warsaw Ghetto, and read a report of a killing centre based on eyewitness testimony. Jan Karski had been dispatched in search of the deportees and reached the village of Sokolow Podlaski near Treblinka, where he learned about the new side track that ran right up to the gas chambers. Later he met with Uziel Wallach, another escapee, like Jiri Bachner, who confirmed what was happening behind the barbed wire.

Some of the younger activists in the room had not heard the details before. Syzmek Lustgarten had sheltered them from it. Others were in denial. Tonight, they learned the truth in the starkest of terms

'Thank-you, brother,' Shimson Dawidson said. 'No mistake about it: the Jews of Poland are doomed. Tens of thousands are going to die in this German crusade. Very few will escape. They are being led like sheep to slaughter, without raising a hand to defend themselves. And the world is silent. We have been silent, Gusta and I, preparing the fields of Kopaliny for a harvest that will never come. But we will be silent no more. History summons us all to embark on a new road, and I ask that you take it with us.'

A young man jumped up with clenched fist held high. 'We'll tear those Nazi bastards to pieces!'

'Let's start with the Jewish pigs who wear their uniforms,' another shouted. 'They're the worst of all. Breaking up families and pushing them onto trains while the Germans stand around watching.'

As I lowered my head in shame, I realised he was talking about Symche Spira and his men.

'Another unpalatable truth.' Romek Liebowicz shifted his enormous frame and crossed his arms high on his chest. 'How can we resist the true enemy with this Fifth Column in our midst? It's not just the Jewish Police. There's a whole system of collaborators and informers in place to undermine our every move. Our first actions must be directed against these traitors.'

Murmurs of agreement, and a lone voice of dissent.

Gusta Dawidson threw off her husband's hand to step behind the chair and grasp the headrest.

'Is this not what the Germans want? To turn us against each other? I haven't come here tonight so I can start killing Jews. God will decide what happens to these wretches, not me. The Jewish Police took my father and sister. When I see these turncoats do the German's bidding, of course I want to lash out, to spit in their dirty faces. But what good will it do? More will take their place, and the deportations will continue. Combat operations must be our primary aim.'

Dolek said, 'But we can consider incidental reprisals as useful training exercises, correct?'

'Sniping at German patrols is a legitimate act of resistance,' Gusta said. 'Lynching your next door neighbour is not. To stop the trains, we need to think like tacticians, not gangsters. Sabotaging railroads and blowing up bridges. That is how we halt the madness.'

The guitarist in the corner strummed a mock-flammenco flourish, and those around him yelped excitedly and began to imitate a drum roll on their knees. As the musician keened in Yiddish, I realised I knew the song. I hadn't heard it played before, but I had read the lyrics, handed to me by an informer at Jozefinska.

It's burning, brothers! It's burning!
Oh, our poor village, brothers, burns!
Evil winds, full of anger,
Rage and ravage, smash and shatter;
Stronger now that wild flames grow --
All around now burns!
And you stand there looking on
With futile, folded arms
And you stand there looking on --
While our village burns!

After a stately first verse, Mordecai Gebirtig's finger-picking became more strident, and the rhythm was soon echoed by hand-claps. When a vicious slash of the strings signalled the chorus, the entire room erupted in song. I felt myself lifted into a state of transcendence by the voices.

47

After July 25th, Gusta and Shimson once again became strangers to me. Communication was limited to messages dropped off and collected from the Eagle Pharmacy. Everybody present at the apartment was supposed to have made the same vow; it was too risky to be seen together. The group managed to keep apart, for the first few days. Fellow conspirators passed each other on the street without so much as a nod or wink. But their resolve quickly weakened. Before the end of the first week, clusters of four or five Akiva youths were striding through the Ghetto with heads held high, like the old school gang back on the block. Who could blame them? Everything had been stolen from their lives, leaving only the fleeting joys of fellowship.

My job was to keep the resistance supplied with resources and to allow them to operate below the authority's radar. Acquiring weapons was Gusta's top priority. I had access to the Jozefinska armoury store, but was under strict instructions not to touch a single bullet. Frustrating as it was, I understood her logic: my position in the heart of the SS was too valuable a resource to lose. Stealing weapons from under the German's noses was how the Chaze had finally been caught in Vilno. So the Luger pistol I unholstered and presented to Shimson Dawidson on July 25th was my first and probably last contribution of its kind.

I furnished the resistance with dates of upcoming Aktions and envelopes stuffed full of banknotes from Erich Monhke's safety deposit box. These deliveries to Magister Pankiewicz were the most gratifying. Gusta's group had resorted to extorting forced contributions from the few Jews who still had money, which reminded me of the raids the SS used to lead in Kamierz. I was glad to be able to provide an alternative source of income. If there is time, I will give away every note.

In addition to money, I supplied blank identity papers, work permits and ink-stamps. Shimson Dawidson was an experienced printer and engraver, and ran the group's forgery operation. It was Shimson's workshop I had raided last December in the abandoned bakery, another reason for his dislike of me. In the Ghetto, Shimson had what was called a 'walking office', which was a rather grand way of saying he had to lug all his materials through the streets in briefcases, with assistants lugging boxes and even a typewriter in his wake. At the start of each week, I would send a list of apartments recently cleared by deportations. Shimson would use each one for half an hour, then move on.

Dolek Liebeskind's policy of reprisals was first put into practice with the beating of Karl Mende, loathed for his violence during deportations. Mende was found in the middle of Zgody Square at dawn on the first day of August, reeking of alcohol, with two black eyes and a clutch of broken ribs. It was claimed he had been assaulted by Jews, although there were no witnesses and Mende himself could not recall what had happened.

On recovery, he was reassigned from Civil Affairs to the courtyard cells, for his own protection. The cells were largely empty these days, save for a retarded young girl kept as a prostitue for some of the more debased officers. Most of the Ghetto's non-Aryan criminal element had been shipped to Belzec by now, and the Jews who remained had no wish to follow them. Crime in the Ghetto was at an all-time low. I was baffled then, when one of Gusta's most trusted lieutenant's got herself arrested shortly afterwards, for the most trivial offence. Adina Meed, she of dynamite-smuggling renown, had left her apartment that morning without her Blauschein and was stopped by the first patrol. Punishment was a forty-eight hour stretch in the cell next to Karl Mende.

As her second day in the cells was coming to an end, I heard my old partner shout out in anger. Nobody else in the office seemed to hear but since my desk was close to the back door, so I didn't have far to go and investigate. As I approached the gaol, his shouts grew louder, and climaxed with a single gun-shot.

I found Karl Mende crumpled against the wall outside the

cells, shot through the eyeball.

According to my report, the retarded girl had confessed to summoning Mende to her cell and when he was close enough, she'd thrust her hand through the bars, pulled his pistol from his belt and fired at point-blank range.

But in reality, I'd found Mende's body lying outside Adina Meed's cell, and it was she who'd passed me the gun and told me where to put it.

The retarded girl was put out of her misery on the gallows that evening, and Adina Meed released the next day.

***

Throughout the summer, the resistance forged alliances with like-minded Polish organisations, set up a number of safehouses on the Aryan side and spirited relatives through the walls to escape the August Aktions, including Gusta's mother and Shimson's nephew. I received only fragments of information from the Pharmacy, summoning me to a particular gate at a particular hour. One night I realised the bearded businessman I was smuggling back inside was Gusta Dawidson herself; I hadn't even known she was gone.

The most promising offer of unity came from the Polish Worker's Party. One of its key members was Gola Mira, a Communinst who'd broken out of prison at the beginning of the war and had been successfully evading the authorities ever since. Gola also happened to be a cousin to Dolek Liebeskind's wife. After several weeks of negotiations, it was agreed that Edwin Weiss would lead the first armed group of Akiva fighters out into the forest with a guide supplied by the PWP, in order to join the partisans.

But Edwin Weiss's group were little more than school-children, and four weeks of training inside the Ghetto was all they knew of military discipline. When their appointed guard became lost and abandoned them, the group spent three days wandering around the forest in the heat of summer without food or drink.

Dejected and defeated, they finally came upon a town, where they decided to attack a police station as compensation for failure. But the policemen would not be drawn out to the street. With no fight to be had, Weiss's group returned in shame to the Ghetto.

**

On October 27th, Wilhelm Kunde gathered the office together and informed us that a major Aktion was scheduled for the next day. The time was fast approaching, he crowed, when the District would be 'Judenrein', clean of Jews.

When the meeting broke up, I managed to find a spare Jewish Police uniform, bundled it up in a dry-cleaning bag together with a summary of Kunde's announcement, and delivered the parcel to the Pharmacy, marked 'Urgent'.

By lunchtime, news began to filter back onto the streets. Jewish shops closed early, trading ceased, and a scramble for hiding places began. Fights broke out in cellars and attics and those who had found nowhere to stow themselves resorted to scaling the walls in broad daylight. Hardly any managed to dodge the guards, and those who did were shot to pieces on the way down; a patrol of security police had sealed off the Ghetto from the outside, forming a human chain around its perimeter. At the same time, Gusta Dawidson was hastening back to Cracow to rescue her mother for a second time, the old woman having sneaked back in since August.

Amon Göth and his Sonderkommando arrived early on the 28th to take charge. Today was their sixth major Aktion, and I wondered whether it might be the last. A decree had been issued ordering all bearers of labour cards to appear at Jozfinfksa at 10.00 o'clock for inspection.

Unlike previous occasions, German police began shooting from the start. All pretext of civility was gone. I waded through corpses to conduct house to house searches while all around me victims were struck down and executed. Surviving deportees were driven to Zgody Square and from there we marched to Plaszow station.

On the Aryan side of the city, residents were out in number enjoying the autumn sun. Our caravan of misery across the river Visutla had become a regular sight in recent months, and few even bothered to stop and gape. Two gaunt Polish housewives who did walk alongside us for a while turned out to be Gusta Dawidson and Dolek's younger sister, the raven-haired Mira. They were scanning the line for somebody they knew. When they found Toshka Stark amongst our number, I was not able to let the prisoner slip away with them, but did allow a minute for the three to exchange information.

I overheard mention of the safe-house on Wiapola Street, where Shimson, Dolek and Romek had managed to get to, and were now marooned. The rest of Akiva were trapped inside the Ghetto. I was relieved to hear that the policeman's uniform I'd delivered to the Pharmacy had already found its way to Yehuda Maimon, and had helped bring out a few children before the human chain sealed them in.

Although the Aktion didn't quite fulfil Wilhelm Kunde's lofty expectations, the

Hospital and the House of Orphans were the first public buildings declared 'Judenfrei'. Medical staff who insisted on staying with their patients were shot on the spot. The directors of the orphanage, Anna Feurstein and Dawid Kurzman, had been given permission to stay in the Ghetto, but chose to set off to the railway station with the children, on one final class trip.

The October Aktion was the bloodiest yet. Overnight, the human chain withdrew and the wall once again regained it porousness. The surviving members of Akiva seeped back in to find blood-spattered walls, burnt-out apartments and piles of corpses.

Approximately 6,000 Jews were transported to Belzec that day.

***

The resistance regrouped in the first week of November to agree a new strategy. With the organisation diminished, it was impossible to operate on the same scale. The plunging depths of a Polish winter was only weeks away, which ruled out any idea of joining the partisans in the forest, not that the first attempt had met with any success. The time for grand plans was over. From now on, they would be a tight-knit unit, based in the city.

The Dawidsons' swathe of safehouses were reduced to a core that ran along the Cracow-Lwow and Cracow-Warsaw railway lines, principally for the benefit of the kashariyots. Ghetto resistance groups were beginning to coalesce under the umbrella of the Jewish Fighting Organisation, commanded by Mordechai Anielewicz in Warsaw.

Some of Gusta's leaders reluctantly agreed to move out of the Ghetto, to preserve the power structure. Dolek and Rivka found refuge in Visnicz, with Halina Rubinek. The sleepy-eyed giant Romek Liebowicz preferred to stay in the German quarter of Cracow, where he was joined by Juda Tenenbaum. Gusta and Shimson remained in the Ghetto, sleeping at the apartments of friends and Dolek's parents. Gusta had not been able to save her own mother a second time.

Husband and wife spearheaded a month of thrilling nocturnal surveillances and ambushes. It was exhausting work for all, but Gusta thrived, exhorting Shimson and I 'to strike terror into the hearts of those who presumed to be our lords and masters, the arbiters of life and death for millions of defenceless people'. While they lived on frugal rations, Gusta's words could have fed an entire army.

Although I took part in the majority of these operations, the most audacious one was not led by the Dawidsons. I knew nothing about it until I arrived at Jozefinska the next morning.

The first sign that was something was amiss was Amon Göth crashing through the front doors at 10.00 o'clock. Göth only came to the Ghetto for an Aktion. As far as I knew, none had been scheduled since October 28th. Yet here he was, pasty-faced and sweating, sweeping past the front desk and up the stairs. The shouting started before he'd even reached Kunde's door and only stopped five minutes later when both descended and disappeared into the limousine.

It was left to Rottenführer Ritschak to inform us of last night's attack. Three Jewish terrorists had thrown sulphuric acid into the faces of a patrol of German soldiers on Adolf Hitler Platz in the Old Town. When the rest of their unit came running, the Jews opened up with a machine gun. One soldier disfigured, two blind and four dead.

'Adolf Hitler Platz,' I marvelled. 'Is nowhere safe?'

'The gun was one of ours,' Ritschak said. 'An MG42.'

'Incredible.' For once in these situations I was without an ounce of dissimulation. The machine gun had not come from me. 'There was an acid attack in Nieswiez last month. They hunted down every last Jew, then set fire to the Ghetto. Destroy the lot, it's the only response.'

'It's not that easy,' Ritschak said. 'Cracow isn't some Belarussian backwater. We're the capital of the Generalegouvernment and the eyes of the world are watching.'

He was right. Anywhere else, and the Ghetto would have been razed by nightfall.

As it was, Hans Frank ordered three 'proportionate' reprisals:

The curfew hour was cut back from 11 to 9 pm.

Non-essential staff were deployed to street patrols. This included myself. From now on, Symche Sprira and his informants would report directly to Wilhelm Kunde. Quite apart from the humiliating attacks perpetrated by its supposedly constrained Jews, Jozefinska had another security problem. Large numbers of Poles, mostly teenagers, were getting through the walls to loot whatever they could carry from the mass of vacated apartments. Suits, coats, pots and pans, toothbrushes, chairs and tables, even window-frames were disappearing at an alarming rate.

Hans Frank made one final concession to the families of the Acid Seven, as they were known. Amon Göth was allowed to take a group of seven Orthodox Jews hostage until the terrorists responsible for the attack were caught.

48

In late November, the circle of Akiva gathered at 13 Jozefinska to observe the ritual of greeting the Sabbath. In these moments, they were children once again, with no fear of the future, united in joyous prayer that strengthened and healed the wounds of the last week of hardship. But despite their cheer, a shadow was cast upon the evening. Communal life in the Ghetto was coming to an end.

While Gusta uncorked the wine, the rest of the table launched into the first hymn of praise, *Woman of Valour*:

A woman of valour makes the world change
Her strength is the content that guides through the days
Defined by her actions that bring light to all dreams
Valour is something that's defined by her deeds.

In accordance with traditions for treating the fairer sex, the guests bestowed lavish compliments upon the woman of the house who watched over all. In Gusta Tova Dawidson's case, every extravagance was hard-earned. Everything in that kitchen was the result of one woman's ingenuity and drive, her pride and passion. Without Gusta, there was no Akiva. Without Gusta, there were no Sabbath lights or bedecked table, no food or wine.

For many years the candelabra sockets had not been filled with thick heavy candles scented with paradise. Gusta made do instead with the enfeebled flames of left over Hannukha sticks. The table was still laid with two white cloths, one over the other, but the dishes underneath were scavenged substitutions. No grand spread of challah breads resembling the twelve loaves of the Tabernacle, but two finger-sized rolls. Potato and beans in place of meat and fish, seasoned with Gusta's special sauce.

Tonight, however, there was a special guest. The group was blessed with not just one extraordinary woman, but two.

***

Meanwhile, across the street, drinks were being served to the great and the good in Wilhelm Kunde's office.

A touch of Christmas festivity was in the air. Despite the chill, the party had spilled out onto the balcony above the courtyard. On leather armchairs that had once belonged to deportees, the Ghetto authorities toasted their success. An entire week had passed without further Jewish attacks. Although the acid terrorists had not been brought to justice, Amon Göth believed that taking the Orthodox hostages had been vital in thwarting the terrorists' ambitions. The prisoners had fulfilled their purpose, and were now taking up gaol space, and consuming rations. Tonight, Göth said, we'd throw them a release party.

As a prelude to the main event, the SS of the Ghetto listened to nostalgic songs on the gramophone, serenading the cells below with the chorus of *Lili Marlene*:

Underneath the lantern
By the barrack gate
Darling I remember
The way you used to wait
'Twas there that you whispered tenderly
That you loved me
You'd always be
My Lili of the lamplight
My own Lili Marlene.

Rottenführer Ritschak lifted the stylus off the record and replaced the disc in its sleeve.

A four-man firing squad appeared under the balcony and began to assemble their weapons on the courtyard cobbles. These were not Jozefinska officers, but the surviving members of the acid attack at Adolf Hitler Platz. Working in pairs, one solider fixed the stand of his MG42 while the other crouched at his side, readying a belt of ammo from an open box. The machine gun secured, the first soldier dropped down onto his stomach behind it, propped himself up on his elbows and squinted into the sights.

We watched in silence as Symche Spira led the Orthodox prisoners from the gaol in leg-irons, flanked either side by members of the Jewish Police. In a column six-deep, they stood before the guns but did not raise their eyes to the balcony.

Amon Göth stepped up to the railing and produced a time-piece from his pocket. He studied it patiently, snapping the case shut when satisfied.

'Unchain them,' he called down.

'Yes, sir.'

Symche Spira relayed the command to his officers.

When all prisoners were unshackled and reorganised into a straight line, Spira dismissed his men.

The Jewish Police retreated back into the gaol. I kept my eyes focussed on the prisoner in the middle of the line, a short, burly man clutching his thin overcoat to his neck. The garment had no belt or buttons. Before his year in the Ghetto, the prisoner had been a dapper architect.

'In one minute, turn your back to the guns and face the wall,' Göth told them. 'Run quickly, with no jostling. We will give you a fighting chance. Anyone who reaches the wall will be allowed to return to their families.'

The prisoners turned round, hands twitching at their sides, assuming crouches like athletes on a race track.

Göth called, 'Go!'

Half the men started running immediately. Of the three who remained, the two at the sides looked at each other and shrugged, then set off. Only the burly man in the middle stood his ground, refusing to run.

Göth pulled his pistol from its holster and shot twice at the man's feet, to make him dance. But the man did not move. Göth shot again, bullets sparking the cobbles. Finally, the man brought the tips of his palms together under his chin, put his head down in prayer and launched himself forward.

He got about halfway to the wall when the machine-gunners opened fire.

***

Two days ago, an Akiva kashariyot had been dispatched from the Ghetto to Warsaw, on a gun-run. With her bleached blonde hair, borrowed outfit and elegant handbag, Anka Fischer looked every inch the glamorous Polish sophisticate, and had mastered the accent and withering manner. After purchasing weapons at the seedy Hotel Crsitof, Anka walked out with four pistols taped underneath her frock. Heading back to the train station, her sixth sense told her she was being followed. She stopped at a cinema, and bought a ticket for the new Kristina Söderbaum film, *The Golden City*. Reasonably sure that nobody had followed her in off the street, Anka wasn't one to take any chances. She sat down in the auditorium, leaving halfway through the screening to use the bathroom, where she removed the pistols, placed them in the lavatory cistern and returned to her seat. An hour later, she was arrested on the cinema steps. Her instinct had been right. The Hotel was under surveillance. The Gestapo wanted to know what a woman of such refined tastes was doing in a renowned den of black-marketeers and pornographers like the Cristof. Maintaining her icy demeanor, Anka explained that she was suffering from a delicate condition of female health, and was unable to go more than thirty minutes without needing the bathroom. The Hotel Cristof was the only place she'd been able to find in an emergency. If the Gestapo wanted to know more, they would need to provide an experienced medical practitioner to examine her. Anka was released that afternoon, with an official apology. She returned to Kino Luna, retrieved her pistols from the cistern, dried them with toilet paper, reattached the tape to her arms and thighs and started out again for the train station.

And now she was back at 13 Jozenfinska, just in time for the Sabbath.

With the lights glowing in the candlesticks, Shimson Dawidson blessed Anka, and the rest of the table in turn. He chanted the hymn of praise and salutation, the Lecha Dodi.

'Come, my beloved, to meet the Bride; let us welcome the Shabbat.'

Wine was passed from one to the other, and they began to eat.

After the meal they sung the traditional evening festival prayer, getting as far as the barchu and shma when the machine guns resounded from the courtyard across the street. Shimson jumped up, sidling across to the edge of the window.

'That came from the stationhouse,' he said. 'What the hell's going on?'

Romanek said, 'It's the seventh day.'

'Seventh day of what?'

'The hostages.'

***

After their entertainment, Kunde's guests began to troop back inside to his office. I remained on the balcony alone, watching the Jewish Police load the last of the bodies onto the truck. The hostages had spent their last week in goal, metres from my desk, and I had done nothing to try and help. In truth, I had forgotten about them. And now I had watched them die, standing at Amon Göth's side, forced to cheer their pathetic dash for glory like a Roman senator at the Colosseum.

When I made my way into the office, talk had turned to the subject of the tiny Prokocim Julag encampment, currently populated by a few dozen prisoners laying railtrack. Jews deported from the Ghetto had been marched there, to the Plaszow train station. The site was due to be expanded into a labour camp with its own textile workshop, into which the last remnants of the Ghetto would be transferred, to produce German army uniforms and boots.

I thought back to last summer, to the glory days of Camp Moda. The Chaze had been in my thoughts a great deal recently, and here was Wilhelm Kunde talking about a military uniform workshop just up the road from the Ghetto.

'We're putting together a party to start next week.' Kunde leant against his desk, holding forth to a semi-circle of the men. 'A working group of Jews to build the living quarters. We'll need a guard to escort them there and back until the barracks are ready.'

I stepped closer, joining the edge of the group.

'I'd like to volunteer, sir.'

'For the Barrackenbau?'

'Yes, sir. Now that Civil Affairs has been closed down, I've been thinking about my future. Establishing a new camp on our doorstep sounds like the kind of challenge I'm looking for.'

'Do you have any experience of construction?'

'Not personally, sir. But I have a detailed knowledge of the Jews that do. I understand how they think, and I know how to make them work.'

'Plaszow's going to need all the good men it can get. We're meeting at Oberführer Scherner's office on Monday.'

***

The mood at number 13 did not recover after the shootings. No amount of stirring escape stories from the likes of Anka Fischer could distract the group from what had just happened. While the leaders of the resistance sat around drinking wine, innocent Jews were being slaughtered in their name.

'I think our time here is coming to an end,' Dolek said.

Romanek looked at his watch. 'It's almost curfew.'

'I'm not talking about tonight,' Dolek said. 'I mean this supper, here in the Ghetto. When we lose Dabrowski Street and Janowa Wola next week, they'll only be a few blocks left.'

'Then we need to redouble our efforts,' Gusta said. 'Whatever the consequences.'

'Agreed.' Dolek nodded his head slowly, averting his eyes. 'But if you don't leave, you may not have another chance.'

'Leave?' Gusta said. 'But we've only just come back.'

'And you're more exposed every week. Too many people know you, too many people are talking. I believe you must make immediate preparations.'

'He's right,' Shimson said. 'We all knew the time would come. Now it's here.'

He reached out to Gusta on one side and Dolek on the other; the group linked hands around around the table.

'We are on the road to death, my friends,' Dolek said.

'There can be no turning back. If you want life, don't look for it in Poland. We are at the end of days. I have the feeling that this is the last Sabbath we will spend together.'

49

I had learned a great deal from Gusta Dawidson that summer about Oberführer Julian Scherner. This was the man, above all others, responsible for the tide of blood staining the Polish landscape. In between deportations from the Cracow Ghetto, Scherner had personally ordered the culls in Tarnow in June, in Rzeszow, Debica and Przemsyl in July, Jaroslau, Krosno, Jaslo and Nowy Sacz in August, where 15,000 Jews were rounded up and shuttled to Belzec in three twenty-five car cattle trains. Unsated and unsatiable, Scherner's murderous sweep continued through Novy Targ, Sanok, and Miechow, and then Tarnow again by mid-September.

Now this genial, avuncular man was welcoming me into his office with a handshake as limp as a noodle. I feared my own blood would congeal at his touch, or a fount of nausea issue from my lips and repaint his skirting board. But I managed to control myself. I was here for one reason only: to get as many Jews as I could out of the Ghetto into the shelter of a new camp, sparing them from the final deportations. I would soak up every last drop of Scherer's oily charm, and do so with a smile on my face. It wasn't as if I didn't know how. Only four months ago I'd dined at his penthouse apartment, seated next to his attack-dog, Amon Göth. At least Göth wasn't invited to today's meeting. The Ghetto was his domain; I had to try and make camp Plaszow mine.

My dream of creating a refuge to rival the Chaze's took an early set-back when I saw that the guest sipping coffee with Wilhlem Kunde in the corner of the room was that scar-faced malcontent Horst Pilarzik, one of the worst Ghetto criminals I was hoping to get away from. Kunde's opening words to me brought even worse news. In recognition of the man's thuggery, Scherer had appointed Pilarzik Commandant of the fledgling camp.

As we chatted over cream cakes, the dark part of my brain ticked over, searching for a crumb of comfort. Scherer may have been impressed by reports of Pilarzik's brutality, but had no idea of his unsuitability for leadership, in terms of intellect and ingenuity. The new camp Commandant would struggle to run a bath without a numbered diagram.

The disappointment I felt at Pilarzik's involvement was offset when I met the suave and silver-haired Julius Madritsch, one of only two civilian guests. Madritsch operated a sewing factory in the Ghetto, which, like Oskar Schindler's, was known as a refuge of decency. More encouragingly, he was keen on expansion, recently opening Ghetto workshops in Bochnia and Tarnow. With the debonair Austrian industrialist as an employer, the prisoners of Plaszow would enjoy unrivalled working conditions. All I had to do was keep the Commandant at a distance. Pilarzik was as corruptible as the rest of the SS, and Madritsch was making more than enough money to make sure he was paid off.

But I was getting ahead of myself - the camp hadn't even been constructed yet.

The man responsible for that was the second civilian guest, Rudolf Lukas, the senior contractor from Deutsche Wohmund Siedlunggenossenschaft. It was his blueprint we clustered around after coffee and introductions.

The existing Prokocim-Plazsow railway station Julag occupied the narrow depression between the two enormous hills of the Krzemionki District, a naturally secluded location chosen so as not to affront neighbouring Poles. It was also close to the Ghetto, and had potential for running quarries. The proposed expansion covered the plots of the former Wola Duchacka Commune and the two cemeteries of the Jewish synagogue, land now owned by the Generalgouvernment. Rudolf Lukas' design envisaged the development of a 15 hectare site, with SS barracks, a kitchen, washing room, latrine, laundry and a group of industrial barracks opposite the residential area. The camp was designed to accommodate 4-5,000 inmates.

Lukas' pointed to an empty area of the drawing next to the male prisoners' camp. 'We think this would be the best spot for your workshops, Herr Madritsch. We'll be requesting a designated railroad spur too, for speeding up deliveries.'

'By all means, request away.' Madritsch struggled to conceal his amusement behind a tight-lipped smile. 'Hypothetically, it looks very interesting. But you'll understand I need more than a shaded box on a map before I make a serious commitment.'

Scherer nodded earnestly. 'That shaded box will be a state-of-the-art factory before the year is out, Julius. All mod cons, and all the labour you need, living on site.'

'I have all the labour I need now,' Madritsch said. 'And I'm rather fond of my factory, since I built it.'

'If I may, sir?' I straightened up from the map and crossed my hands behind my back. 'A businessman who's looking to grow won't find a better opportunity. I've spent a year investigating the various skill-sets within the Residential District. Even in its depleted state, we have a mine of untapped potential for ambitious manufacturers. I know for a fact that we have dozens of experienced leather workers available – everything from tanners to clickers, cutters, gimpers and hole-punchers.'

'Your man's certainly done his homework, Oberführer.' Madritsch turned to me. 'You seem to know as much about the textiles industry as I do. Perhaps you have a family business?'

Scherer looked nonplussed. As a family friend, he knew the Mohnkes were no factory owners.

'I learned it all in the District,' I said. 'It's been quite an education. We've got tailors washing dishes, upholsterers unloading crates, jewellers sweeping the floor. With the right partners, this camp could be a very rewarding concern.' I held Madritsch's gaze. 'For everybody involved.'

'And I am not immune to that line of argument. But this great untapped potential could just as easily be mined where they are, could they not, without the need for supplanting? And for a fraction of the cost.'

'Imagine showing potential investors around the Ghetto,' I said. 'It's filthy and dangerously overcrowded, despite our best efforts to thin the herd.'

'The problem is, my workers seem to like it there.'

'Who gives a damn what they like?' I said, calibrating a little pop of anger. 'Forgive me.'

I stepped forward to grip the edge of the table and lowered my head in mock contrition.

'My profit margin cares,' Madritsch said. 'We're not just churning out identical kits on a production line. Some of these workers are highly skilled artisans. It's a word I never thought would apply to Jews, but it's the truth. If they feel at home, productivity rises and so does the quality of their finish. In a forced labour camp, with watchtowers and patrols... it would be impossible to replicate Ghetto conditions. My clients are very demanding people, with very high standards. They won't tolerate inferior products.'

'And they won't receive any,' Scherer said. 'At least, not on account of us. Commandant Pilarzik will forbid his men from interfering in any way with your internal practices. Their job is to oversee the smooth functioning of the site as a whole - to assist businesses, not meddle in them.'

'No interference,' Madritsch said. 'You guarantee?'

'Absolutely. As long as we don't have another Camp Moda on our hands.'

I kept my head down, squinting at Rudolf Lukas' blueprint as my face flushed again with blood. Silence filled the room, leaving two words to echo between my ears.

Camp Moda.

It had been eighteen month since I'd heard a German speak those words. I'd assumed the Chaze's forest workshop had become a forgotten footnote in the Lithuanian campaign. Instead it had entered the Nazi lexicon as a byword for subversion.

Julius Madritsch said, 'What's Camp Moda?'

Scherer savoured a sly smile. 'Let's just say it's what happens when the lunatics take over the asylum. You have to understand, Julius, there is simply no future in the Ghetto. I've been telling you that for months now. Now Reichsführer Himmler has made it official. From the end of November, all Jews working for the needs of the army are to be concentrated in labour camps. And that's Plaszow. The Ghetto will be gone within six months.'

Madritsch bristled. 'So this isn't really a consultation.'

'It's a consultation about what kind of camp you'd like to

see, and the scope of your role.'

'Very well.' His throat ticked several times as he digested the news. 'So where do we start?'

The project was an extension of the three small Jewish labour camps in the compact Plaszow, Prokocim and Bielzanow districts. Julag I would be the nucleus of the new camp. The project was due to commence with ten barracks on the plot of the synagogue cemeteries at Jerozolimska Street and Abraham Street.

'We know how close Jews feel to their ancestors,' Scherer said. 'They'll be sleeping right on top of them now.'

Madritsch flashed a grin as mirthless as my own.

Ghetto workers would soon be marked in accordance with the nature of their employment with one of three identification letters: R for Rüstung, the armaments industry, W for Wehrmacht, the army and Z for Zivil, or civil work. According to Himmler's new regime, companies and military facilities would only be able to hire workers on the basis of a special permit. Orders had to be forwarded to the SS camp management headquarters in Berlin, which Scherer would expedite.

The meeting ended with assurances that ground on the new Plaszow site would be broken as soon as possible, hopefully by the end of the week. Rudolf Lukas rolled up and sheathed his map and left the office chatting with Julius Madritsch. Kunde, Pilarzik and myself were to head back to the Ghetto by car to begin putting together the first construction team. My colleagues were out the door when I felt Scherer's hand on my shoulder.

'I'll keep Mohnke for a minute or two,' he called. 'Don't bother waiting.'

Scherer's fingers tightened, squeezing the collarbone.

With the door closed, he opened his drinks cabinet and poured two whiskeys from a crystal decanter.

'Congratulations, Harry.'

We chinked glasses. I tossed mine back and held it out for a refill. Sportingly, Scherer obliged.

'I can't tell you how pleased that you're on board for this,' he said. 'You wouldn't have wanted me to pull any strings, so

I held back, much as it pained me. Willi Kunde put your name right at the top of his list. All those hours you've put in to the Ghetto have not gone unrewarded. Plaszow is a new chapter, and it's going to be a very profitable, for the Reich, and for ourselves. To 1943.'

We raised another toast. 'Thank-you, sir.'

'You're here on merit. Your father would be proud.'

'I hope you're right.'

'On that particular front.' Scherer set his glass down on the tray and pulled his tunic away from his belly. I take no pleasure in reminding you of this, but it's almost a year now that you've been promising to pick up the phone.'

'Time's gone so quickly.'

'Your father's an old man, Harry. This is only making him weaker.'

'It's not easy for me, either, sir.'

'Christmas is approaching, and it might be his last. Do the decent thing and pick up the damn telephone.'

50

Two days later, the first Barrackenbau group assembled
outside Jozefinska in the dawn drizzle. Back-breaking
construction work in harsh winter conditions - yet there'd
been no shortage of volunteers. The final list comprised fifty
men, five Jewish Police, and myself. I'd sent a message via the
Pharmacy asking Gusta for any names she wished included,
but there was no time to await her response. More lists would
be compiled as Plaszow continued to grow.

Walking in a column, we set off out the Ghetto. The
prisoners were pleased to be leaving, but their mood was more
subdued than I expected. I should have realised why: their
loved ones had been marched along exactly the same roads
during the Aktions, before being shunted off to Belzec. I
allowed a leisurely pace and hoped the mood would lift when
we arrived.

Situated on the stony hillsides and malaria-infested
marshes of the Liban quarry, Julag I was no promised land.
Any notion that the men were destined for a better life was
dispelled by the electric double-apron barbed wire fence
which extended around the camp's perimeter. Between the
two fences was a ditch filled with swampy water. The fence
was guarded by thirteen watch towers, equipped with
machine guns, telephones and revolving spotlights. The
personnel were snarling black-uniformed Ukranians,
supplemented with their own uniformed Ordnungsdienst,
armed with rubber truncheons. There was no beaming Chaze
to greet us, no whistling Oswald Zgismond to give a grand
tour.

Prior to Pilarzik's appointment, the sole source of
authority had been Franz Jozef Muller, Kommandant of Julag
III. His regime was lawless. There was no system of
administrative control or camp by-laws. The Julag had been
Muller's personal fiefdom for the past year, and the existing
prisoners despised him. Conditions were unbearable. Men

had to run to and from from the railway line, while the Ukranians shouted, screamed orders and threatened to shoot them. Muller had executed one sixteen year old boy for muddying his favourite horse. The Julag barracks lacked sanitary arrangements or even beds.

I inquired about getting my men some food and drink before they began work. The four mile walk from the Ghetto had left them tired and hungry. But I learned that prisoners would not be provided with meals and had to bring their own food. For the residential Julag inmates, breakfast was one slice of bread and black coffee. Lunch was a cup of soup, in four hours time, and evening meal was a second cup. I loitered by the garbage pile outside the kitchen, moving away when a guard approached a Jew digging through the scraps and fired a gun into his neck.

I gathered my Barrackenbau and explained what had to be done. The two Jewish cemeteries were to be levelled to make way for the new buildings. Buried bodies would be relocated to a mass grave while the coffins needed to be chopped up for firewood for bombed out families in Germany. The headstones had to be broken up with pick-axes and hammers, the smaller pieces ploughed back into the earth as part of the barracks's foundations. In a typical display of Nazi theatricality, larger sections would be used to pave the roads in front of the SS offices and residences.

According to Oberführer Scherner's instructions, only one monument was allowed to remain standing. At the edge of the Jerozolimska Street cemetery, at the camp's new entrance, a modest sandstone marker bears the following inscription:

Here rests
Chaim Jakob
Abrahamer
Died on 25.5.1932
In the 74th year of his life.
Peace to his soul

I have no doubts as why Scherer chose to spare Chaim Jakob Abrahamer's tomb from desecration. As you may imagine, it had precious little to do with sentimentality or respect. Abrahamer's stone is a reminder to Plazsow's Jews of all they'd been denied: a long life during peacetime, and a death from natural causes.

***

When the walls of the third hut went up at the end of November, I told the workers they would not be returning to the Ghetto. They moved in to the barracks the next day, with no electricity or sanitation. As rough and dreary as the camp was, it was better than life in the Ghetto, which limped on fearfully in our absence, day by bloody day.

The end of the Ghetto was nigh, and even the Judenrat couldn't deny it anymore. Constant searches were carried out by the SS, with maximum violence and brutality. Houses were raided around the clock, people dragged from their apartments or rounded up on the street, regardless of age and sex, marched to Prokocim and loaded onto trains. The transfer of able-bodied inhabitants into Plaszow went on at a slower pace, with approximately 100 new admissions a day.

With every deportation, the Ghetto area was diminished. New working squads were assigned to sort through Jewish property in the vacated streets. Furniture and other valuables were carried out and stored on Jozefinska. But that space was now full, and talk had turned to setting up new warehouses in the camp.

A particularly bitter winter morning brought a team of engineers into the dazed streets with new plans and diagrams. The Ghetto was to be divided into two sections: A and B. A new decree proclaimed that all R, W and Z workers must henceforth relocate to section A, and any unemployed residents must move to B, which became a holding pen for the elderly, the sick and the children. Within a few days, Section B was emptied out in the usual manner, via trains to Belzec, while overcrowding in Section A drove able-bodied workers to fling themselves from fifth floor windows, as if driven out by tongues of fire.

51

A young Ordungsdienst called Poldek Hackl was supposed to be guarding the main Jerozolimska Street gate while my Barrackenbau were having evening soup. Like most who wore the German uniform, Jackl was seen as a collaborator and widely despised. For his own protection, I kept him away from the prisoners and put him in charge of the gatehouse, even though I suspected he was not up to the job. Hackl was a broken man following the October Aktion. When Amon Göth's troops formed a human chain around the Ghetto, Poldek was assured his own wife and son would be spared. Symche Spira arranged for them to be transferred to the Prokocim Julag, to work on the railways. But amidst the chaos of the day, mother and child ended up in the wrong column and were last seen being herded into a cattle-car to Belzec. As if this was not bad enough, two days later Gusta Dawidson tracked Hackl down with good news: she had arranged for his son to be saved.

'From Belzcec?' Hackl hardly dared to believe what he'd heard. From the whole of the Ghetto, only one man was ever known to have escaped.

A rare note of doubt dulled Gusta's voice. 'Which son are you talking about?'

'I only have one.'

'Jiri?'

Hackl gave a sombre nod. 'He was deported with my wife. What did you mean, he was going to be saved?'

Eventually, Hackl managed to get the truth out of her. Gusta had secured a place for Jiri outside the Ghetto, to be raised as a Christian. Jiri had been due to be smuggled out that night.

For my own peace of mind, I rigged a bell wire from Poldek's guardhouse to the officers' quarters, for advance warning of important visitors. The idea came to me during a rare return to Erich Mohnke's apartment. Much as I disliked leaving prisoners under the replacement Ukranian guards, I hadn't yet recorded the camp's brutalities in my ledger. If I died tomorrow, the truth would be buried with me. When I got back to Erich Mohnke's apartment, I fell into my usual procrastination, rereading previous entries. I turned back to one of the very first, the story of Shoshana's Magic Bell.

Nights in Plaszow were eerily quiet. The German residential quarters were situated in the nucleus of the emerging sprawl, just acoss SS Strasse, opposite the administration offices. Most of the guards had gone out to the Cyganeria Café; I'd come down with another migraine - so I told them - the perfect excuse for solitude. The guards lived a life of luxury, with electricity and hot showers, but preferred to spend evenings in the city, socialising with Polish sweethearts. Most of them were young, at least half my age. Who could blame them? Their bedrooms were decorated with the finest rugs and curtains and silk-covers looted from the Ghetto. On the other side of cemetery, the former curtain-owners were herded into cold, bleak barracks without roofs.

I was reading about the sinking of the British destroyer HMS Blean, torpedoed north-west of Algiers by a German U-boat, when our house-help appeared at my door. Radka was a timid creature who rarely ventured into private quarters when they were occupied, so I knew something was amiss.

'Oberführer Scherner would like a word with you, sir.'

I peered over the top of my newspaper. 'Did he say in connection with what?'

'No sir, and I didn't like to ask.'

'Very well, Radka. I'll call him right back.'

'Sorry to say, sir, I haven't made myself clear. The Oberführer has just arrived in the camp.'

'He's here?'

'He's waiting for you outside.'

'Good God. Why didn't you say?'

There must be something wrong with Poldek: the Magic Bell hadn't rung.

I threw my jacket and boots on and scrambled out onto the new road, paved with shiny Jewish headstones. The sight of the Oberführer approaching in a smart black tuxedo went some way to quelling my nerves. His limousine was idling on the main road, on the other side of Jerozolimska Street. Through the tinted glass I could make out the tiara-topped curls of his wife in the backseat, regal as the Queen of England. Poldek Hackl was nowhere to be seen. The sickness in my stomach quickly returned.

'Evening, Harry,' Scherer said.

I wasn't sure whether to salute or shake hands, and ended up lurching awkwardly from one to the other, almost jabbing the Cracow Polizeiführer in the stomach.

'Is everything alright?'

'Yes, sir.'

'You look worried,' Scherer said. 'What were you doing in there?'

'Reading the paper,' I said. 'It is 7.30 in the evening, sir.'

'Come.'

I followed him across the road to the guardhouse. Scherer paused, hands on hips, leaving me to approach the hut. The guard's chair was empty. I leant forward, nosing through the window. A pair of ragged trouser-legs stretched out on the floor, bare footed. Socks were balled up and stuffed inside the boots. Muffled snoring came from underneath the guard's desk. Poldek Hackl was sleeping on his shoulder, tunic bunched under his head as a pillow.

'The entire workforce could have fled through the gates and your security wouldn't have woken up,' Scherer said at my ear, tossing a filter-tip into his mouth. 'Put the man down, Harry.'

I heard the spark of Scherer's lighter and smelled a faint tang of smoke as he withdrew to savour his cigarette. I unholstered my Luger, slowly opened the guardhouse door and tiptoed inside. Poldek didn't stir. I crouched at the desk, slipped the fingers of my free hand under his jaw and when he finally woke with a start, clamped his mouth shut.

'Scherer's outside,' I whispered. 'He's going to hear a gunshot, and you're going to lie there, completely still, until you hear his limo drive away. Understand?'

Hackl's head nodded under my fingers. I drew back, cocked the trigger and fired into the floorboards.

Outside, Scherer had turned around and was gazing at the prisoner barracks.

'This was inexcusable, Oberführer,' I said. 'I don't know what to say, after the trust you've placed in me.'

'I'm sure one bad egg doesn't spoil the box. But at the same time, if word got out this was some kind of holiday camp we're running ...'

'It won't, sir. These inmates work until they drop. You can see what we've accomplished.'

'Yes I can. But now I wonder how much more if everybody was pulling their weight. You need more eyes on the ground when the guards are off duty. As of tomorrow, you'll get 500 extra men, prisoners and Ordungsdienst.'

'Yes, sir.'

I would take them, and gladly so. Every soul that came to us meant one less for the greedy gas chambers. The problem was keeping the prisoners busy. There'd been a bottle-neck in supplies somewhere along the chain, and we'd had no timber for days. We were having to make up pointless jobs to keep the prisoners busy. One group would dig stones all day in the quarry, another would carry the stones and pile them up few hundred feet away. Then, a few days later, they'd have to take the same stones from the same pile and move them back to the original spot.

'Elsa spoke to Kate today,' Scherer said.

'I'm sorry?'

Elsa was his wife, but who was Kate?

'Kate Becker. Your aunt.'

I had forgotten about the skiing accident. 'How is she?'

'Back in a wheelchair, I'm afraid. Not that it's slowing her down, the woman's indomitable. She's invited us up for lunch on New Year's Day.'

As far as awkward meetings went, this was bad, but I had survived worse. Coming face to face with Amon Göth again, for instance. Aunt Kate would be no match for him. She had to be in her seventies, and with any luck her eyesight would be failing. I'd pass as Harry Mohnke, as long as I kept a distance.

'The Vienna Philharmonic are broadcasting live on the radio,' Scherer continued, 'and you know how he feels about them. He's too weak to get even get to Cracow at the moment, so we thought this would be the next best thing.'

I'd lost the thread again, and Scherer could see it.

'Your father,' he explained kindly. 'He'll be meeting us at Kate's.'

***

While Julian Scherer was sitting in his opera box that evening, Dolek Liebeskind was arrested in the Ghetto. The Jewish Police traced him to his parents' apartment, and found the fugitive sleeping in the back bedroom. After subduing him with truncheons, they marched their prized prisoner to Jozefinska, but didn't think to frisk him before setting off. Liebeskind was carrying one of the pistols that Anka Fischer had smuggled from Warsaw. Seizing his chance when a policemen was hit by a stone from a high window, Liebeskind pulled his weapon. The unarmed policemen fled, and their prisoner disappeared into the night. A building-by-building search ensued and lasted until dawn, but Liebeskind wasn't found. He was rumoured to have escaped via the sewers.

Understandably, his flight was the talk of the Ghetto. I found out the next day when Poldek Zygoti returned with Scherer's 500 new recruits. We forbade the prisoners from speaking about Liebeskind amongst themselves, but the guards talked of little else. The fact that Liebeskind had come back to the Ghetto at all confirmed speculation that the resistance were preparing a large-scale offensive. I hadn't received any messages from the Pharmacy for weeks by this point, and was as reliant on gossip and scuttlebutt as the next man. Depending who you listened to, the Jews were either planning on blowing up a section of the Ghetto wall, or had assembled enough of a weapons cache to mount an armed uprising.

***

Most of the new Plaszow prisoners were put to work transporting materials for the Latrines. Through fierce wind they trudged up and down the hills, carrying planks and pipes and stones and bricks, depositing pile after pile on the muddy slopes. From there, the skilled builders took over - the carpenters, plumbers and tinsmiths – and slowly the building began to take shape in the icy mud.

At the end of the first day, Horst Pilarzik arrived to direct the evening roll call in person. He made Poldek Hackl count the prisoners as they stood to attention in a blizzard. Hackl's first tally showed two short of the expected 500 men, and a recount was ordered, which came in at 497. Instead of ordering a third, Pilarzik turned round and put a bullet through Hackl's left eye.

52

Concern continued to grow about Plaszow's slow pace of building works. Only three barracks had so far been completed: the Kommandantur's hut that contained the Building Administration, and two workshops for the industrial side of the camp. Himmler's deadline for clearing the Ghetto was less than a mere two weeks away, but there were still 12,000 residents within the walls. If we proceded at the current rate of transfer - about 100 prisoners a day - the Ghetto wouldn't be empty until April 1943.

The main reason for Plaszow's lack of progress was obvious, or at least it was to me. The vast majority of workers were still commuting from the Ghetto every morning, and returning before curfew. I argued that the long walk rendered them less productive, and that we could maximise the working day if all lived on site. But my superiors regarded prisoner barracks as a luxury. I began to worry that I looked 'soft' on Jews, so abandoned my persuasion.

Kommandant Pilarzik blamed Rudolf Lukas and replaced the civilian contractors with three Jewish engineers from the Ghetto, who were given overall responsibility for construction and solving all technical problems. Zygmunt Grunberg headed up this team. The engineers worked at a frenzied pace in the hothouse of Building Administration, desperately trying to execute the new Kommandant's crazy completion schedules. But by now Pilarzik himself had been moved aside. Franz Jozef Mueller had been promoted from the Julags to camp Kommandant, and the demands on Jewish labour went overnight from unreasonable to unfeasible.

All prisoners bore the brunt of this new regime. My Barrackenbau laboured without relief, day and night, at a running pace, under work norms which were first doubled, then quadrupled, in order to complete the latest demand. Builders were disposable. The dozen that dropped dead of exhaustion in an average week could easily be replaced. But the newly ordained engineers were indispensable. When it came to putting the Kommandant's rantings into effect, nobody else would or could do the job. In the whole of Cracow, here were three Jews who couldn't be killed, at least not until the camp was up and running. But that didn't mean they weren't beaten, and often to within an inch of their lives.

It was one such punishment I interrupted by chance on the afternoon of December 17th. I'd been summoned to the Building Administration office to receive a telephone call – Scherer's customary progress check, I imagined - only to find Mueller laying into Zygmunt Grunberg as if he were a punch-ball. The engineer was every bit as compliant, but did fail to obligingly right himself for the next pummelling, slumping instead against a map of the camp on the wall. The Kommandant had to pull him upright by the collar before he could demolish the other side of his face. When I cleared my throat and picked up the telephone, Mueller finally stopped, leaving Grunberg to slide down to the floorboards. Still seething, the Kommandant walked out. Grunberg's colleagues unglued their behinds from their stools to venture out and hold the stricken man's hand, but he flapped them away. If their work stopped, even for a minute, men would die. Besides, there were no doctors at Plaszow; medical attention was only available in the Ghetto.

The black receiver buzzed in my hand and I heard a tiny, shrill echo from the ear-piece. It sounded more like Scherer's wife than the man himself.

'This is Oberführer Mohnke,' I said. 'Who's calling?'

'Oh, at last. Harry, is that you?'

Definitely an older woman, but it was too high for Elsa Scherer.

'Who am I speaking to?'

'Katherine.' The name meant nothing to me, until I ran through its various abbreviations. Just as I guessed who I was speaking to, she confirmed it: 'Kate Becker.'

'Aunt Kate. How nice to hear from you.'

'I have sad news, dear. Are you sitting somewhere quiet?'

Against the wall, Grunberg began to stir. He grabbed a handful of writing paper from the desk and started to wipe away the blood, but the paper had no absorbency and merely smeared it around his face.

'What's happened?' I said.

'It's your father. He never woke up this morning.' She paused to let this sink in. 'The housekeeper found him passed away in bed, as peaceful as anything.'

'He's dead?'

Grunberg was looking at me through blood-slicked eyes. I wondered if he'd seen the involuntary pump my fist had given the air.

'I'm so sorry to be the one to tell you,' Kate Becker said. 'Mr. Scherer offered – I called him to get your new number – but I thought it should come from me.'

'Thank-you, Aunt Kate. I appreciate it. How - what happened?'

'The doctor thinks it was his heart. Otto wouldn't have suffered. Chances are, he didn't even know. None of us can ask for more than that.'

'I can't believe it. We were only talking about him a few days ago.'

'So sudden, I know. But better this than long and drawn out.'

'Yes. He'd lived a full life.'

'He certainly had.'

'Are you alright, Aunt Kate?'

'Me?'

She seemed almost amused at this questioning of her self-sufficiency.

'Do you have anybody with you?'

'Not yet, thanks heavens. I've got the whole brood arriving tomorrow. I suppose they'll be staying until the funeral now.'

My God. Another bloody funeral. What was it with this damned family?

'You leave all the arrangements to me, dear. I expect the service will be in about a week, but I'll let you know when we have a date. You're still living on Tragutta Street?'

'Yes. Although I have quarters here in camp now.'

'Well I know where to reach either way. Please call if there's anything you need. Absolutely anything.'

'You're very kind.'
'God bless, Harry. We'll speak soon.'

53

Unsure of the protocol for Christian burials, I estimated five to seven days before Otto Monhke's coffin was lowered into the ground. Which meant I had a week left in Cracow. There was no future for me after that, whatever I decided. If I went to the funeral, Harry's friends and family were sure to realise I was an impostor. If I didn't go? Scherer would never stand for it. He almost certainly blamed me for hastening his old friend's demise, by prolonging the rift. Out of loyalty to Otto, Scherer would do everything in his power to ensure I discharged my final filial responsibility. Even if I managed to wriggle out of it, Scherer and Elsa would travel by themselves. My absence would cause as many questions as my presence. The gossip was not hard to imagine:

Harry's become a virtual recluse.

Nobody's seen him for such a long time.

Probably not since Erich's funeral.

He was never the same after his brother died.

That was over a year ago, November 1941

The truth of what happened outside Lublin train station was buried along with Augustus Brühl, but it wouldn't take much digging to bring both to the surface. Particularly when the timeline was established. Camp Moda had evidently entered into Nazi folklore, which meant that Jozef Siegler's breakout in the autumn of 1941 was also common knowledge. If the Gestapo set about tracing an escape route south, they'd put Siegler in Lublin at the same time as Harry Mohnke's train had broken down, en route to Cracow.

Laying it all out like this was terrifying. It was only thanks to the quotidian anarchy of war that nobody had yet made the connection. Otto Mohnke's funeral finally provided the opportunity. I worked myself up into such a state after Kate Becker's telephone call that sleep was impossible. I spent the early hours wandering the camp, throwing chunks of bread through barrack windows.

How could I abandon the last of the Cracow Jews now? And where could I run to? I knew from bitter experience I lacked the skills to survive alone. It was only by donning the enemy's uniform that I had given myself any kind of future. But those lightning bolts came with a heavy price: the burden of responsibility. I'd been with my Barrackenbau since the start; everything that happened to them was down to me. It wasn't just life in the camp. The remainder of the Ghetto would be emptied any day now. I was using my influence to see as many residents as possible transferred to Plaszow. Without my demands for labour, thousands more would end up on a one-way train ride to Belzec and Auschwitz. If I stayed here, I risked certain capture. It wasn't death that I feared most, or even torture; I already knew my capacity for withstanding physical pain was pitifully low. What terrified me was the knowledge that, under duress, I'd betray the names of my brothers and sisters in the underground.

There was only one person I could turn to for advice. The next day I volunteered to lead a prisoner detail back to the Ghetto and while there, I posted a message through the Pharmacy's letterbox. I didn't know where Gusta was living, but I knew how to reach her.

***

Meanwhile, preparations for Otto Mohnke's funeral continued apace. Kate Becker was keeping me updated on a daily basis. In a perverse way, I had come to look forward to our conversations. Kate's consoling tones soothed me, even if her actual words were nailing shut my own coffin. The doctor's initial assessment was correct; Otto Mohnke had died aged 73 of a massive heart attack. The funeral was to be held at noon on December 24th, at St. Mary's in Dahme, the same church where Erich Mohnke was laid to rest thirteen months previously. I was due to make the thousand mile journey on the 23rd, and return after the reception. Julian Scherer had already reserved three first-class tickets on the 7.02am Berlin express from Cracow Hauptbanhof, changing first at Lublin, of all places.

After speaking to Aunt Kate, I telephoned the Pharmacy to check for any messages, but the answer was the same again. Three days and no reply. In another three, Harry Mohnke's father would be buried.

How long does Scherer wait in his first-class carriage before realising I'm not joining him? Let's hope a son is given a little latitude on the day of his father's funeral. Say 8.02am comes and goes and Scherer delays the train's departure. It's within his power. As SS Commander for Cracow, he could order the city to a stand-still if he so chose. When after half an hour I've still not taken my seat, he sends men to the apartment on Tragutta Street. Finding it empty, he calls for a city-wide search. By this point, Scherer has done as much as he can. It's 9.00am. He can't postpone the journey any longer. Otto was his dear friend, as well as Harry Mohnke's father. Three hours later, Scherer explains my absence to the St Mary's congregation, and the questions begin to fly. By the end of the day, 'Harry Mohnke' has been correctly identified as Jozef Siegler. The German people have a new Public Enemy, one a lot closer to home than the last fugitive to hold the title, Hitler's former Nazi Party rival Otto Strasser, currently on the run in Canada. I'd be lucky to make it across the river Vistula.

***

While my Barrackenbau were excavating a building at the main Jerozolimska Street gate, I overheard a kindly buck-toothed prisoner called Szei Dreiblatt approach the OD and explain that he was feeling ill. Szei was a former high school chemistry teacher, a patient, hard-worker respected by inmates and staff. The OD had no reason to think he was shirking, and granted permission to step away for a couple of minutes to use the newly constructed Latrines.

To me, watching from the fence, the timing seemed odd. The rest of the men would be stopping at noon for lunch-break. Szei Dreiblatt didn't look sick enough that he couldn't wait another half an hour. And that was the other thing: he'd told the OD he was ill at 11.30 on the dot, not 11.28 or 11.33.

In my experience, sickness was rarely so punctual. Szei Dreiblatt was up to something. I needed to know what in order to protect him.

In no time at all, the Latrines had become the spiritual and commercial centre of the camp. Prisoners lingered at the taps before morning roll call, to trade gossip and cigarettes, and the OD often chased them out with whips. Szei Dreiblatt was not one of these idlers. He only used the latrine for its designated purpose, and to brush his large yellow teeth. My suspicions were right: he walked straight past the building now and carried on up the hill towards the barracks. Perhaps he needed to lie down. But he didn't look tired; I was struggling along the fence while he threw himself into the wind.

He disappeared inside the barracks and closed the door, two punishable crimes in themselves. I approached the side, pretending to give the windows their daily inspection for smudges or smears and stopped at the corner where Dreiblatt bunked. I peered in through the glass past the stove and water pail.

There were three men clustered around the bunk, two other prisoners having left their details at the same time as Szei Dreiblatt, as I suspected. His accomplices knelt while the teacher unwrapped the striped jacket he used as a pillow. This was where prisoners stored their only personal property, the dish and spoon and washcloth. From his bundle, Szei Dreiblatt extricated three highly-illegal metal tins, jam or honey from the looks if it. The school teacher was smuggling contraband after all. Good for him. Now I knew, I could pay off the OD to ensure his bed wasn't searched.

As I pretended to finish off my inspection of the glass, Szei Dreiblatt removed a handkerchief from his pocket and carefully laid it out onto his straw bedding. I stopped, curious to see what else he was trading. He lifted the first tin to pour and out came a fine rain of black powder. From the second tin, a hail of scrap fragments and ball-bearings. He stirred the metal into the gun powder with his hands, lifted the corners of the handkerchief, tied the ends and stuffed the ball down into the third tin. Leaving a length of cloth projecting from the top as a fuse, he screwed the lid back on.

Szei Dreiblatt emerged through the door five minutes later, threw himself into the wind and pushed back up hill towards the Latrines.

Just when I'd decided to follow, the barracks door opened again and the second prisoner emerged. Without acknowledging Dreiblatt, he turned and set off in the opposite direction, towards the work detail levelling the Old Cemetetry. I watched the two men drift apart, until they were random specks in the snow. The door opened a final time. The third prisoner stepped out, and headed east, disappearing between the barracks.

54

It was time for me to leave Cracow for good.

After evening roll call on the 22nd, I wrapped my toothbrush and razor in my washcloth and hitched a ride to the Ghetto. There was nobody at Plaszow to say goodbye to, and nobody at Jozefinska, now that Brühl and Mende were gone. This time last December the courtyard rang out with pagan carols and Lili Marlene. Now the stationhouse was quiet, the rest of the street deserted. I hurried past. Up on the fourth floor Syzmek Lustgarten's apartment had been gutted, its windows smashed.

Tadeus Pankiewicz left his scales unbalanced to usher me into the Pharmacy office. He handed me a cream envelope.

'She said it was urgent.'

'Gusta?'

Not hearing an answer, I tore the seal and pulled out the single sheet of paper. Two words in Hebrew in the middle of the paper, the sign of the cross underneath:

Be Strong, Sacred Flame
X

Nothing on the other side.

'Be strong,' I said. 'Is that it?'

Pankiewicz's face was as impossible to read as ever.

I showed him the message. 'She's joking, right?'

'Could the X be a Roman numeral?'

'You think? Number ten. An address? Be Strong, Ten.' It meant nothing to me. 'Is there a Strong Street in the city?'

'Not that I know of.'

'A tenement building? Strong House, maybe?'

I held the paper up to the light-bulb: no watermark. I ripped the envelope apart and examined every corner.

Nothing.

I exited the Ghetto for my apartment on Tragutta Street. The priority was to finish documenting conditions in Plaszow before I left the city for good. The camp had mushroomed since Poldek Zygoti's death, and there was a great deal to record. I brewed black coffee, fetched the book from behind the Caravaggio and took my usual seat in the living room. Conscious the words could be my last, I chose each one obsessively, weighing the rhythm of sounds and sentences in my mind before laying them down on paper. Progress was slow, but I finished before 10.00pm.

It was too risky to take my journals. I already had the safest of safe places to leave them. If Harry Mohnke was arrested after failing to appear at the funeral, and his property searched, there was a good chance the wall-safe would elude detection. I'd been living in the apartment for weeks before I found it. My books could survive untouched for decades. They might need to. If Germany won the war, the Jewish people were in danger of becoming extinct. We'd be a rumour of an ancient people, like the myth of Atlantis.

I tied the three volumes together with string and laid them on the metal plate. On top I placed the dog-eared Torah of my night prayers, the folded prayer shawl taken from the old woman at the village massacre, the copy of Mordecai Gebirtig's *Our Town is Burning* handed in by his informer, the first anti-Hitler postcard I found in the stairwell last December and Augustus Brühl's Christmas present, *The Lyrical Ballads of Heinrich Heine*. That was it, my collection of relics. I locked the safe and rehung the painting.

It was time to go. My plan (such as it was): head for Paskow, where my mother and sister had last been sighted. Follow their ghosts towards the Ukranian border. From there, travel south, through Georgia and Turkey and finally on towards Palestine. Shoshana and I had often spoken of emigrating there from Vilno, the so-called Jerusalem of the North. I dreamed we would be reunited in its namesake.

While I was making a sandwich, a dull thud boomed beyond the windows. Time was, the noise would have shaken me. But now my knife didn't even wrinkle the butter. Two years in the Ghetto had accustomed me to the hail of nightly gun fire. This sounded different, though. Further away than the old wall, but louder than bullets.

I wrapped the bread in brown paper, ran the knife under the tap and turned off the kitchen light. I was donning my leather greatcoat in the hallway when a second explosion detonated, rattling the panes in the living room.

I was right: this was the wrong direction for the Ghetto. And it definitely wasn't gun fire.

The third and fourth explosions went off one after another, like echoes.

Good God.

I raced towards the living room window as the sky above the river lit up in a juddering orange flash. The city was under attack. I'd lived through the bombing of Vilno; this was no aerial assault. Where were the roaring planes, the air-raid sirens? These explosions were coming from the streets, the very heart of the city.

About twenty minutes after the last blast, my neighbours began venturing out of their apartments and gathering on the streets below my window. I changed out of my uniform and went to join them. The first few Christmas revellers had returned from the Old Town, stumbling over the bridges.

Dazed and dusted, the survivors brought wild stories of cafes and bars reduced to rubble. A husband and wife had been enjoying a concert at the theatre when an explosion rocked the street outside. Everywhere they looked, German soldiers' corpses were being loaded onto ambulances. For the first time since the invasion, the city was plunged into confusion, but this time, it was the Germans on the back foot. The streets were full of frantic Nazis dashing in all directions, trying to find out what had happened, while police cars and fire trucks screamed from scene to scene. It seemed that half the city was on fire.

A crawling flotilla of loudspeaker trucks came next over the bridges, announcing a curfew. We returned to our apartments, to windowside vigils and silent radios. Either the bombers had hit the transmitters, or the Germans had taken themselves off air.

At 11.50pm, my telephone rang.

Gusta Dawidson, I was sure of it. Her final coded message wasn't an address, it was a warning. X = 10.00pm, the first wave of bombs.

'Hello?'

'Harry, I've been ringing for ages. Thank God you're safe.'

'Who is this?'

'Julian Scherer. I thought you might be caught up in all this.'

'I was out on Traguta, until the curfew. What's happening?'

'Jewish terrorists. They've blown up cafes and bars, God knows what else. Bridges, boats, you name it.'

'Jesus Christ.'

'The bastards will be utterly crushed, mark my words. You do realise what this means?'

'Sir?'

'There's no way I can leave town in the middle of this shit-storm.'

'Oh. The funeral.'

'We wouldn't have got through to Lublin anyway, they took out the main signal box. I've shut down all buses, trams and trains.'

'Jesus Christ.'

This was it. Gusta Tova Draenger had answered my prayers. With a valid reason not to attend the funeral - and they didn't get any more valid than the bombing of the seat of the Generalgouvernment - I would be free of Harry Mohnke's cursed family for good.

'I'm afraid I won't be leaving Pomorska for days,' Scherer said. 'But it doesn't mean you can't go by yourself. Why don't you take my driver?'

'To Dahme? It's a thousand miles by car.'

'Get a couple more hours sleep, leave bright and early and you'll make it in plenty of time.'

'It's a very considerate offer.'

'What time shall I tell Kahlert, four, five?'

'I can't go back to bed with this going on.'

There was a lot of shouting in the background, then

Scherer broke off to add his own bark.

'Sorry about that,' he said, a minute later. 'Do you mean you're ready to leave now then?'

'If you're not leaving, sir, neither am I.'

'Otto's not my father, Harry.'

'And I know what he'd tell me, if he could: when you're under attack, son, stand and fight your corner. How can I run when we're being blown to pieces in the streets?'

'We can manage without you for the day.'

'Aunt Kate can cope without me. Right here is where I can do the most good. Wherever they are, this Jewish menace can be traced back to the Ghetto. With my knowledge of informants, there's nobody better placed to root it out. The first twenty-four hours will be vital. If I'm stuck in Dahme, I won't be able to do a thing. God forbid, if there are more attacks, I won't even be able to get back.'

'That thought had crossed my mind,' Scherer said. 'There's Plaszow, too, of course. Kommandant Mueller's lost men at the Gipsy Club. When you didn't answer the phone, that where I thought you were you were.' He paused. 'You know, it's amazing how much you sound like him.'

'Who?'

'Your father. Quite uncanny.'

'Who did we lose sir, at the Gipsy Club?'

'Knaup, Leopold, Thiele and Sefas. That we know of. And that's just one café.'

'God damn it. I should be at Plaszow.'

'Tonight?'

'Knaup and Sefas were Blockfuhrers. We're going to be short-handed. What if the prisoners have bombs too? They might be planning a break out.'

Evidently Scherer hadn't thought of this.

'I'll have Kahlert pick you up,' he said. 'It's too dangerous to be out by yourself.'

'Thank-you, sir. Could you contact Kate Becker on my behalf?'

'Of course. I shall send a cable from Elsa and myself in the morning.'

'Thank-you.'

'They'll pay for this, son. By the time I'm through with them, they'll be begging for the gas chambers.'

Separated from the Old Town by seven miles and as many hilltops, Plaszow wasn't troubled by the explosions that shook the windows of Podgorze. At midnight I found the camp at rest, the prisoners' barracks dark and quiet. My own guess was that Szei Dreiblatt had no idea that his handiwork had been put to such spectacular use. The youths I'd seen him training two days ago had probably escaped back to the Ghetto that night to make more bombs; Dreiblatt's work was done.

The only noise I could hear now was coming from the guards' kitchen, where an emergency meeting was taking place. I entered the room and squeezed in at the corner of one of the packed tables.

'Thought you had a pass for the holidays,' Kruger whispered on my right, shifting his chair to accommodate mine. Nobody knew about my father's funeral. I'd told Kommander Mueller I didn't want a fuss.

'No trains running,' I said. 'It's bedlam out there.'

The mood in the room had already passed from shock to anger. Revenge was on the cards, an eye for an eye. If four Germans had died in the attack, each barrack should lose four Jews. The men were currently arguing whether their psychotic Kommandant would stop screaming into his telephone long enough to authorise reprisals, or whether they should seize the moment and act unilaterally, out of loyalty to their fallen comrades. A vote was being taken round the tables. It seemed close, a 'Yes' for every 'No', but I was worried. The crowd scented blood.

'I say we wait,' I said, when my turn came. 'Right now, our Jews don't know what's happened. Why wake them up and give them a chance to gloat? So we shoot four dead. It won't begin to wipe the grins off their faces. We'd need to liquidate four hundred to even come close.'

'Sounds good to me,' Fricke said opposite. 'Where do I start?'

But his bluster failed to convince. In the end, the guards were split fifty-fifty and decided to await further instructions.

Kommandant Mueller scared the Germans almost as much as he did the Jews.

In the aftermath of the attack, more detailed reports began to circulate. Eight of Gusta Dawidson's Akiva Youth units had broken loose from the Ghetto at lunchtime on the 22nd December, joined by members of the Jewish Fighting Organisation and partisans from the Communist People's Army, comprising forty fighters in total. Signs of an upsurge in underground activity were first noted shortly afterwards: small cells of resistance fighters spent the afternoon hanging protest flags in Matejko Square, on Batory Street and, most audaciously, from the great bridges of Pilsudski and Debinicki, two men suspended above the Vistula on harness and rope. But the authorities were too busy preparing for Christmas to pay much attention, as Gusta had hoped. Last minute gift shopping, veritable feasts to be carted home after work, office parties to head back out for. The resistance had the run of the city.

As dusk descended on the teeming Old Market Square, groups of wan youths left flowers in a shrine for Adam Mickiewicz, the National Poet whose statue was torn down by the invaders. Bundles of leaflets blew like confetti in the surrounding streets, exhorting Poles to rise up against their oppressors.

At 10pm, fighters approached the Café Cyganeria on Szpitalna Street, a popular meeting place for the SS and Gestapo. Three Jews ran into the loud, smoke-filled room, opened fire with pistols, lobbed home-made grenades across the tables and fled. Eleven Germans died, and many more were wounded. Two similar attacks were launched simultaneously, at the Esplanada and Zakopianka, an Officer' Club. It wasn't just cafes and bars. Railroad stations were sabotaged, military garages blown up and soldiers assassinated. Two coast-guard boats were sunk on the Vistula. A major assault on the Sztuka Theatre was supposed to have been the crowning glory, with its capacity crowd of Nazi sitting ducks. But a last minute change to the bill brought a bigger Polish audience than expected. Frustrated, the bombers aborted, venting their frustration on a startled posse of Gestapo agents outside the lobby, and eventually seizing their weapons. While the attacks were underway, another cell started compounding the chaos by phoning in dozens of hoax calls to the emergency services. It must have seemed to Julian Scherer that the entire city was under attack.

The next morning, the transfer of prisoners from the Ghetto was halted in an attempt to contain the insurrection. But, thanks to me, news had already spread to the barracks. I'd spent the rest of the night on patrol, pushing notes under doors, detailing what I knew. I lingered long enough to see a candle flicker to life and hear an excited gasp, 'The Gipsy Club's been blown up!' or 'Good job Shimon and Syzmek!'. The effect on the prisoners' morale the next day was profound. Old men were revitalised in a way that put Tadeus Pankiewicz's hair-dye to shame. Instead of trudging through the mud, prisoners bounced with a spring in their stride, hailing each other with hugs and embraces. It didn't take long for a new work-song to pass from detail to detail, sung to the jaunty tune of *Horst Wessel*:

> We Jews, we're not dead yet!
> God is watching over us! God is watching over us!
> Hitler will end up hanging upside down.
> Good health to him and cholera, too!
> We'll slice him into little pieces!

When the camp authorities prohibited the verse, the prisoners started humming. This infuriated the guards even more, it sounded like the prisoners were humming the Nazi Party's anthem. Even Kommandant Mueller couldn't ban that.

In the end, he didn't need to. Jewish jubilation was short-lived. December 22nd was meant to herald a new era of resistance. Instead it turned out to be the swan-song. Gusta's young fighters, barely out of their teens, made one crucial tactical mistake, agreeing to rendezvous at a single safe-house after the attacks instead of dispersing throughout the city.

It didn't help that two of the members moonlit as Gestapo

informers. Julek Appel and Nathan Weismann were able to get word to their paymasters; German soldiers were lying in wait outside 24 Skawinska Street before the fighters arrived. A fierce battle broke out in the streets of Kazimierz, lasting several hours. By dawn on the 23rd, half a dozen more Germans had been injured. But three-quarters of the resistance were either dead or in Gestapo custody.

When news of this defeat was broadcast throughout Plaszow at lunch, all humming stopped.

After putting in a twenty-hour shift, I was summoned to Kommandant Mueller's office, where it was explained that I'd be escorted back to the city, 'to rest'.

Even for a friend of Scherer's, such indulgence was unheard of at Plaszow, the guards being worked almost as mercilessly as the prisoners. Naturally, I feared the worst: somebody had seen me delivering messages to the barracks. But there was nothing to be done at such short notice; my escort was waiting outside. We left immediately. I hardly need say the twenty-minute ride was the single-most terrifying experience of my life. But when the driver failed to deliver me to the basement at Pomorska HQ and stopped instead at my corner of Tragutta and Dabrowskiego, I stumbled out, drunk with relief.

No Gestapo agents lurked inside the lobby; my apartment was exactly as I'd left it.

I took a long, hot bath and slowly realised what had happened. Mueller didn't let on, but the order to relieve must have come from Julian Scherer himself. Otto Mohnke was being buried in the morning. If Harry couldn't be at his father's service, at least he could observe the day at home, in peace.

The next morning, December 24th, I rose bright and early. Avoiding Jozefinska, I entered the Ghetto via the Zgody Square gate and sought a private audience with the pharmacist. As usual, Pankiewicz knew enough to put my mind at ease. The betrayal of Skawinska Street was a set-back, but not fatal. The Undergound was still active. Survivors had regrouped outside the confines of Cracow, withdrawing into the forests to construct bunkers and hiding places. Pankiewicz wouldn't divulge names or specific locations, and I didn't blame him. Three-quarters of the command structure were still intact (Gusta, Shimson and Dolek Libeskind), and needed to be preserved at all costs.

I returned to the apartment to chronicle the attacks that had brought the city to an extraordinary – if brief - stand-still. As I was writing, a worry-worm began to twist in my stomach, and it took a few pages to realise why. There'd been a lot of noise that morning as the city regained its equilibrium after the attacks, but I'd been able to write through it. The wealthy Aryans of Podgorze were bundling their families into automobiles, leaving the city for country cottages and the traditional Christmas Eve. Nothing, not even armed insurrection, came between a Pole and his fried carp and beetroot supper.

Hungry at the thought, I boiled an egg for breakfast. As I mopped my yolk with a slice of buttered toast, my knife started vibrating on the table-top. From beyond the window came the low lumbering rumble of heavy-duty vehicles, as if my neighbours were escaping en masse in a fleet of omnibuses. Empty plate in hand, I made my way over to the glass. As I looked out, the plate slipped through my fingers and broke on the floorboards.

Tragutta was filling with a convoy of German army trucks.

The first one stopped a hundred metres away on Dabrowskiego, and four more came to a halt behind it. SS soldiers jumped down and spread out across the street, setting up a series of security cordons, a tight dragnet with my apartment block dead centre.

I jumped across the room, grabbed my journal, thrust it into the safe, slammed the door, set the lock and hooked the Caravaggio back into place. Running out to the corridor, I stopped at the railing, peered down through the four flights of concentric rectangles to the coffin-shaped patch of light on the lobby floor.

No echoing march of boots, no bobbing throng of helmets.

Where had they got to?

A minute ago the SS were right outside the apartment

building.

Back at my living room window, I watched the last of the soldiers run past towards the corner of Kacik Street, where a batalion of machine-gunners were setting up along the pavement, aiming their sights on the balcony above the entrance of a three-story apartment block, the one sandstone building sandwiched between a row of dark red-bricks. It was this otherwise non-descript doorway that the last of the SS squadron now filed through, flooding into the lobby. Back on the pavement opposite, I saw Amon Göth and Wilhelm Kunde behind the machine-gunners, the latter holding an ear-piece to the side of his head and berating the radio-signaller crouched at his side.

Then, on Kunde's order, the gunners opened fire. MG42 rounds decimated the balcony's iron railings and glass shattered in a crystallised cascade. After a short blast, the guns fell silent. The building seemed to exhale, releasing a cloud of dust and smoke through the ragged remains of the window frame. But the respite was illusory: the end of the first onslaught signalled the commencement of a second attack, pincer-style. The squadron stormed the apartment from the inside and once again the window lit up with gunfire. A series of distinct pops went off off between the blitzkrieg as the inhabitants attempted to fight back, but such a one-sided battle could only end one way, and did. After several minutes of silence, the SS squadron leader appeared on the balcony and gestured to Göth and Kunde. Two targets inside, both dead.

I learned later that the men were Idek Tenenbaum and Dolek Liebeskind. Their safe-house was on the edge of the Ghetto, less than two hundred metres from my own and I'd never known. It was the Command Post for the 22nd December attacks. In addition to their bodies, the SS brought out the duplicating machine used to print the leaflets distributed in the Old Market Square, and a cache of arms, money and uniforms used that night.

Two German soldiers were killed in the shoot-out, and four more wounded. The distinct pops I had heard earlier were not the sound of the Jewish Resistance fighting back, but taking their own lives. First Dolek shot Idek, then turned the pistol on himself.

55

In the aftermath of the Cyganeria crack-down, I was so paranoid about my journals that I decided not to write another word. If the Gestapo ever found my books, they could shut down what remained of the Underground in a day. The books were bound with a tatty piece of string, but they might as well have been gift-wrapped. Even taking a volume out the safe to glance through was enough to give me a heart attack. Part of me wanted to drop the whole lot in the sink, douse them with gasoline and watch them go up in smoke. At least that way no harm would come.

But I couldn't. Writing had become a compulsion for me. I didn't know how to stop. Like an addict, I feared that one day I'd break down and reach for the ink-pot again. If I couldn't trust myself, I would have to physically remove the temptation. And the books weren't going anywhere. So I made another pledge: I would not return to Traguta Street until the war was over.

***

The swift elimination of Commander Dolek Liebeskind on Christmas Eve 1942 was considered a victory for Julian Scherer, who took the unprecedented step of cabling Adolf Hitler on December 25th to announce the uprising had been quashed. It is not known how this telegram was received, for that same morning Hitler received grim news from Stalingrad. German troops were encircled and outnumbered by the Red Army, in temperatures of -25 degrees. Hitler sent the following telegram to General Friedrich von Paulus: 'You should enter the New Year with the unshakeable confidence that I and the whole German Wehrmacht will do everything in our power to relieve the defenders of Stalingrad'. Neither is it known if General Paulus was aware of the attacks in Cracow. If so, we may speculate that the Führer's words provided little comfort. The German Wehrmacht hadn't been able to defend the jewel of the Generalegouvernment, never mind the wilds of Southern Russia.

Dolek Liebeskind's death paralyzed the movement, and Jewish informant Adek Lipszitz was responsible for a subsequent spate of high-profile arrests, but the Underground lived on. Hilel Wladyslawski led a group of twenty fighters into the Wisnicz Forest in Buchnia, where the base reorganised. On January 1st, Underground units invaded the Ghetto's employment centre, destroying all documents and liquidating several German employees. A few days later, Cracow Haupt Banhof was attacked by Jews guided by a Polish friend, Janina Bigai. Dozens of Germans were killed and much cargo was destroyed. The Germans killed twenty-two Jews in the Ghetto as reprisal. On Janurary 16th, Janina Bigai struck again, having been invited to a party attended by many Nazi officers at Commandant Keper's house. Bigai immediately informed her contacts, and a raid was planned. One fighter gained entrance by posing as an electrician, then let in four more hiding outside. They tied up all guests, including Janina, and seized machine guns and rifles. The fighters changed into military uniforms and returned to the Ghetto in a captured German truck. Reprisals in the Ghetto were horrific, and some within the Underground questioned the wisdom of continuing.

In 1943, the Nazis renewed their liquidation with renewed vigour. Thousands were sent to Treblinka and Auschwitz-Birkenau, whose crematorium had recently been converted into a killing factory, complete with sealed gas chambers for the dispersal of Zyklon B. Apart from the lucky few in the workshops of Oskar Schindler and Julius Madritsch, the inmates of Ghetto B were no longer able to escape deportation by being useful to the German war economy.

On January 18th 1943, Shimson Dawidson was arrested. Gusta turned herself in immediately, for they had vowed to die together. The thirty-three men of the Underground were sent to Montelupich prison, while twenty-two women were held at Helclow. Husband and wife kept in contact, promising to break out to see each other one last time. Briefly, after the liberation, I met a survivor of the women's prison. Pesia Warszawska told me that being confined with Gusta was her happiest memory of the war, possibly of her entire life. Despite the fact the women knew they were facing certain death – indeed, perhaps because of this knowledge - they lived their last days in absolute harmony. The tingling excitement and spiritual uplift experienced by Pesia at Helclow was a gift from God.

Meanwhile, Frank Jozef Mueller was relieved of his command of Plaszow by Untersturmführer Amon Leopold Göth, who assumed control on February 11th. Julian Scherer wanted all Jews from the Ghetto transferred to the camp as soon as possible, and Göth was the man for the job. The new Kommandant was rising fast upon Jewish flesh. On the day of his arrival, Göth ordered a young girl to be hanged for attempting to leave the camp to visit her mother.

Death was now the punishment for any misdemeanour at Plaszow. Immediate death, without judgement and - in most cases - warning. Shooting and hanging were commonplace. The new Kommandant had two Dobermans, Ralf and Rolf, both trained to attack and maul. Göth's adjutant Grün was another notable sadist, renowned for being able to materialise out of thin air and to discover a punishable victim wherever he appeared. Assisting in this mayhem were the Jewish Police, now known as Kapos, and recruited exclusively from the criminal community. Göth's gang of murderers pursued a reign of terror that allowed him to push through stage after stage of Plaszow expansion, all of it done at lightning pace. If the prisoners couldn't keep up, they were shot.

At night, Göth worked alone, drawing up plans for the final liquidation of the Ghetto. The date was set for March 13th, Purim in the Jewish calendar, one of the most joyous of holidays. When the day arrived, every guard wanted to play their part in bringing 700 years of Jewish Cracow to an end. For once I volunteered to stay behind at Plaszow.

The order was given by SS Oberführer Julian Scherner and the Aktion overseen in two phases by SS Untersturmführer Amon Göth in conjunction with SS Sturmbannführer Willi Haase, the Chief of Staff of the SS and

Police. On March 13th, the remainder of Ghetto A was liquidated and Ghetto B, home to the elderly, the sick and children aged up to 14, went the following day. A total of 2,000 Jews deemed unfit for labour were killed in the streets. 8,000 healthy workers were marched to Plaszow. 3,000 more were transported to Auschwitz-Birkenau. Camp authorities selected 499 men and fifty women for forced labour. The rest, approximately 2,450 people, were murdered in the gas chambers.

From his bunker in the Wiznicz Forest, Hilel Wladyslawski sent communiques to the prisoners of Montelupich, offering to try and free them. But Shimson Draenger refused. Together with Laban, he'd been working on his own plan, now only days away from being put into action. There was only one problem. Communication with Helclow had become too dangerous: Gusta didn't know what was about to happen.

All imprisoned Underground members were scheduled to be executed on March 23rd, at Plaszow. The enormous mound of Hujowa Gorka was selected as the site for their gallows, as it dominated the camp and could be seen from all quarters. For this reason, some of the cruder inmates referred to it as Prick Hill.

On the morning of the 23rd, the men were driven from Montelupich to the Jerozolimska Street entrance gate, where an armed platoon of six of Shimson's comrades ambushed the driver. As rehearsed, all thirty-three prisoners jumped from their benches. Syzmek and Laban knocked out one guard each, took their keys and weapons and and made sure the men didn't rise again. Laban was killed in the subsequent fighting. Twelve of the thirty-free managed to get away, including Shimson Draenger. They were hustled into a side alley by their comrades, who gave them new clothes and led them to a safe bunker inside Ghetto B.

The twenty-two female prisoners were also in transit that morning, removed from Helclow by foot to the same destination. When they spotted the men's truck approaching Jerozolimska Street, they were overcome with joy, and began to run towards them. But the men were still in chains and had no idea what was happening outside. Most women were recaptured. One woman was shot to death, but two got away, including Gusta Dawidson.

Within days of being reunited, Gusta and Shimson resumed publishing and distributing copies of their magazine *Hehalutz Halohem (The Fighting Pioneer),* expanding to the workshops of Optima, Madritsch, Tarnow, Reichstof, Przemyszl and Rjebnos, near Jaslo. After a week of hiding in Ghetto B, the Dawidsons joined Hilel Wladyslawski in the Bochnia forests. From mid-April, the group conducted eleven sabotage operations on the Cracow–Lwow railroad, a main supply line to the front. In order to raise money, they removed spirits and cognac from cargo, and tobacco from Podlenze station. In a rare foray back to Cracow, the group assassinated the Jewish collaborator Adek Lipszitz. Disguised as German soldiers, they kidnapped him from his bed, stabbed him to death and disposed of his body.

For all the group's idealism and courage, they lacked the military experience to evade the Gestapo for long. The twenty fighters were captured again in the autumn of 1943, and this time there was no last minute reprieve. In all likelihood, the Germans sentenced the group to immediate execution. The only certainty is that all trace of the Cracow Jewish Underground vanished that day.

***

After his successful liquidation of the Ghetto and expansion of Plaszow from 25 acres to 200 acres, Amon Göth was given a two-grade promotion to Obersturmfuehrer, on 1st August, 1943. The following January, the SS Economic and Administration Main Office started converting the site into the Cracow-Plaszow concentration camp. All other forced labour camps in the Cracow and Radom Districts were closed, their prisoners transferred to Cracow-Plaszow. In the spring of 1944, the SS also began to transport Hungarian Jews to the camp.

It was while supervising one such delivery from Auschwitz-Birkenau that I was brought face to face with a ghost from my past. As the prisoners clambered out of the cattle-cars, one woman became particularly agitated and began screaming curses. Kapos beat her down until she could only crawl. I later learned that the woman's anger was directed towards myself. Gaunt and shaven-headed, I no longer recognized the proud figure of Devorah Montefiore. Devorah and Moses had remained in Ghetto A until last year, but when it came to the final liquidation, Moses was murdered with the rest of the children and Devorah transported to Auschwitz. She survived the first selection of the gas chamber and was put to work in the Siemens factory. Almost a year later, after volunteering to join the Hungarian transport, she was back in Cracow.

Shortly after this strange reunion, building materials were delivered to Plaszow for the construction of crematorium and gas chambers. But due to spiraling costs and the relative proximity of Auschwitz, the construction was never completed. Amon Göth had to find another way to make room for the hundreds of Hungarians now arriving on daily transports. A cull was suggested, and SS-General and Inspector of Concentration Camps Richard Glücks agreed. Under the euphemistically named 'Health Aktion', measures were drawn up to create space for an anticipated 10,000 Hungarian Jews.

Selections began on the morning of May 14th 1944. Prisoners were ordered from their barracks to stand in formation on the Appellplatz, and marched to the reception area. After stripping naked, each prisoner was called out to be examined by teams of doctors headed by the SS Dr Blancke.

I spotted Devorah Montefiore in one of the lines, and wondered how to intercede on her behalf if selected. I had tried doing so once before, during a Ghetto Aktion, without success. The doctor quizzed her in much more detail than the other women, and spent an unnecessarily long time fondling her breasts, one after the other. After this, Devorah Montiefiore was directed on to the obstacle course of holes that would decide the prisoner's right to life. While the adults threw themselves across the open pits, 286 children were rounded up and transferred to a separate compound. Upon discovering their off-spring missing, parents veered off course and began running after them, begging for their return.

A wall of SS moved in, swiftly regaining control. As the children were driven away, Göth ordered the camp orchestra to play traditional German nursery songs, such as *Mother, Buy Me A Little Pony*. Their parents were serenaded to the Auschwitz wagons later that day by radio technicians singing 'Goodnight mama'. Approximately 1,400 Jews were sent to the gas chambers on 14th May, but not Devorah Montefiore, who had been passed fit and healthy.

In late August 1944, with defeat in the air, the Nazis began erasing all traces of the horrific crimes commited at Plaszow under Göth's command. 200 of the strongest male prisoners were isolated from the rest and tasked with the removal and burning of all corpses from the mass graves, an infernal job that took two months to complete. As ever, Göth grew impatient with their lack of progress, and couldn't keep his finger off the trigger. As fast as corpses were dug up, he added fresh ones. Meanwhile, the Soviet Red Army drew ever closer. Evacuations of prisoners began in September, for swift disposal at Auschwitz.

Then, without warning early on September 13th 1944, Amon Geoth was arrested at his villa. Following an investigation into corruption and black market activities within the camp, Göth was accused of misappropriating valuables from camp prisoners, property which rightfully belonged to the Reich. Management of Cracow-Plaszow was turned over to SS-Obersturmführer Arnold Büscher. But by this point in the war, there was barely anything left of the camp to administer.

On 31st January 1944, some of the last prisoners were evacuated on a train to Auschwitz-Birkenau. There were two boys and 178 women, including Devorah Montefiore. I still had no idea about her condition at this point, and if her friends had told me, I wouldn't have believed them. I volunteered to accompany the transport west, to keep the prisoners safe for as long as I could. The war was almost over, any day now. With God's grace, the Red Army would liberate Auschwitz before we arrived.

But I miscalculated. If we'd stayed in Cracow three days longer, my prisoners would have survived. Hans Frank's government fled the castle on January 17th; Soviet troops entered the city on the 19th. But by this point, the last prisoners of Plaszow had already passed through the gates of hell into Auschwitz-Birkenau.

A grey hive of industry in which every action was devoted to death and destruction. My prisoners were put to work immediately, lifting corpses onto trolleys, pushing them into massive burning pits, all day long, body after body. The bullies and clowns of the SS screamed, while the women - and most prisoners were women by this point, women who resembled cancer patients, pencil necks, enormous dark eyes and head scarves - remained completely silent, too numb to utter a word. For a week they worked in ceaseless squalor, feeding the furnaces, caked from head to toe in ash.

The SS set fire to the vast warehouses of Jewish property dubbed Kanada, and destroyed their own records offices. While I was meant to be burning files in the Gestapo offices, I came across a back room containing over three hundred Death Books: handsomely-bound compilations of death certificates of prisoners who died in Auschwitz-Birkenau between July 29, 1941, and December 31, 1943. Most of the reasons of death were fictitious; there was no mention of the hundreds and thousands of victims who'd died in the gas chambers. But it was in these pages that I finally discovered the fate of my mother and sister. They had died together 'of Tuberculosis' on March 1943, three months after last seen fleeing towards the Ukraine.

56

That night I had a long and vivid dream. *I was
leaving Auschwitz on a forty-eight hour pass, clutching a
brown paper package tied with a dainty pink ribbon. Inside
were two hobnailed boots wrapped in a shirt and a pair of
size forty trousers, brown and belted.*

*'You're in a hurry tonight,' observed the guard at the
gatehouse, Jan Breyer.*

*'A train to catch.' Pushing the package up against my
chest, I flashed my watch. 'Hurry it up if you can.'*

'May I ask where you're going?'

*'If you're trying to be as impertinent as possible, yes, you
may.'*

'It's just... the parcel.'

'My youngest sister's getting married in Berlin.'

*'Berlin will look beautiful in the snow. I wish you all a
very happy occasion. Do you mind if I quickly check the
parcel?'*

*'Of course.' I handed it through the open window.
'Wedding gift.'*

*The guard gently felt the contours of the parcel.
'Clothing and...?'*

*'A dress and some fancy shoes I bought from town. If you
open it, wrap it up better than I managed. Not very good at
this kind of thing.'*

*The guard sniffed and studied the parcel once more,
feeling the ribbon between his fingers.*

*'Not at all, sir,' Breyer said finally. 'It looks fine to me as
is. Enjoy your Christmas.' He returned the parcel unopened.*

'Thank-you, Breyer. Heil Hitler.'

'Heil Hitler.'

*One first-class ticket to Berlin, returning on the 29th.
There was a single stop at Wroclaw, although if I got that
far, my mission had already failed. I waited on the platform
under the vast brick archways, mingling with a group of*

soldiers, making sure to mention my holiday plans to at least three different youths. When the 19.30 train puffed into the station, I bid them goodbye, stepped on board and guarded the first-class cabin nearest the exit until I was sure all other passengers were seated. I had the luxury of the oak-lined snug all to myself, for five whole minutes.

Right on cue, the train clacked to a stand-still in the eastern suburb of Bronowice, the first and only unscheduled stop. I rose with the parcel, slipped out into the scarlet corridor, checked both ways before lowering the door handle and stepping down into the cold black night. I slammed the door shut, jumped onto the gravel beside the tracks and scrambled underneath where I waited for the engine to pull away, remaining hidden until the last carriage rumbled over my head.

Bronowice station was deserted, outside and in. The area had been chosen because of the generous amount of wooded cover provided. It didn't take long to find Jordan Park and then the much larger Blonia Meadow.

I walked south, traversing Cracow through its pleasant, leafy suburbs until I found the banks of the Wizla. I followed the river east as it wound its way through Plaszow and Rybitwy as far as Popielnik, where I scrambled up the slope towards Nova Huta and the scattered remains of Austro-Hungarians forts. I kept moving uphill until I found the remains of the aristocratic country house with the roadside shrine outside, and two kilometres beyond it, the half-rotten wooden church.

Inside, hanging behind the desiccated altar, exactly as promised, was the wire coathanger and the canvas garment bag. I tore open my parcel, shed Harry Mohnke's SS uniform and changed into the loose peasant clothing I'd brought from the Auschwitz warehouses, trying not to think about the fate of the garment's previous owners.

I hooked the wire beneath the epaulettes of my jacket, folded the trousers over the base of the flattened triangle, remembering to remove the Nordland cigarettes and matches from the pockets, then wrapped the dust-bag around the whole thing, replaced the hook behind the altar and tucked my officer boots into the apse. As I watched the brown packing paper curl and blacken under match flame in the dry water font, I heard the truck approach outside and idle to a stop.

I approached the driver's window to get a better look at the man. Grey stubble, scar over his left eyebrow, black cap pulled tight over sparse curls.

The driver revved his accelerator and said in Polish, 'Name?'

'Which one?'

'The one that matches what I was given or I'm out of here.'

'Jozef Siegler.'

The driver nodded. It was good. 'You got a cigarette, Jozef Siegler?'

'Here.' I handed over the pristine packet. 'Keep them.'

The driver grunted his appreciation and struck one up with a silver lighter that was almost certainly stolen and blew the smoke out the window into my face. 'Want one?'

I coughed.

'Suit yourself,' he said. 'Let's go.'

I walked round between the headlights and had my hands on the passenger door handle when the driver said, 'The fuck are you doing? In the back. Under the tarpaulin. You need to piss, knock. Maybe I hear you, maybe I don't.'

For four hours we rode, every bump in the road jarring my bones. The tarp and floor were sticky with a dark substance that I hoped was oil, but whatever it was, I was on my way, alone and outside. Almost free. I turned up a corner of the tarp and gazed at the jagged shadows of pine forests and mountain peaks that glided past like icebergs, at the burning stars and the cold, cold moon.

We stopped a little way into Eastern Czechoslovakia just after 04.00. I climbed off the back outside an empty bus-stop and approached the truck window. The name of the small town - Čirč - was all the driver muttered before putting his vehicle back into first gear, executing a wide turn in the road, and trundling back the way he'd come. I watched the truck's tail-lights disappear into the morning dark. For all his grumpiness, the driver had made good time.

The football stadium was easy to locate; its rickety stands loomed over the northern quarter of town like a hair-raising rollercoaster. And there, beneath the litter-strewn wooden slats next to the main turnstiles, painted in the home team's red and white stripes, was the entrance to the cellar bar, the Čirč Pivnice. The door was open. Even at this hour, rude laughter bubbled up and out. I tucked the shirt into his baggy trousers, spit-flattened down a tuft of hair and squeezed down the narrow stairway.

Had the sworn enemies of Čirč FC wished to construct a tinder-box under the stadium, they couldn't have done a better job. The cellar's interior walls were lined with bamboo, the tables were oak, the chairs wicker, and the only source of light were a dozen sputtering candles. Bestowed into the careless custody of a gang of town drunks, it was a miracle the whole shebang hadn't gone up in flames.

I lingered at the bottom of the stairs, but was spotted by the tall purple inn-keeper as he made his rounds collecting empty tankards. The man's face was really quite an extraordinary colour, offset by silky white wisps of thinning hair.

On making eye-contact, the inn-keeper slammed a fistful of handles back down onto the corner table, hiked his trousers up by the belt and waded towards me, grinning. His enormous hands rose and fell in front of his white shirt as if juggling in slow motion. The curve of his lips threatened to crack his jaw in two. I shuffled back, bumping into the bottom step. The purple inn-keeper yucked a laugh, extended those large hands and smothered my shoulders in the warmest of embraces.

'Vel-com, vel-com!' he boomed in broken English.

The patrons flashed watery eyes in our direction, but resumed quickly enough their patter, as if such intrusions were commonplace.

'I'm Jozef Siegler.'

'No kidd-ing,' the inn-keeper said. He laid his right hand over his heart. 'I, Petr.'

'Petr Zeman?'

Nodding, the inn-keeper smiled again and backed away, sensing the imposition of his own hulking frame. 'Come, come here. Beer. Good very beer.'

I followed over to the counter and sat on the stool Zeman pulled out before opening the hatch and pouring a tankard of Pilsner, wiping the foam off with a flat wooden stick. 'Cheers,' he said.

'Na zdravie,' I responded. We switched to Czech, which Petr preferred.

'Good?' He asked as I drank. He poured himself a smaller glass and answered his own question. 'Good.'

Half the tankard gone and I was already light-headed. 'Are you just open or just closing?' I asked.

'Closing? What is the meaning of the word?' Petr placed a bowl of peanuts on the counter and I scooped a handful, ravenous. 'If this war's good for one thing, it's business. I haven't had a holiday in years.' Several seconds passed in which I became aware of the bar's ambient hum. Petr lowered his voice to a good-natured growl. 'Is it true they've got you into a camp?'

I nodded, drained the remainder of his beer. 'Auschwitz-Birkenau.'

Petr's cheeks puffed. That was something, I thought. The name meant something to the outside world.

The remaining conversation was limited to details of my onward journey. The brewery man would be arriving shortly and in a change of plan would take me as far south as Hatvan, an hour from the Hungarian border. I queried this repeatedly, having been advised to accept no alterations to the route previously agreed. But Petr was adamant, and I had no choice but to trust him. Arrangements from Hatvan were already in place, he assured. All subsequent connections would be met. The only difference was, I now would be arriving in Turkey a half day earlier than originally anticipated. With any luck, I'd make up more time with the Brits going south. Win-win: everything to be gained and nothing to lose.

But I remained sceptical, and was not particularly reassured by the sight of the brewery man stepping down from his lorry onto the kerb: a bearish brute taller than Petr (what were these Slovaks eating?) and three times as wide. The kindly barman read the doubt flickering across my eyes.

'He's a decent enough guy.' Petr pumped his hand good bye. 'He just doesn't talk that much.'

'That much' turned out to be 'at all.' I was initially relieved to discover I was allowed to ride up front in the cabin and not hidden on the flat-bed. But before long I found the driver's stony-faced silence more of an ordeal than being stuffed into any hoppy barrel. I couldn't even get the man to utter his name, not so much as a grunt.

By the time we crossed the Tatra Mountains, I had abandoned all attempts at engaging the brewery man in conversation and had decided that he was in the presence of what physicians called aphasia voluntaria, or a selective mute. I remembered stumbling onto a lecture at Kiel about children who were able to speak normally, but refused to. Maybe the brewery man had been bullied as a child, then later mailed away to the USA for the Charles Atlas course and trained every muscle in his body apart from his tongue.

The longer the driver maintained his silence, the more my own words seemed take on a mocking air, and so I too stopped talking. The remaining four hour journey was undertaken in complete and utter silence. Clambering out the lorry at a small café on the edges of Hatvan late that afternoon, I didn't even bother saying goodbye.

All subsequent connections were indeed met, as Petr Zeman had promised. But the brewery man had set the tone for my subsequent reception in southern Europe. I had the distinct impression that rides were being given grudgingly from that point forth. That I was being helped despite my Judaism, not because of it. True enough, I was not at my most sociable. Beyond exhaustion, having already endured twenty-four hours on the road without sleep or sustenance, save for two Pilsners and a bowl of peanuts. And as far as tokens of gratitude for my benefactors, all I'd thought to bring was one packet of cigarettes, which now seemed laughable. Throughout Hungary and Yugoslavia and on into Romania, I was passed from van to school-bus to – on one occasion – horse-drawn hearse.

Dropping down the continent, the local citizens' skin grew darker and their hair more prone to curls and I swore I could feel the bitter breath of resentment on the nape of my neck.

The last day on European soil passed in a blur of nightmarish visions and rude awakenings, a grim cyclone of anti-sleep. One time, between Sofia and Haskovo, I opened my eyes to find I'd been lifted from the vehicle while unconscious. Any manner of physical abuse could have been visited upon me in that condition. And yet it was not. The rides kept coming and the sun grew fiercer and suddenly the church spires that had pierced the landscape slowly gave way to the smooth, breast-like domes of mosques.

I was dropped on the outskirts of a sprawl I correctly identified as Istanbul and waited on the side of a dusty street for two hours, with only a forlorn three-legged dog for company. The mutt wanted nothing from me but affection, which was all I had to give. After I stroked its tufted haunches to a sheen, the dog collapsed onto its belly and fell asleep with its long chin resting on my boot. When the British army jeep tore round the corner with a jolly toot-toot, the dog flung itself up and scrambled away, fur spiked in fright like a Loony Tunes cartoon.

'Sorry we're late, Jozef old boy,' a familiar voice called over the clanking engine. 'The roads here are worse than bloody Nottingham.'

It couldn't be. And yet it was. There in the flesh: I was shaking the pale, pencil-thin fingers of Lieutenant James Rogarden. Four years since any kind of contact, and they'd sent me the same bloody man who'd recruited me: you had to hand it to the Brits.

'Hop in, Dr. Doolittle,' Rogarden said. 'The dog stays put, I'm afraid.'

Still dazed by the apparition, I climbed onto the back seat and pushed up into the middle, between Rogarden and the driver. I couldn't see much of the other man apart from the tip of blistered nose and a badly-scabbed ear, neither of which I recognized. The driver was testament to the old joke that redheads didn't tan, they burnt. This one could certainly handle a jeep, though, executing a hairpin turn up a cramped alley at a cool forty miles an hour. Laundry lines flapped over our heads like great winged beasts.

Rogarden was thriving, fulfilling his manifest destiny as apprentice master of this brave New World, eyes crystal blue as the Bali Ocean as he turned and grinned. 'Good to see you again, old chap.'

'You too, my friend,' I said, nodding. 'You too.'

Rogarden's face had filled out since '38, the finely pointed moustache he now sported nothing more than a tragic inevitability. Errol Flynn, that was who he looked like. I saw he still travelled with his trusty black ledger, stuffed into the passenger door pocket between a spray of maps. Debrief-on-wheels, it made sense. The information I had about what was happening in Poland couldn't wait.

'I'm disappointed your chum's not here too,' I said, relishing the smooth feel of the English tongue after the days' deprivations. 'I thought you two were inseparable. What was his name, Bellamy?'

'No,' Rogarden said, and gazed off at an oil refinery in the distance. 'Bellamy didn't make it.'

I knew he was talking about more than the trip. 'I'm sorry.'

'And what more is there to say than that? Let's hope Corporal Fleck's got more staying power.'

'It's an honour to meet you, sir,' Fleck said. I saw from the squint of the driver's eyes in the mirror that he was being entirely serious. An honour.

'I hope you can put aside your first impressions,' I told him. 'Bear in mind I've been on the road for two days already. One day dragged by a knackered horse in a coffin. I was in the coffin, I should point out, not the horse. But it was close.'

'Stop complaining, man,' Rogarden said. 'You people should have the wandering down to a tee by now, all those centuries of practice.'

'There's wandering,' I said. 'And there's hostile abduction.' Poor choice of words: I tried not to think about

the thousands of windowless cattle-wagons criss-crossing the Reich. 'Anyway, here I am. Safe and sound and in about a million tiny pieces.'

'Why don't you sit back and nod off? Twenty hours or so before we get there. Plenty of time.'

'Later. I've always wanted to see Istanbul.'

'Really? I always enjoy seeing it in the rear-view mirror. Ghastly place. The last time I ate there, it was three days before I could stand up without shitting myself. Bloody fish sandwich, of all things.'

'You're British,' I said. 'I thought the pursuit of the inedible was your national sport.'

'World-beaters, you know us.'

I slumped back against the seat and let the city wash over me. The high palace and mosques of Sultan Ahmed gleamed like Faberge eggs as a golden dusk descended over the Horn. My view was confined to snatched glimpses as the jeep patrolled the polluted northern quarters between the bridges until a car ferry agreed to take us over the Bosporus.

We decamped unmolested to a café on the sun-dappled western deck of the good ship Fatih and ate salt-cod sandwiches, Rogarden abstaining, washed down with Turkish tea from hot glass tumblers.

The city's jewels glittered against the skyline as the ferry pushed into the harbour, the lush green courtyards of the Topkapi unfurling down the hillside like enchanted velvet. I could have studied the complex for the rest of the evening as if preparing for a great heist, but Rogarden had other ideas. The ledger was open, propped between his knee and the lattice table-top. He was busy scribbling away, seemingly as lost in his own thoughts as I had been in mine, but the invitation was unmistakable. Debrief-on-water.

'You've shown me paradise on earth,' I said. 'Now I give you the guided tour of hell, is that it?'

'In your own time.'

'What do you want to know?'

'Are you sure you're ready?'

'I've been ready for two years,' I said. 'It's you I'm worried about.'

Rogarden scratched a fresh heading in his book. 'Let's start with Auschwitz. What are the conditions like?'

'Conditions?' I rubbed my nose. 'Conditions would be nice.'

I turned away from those blue eyes, back across the water. The ferry was slowly turning now towards the East, Sultan Ahmed receding from view. Strange the mosques and sacred Muslim relics of the Byzantium era now found themselves stranded on the European side of the city. The nightmare of history: for once James Joyce hadn't got it quite right. Sometimes you did wake up.

I talked uninterrupted for thirty minutes, the condensed tour of the underworld. My first day through the Auschwitz gates, the first trains, the prisoners' last walks towards the waterless showers, the heaps of tangled bodies pulled out and swallowed up by a greedy earth. The lies of the Ghetto before that, the vile language of liquidation, the ceaseless routines of Special Selections. I couldn't look Rogarden or Fleck in the eye until I'd finished. Turning towards them, steeling myself for a sceptical British inquisition, there was still no way I could have expected Rogarden's response.

'It's almost verbatim,' he said. 'Word for word. Jesus Christ, Fleck. He was telling the truth.'

'Verbatim to what?' I said. 'What are you talking about? Who was telling the truth?'

The two Brits looked at each other; Fleck shrugged.

Turning back several pages in his ledger, Rogarden said, 'Does the name Jan Karski mean anything to you?'

'Polish resistance fighter, infiltrated the Warsaw Ghetto.'

'He posed as a guard at the Izbica transit camp, witnessed Jews being herded on to train cars, saw they never came back. The Polish government in London smuggled Karski out with a microfilm detailing atrocities. He addressed the governments of the United Nations two weeks ago.'

'In New York?'

'The mass extermination of Jews in German occupied Poland, that was his talk.'

'Two weeks ago? So you mean to say... you know? Why

the hell are these camps still standing?'

'The Americans didn't want to bomb civilians.'

'Believe me, bombing would be a blessed relief.'

'And Karski's only one man,' Rogarden said. 'Churchill was worried of the lone Pole with an Occupation axe to grind, exaggerating for dramatic effect.'

'Exaggerating? Did you listen to a word I said?'

'Every one of them, old fruit. Dictated to the best of my ability. Here.' Rogarden pushed the ledger across the table for me to check. 'Sign and date underneath for now, I'll get copies typed up ASAP. This changes everything.'

I pushed it back untouched. 'This changes nothing. Not if you already knew.'

The ferry docked and we spoke again only briefly on the subject of which deck we had left the jeep on. I debated remaining onboard and heading straight back to the European side. But I was more than halfway to Palestine now, and could almost smell the scent of my mother's jasmine. A sullen child, I mutely followed Rogarden and Fleck down to the vehicle.

Throughout the rest of Turkey, Syria and down into the dustbowl of Lebanon, I resisted all further impulse to talk, even when the two men up front were discussing my favourite actor's latest film, a Resistance romance set across the Med in Morocco. I hadn't seen Bogart on screen since They Drive By Night, when the presentation of American films had become illegal across the Reich and its protectorate, and I was eager for gossip. But I wasn't about to break my silence for anybody, not even Bogie. I had said all I had to say about my life in Poland. The truth was in Rogarden's ledger now. What happened next was up to him.

We arrived in Nablus at night, not that I knew which night it was exactly, or that I was even in Nablus. In blackness, all deserts looked the same. From what I'd seen, they didn't look much different by daylight, either. But for the first time since leaving Istanbul, Fleck had taken his foot off the accelerator.

The two Brits were peering at a row of squat one floor houses that had sprung up out of nowhere in the middle of the darkness. They drove slowly past each one, conferring briefly until one of them said 'no', and moved on. The British army knew where the house was; the prodigal son did not. It was as if I was being led to my mother's house blindfolded.

And then, at the last but one in the row, they came across a sign. Hanukah candles burning in the front window, the only light in the street.

The jeep stopped outside and Rogarden said, 'Here we are.'

I studied the house. 'That's it?'

'What were you expecting?'

'I don't know.'

'Well. This is the place. Take as long as you need, my friend. We're not going anywhere.'

'I haven't seen them for many years.'

'So stop wasting time,' Rogarden urged gently. 'Don't worry about us. Whenever you're ready to go. It's entirely up to you.'

'You'll come in, surely.'

'Thank-you, but no. Perhaps later. Certainly not for a decent while.'

'Alright, then.' I opened the door. It was another half a minute before I found the strength to climb out. 'I would offer to bring you a fish sandwich, but…'

'If you managed to find any fresh fish out here, I might eat it. I'm sure Fleck would appreciate a bite later, if it wasn't too much trouble. Now go on. They're waiting for you.'

Rogarden watched as I stepped slowly up to the front door, which opened without being knocked, displaying the fanned arms of two beaming women, my mother and sister. I lifted my boots over the threshold into their collective embrace and the door closed behind them. In the front window, the curtain lifted and a child's mouth blew out the Hanukah candles.

57

The end came on January 17th 1945, as the first Red Army guns boomed over Auschwitz' evening roll call. Although for you, my child, it was just the beginning.

We expected the Soviets would enter the nearby town of Oswiecim in the morning. They would find our camp shortly after. Evacuations had been underway for days by this point, with tens of thousands of prisoners forced to trudge west through heavy blizzards, towards the subcamps at Gliwice and Althammer. The Death Marches. One simple rule: any prisoner who slowed, for any reason, was shot. Nobody could be left behind alive.

Before the Soviets could arrive, the decision was taken to evacuate the remaining 30,000 prisoners towards Loslau some forty miles away, where survivors would be put on freight trains to the furthest flung territories. This would be my final job: to accompany the Death March. When prisoners stumbled in snow drifts, they would still need a helping hand. Most were in various stages of starvation; many had only wooden shoes or rags to cover their feet.

Overnight temperatures in Upper Silesia plummeted to −20 °C. When I assembled my prisoners under the Appelplatz floodlights for the final dawn roll call, two women were missing. According to the block twelve Kapo, Devorah Montefiore, your mother, was too ill to move from her bunk. Another woman had stayed behind to nurse her. Ernst Hanning, the superior SS officer in charge of the count, ordered me into the women's dormitory. I knew what was expected: bring them out, or leave them dead. As I hustled across the snow, I conjured a third way. I could certainly make it sound like I'd killed them: two shots fired into an empty mattress. I could come out alone, and we could leave the women to fend for themselves. Unfortunately, Ernst Hanning changed his mind at the last minute and decided to accompany me.

'This could be a trap,' he said, brushing past with his pistol unholstered. 'What do you know about Montefiore?'

'Nothing,' I lied.

I had seen the strange way the doctor examined your mother during Amon Göth's Health Aktion last October, ripping her tunic off to fondle her breasts. For once there was nothing sexual in the doctor's actions. Suspecting Montefiore of having fallen pregnant, he was trying, unsuccessfully on this occasion, to stimulate milk.

I held the dormitory door open and followed Hanning across the threshold. Devorah Montefiore was pale and still, the thin blanket pulled up over her breathless face. Standing at her side, the friend cradled a bundled and bloodied sheet. The fingertips of the woman's other hand poked out from the sheet, supporting the back of a tiny pink head, matted with raven curls. You have your mother's curls, my sweet.

'And that one?' I said, pointing to the body under the blanket.

The friend nodded, dry-eyed. 'Devorah didn't make it. What will happen now?'

'What happens is up to you,' Hanning said. 'We either leave the mother and child or we leave all three of you. Makes no difference to us.'

Before she could answer, I tried one vain appeal, to Hanning's survival instinct. 'If we have to negotiate our terms of surrender with the Soviets, the baby could be a bargaining chip.'

'One baby's not going to save us now, man,' he said. 'Take it out back. Not in front of the others.'

There was no point pleading the case. Devorah Montefiore's friend transferred your bundled warmth into my arms and then followed Hanning back out to the Appelplatz.

I waited for his long column of prisoners to start marching past the chimneys that were supposed to be their only exits, and then file out through the mendacious gates. When I could no longer see Hanning through the frosted glass, I took a blanket from an empty bunk and tied it around my shoulders, fashioning a sling. Lodging you inside, I drew on my greatcoat, leaving two buttons open in the middle for you to breathe, and hurried through the deserted camp towards Kanada, the vast repository of purloined Jewish clothing relieved from prisoners upon their arrival. Most warehouses that comprised the complex had been razed in the last few weeks, but not all. According to subsequent newspaper reports, the Soviet Army's 322nd Rifle Division would find 370,000 men's suits, 837,000 women's garments, and 7.7 tons of human hair.

I didn't have much difficulty shedding my uniform and finding civilian clothes that fit. In my new guise, we left the camp and turned east, away from the Death March. Instead of being fastened beneath my rough SS greatcoat, you were now slung beneath a rich fur coat, a far more accommodating skin. Within five minutes you were snoring.

Walking on the highway towards Zaborze, we eventually encountered our first group of Soviet soldiers. But they were far from friendly faces. I wondered if they suspected me of being a disguised German. They asked for my Grana wristwatch, which I had forgotten to take off and leave with the rest of Harry Mohnke's possessions. When I handed it over, they asked for money.

I told them, 'My name is Jozef Siegler. I am Juden. Juden. I have no money. We've come from the concentration camp.'

'Jew,' the soldier said to his comrades. 'Just our luck. Nobody likes Jews. Germans don't like Jews, Poles don't like Jews, and we don't like Jews.'

'Please,' I said, opening my fur to show the baby. 'She is all I have left.'

'Not quite,' the soldier said, and motioned for me to remove the coat. Wearing it draped around his shoulders, he lifted his rifle and chased us off the road into the forest.

***

We ended up in Dusseldorf in 1946, where I found work with a shoe-maker, and from there passed through a series of Displaced Persons camps, set up by the US Army. Once more we were transported cross country in German railroad cars. Conditions in the D.P. camps were not much better. Ten GI's in charge of thousands of Jews, housed in pig sties and fed on slop.

Eventually we travelled to Bremerhaven, a German port in the English sector. Yet another camp. We shared a room with four other couples, all newlyweds, keen to make up for lost time. For the first time in a year, you were not the one who kept me awake all night, my child.

In Bremerhaven we lived on nothing but dried potatoes. Meat was a rumour. Packages of food that arrived from the Red Cross were stolen by Germans working at the camp.

***

The SS Marine Flasher was completed as a C4 type troopship shortly after V-J Day, and first set sail from San Francisco for Okinawa and Inchon, Korea in September 1945. She returned to Seattle in November, and left again on Christmas Day for Shanghai. In February she arrived once more in Los Angeles, and on March 7th, departed for New York via the Panama Canal. On the 25th April 1946, she left Manhattan for the heavily-damaged north German port of Bremer, in what we now call the English sector. Now, thanks to President Truman's Displaced Persons Act, which reopened immigration to the United States by allowing a maximum of 38,681 refugees to enter the country each year, the Flasher is set to be the first ship to leave Europe with 795 refugees on board.

Paperwork from the American consulate took several months to complete, but now, finally, we are ready. It is 13th May, 1946. In four days' time, the SS Marine Perch follows with another 566. No other country has yet offered asylum.

I stood on the Flasher's deck with you in my arms. Down below, Bremen was strung with banners to mark our departure. A band of American servicemen played Glenn Miller jazz tunes to prepare us for our New World home. If we find ourselves in the mood at Tuxedo Junction on a juke box Saturday night, the conductor told the baffled passengers, at least we'll know the moves for the Chatanooga Choo-Choo.

Once at sea, with Europe safely behind us, we headed downstairs. Since the Flasher was a troop ship, designed for marines, there are no cabins. We have a hammock in a stateroom with some forty other refugee families. At mealtimes, we eat at table number eight on the B Deck Dining Room. The first meal was served at noon, while the crew were preparing for departure. After lunch, each passenger received a shiny orange. This simple piece of fruit reduced grown men and women to fits of tears. Several of the older passengers fainted. One woman explained that she had not seen an orange since 1939.

The weather turned very cold as we left the English Channel, and women were soon sorting through their trunks and boxes for winter coats. The cold snap heralded an enormous storm that has so far tracked us for eight days, almost the entire length of the voyage. Although the passengers continue to be overwhelmed by the variety of the B Deck Dining Room's daily buffet, most were unable to eat due to chronic seasickness. Even the hardy American mariners had seen nothing like it before, the ocean transformed into towering mountains of water over which we climb and drop, climb and drop.

Today brings the first calm we have known for over a week, and in the relief from the crashing waves, I hear shouts from outside in all kinds of languages. They are calling the names of famous skyscrapers and bridges.

But there is one American word that I hear above all others, and it is the sound of freedom.

I lift you from the hammock and run up to the deck. Hundreds of fellow refugees have coalesced into a single cheering crowd, jostling for the first view of New York over the railings. I hold you aloft, and there she is, standing tall on Ellis Island, the new colossus, her torch aloft.

Liberty.

What Did You Think of *I Am Juden*?

First of all, thank you so much for purchasing **I Am Juden***. I know you could have picked any number of books to read, but you picked my book and for that I am extremely grateful. I hope that it added some value and quality to your everyday life.*

If you enjoyed this book and found some benefit in reading this, I'd like to hear from you and hope that you could take some time to post a review on Amazon. Your feedback and support will help this author to greatly improve his writing craft for future projects.

If you're in the UK, you can follow this link to https://www.amazon.co.uk/I-Am-Juden-Undercover-SS-ebook/dp/B07MRL9TX3/ref=sr_1_1?ie=UTF8&qid=1551480404&sr=8-1&keywords=i+am+juden now.

Or Amazon America, Australia, or India, or wherever you may be!

I want you, the reader, to know that your review is very important and so, if you'd like to **leave a review***, all you have to do is click and away you go.*

A follow-up to this novel The Ballad of Liberty Siegler is now available. For more information about the real-life characters in I Am Juden, please follow me on Twitter: @StephenUzzell2

Also visit NO HOOPTEDOODLE, my new book blog for reviews and author interviews:
https://stephenuzzell.wixsite.com/website

I wish you a long life of many happy reading adventures to come.

Stephen Uzzell

Made in the USA
Middletown, DE
11 December 2020